MISTRESS OF ELVIRA

The path that led Lizzie Desmond to the great Virginia plantation of Elvira was a long one. She was a world away from the England of her girlhood, the Paris of her youthful triumph, and the irresistible lover she had lost. She was wife to dashing, debauched Jack Cavanagh, who used her for his pleasure and displayed her for his pride. She faced a new life in a new world while still haunted by a love that time could not dim or any odds defeat. Lizzie played out her role as mistress of Elvira with exquisite perfection . . . but she never stopped striving to become mistress of her fate. . . .

POMP AND CIRCUMSTANCE

lovers . . . dark deeds and derring-
—*Kirkus Reviews*

. . meshes many elements of fact, ro-
d historical controversy.”
—*Booklist*

POMP AND CIRCUMSTANCE

A Novel by

Fred Mustard Stewart

A SIGNET BOOK

SIGNET
Published by the Penguin Group
Penguin Books USA Inc., 375 Hudson Street,
New York, New York 10014, U.S.A.
Penguin Books Ltd, 27 Wrights Lane,
London W8 5TZ, England
Penguin Books Australia Ltd, Ringwood,
Victoria, Australia
Penguin Books Canada Ltd, 10 Alcorn Avenue,
Toronto, Ontario, Canada M4V 3B2
Penguin Books (N.Z.) Ltd, 182–190 Wairau Road,
Auckland 10, New Zealand

Penguin Books Ltd, Registered Offices:
Harmondsworth, Middlesex, England

Published by Signet, an imprint of New American Library, a division of Penguin Books USA Inc. Previously published in a Dutton edition.

First Signet Printing, May, 1992
10 9 8 7 6 5 4 3 2 1

REGISTERED TRADEMARK—MARCA REGISTRADA

Printed in the United States of America

PUBLISHER'S NOTE
This is a work of fiction. Names, characters, places, and incidents either are the product of the author's imagination or are used fictitiously, and any resemblance to actual persons, living or dead, events, or locales is entirely coincidental.

As always, to my darling wife, Joan.

AUTHOR'S NOTE

Every writer frets about the authenticity of his characters' dialogue as, at the same time, he wants to protect the English language by putting it down on paper correctly. As William Safire pointed out in the *New York Times*: do writers wish to contribute to the slow strangulation of the beautiful English language by writing it the way even the best-educated actually speak it?

When researching the speech patterns of the antebellum slaves, I found an excellent source of how the slaves actually talked. During the Depression, the Federal Writers' Project, part of the WPA, dispatched interviewers to seek out and question the approximately two thousand former slaves who were still alive in America during the mid-1930's. Their reminiscences, recorded in *Bullwhip Days*, edited by James Mellon, are not only fascinating and haunting but also give us today an accurate "recording" of how the slaves talked more than 130 years ago. Although I have eliminated such things as "Ah" for "I" and "gwine" for "going," I will stand by what I have written as being accurate.

In the transliteration of Hindi words, I was faced with a bewildering variety of spellings. To track through this maze, I relied on what seemed to be the most consistent orthography. I did the same with the names of towns.

From our modern viewpoint, it is easy to poke fun at the Victorian Age and the woman who gave it its name. But the more one gets to know Queen Victoria, the better one likes her. Even her severest biographer, Lytton Strachey, ended up falling under her spell. Oddly, while most of her subjects were what we would call racists, the

Queen herself was not one. I have read many of her letters. There are also dozens of quotes in Lady Longford's excellent biography. Her epistolary style was idiosyncratic but, somehow, quite wonderful. She of course used the royal "we" and referred to herself in the third person: for example, "The Queen thinks . . . ," "The Queen believes . . . ," etc. I have done my best to imitate faithfully her style in this book.

PROLOGUE

ADAM AND LIZZIE

"I love you, Lizzie," said Adam Thorne. "I expect I'll love you till the day I die."

"Oh, Adam, you know I love *you!* We are like one soul: nothing can ever separate us."

These lovers' vows were spoken without a trace of self-consciousness and with passionate sincerity as the two ten-year-olds stood holding hands in the ruins of Newfield Abbey. A strong wind was blowing over the dun-and-purple Yorkshire moors, bringing the first blast of fall and blowing the children's hair. Adam's, thick, black, and uncut, and Lizzie's blond, bleached by the summer sun to the color of wheat. Newfield Abbey, once a monastery, had been burned by the soldiers of King Henry VIII when that monarch had dissolved the monasteries and founded the Church of England. What was left of its stone walls, its half-destroyed Gothic windows, its floor overgrown with weeds and wildflowers, all made the Abbey irresistibly romantic and the favorite meeting spot for Adam and Lizzie.

Now the dirty-faced boy in the white shirt and ragged trousers knelt before the beautiful girl in the homespun dress and took her hands.

"I, Adam Thorne, do solemnly swear to be thy knight," he said, his dark eyes looking up at the face that he adored. "I swear to protect thee from the cruelties of this wicked world and to love thee with a love that is pure."

"And I, Elizabeth Desmond, do accept thy pledge, Sir Knight, and vow to return thy love with my own truest love."

The wind continued to moan over the moors as rain-swollen clouds scudded across the sky.

Eight years later, in 1856, a naked Adam Thorne eased himself on top of a naked Lizzie Desmond, who was lying back-down in the wildflowers of Newfield Abbey.

"My sweetest Lizzie," whispered Adam. "My beautiful Lizzie."

He held her in his arms, kissing her breasts. Lizzie closed her eyes and clenched her fists.

"Dear God," she whispered, "forgive me my sins."

"Hush. It's no sin. In the eyes of God, we're man and wife. We've always been that."

"Not in the eyes of my father."

"Your father's pious enough to get us all into Heaven, though I'm not too sure I'd want to be there if he's there."

"What a wicked thing to say, even though it's true."

I can't help myself, she thought as she opened her fists and put her hands on his warm, smooth back. The pure, innocent love of two children who had grown up together on the moor had, early that summer, turned into something far from innocent. Lizzie was obsessed by Adam Thorne, who had grown into an adult of dark good looks and imposing physique, a man whose kisses had led to fondles and feels, a man whose periodic bouts of moodiness fascinated as well as perplexed her. Lizzie was the daughter of the vicar of Wykeham Rise, and she knew what fire she was playing with. Reverend Hugh Desmond, a widower since the death of Lizzie's mother twelve years before, was a firm believer in hellfire for sinners. Lizzie knew that if she lapsed into a "state of sin," there would be hell on earth to pay.

But she had already lapsed: six times, by actual count, and she was counting. Newfield Abbey, that scene of so many childhood idylls, had become their setting for what she was beginning to think of as their perpetual orgy. Despite the fact that technically she was already "fallen," Lizzie had no intention of becoming a "fallen woman," that subject of so many of her father's endless sermons. The answer, of course, was marriage, but so far Adam had not brought the subject up. Lizzie had determined to bring the subject up for him.

"Oh, God," she cried, her hands squeezing the flesh of his narrow waist as he brought her to orgasm. "Oh my love . . ."

He rolled off her onto his side, panting, his body slick with sweat. Even though, as usual, a wind was blowing, the August sun was warm; besides, Adam Thorne was a passionate lover. He picked his shirt off the grass and wiped his face.

"My aunt's coming tomorrow," he said. "I have an idea she's going to bully my father into sending me up to Oxford. Father got the letter this morning, and it made him so upset he was drunk before noon."

"Why is he upset?"

"He's terrified of the old girl. I met her once when I was ten, and she terrified *me*. She's a real dragon. She's my mother's older sister, Lady Rockfern."

Lizzie sat up, waving away a fly. "Would you want to go to a university?" she asked.

"I don't know if I could get in. You know I'm no scholar. Besides, who's to pay for it? Father has drunk up most of his money, and my grandfather hasn't sent a farthing in twenty years. But it *is* the family tradition to go to Oxford, and I suppose they might try to talk me into it. Maybe I could get some sort of job to pay the fees . . . I don't know. At any rate, I can't think why else my aunt would come slumming to see me."

"You don't really think she looks at it as slumming?"

"Don't I?" He gave her a look with his dark eyes, and she saw the anger smoldering in them. "I know what the de Veres think of me, or at least I can guess. I'm the poor relative, the wild child who hasn't proper manners and can't spell worth a damn and you'd be embarrassed to have him to dinner. I wouldn't last a term at Oxford anyway. They're all a bunch of snobs."

"But you're the grandson of an earl!"

"Oh yes, an earl I've never met, who disowned my mother for no good reason . . . a man I hate!" The rage in his eyes spilled over onto his face as he got up and went to the door of the Abbey to look out over the moors. The wind blew his hair as he leaned one hand on the empty door frame and raised his right fist in a gesture of defiance to the world. "Be damned to hell, Lord Pontefract!" he shouted. "May the devil chew you up and spit you out—and if the devil won't, I will! For I'll rot in hell if I don't pay you back for your damned pride!"

"Adam!" cried Lizzie, shocked at the vehemence. "He *is* your grandfather, after all."

Adam turned to glare at her. She decided it wasn't a good time to bring up marriage.

PART I

THE PONTEFRACT INHERITANCE

CHAPTER 1

Thorne Manor indeed! thought Lady Sidonia Rockfern as her open carriage pulled up in front of the weathered stone house that belonged to her brother-in-law. It might have been a manor once, but now it's a wreck. It's shocking that my dear, dead sister could have thrown away her beauty and all her glittering social prospects to come bury herself in this godforsaken part of the world with that disgraceful, drunken husband! Well, he'd better be sober today, or I'll give him what for what!

Lady Rockfern was a tall, imposing woman in her fifties who had a long, horsy face. She sat ramrod straight in her carriage, a black parasol protecting her from the sun and a black bonnet protecting her gray hair from the wind. When the carriage stopped, one of her two coachmen jumped down to open the door and lower the steps. Lady Rockfern alighted onto the weed-filled patch of grass that passed for a lawn and looked around. Thorne Manor seemed deserted. Its wooden shutters hung from their hinges in places, the windows were filthy, and several panes were missing entirely.

Lady Rockfern's lips pursed with disapproval. "Announce me," she said.

Her coachman hurried up the gravel path to the front door and banged the iron knocker. As she waited impatiently, Lady Rockfern's green eyes swept the windows of the two-story house, looking for signs of life.

"Sidonia! Dear sister!" cooed a voice, and a tall man with gray hair stumbled out the front door. His arms were open wide as he weaved down the path toward her, a wine bottle in one hand. "Welcome! Welcome to Thorne Manor! Well, well, dear lady, you haven't lost your looks, hey? Still a beauty, but then, you de Vere girls were all stunners."

"You're drunk," snapped Lady Rockfern. "And don't try to butter me up with your sweet talk. I never had any looks to lose. It was Lavinia that was the beauty, though the good Lord knows she wasted her looks on you. Now, put down that bottle, sir. We have things to discuss. Where's the boy?"

Sir Percival Thorne stopped a few feet from his sister-in-law, staring at her as he weaved precariously back and forth.

"How now, dear lady? You speak so harshly. Drunk, you say? 'Tis a lie, madam, and one to which I take offense. I have merely been sipping a cooling claret on this sulfurous day—"

"Enough, sir!" She rapped her parasol on his shoulder, her voice booming like a cannon. "I have driven a long way from Pontefract Hall and I have no time for your drunken buffoonery. Fetch the boy. I wish to see him."

Pushing Sir Percival aside, she strode down the path to the front door and entered the house. Sir Percival took a long swig from the bottle, then squirted the wine out in his sister-in-law's direction.

Inside the house, Lady Rockfern crossed the stone entrance hall and went into the drawing room. "Filthy," she said to herself, running a gloved finger over a walnut Jacobean chest. Clouds of dust swirled. The red velvet curtains were equally dusty, in places moth-eaten, the dull gold fringe torn and dangling. The paneling on the walls, though, was good, dating from the seventeenth century when Thorne Manor had been built by one of Sir Percival's ancestors, and the elaborate ceiling was a masterpiece of the plasterer's art. "What a crime to let a place of this quality go to ruin," she muttered, pounding the cushion of a high-backed chair. More clouds of dust. Then she took a seat on the cushion, resting both her hands on her parasol, watching the entrance hall, waiting for the arrival of Sir Percival.

She was enormously upset. Murder! The very word was so violent, so vulgar. Murders didn't happen in families like the de Veres. And yet, it *had* happened: violent, vulgar murder. Oh, yes, her father had instructed her not to tell Adam; it must be kept a secret, passed off as an accident. But this one horrible act had turned the de Veres' world upside down. And Adam? How would he react to the news?

She burned with curiosity to see her nephew. She knew he had turned eighteen the previous month. She knew he had graduated from some obscure school near Wykeham Rise, but that his life was unstructured, mostly the fault of his drunken father, who had offered no guidance to the boy, set no Christian example. Adam had grown up totally outside the pale of polite society, like some wild young animal. Perhaps it was partially her father's fault: she would concede that. And she knew Adam was probably bitter toward his own family. But now everything was so different. She wondered if this wild young man who she had heard galloped over the moors for hours on end . . . could he ever be civilized? It might be difficult, but it had to be done. And Sidonia had already picked an ally: Lady Sybil Hardwick.

She checked her gold lapel watch. "Where has that idiot gone?" she said irritably. "Does he think I have all day? Percival!" she called out.

A distant clock ticked somnolently as the sunlight strove to pierce the dirty panes of the tall Jacobean window. Lady Rockfern was about to snort again with annoyance when a young man appeared in the door. He was tall, well over six feet, she judged, and strappingly built with broad shoulders and narrow hips. He had on a dark, rather threadbare suit and a clean white shirt, although he wore no cravat and his black, curly hair looked uncut.

"Adam?" said Sidonia.

"Aunt Sidonia?"

He came into the room, crossing it to present himself before her chair.

"You may kiss my cheek," said Lady Rockfern.

"Yes, Aunt."

He leaned down and kissed the right cheek she had proffered. He smelled of strong, homemade lye soap.

"Well, let me look at you," she said as he straightened. She pulled a lorgnette from her purse to examine him. "You got your mother's looks—and your father's. I'll grant him that: he's a blackguard, but he's a handsome one. My poor sister took one look at him, and that was the end of her. Where *is* he, by the way? Can't he stay sober for one day?"

"I think that Father is afraid of you. He just got on his horse and headed for the tavern."

"The tavern? Outrageous! Well, he has a right to be afraid of me, the way he ruined the life of my sister."

"And how about you, Aunt?" said Adam softly, barely containing his rage. "And how about my grandfather? Didn't he ruin my mother's life by turning her out the door like a common slut? Yes, my father drinks. It's a wonder *I* don't drink."

Lady Rockfern frowned. "Your bitterness is understandable, Adam. But there is a reason for what happened—a reason I will let your grandfather tell you. Meanwhile, I assume you have not heard the tragic news?"

"What news?"

"You see that I am in mourning, Adam. There has been a death in the family. In fact, there have been four deaths. All of which has drastically altered the Pontefract inheritance—as well as your future." She stood up. "Come, boy. Pack your things in a bag. You must come with me to Pontefract Hall today. Hurry! It's a three-hour drive, and I wish to be home before sunset."

Adam stared at his aunt, wondering what in the world was happening.

"Look, Lizzie: my wedding invitations! Aren't they beautiful?"

Lettice Desmond, the eldest of the three Desmond sisters, thrust a box of cream-colored envelopes into her younger sister's hands and smiled haughtily. "The engraving is of the finest quality," she went on. "Papa has been surprisingly generous, but then we all want the wedding to be impressive, don't we? After all, Mr. Belladon is quite a catch for the family, and *I* caught him."

You *threw* yourself at him, thought Lizzie as she took out one of the invitations and read its Gothic script:

The Reverend Hugh Fitzalan Desmond, M.A., D.D.
Requests the Honor of the Presence of ———
At the Marriage of His Daughter,
Lettice Winifred,
to
Mr. Horace Belladon
at St. Giles Church
Wykeham Rise
The Ceremony to Commence at Eleven O'Clock
October 28, 1856

"You *will* help me fill them out, dear Lizzie?" Lettice added. "You have such a fine hand. Oh!" She waltzed a few steps around the small bedroom the three sisters shared on the second floor of the parsonage. "It's going to be such a beautiful wedding. And just think, Lizzie: you and Minna can come visit me at the Priory and stay as long as you like. And we'll be waited on by servants and have all the chocolate we can eat. Dear Mr. Belladon promised. He's so generous, you know. And so rich!"

"And so old," said Lizzie, putting the invitation back in the box and getting off her bed.

"You're just jealous," retorted Lettice. "Because you don't have a fiancé, or even a regular beau except for that alley cat Adam, who's not even presentable in polite society."

Lizzie grabbed one of her sister's long blond curls and gave it a swift yank. "You hush up about Adam."

"Ouch—that hurt! And you *are* jealous! Everyone knows that Adam Thorne will never amount to anything, with that drunken father of his."

"You think I'm jealous of Horace Belladon, that fat weaver who puts on ridiculous airs and slurps his soup?"

"He's *not* a weaver! He owns Belladon Textiles, Limited, and he has three factories and makes twenty thousand pounds a year—"

"He's fat, he's twice your age, and he picks his nose."

Lettice bit her lip. Though many people had commented on the physical similarity between Lettice and Lizzie, who was one year her junior (many people in fact thought they were twins), Lettice was fully aware that most people also said Lizzie was the prettier sister, a fact she had never forgiven Lizzie for. Now she put her hands on her hips and gave her sister a superior look. "At least he bathes, which is more than your precious Adam does."

"I *love* Adam's smell!"

"Oh? And you've been close enough to smell him, I'll wager. How close have you gotten, Lizzie? Close enough to kiss? Hmmm?"

Lizzie picked a book off her bed table and threw it across the room at her sister. Lettice ducked. The book hit a blue china pitcher and knocked it off the dresser. It crashed to the floor.

"*Now* you're in for it," said Lettice, running to the door. "I'm going to tell Papa, and he'll thrash you the way you deserve."

"I wish the book had knocked your *head* off!" yelled Lizzie.

"You put on airs, miss, but I have a good idea what's been going on at Newfield Abbey—and I'll tell Papa that, too!"

She opened the door to run out, almost bumping into her second sister, Minna. "Oh, Minna, you're such a booby—you're always in the way."

Angrily she pushed by Minna and went into the upstairs hall. Minna, who was so shortsighted she had to wear glasses, came into the bedroom. "What's gotten into her now?" she asked, closing the door. Of the three Desmond sisters, Minna was the shyest.

"Oh, she's bragging about Horrible Horace," said Lizzie, flouncing into a chair by the dormer window.

Minna said, "Well, Lizzie, it is true that Lettice is the only one of us with prospects."

Lizzie smiled at her sister. "I certainly don't worry about

you, Minna. Every eligible suitor in the country will be after you one of these days. And while Adam hasn't proposed *yet* . . ."

"Speaking of Adam, old Jethro from Thorne Manor just rode over with this."

Minna pulled an envelope from the pocket of her skirt and brought it to her sister.

"You goose, why didn't you tell me?"

Jumping from the chair, she snatched the envelope and pulled out the note.

"My deerest Lizzie," it began, and she cringed at Adam's spelling and crude handwriting. Lizzie was a star pupil at the Clergy Daughters' School at nearby Castleton.

> My ant, Lady Rockfern, is taking me to meet my grandfather at Pontefract Hall. I have little time as ant is in a hurry. I will writ you more later. I love you.
>
> Your true knite,
> Adam.

"What's he say?" asked Minna, burning with curiosity.

"He's going to meet his grandfather, Lord Pontefract," said Lizzie. "How very odd. I wonder what it means?"

"I am aware that the unfortunate state of your finances prevented you from going to any proper school, like Eton or Harrow," said Lady Rockfern to Adam, who was sitting opposite her in the carriage, which was bouncing through the golden afternoon. "But I have been told you just were graduated from some local institution?"

"Yes. I spent four years at Mr. Cadbury's classes."

"Do you know any Latin?"

"Well, a little. I never understood the vocative case. I mean, why should I learn how to say 'Oh, table' in Latin? I never talk to tables."

"You have a point. I am firmly convinced that one reason the Roman Empire fell was their ridiculous grammar. Why should anyone address inanimate objects? Do you know French?"

"No."

"Can you parse an English sentence?"

"Yes, but my spelling's wretched."

"Hmm. It seems you have enough education to become an English gentleman. I personally do not believe in all this talk of educating the masses. Too much education can warp a man's character."

"Then you're not going to try to send me to Oxford?"

"Oxford? Of course not. Attend to me, Adam. I assume you know something of your family history?"

"No. Mother never spoke of it, at least in any detail."

"Then I shall have to explain at rather tedious length, because it is important for you to know. My father, Lord Pontefract, who is also your maternal grandfather, sired three children. The firstborn was my brother, Lord Augustus de Vere, who was heir to the earldom which descends through the male line. I was the second born. I married the late Lord Rockfern, and we had one daughter who died in childhood. As you know, your mother became estranged from her father.

"The succession seemed assured by my brother, especially after he sired two fine sons. But a disaster has happened to the family. Lord Augustus, his wife and two sons had embarked on a steam yacht belonging to Lord Willoughby Fane en route to India. They were less than half a mile down the Thames when there was an explosion on board and all hands were killed—we assume the boiler blew up. In one blow, so to speak, the Pontefract inheritance was changed forever." Sidonia had lied, as she had been told. She knew it was murder.

Adam was staring at her. "Do you mean . . ." He hesitated. ". . . that I might be the next Earl of Pontefract?"

"Might? I mean you most certainly *will* be."

How many nights he had huddled in his bed, listening to the wind of the moors whistling around the ancient, unheated manor house, and cursed the perverse fate that had left him the poor relation and his cousins the heirs to what he knew was a large fortune. The whimsies of birth seemed unfair enough, but the bizarre behavior of his grandfather toward his mother made it all seem cruel as well as unfair. But in his wildest fantasies, it had never occurred to him that he might one day inherit. All he could say was, "And . . . and my grandfather doesn't mind?"

"Of course he minds that his son and grandsons have been killed. It has come to him as a great blow. But he is eager to meet you, Adam. He has a great number of things to tell you, as do I. First, let me acquaint you with the details of the estate. Lord Pontefract, who is the second earl, owns forty thousand acres in England, mostly here in Yorkshire. In the last century, rich seams of coal were discovered beneath it, and the mines bring in an annual income of approximately fifty thousand pounds."

"Fifty thousand?" Adam whispered, almost unable to conceive of such a huge figure.

"In addition, there are some twelve thousand acres in Scotland—Ayrshire, to be exact—and Pontefract Square in the West End of London, the rent roll of which brings in another twenty thousand pounds per annum. There is also an additional half-million pounds invested in the Funds. Naturally, as third earl you will also inherit Pontefract Hall, Pontefract House in London, and a perfectly ghastly suburban villa on the Scottish coast."

"Aunt," he said, almost in a state of stupefaction, "you're not . . . this is not some joke?"

She stiffened. "Joke, sir? I do not consider inheritances a joke."

"Then it's true? Someday I'm going to be . . . well, rich?"

"Your swiftness of comprehension does you credit, my nephew. But now perhaps you can begin to appreciate the enormity of the task that lies before us. You were nothing: you will be everything. We must polish you to take your rightful place in society. We must also find you a proper wife. Happily, your quite remarkable good looks, as well as your prospective income, should make that task a simple one. I am in the process of drawing up a list of suitable heiresses—"

"Wait a minute. Aunt, that's very kind of you, but you see, I'm already in love."

Lady Rockfern frowned. "You are? And with whom, pray?"

"The most beautiful girl in England, as well as the sweetest: Lizzie Desmond."

"Lizzie? I was not aware that Lizzie is a name one encounters in polite society. Who, pray, is this Lizzie?"

"Oh, she's quite respectable. Her father's the vicar at Wykeham Rise. They're poor as church mice, but Lizzie's got a smart head on her shoulders—she's a lot better educated than me. So forget your list. When I become the third earl, I'll marry Lizzie and make her the third countess. . . . The third Earl of Pontefract." He repeated the name, savoring it. "It doesn't seem possible. And all these years I've hated you and Grandfather. But now . . ." He hesitated. The incredible news had left him as dazed as he was excited.

"As I said," his aunt continued, "your bitterness is understandable. But you must strive, Adam, to forget the past. Fate has brought you a splendid inheritance, and someday—probably soon, alas—you will be the head of our family. Great position also carries great responsibilities. Until you marry and sire children, you are the last of the de Veres, and you must make us proud of you. Whatever we have done to you before, you must try to overlook. It is your Christian duty to forgive, dear Adam. And happily for all of us, you are now in a position to be generous."

"Yes," he said, thoughtfully, "perhaps you're right. I must try to forgive . . . What's Grandfather like, Aunt?"

"He is not the ogre you may have assumed. He's like all of us: he has his faults and his virtues. He's also very old, Adam. You must be gentle with him. You might even be surprised to find you like him, after all."

CHAPTER 2

If Adam could hardly believe his ears when Lady Rockfern told him he was to become an earl, he could hardly believe his eyes when he saw Pontefract Hall. He had vague memories of his mother telling him about the huge place she had grown up in, but she had died of consumption when Adam was seven.

"The house was begun in 1760," announced his aunt as the carriage rattled down the enormously long drive toward the distant mansion. "It was built by the first earl, your great-grandfather, who was a Calcutta Nabob."

"A what, Aunt?"

"A Calcutta Nabob. Your great-grandfather, Algernon de Vere, went out to India in the last century as a writer, or clerk, for the East India Company. You *have* heard of the East India Company?"

Adam gulped nervously. History was not his long suit. "Yes."

"Algernon was quick-witted and industrious and rose in the ranks of the Company. Along the way, he became a friend of Robert Clive. You *have* heard of Clive of India?"

Another gulp. "Yes."

"You *have* heard of Calcutta?"

"It's in the east of India, isn't it? On a river?"

"Bravo! It's in Bengal, to be precise, on the Hooghly River, and the climate is beastly. At any rate, Great-grandfather not only possessed a splendid head for business—balanced by a rather, shall we say, adaptable sense of business ethics—he was also a man of great physical courage. You *have* heard of the Battle of Plassey?"

Adam frowned. His aunt was throwing a lot at him, but

he didn't want to appear a total nitwit. "Wasn't that when we beat the French in India?"

"Precisely. In 1757, almost exactly one hundred years ago. Calcutta was under the control of the Nawab of Bengal, a despicable little man by the name of Siraj-ud-Daula—they have peculiar names, one might as well get used to it. This Nawab, the year before, had been responsible for the Black Hole of Calcutta. You *have* heard of that?"

"Wasn't that when all the English hostages were squeezed into a single room and most of them died?"

"Precisely. Perhaps a hundred and fifty people—the exact number is in question—were squeezed into a room eighteen feet by fourteen feet with two air holes on the hottest night of the year. The next morning, when they opened the door, all but twenty-three were dead from suffocation or heat exhaustion. It was a shocking, brutal incident. Your great-grandfather and Clive organized a punitive expedition in Madras against the Nawab and marched to Calcutta, which they recaptured. They then chased Siraj-ud-Daula to a place called Plassey, where they defeated the scoundrel's forces as well as the French troops. Siraj-ud-Daula was later murdered, which he richly deserved. Clive made a pro-English Mogul general the new Nawab of Bengal, thereby founding our empire in India. Clive, Algernon de Vere and other leaders of the East India Company were then given large sums of money as rewards from the new Nawab, Mir Jafar. Your great-grandfather received 285,000 pounds, an enormous sum at the time."

"It's an enormous sum *now,*" said Adam.

"Your great-grandfather and the others, described as 'arrivistes' by their jealous contemporaries, were known as Calcutta Nabobs. Algernon returned to England, bought this land, built Pontefract Hall and bought a seat in the House of Commons. Later, during the unfortunate American Revolution, he supported the King's Men of George III, who rewarded him with a peerage. Algernon de Vere became the first Earl of Pontefract. I trust you have paid attention, my nephew? I am telling you your family history."

"Yes, Aunt. But . . . it's huge!"

" 'Huge'? An odd way to describe one's family history!"

"No, I mean Pontefract Hall!"

Adam, his excitement mounting, was staring at the baronial pile, which they were now nearing.

"It is said to have more than one hundred rooms, though I have never counted. Counting one's rooms strikes me as inexpressibly vulgar. However, I can tell you the staff numbers about fifty, although with all these radical ideas in the air, it is becoming increasingly difficult to find servants."

Adam's eyes were drinking in the splendor of the house looming before them, if "house" was the applicable word. The classic facade of the stone building stretched, Adam estimated, over six hundred feet. It appeared to be one central building, dominated by a templelike portico, with somewhat lower symmetrical wings extending on either side, each terminating in a square tower with a cupola. The center portico, with its six columns and triangular apex surmounted by a statue of a goddess, was approached by a double staircase, each being a zigzag ramp. The great multipaned French doors of the main floor were eyebrowed by classic pediments, alternating half-moons and triangles, and the roof bristled with stone urns and gods and was surrounded by a stone balustrade. The house was set in an enormous park with lovely trees. In front of the mansion was a circular fountain with a fifty-foot jet which sprayed slightly in the evening breeze.

Adam fell in love with this architectural masterpiece at first sight. "Aunt Sidonia," he exclaimed, turning back to her. "It's more beautiful than I ever imagined. Lizzie's going to love it. How happy she'll be!"

Lady Rockfern sniffed. A vicar's daughter named Lizzie? she thought. We'll see about that. No, the perfect wife for Adam is Sybil Hardwick, and the sooner I bring those two together, the better. Like most of the aristocracy, when it came to marriage, Sidonia thought much more in terms of family trees than love. If a bride and groom fell in love, that was a pleasant dividend. But as with horses, the important thing was breeding, and Sybil's bloodlines were some of the best in England.

Adam, turning back to Pontefract Hall, wasn't thinking of breeding. He was thinking of how proud he would be to show this to the woman he loved.

"You'll like Lizzie, Aunt. She's the most wonderful woman in England!" He looked back at Sidonia and smiled. "Present company excluded, of course."

His aunt said nothing. He has some natural charm, she thought. He's far from hopeless.

The parsonage at Wykeham Rise was a humble building, albeit not without a certain gloomy charm. The village of Wykeham Rise consisted of four hundred souls, most of whom worshiped at St. Giles at the edge of the town. The parsonage stood next to the moor, separated from the church by the town graveyard. The village was on a rise, or hill, and the High Street was paved with flagstones laid endways in order to give a better hold to the horses' hooves. The High Street led down to the church and parsonage, both built of the same gray stone as the houses in town. The parsonage roof was made of the same flags used to pave the street (any lighter roofing could not have withstood the strong winds). The building was flanked by two chimneys and surrounded by a low stone wall that enabled the Desmond sisters to plant a few hardy bulbs in the front garden, along with elder and lilac. With the cold, rainy climate of the moors, the parsonage generally looked somber, although when the sun shone the house seemed to cheer up a bit. Growing up in such a place, next to a graveyard, might have given Lizzie a morbid personality. On the contrary, she was usually cheerful.

She had to be to live with Reverend Desmond. Her father, a big man with a bushy white beard, compounded all the worst faults of his mid-Victorian contemporaries. He was pompous, self-righteous, humorless, bigoted and mercilessly sincere. The only thing that made him bearable was his love of animals—in fact, many said the reverend was fonder of animals than people—and the parsonage crawled with cats, dogs and birds. When Lizzie was summoned to her father's study, he was seated behind his littered desk stroking the back of Ezekiel, his favorite Persian.

"Ah, Elizabeth," he said in his soft voice that contrasted with the booming diapason he employed in the pulpit. "Sit down, my dear."

"Yes, Papa."

Lizzie took a seat before the desk. The small study was cluttered with junk as well as with shelves sagging with books. A fire smoldered in the hearth as two other cats stretched and lazily circled the room.

"Lettice tells me you threw a book at her and broke a china pitcher. Is this true?"

"Yes, Papa."

"The Lord does not approve of temper tantrums."

"The Lord doesn't have to put up with Lettice."

Her father's brows, which bristled and curled, now frowned. "You have a sharp tongue, but to use the Lord's name in a flippant manner is most distressful to my ears. You will apologize."

"I am sorry, Papa."

"I understand that Sir Percival Thorne's man, Jethro, delivered a note to you this afternoon. Who was it from?"

"Adam. He told me he was going with his aunt to Pontefract Hall. Apparently they are going to try to send him up to the university."

"It would be a blessing for Adam, poor crude thing that he is. Lord Pontefract has treated him shabbily, but then, the de Veres have the curse of great pride. Pretty pussy, pretty pussy." For a moment he seemed to forget Lizzie as he tickled Ezekiel's ear. But she knew her father well enough to realize this was a device to throw her off-guard, the calm before the storm. After a moment he looked back up at her. "Lettice seems to think your behavior with Adam is open to some question in terms of propriety. She tells me you and he have been going to Newfield Abbey."

"We've been going there since we were five."

"But Lettice says she saw you kissing."

His look became deadly. He continued stroking the cat.

"I won't deny it, Papa. I have allowed Adam to take certain liberties with me." That's putting it mildly, she thought, crawling with guilt.

"Your mother had a somewhat frivolous nature which I fear you have inherited. You know I am a man of God and inflexible in matters of morality. Let me warn you that if you become tainted with sin, I will not only cast you from this house and pray for the damnation of your immortal soul"—he leaned forward and lowered his voice—"I will also thrash you within an inch of your life. I quote Proverbs, Chapter Five: 'For the lips of the harlot drip as in an honeycomb, and her mouth is smoother than oil: but her end is bitter as wormwood, sharp as a two-edged sword. Her feet go down to death; her steps take hold on hell.' " He paused, then leaned back in his chair. "Think about it, my dear. You may go now."

Lizzie stood up, her face white. She curtsied and left the room. As a young man, her father had been one of the leaders, with William Wilberforce, in the fight for the abolition of slavery in the English colonies. Lizzie knew little about slavery, but she admired her father's courage for fighting for principle. But she knew he had an explosive temper. As she left the study, she was not only riddled with guilt, she was also afraid. She knew her father's threats were not idle.

"So this is Lavinia's son?" wheezed the old man seated in a wheelchair before the great fireplace. Augustus Gascoigne Grimthorpe de Vere, second Earl of Pontefract, squinted his rheumy eyes trying to bring Adam into focus. Lord Pontefract was eighty-seven, a wizened mummy of a man in a long white nightgown and tasseled nightcap, whose hands, clasped in his blanketed lap, had skin as thin as crepes through which the blue veins showed, crawling like painful worms over arthritic joints. Adam stared back at his grandfather. It occurred to him that this old man must have been good-looking once, although his skin was surprisingly swarthy.

Lord Pontefract's bedroom was a palatial setting for this aged wreck. The room was twenty feet high with walls lined in faded blue Spitalfields silk and hung with magnificent paintings in elaborate frames. A huge state bed, its four high carved posters crowned by dusty ostrich plumes, stood against one wall. Beside the bed, a portly nurse was putting some medicine into a glass.

"Come here," said Lord Pontefract. "Come closer."

Adam came up to the chair. He thought that, in fact, it was hard to hate such a pitiful old man. Forget the past, he thought. Forgive. And yet, years of bitterness weren't that easy to throw off. When he thought of his mother's miserable life, the old fire inside him rekindled.

"My eyes aren't so good anymore," said the old man, squinting into Adam's face. "Yes, yes . . . you look like Lavinia. The same eyes, the same thin nose. Lavinia was a beauty, but she was impetuous. I loved her, though. A pity she ran off . . ."

"Ran off?" Adam exclaimed. "You threw her out of her own home. If you loved her, why did you disown her?"

"There were reasons."

"What reasons? What could possibly justify such cruel behavior?"

"I'll explain . . . all in good time."

The old man went into a coughing fit. The nurse hurried to his wheelchair with the glass. "You mustn't upset his lordship," she growled at Adam, handing the earl his medicine. "Drink this, milord."

"Go away," he snarled at the nurse. "Damned harpy, always trying to pour some god-awful pee down my throat, as if anything's going to keep me alive much longer."

"You're being difficult, milord."

"Don't treat me like a damned nanny!" The old man looked at Adam, who felt rather ashamed of his outburst against his grandfather. Lord Pontefract was so obviously running out of time. "You're the heir now, you know," he said. "Damned perversity of fate that you . . . My son had a brilliant career ahead of him. He was on his way to India to serve the Company, and then, BOOM!" He started coughing again. The nurse forced the glass into his hand.

"Now drink this, you stubborn old man," she said.

Lord Pontefract tried to scratch her face with one hand as his other took the glass. Then he put it to his mouth and drank its contents, dribbling some of the medicine down his chin. The nurse, whose shadow from the fire loomed up on the wall and ceiling like some dark monster, watched. Then she took the glass and wiped his chin.

"That's better," she cooed.

"Life," sputtered Lord Pontefract, "what's the point of it? You end up worse than a baby, helpless . . . Sidonia?"

"Yes, Father?" said Lady Rockfern, who was standing beside Adam.

"Get a tailor to make him some decent clothes. Then give a ball to introduce him to the county. Spare no expense."

"But Grandfather," said Adam, "am I to move in here?"

"Of course. You're the heir, ain't you? Nurse!"

"Milord?"

"Wheel me to my desk, then get out. All of you get out except Adam."

As the nurse wheeled the old man across the room to a magnificent gilt-and-marquetry *bureau à cylindre*, Adam looked at his aunt, who gave him a nod, signifying "Do what he says." Then she left the room.

"Come here, boy," said the old man, whose shaking hand was fitting a key into the rolltop desk. Adam obeyed, passing the nurse on her way to the door.

"I daresay all this has come as a bit of a surprise to you, eh?" said Lord Pontefract as he rolled up the top. "But there's another surprise in here that may not be as welcome as becoming my heir. Because you're not only inheriting my title and my fortune. You're inheriting something else: the family secret."

Adam watched as the old man put his hands on a wooden box, beautifully painted on its side and lid with sloe-eyed, bejeweled Indians—the men in white turbans and white *achkans,* or three-quarter-length coats, the women in filmy saris. The figures, delicately painted in the almost surreal Indian style, seemed to be floating through a stylized garden. Before opening the box, Lord Pontefract looked up at his grandson and spoke in a whisper:

"What I am about to reveal, you must swear to keep secret. Only my late son knew this, and the only reason I'm telling you is that you are now the heir. Do you swear to keep the secret?"

The look on the old man's face was so intense, Adam wondered what demon lay in the box. "Yes, I swear," he said softly.

"God strike you dead if you betray me."

The ancient hands slowly opened the box. Adam watched as his grandfather pulled out a small watercolor in a simple gold frame. He looked at it a moment, then handed it to Adam, who took the picture and examined it. It was a portrait of a young and quite beautiful Indian woman sitting in a cane chair. She wore a pale blue sari with a veil over her black hair, although her face was unveiled. She stared at the artist with large, defiant dark eyes.

"She's beautiful," Adam said. "Who is she?"

"Her name was Kamala Shah, and she was the daughter of a wealthy Brahmin from Calcutta. She was my mother."

Adam stared at him. His grandfather nodded slowly.

"Yes, Adam: I, you, your mother, your Aunt Sidonia—all the de Veres have nigger blood in their veins. But only you and I know it."

Of all the surprises that day, this, at least initially, came to him as the least shocking. As Lizzie had only a vague notion of black slavery, Adam had only a vague idea of India, having never seen an Indian in his short life. In fact, his first reaction was one almost of fascination. But as he watched his grandfather, he began to catch a flavor of the ugliness of a word that had yet to be coined: racism.

"I've hated India all my life," his grandfather continued. "Hated the mother I barely knew—she died of cholera when I was five. Oh, my father hushed it up as well as he could. He brought me to England and raised me as a white man. His friends from India who knew kept the secret for him, as well they might: many of them had married Indians, or bedded them. They said what my father said:

that my mother had been a *firinghi* from *Belait*—Hindi words for a 'foreigner' from 'England.' People came to believe them, and as the years passed it never occurred to anyone that I wasn't an Englishman through and through. I went to Eton and Oxford as the son of an English earl whose skin just happened to be tanned all year long. But I always knew the truth, and I was ashamed of it." The old man sighed. "Now, as I approach death, I wonder if I haven't been terribly wrong all my life. If my mother had lived, perhaps it would have been different—who knows? But now I'm paying for my sins, and one of my sins, Adam, was what I did to your poor mother. I tried to be more English than the English, and when your mother fell in love with a man I didn't approve of and ran off with him, I punished her by cutting her off from the family. Now I can see I was wrong. But at the time, while I was still trying to be so proper, I thought I was doing the right thing. Can you ever forgive me?"

Now Adam saw how vulnerable his grandfather was, and he felt a surge of pity for him. He took the gnarled hand and raised it to his cheek. "I forgive you, Grandfather," he said gently. "As Aunt Sidonia said, the past is over. And I guess, in a way, you suffered as much as Mother did."

"I wonder if she'll forgive me," the earl sighed. "That is, if we ever meet in the afterlife. My real attitude is that all religion is twaddle and there is no afterlife, but I could be wrong. But I'm paying for my sins in another way. Sidonia told you Lord Fane's yacht blew up by accident, but that was a lie. It was murder." Adam released his hand. "Here, wheel me across the room. I have something else to show you."

Wondering what new revelation was in store, Adam took the rear handles of the chair and pushed his grandfather in the direction he was pointing.

"There's a safe behind the painting," said the old man, indicating a Constable landscape. "Take hold of the right side of the frame and swing it out." Adam obeyed. In the wall was a steel safe. "Here are the keys," Lord Pontefract said, pulling two keys from the pocket of his nightgown.

"The copper key goes in the upper lock, the steel in the bottom. Turn them to the left, not the right." Adam did as he was told. "Inside is a black velvet box. Take it out and open it."

Adam removed the box from the safe and opened the lid. "My God," he whispered. "What is it?"

He was staring at an enormous pink diamond, the size of an egg.

"It's called the 'Idol's Eye.' "

"The great jewel," said Adam in awed tones. "I remember my mother saying something about it . . ."

"My father stole it from a temple in Lucknow shortly after the Battle of Plassey. It wasn't an eye: it was held in one of the four hands of a statue of the goddess Kali. I daresay you know little of the Hindu religion, but their three principal gods are Brahma, the Creator; Vishnu, the Preserver; and Shiva, the Destroyer. Shiva's wife is Kali, who is the bride of destruction and death. Perhaps you've heard of the *thuggees*?"

"The stranglers?" said Adam, his eyes still entranced by the fiery beauty of the stone.

"Yes. Hindus who went around strangling twenty or thirty thousand people a year, all in the name of Kali. They'd stick a coin in a piece of cloth and dispatch a man in seconds. Lord Bentinck led the campaign to stamp them out twenty years ago, but not before they'd murdered God knows how many Englishmen and Indians. The point is, Kali is a powerful goddess. Her statues usually present her as a black figure with gaping mouth and protruding tongue, adorned with snakes and dancing upon a corpse. Her earrings are dead men, her necklace a string of skulls. She is meant to terrify, and she *does* terrify the Hindus. It was a damned foolish thing for my father to steal this stone—perhaps 'arrogant' is a better word—but he didn't believe in the Hindu gods. At any rate, I started receiving anonymous notes several months ago threatening my family unless I returned the Idol's Eye to the temple at Lucknow. I discounted the notes as the work of crackpots until now."

Adam looked at his grandfather. "So you think your son and his family were murdered?"

"I do. It's too much of a coincidence otherwise. And then yesterday I received this note in the post."

He pulled a piece of paper from under his blanket and handed it to Adam, who unfolded it. The paper was cheap and ink-smudged, but the crudely scrawled message had an impact nevertheless. It read: "First your family. Then you. In the Name of Kali."

For the first time since arriving at Pontefract Hall, Adam felt a chill of apprehension.

"But Grandfather, you're in danger," he said.

The old man shrugged. "Perhaps. I've hired on two extra night watchmen. Besides, how much danger can exist for a man my age? I haven't got long anyway, so if some dirty beggar does me in, perhaps I deserve it for turning against my mother's people all these years. But, Adam, there's a reason I'm telling you all this. It's not only myself who's in danger. It's you and Sidonia too. If these people are bloodthirsty enough to blow up a yacht, then we're all in danger, ain't we?"

"Obviously."

"So, Adam, you must return the Idol's Eye to the temple in Lucknow. Kali may be a heathen goddess—although for all I know, she may be a real one—but she's theirs, and so is this stone. Will you swear to me you'll take it back to the temple?"

Adam had been a total outsider. Now he had become the ultimate insider, heir to one of the great fortunes of England, only, just as swiftly, to be made a secret outsider yet again, a man with Indian blood. But the greatest irony was that the proud de Veres were now paying in blood for their theft of a century before. Although Adam didn't understand why, after a hundred years, some mysterious person or persons were suddenly demanding the return of the stone, there was no question in his mind that he must grant his grandfather's request. He was now the last of the de Veres, the head of the family, and it was his responsibility to redress this crime from the past. Besides, it sounded like a grand adventure. His young blood tingled in anticipation.

"Of course, Grandfather," he said.

The old man sank back in his chair, a look of relief on his face. "There's a ship sailing from London for Bombay in six weeks—the *Eastern Star*, it's called. I'll have my estate manager book passage on it for you, and you can sail after Sidonia's ball. India's a strange country, but it gave us our wealth and it's in our blood—literally. It won't be a bad thing for you to see it."

India! Adam returned his gaze to the huge pink diamond in his hand. For a young man who had never even been to London, India held all the magic allure of the fabled East.

His eyes indicated the great diamond. "Of course," added his grandfather, "you'll carry a gun."

"Well, dearie, there's no doubt about it: you're with child."

The crone was Mother Crawford, Wykeham Rise's midwife. Lizzie closed her eyes. "Poor dear, I know what you're thinkin': how to tell your dad, the vicar? It's a problem, I grant ye." The old woman cackled. Mother Crawford thought that the vicar's daughter in the family way with no husband had its amusing aspects. But Lizzie wasn't amused. She was sitting before the fire in the tiny parlor of Mother Crawford's house on the High Street. It was after dark on a stormy night, but Lizzie hadn't dared come here in daylight for fear of being seen. "Who's the dad, sweetie?" asked the midwife, who looked very much like a witch.

Lizzie's eyes opened. "I won't tell you that."

"You don't trust me?" cooed the old woman.

"Not particularly. But what does it matter who's the dad?"

"I can kill it, sweetie," whispered Mother Crawford. "And for you, bein' quality, I'll give a nice discount."

Lizzie stood up. "There'll be no need to kill it," she said. "Because it's going to be legitimate. How much do I owe you?"

"Oh, for the vicar's daughter, a guinea will do nicely, pet. But you'd be better off killin' it. What's one human bein' more or less on this miserable planet, eh?"

Lizzie opened her small purse. She had taken all her savings with her from the parsonage, for she had known in her heart she was pregnant, and she knew if she were, her only hope was to go straight to Adam. All would be well when she found Adam. Wasn't he her true knight, pledged to protect his lady fair?

She gave Mother Crawford the coin. "Thank you," she said. "And please, try to keep this to yourself. The child is going to have a father."

"Ah, sweetie, I won't tell a soul. You know that! Why, I'd be out of business if I blabbed everything I know. Good luck, darlin'. Good luck."

Lizzie went to the oaken door of the low-ceilinged, chestnut-beamed room. "When the father knows, he'll do the right thing."

She went out into the night. It was raining and blowing, a miserable night to have to be out, but she didn't have enough money to take a coach to Pontefract Hall, and the railroads had not yet reached this remote corner of Yorkshire.

She would have to walk.

Bending into the wind, she started for the crossroad at the edge of town to take the pike to Pontefract. She didn't walk alone: she walked with terror. The thought of what her father would do to her if Adam *didn't* do the right thing . . . but he would. He would.

He was her love, her own true knight.

CHAPTER 3

"So that's the new heir?" mused Lady Sybil Hardwick, looking out the window of Pontefract Hall. "He's wonderfully romantic-looking. I love his black hair. I always find dark men so attractive."

"Yes, he's handsome," said Lady Rockfern, who was standing beside the statuesque beauty. They were in the grand salon of Pontefract Hall, a room of palatial splendor, looking out one of the ten-foot-high windows at Adam, who was dismounting from his horse, Grayling, as a groom held the bit. "Handsome and subject to moods—I've found *that* out in only two days. He has a temper and isn't afraid to use it. But I've also seen him staring into a fireplace, brooding like some lovesick Hamlet. Who knows what goes on in his head?"

"Ah, who knows what goes on in *any* young man's head? But I like the head."

"I thought you might, dear Sybil. Of course, there is so much talk in the county about you and Edgar Musgrave having a deep attachment." Sidonia was playing cat-and-mouse. She wanted the best for her nephew, and in Sidonia's opinion the best was Sybil, the daughter of the Earl of Nettlefield, this beauty with the green eyes, the rich chestnut hair, and the impeccable—if impecunious—family tree.

"Edgar and I are childhood friends," Sybil said, her eyes still on Adam, who was talking with the groom. "Of course, we ride together, and he has been my escort at numerous balls, as you are aware. But I am not expecting a proposal from Edgar, if that's what you're hinting at.

Everyone knows Edgar is a fortune-hunter, and I'm far too poor to interest him as a wife."

"I admire your perspicacity, as well as your frankness. Then I, too, will be frank. I have known you all your life, as I have known your family. I would consider nothing more felicitous than if our two families—neighbors in so many ways—were to be united by the bond of matrimony. I have known Adam only a short time, but I believe he has many promising qualities, despite his moodiness. Yet, alas, the position he will assume in society will be difficult for him if he does not have a wife who is at home with the great world, if you see what I mean. Adam was raised without the benefits of loving parents or a gentleman's education. How perfect for him you would be, dear Sybil. That is, if you were interested."

Sybil was still watching Adam through the window. Dear God, she thought: How could I not be interested? He is *the* most handsome man. . . .

"I need hardly point out," Sidonia continued, "that Adam will inherit a considerable fortune."

Sybil smiled slightly. "There's no need to mention the money," she said. "I'm fully aware of that, and I'd be a hypocrite if I said the money were not an added attraction. The Countess of Pontefract, whoever she is, will be one of the greatest ladies in the land, for your nephew is a prize catch. But I would not marry him for the money alone. I may be poor, but I won't stoop to fortune-hunting like Edgar. No, I will marry for love, or I won't marry at all. If a tender sentiment forms between your nephew and myself, then I will be glad to accept if he honors me with a proposal. Otherwise, we shall remain neighbors and, I hope, friends."

She's proud, thought Sidonia. And Adam's headstrong. "Again, I admire your frankness," she said aloud. "Well, we shall see what develops. Ah, Mr. Hawkins has brought the tea."

Sidonia took Sybil's arm and led her to a corner of the salon where Mr. Hawkins, the steward or butler, was directing two footmen in the setting out of the tea service. In the intricate hierarchy of the servants' belowstairs world, the butler was always called "Mister" as an indication of his authority.

Algernon de Vere, the first earl, had instructed his architect to spare no expense in the construction of Pontefract Hall. The son of a York tailor, Algernon was dazzled by the enormous fortune he had made in India, and he had every intention of dazzling everyone back home in England. Fortunately, his architect, who had worked with Robert Adam, the genius who had built—or was to build—such magnificent stately homes as Syon House, Kedleston, Harewood and Osterley, had good taste and a fine eye and had been able to create pomp without pomposity. The grand salon was one of the showrooms of the house, and was a space of haunting beauty. The walls were hung with crimson Spitalfields silk brocade. There were elaborately carved classic surrounds at the doors, with gilt pilasters and pediments, and the tall windows were hung with rich blue silk curtains which framed the view of the front terraces, the fountain and the great lawn. The chairs and settees were all in the delicate style of Louis XVI, their arms and legs graceful and gilt, their seats and backs upholstered in pale peach. The Moorfields carpet—an immense thing to match the immensity of the room—was woven in a splendid classic design with gorgeous reds and blues. But the glory of the room was the coffered ceiling, a firmament of gold, blue, crimson and cream with oval paintings of classical figures done by the well-known artist Angelica Kauffmann.

"I must warn you that he tells me he's in love," said Sidonia, sitting on a settee to pour the tea from the silver service. "A certain Lizzie Something-or-other, the vicar's daughter in Wykeham Rise. Of course, such a match is totally unsuitable. But we must proceed with caution. As I said, Adam is moody, and we know too well, dear Sybil, that the male heart is subject to caprices. Fortunately, I was able to dissuade him from inviting this Lizzie creature to the ball Saturday night. I told him it would be unfair to her, that she wouldn't have the right clothes, though what I meant was that the poor girl would be totally out of her element. He didn't like it, but he finally gave in, which leaves the field open for you, my dear. But hush. I think he approaches . . . Ah, here he is! Good afternoon, dear Adam. Just in time for tea. I want you to meet one of our neighbors, Lady Sybil Hardwick."

Adam looked at Sybil. Though she was on a tight budget, she had a fine eye for fashion, and the pale blue silk dress she had on with the bolero jacket was the latest look from Paris. Even though she was seated, Adam could tell she had a splendid figure.

"Lady Sybil lives at Nettlefield Park," Sidonia went on. "Her father is Lord Nettlefield, such a dear man. The entire family is coming to the ball Saturday."

Adam came over to kiss Sybil's hand. "Then I hope," he said, "I may have the honor of a dance, Lady Sybil?"

Bravo, thought Sidonia. That was well done.

"However," Adam went on, "I must warn you: I'm a terrible dancer. Actually, worse than terrible. I don't know any dances at all except for a few reels."

Sybil gave him her most seductive smile. "Then I'll have to teach you how to dance, won't I?" she said. "And I won't even charge you for the instruction."

Clever, thought Sidonia.

He's no clod, thought Sybil. Far from it. And he is the most exciting man!

I gave in to Aunt Sidonia, thought Adam, because I know she's trying to push this woman on me. I don't want to upset my aunt needlessly, but the next Countess of Pontefract is going to be Lizzie. And Aunt doesn't know it, but tomorrow I'm going back to Wykeham Rise and propose.

The night that had begun with a storm had, by midnight, turned into a gale and Lizzie was soaked to the skin and wretched. She was wearing a black shawl over a blue dress, clutching a small bag that held the few belongings she had taken from the parsonage. She realized she had picked a terrible night to walk to Pontefract Hall, but she was so terrified that her father might follow her she had decided she had no choice but to try and reach Adam as quickly as possible. But as she stumbled along the pike, lashed by sheets of rain blown by a fierce north wind, her skirts spattered by mud, she told herself she had to find some sort of shelter, the weather was too much for her. Though the moor was sparsely settled, she knew there was a crofter's cottage called the Grange not far down the road. She was under the impression it was inhabited by a sheep farmer named MacGee or MacDuff, and while she wasn't happy about the thought of spending the night with a stranger, she realized she had no choice. Although there was a possibility of her father trying to follow her, she discounted it because of the frightful weather.

Five minutes later, she spotted the cottage and hurried toward it. It had a thatched roof off which the rain was pouring. Standing beneath the deluge caused by the lack of gutters, she knocked on the wooden door. After a few minutes, it was opened by a huge, bearded man in a red flannel nightshirt. He had an oil lamp, which he lifted high to stare at Lizzie's face.

"What in the name of God would you be doin' out on a night like this?"

"Sir, I'm on the way to Pontefract Hall, and—"

"Come in before I get soaked too! Damn, what a night! You're lookin' for shelter, I wager?"

He slammed the door and bolted it. A shivering Lizzie squished across the low-ceilinged room to a hearth where a fire was smoldering. The man hurried up behind her to put fresh logs on.

"My name's Stringer MacDuff. And what be yours, miss?"

"Lizzie Desmond."

"Desmond? Any relation to the vicar of St. Giles?"

"I'm his daughter."

"Ah. And why would the vicar's daughter be out on the moors on a night like this?"

As he began lighting more lamps, she could see that the room was sparsely furnished but cheerful enough, with homespun curtains over the windows. She wondered what to tell him, since the truth was out of the question.

"I'm on my way to pay a call on a relative of Lord

Pontefract," she said, figuring that was at least partially true.

"The Nabob? Well, you're travelin' in high circles. And why would you be walkin', if you're so grand?"

She noticed he was leering at her. "Is there a Mrs. MacDuff?" she asked coolly.

He grinned. "Ah no, miss, I live here by myself. It's a real pleasure to have some company, especially such a fine-lookin' lass as yourself. But you're soaked to the bone! Maybe you should take your clothes off so they can dry. Here, I'll go get a blanket . . . No, better yet, you go in the bedroom where you'll have some privacy. There's a blanket on my bed. Put it around yourself, then come out and I'll give you a nip of whiskey to warm you up."

She looked at him. She had a good idea what was going on in Stringer MacDuff's head. On the other hand, if she didn't get out of her soaked clothes she might catch a cold or worse, which could endanger her baby. Her eyes fell on a long iron poker leaning against the stone hearth. She decided that in an emergency she could hold off MacDuff with the poker.

"Thank you," she said. "I'll accept your invitation."

She started toward the bedroom door.

"Here, take this lamp."

He gave her an oil lamp. She went in the bedroom and closed the door. Setting the lamp on a low chest, she sat on the edge of the rumpled bed and started unlacing her boots.

"This is a fine kettle of fish," she muttered, pulling off her left boot and holding it upside down to drain the water onto the plank floor. Stringer MacDuff looked about thirty and he looked strong. But if he had ideas about getting her to join him in this bed . . .

It was then she heard the knock on the front door of the cottage: a loud, persistent, angry knock. She froze, listening. MacDuff opened the door. She heard voices. Then footsteps coming toward the bedroom. The door opened.

"Slut!"

It was her father. He filled the doorway, his black cloak dripping. In his right hand he held a whip.

"HARLOT!"

He lumbered toward her, raising his whip. As she screamed, he started whipping her about the head and shoulders. She got off the bed and tried to run past him to the door, but he grabbed her by the arm and flung her halfway across the room. She stumbled against the chest, still screaming.

"Father, don't . . . the baby . . ."

"You mean the bastard!" he roared, starting to whip her again. She tried to protect her face with her left arm. The whip hurt. "Mother Crawford came to the parsonage three hours ago and tried to blackmail me!" he raged, continuing to whip her. "She said she'd tell all Yorkshire that Reverend Desmond's daughter is a WHORE!"

"Father, stop . . ."

"I'll KILL you, strumpet . . . WHORE!"

"No you WON'T!"

She grabbed the oil lamp and threw it at him. It hit his chest and shattered. She watched with horror as flames spread up his front. He writhed, screaming, as his beard caught on fire. He staggered back, dropping the whip.

"Oh, my God . . . Father! Mr. MacDuff, bring some water . . . oh, God!"

Her father fell backward on the bed, by now half in flames. She grabbed a pillow and started beating him. MacDuff ran into the room carrying a pitcher. He dashed the water on Desmond, but by now the bedclothes were burning.

"Get out!" he yelled.

She was panicking as she hurried toward the door. I've killed my father! The thought raged through her mind. At the door she turned. MacDuff had jerked a quilt that hung on one wall and thrown it over the bed, smothering the flames. But a horrible smell was filling the tiny room, and when the panting crofter pulled the quilt off, Lizzie realized what it was: the stench of cooked human flesh. Her father's face was a mass of black. Wisps of smoke rose from it.

"Is he . . . ?" she whispered.

"Aye, he's gone. And I wager it wasn't an easy way to leave this planet." He threw the quilt on the floor, then went to one of the windows and opened it. Wind and rain poured through. "The room stinks," he said, coming to Lizzie. "Let's air it out a bit."

She was numb. She went into the front room as he closed the door behind him. She stared at the fire, wondering why she couldn't weep.

"I'm beginning to understand your story now," he said. He was beside her, gazing at her with a queer expression. "Your father knocked at my door to see if you'd sought shelter here in the storm. And so you got a wee one in your belly? What are you going to tell the police?"

"The police?"

"Well now, there's a dead body in there, in case you've forgotten. I'll have to report what happened to the authorities. It should be an interestin' trial. I can see what they'll say in the newspapers: 'Unmarried Mother Murders Vicar Father.' "

Her eyes widened. " 'Murders'? You saw what happened. I was only defending myself!"

Stringer MacDuff grinned. "Oh sure, and the jury's going to believe *that* one. An unwed girl who let herself be laid? When the barristers get through with you, they'll be laughing all the way to the gallows."

She turned white. "The gallows? But that's not fair . . ."

"What's fair in this rotten world?" he said, going to the front door and removing a pair of trousers from a peg on the wall. "But it's you or me, my lass. The police are going to say one of us killed your father, and I'm goin' to be there with my story first. I sure as hell don't intend to swing."

"Wait! Please!"

She tried to argue with him, but it was useless. He put his trousers over his nightshirt, pulled on boots, then got into a mackintosh, put on a hat and left the house, slamming the door behind him. Simultaneously the wind blew the bedroom door open again. She stared at the blackened bed with the horrible corpse of her father on it. She put one of her hands to her cheek.

"What have I done?" she whispered. Then she frowned. "More to the point, what am I going to *do*?"

The two Indians crouched on the terrace of Pontefract Hall, watching through the end French door of the ballroom the beautifully dressed dancers inside. The Indians had dark complexions—one of them being almost black—but they wore Western-style clothes. However, they wore turbans and had beards.

From inside the ballroom came the delightful, lilting strains of Weber's "Aufforderung zum Tanz," or "Invitation to the Dance," composed in 1819. The ballroom, on the opposite side of the entrance hall from the grand salon, was another masterpiece of decor, its white-and-gilt walls supporting a barrel ceiling from which depended two magnificent Waterford chandeliers. The eight-man orchestra hired by Sidonia was at one end of the room, playing for the fifty-odd guests who had come to meet the new heir of Pontefract Hall.

"It's the *chowkidar,*" whispered one of the Sikhs, pushing his companion out of the light streaming through the French door. Just then one of Lord Pontefract's watchmen walked by the terrace.

"Congratulations," said Lady Sybil Hardwick, who was dancing with Adam. "You're waltzing extremely well. You're undoubtedly my best dance pupil."

"I'm your *only* dance pupil," said Adam glumly. He was wearing his new black tailcoat and a white silk bow, flawlessly tied by Sidney, his grandfather's valet.

"Ah, but you are too modest, sir." Sybil smiled. She looked ravishing in a dress of ivory satin, its enormous skirt supported by no fewer than four underskirts which in turn were supported by an iron case called a crinoline, which had an unpleasant habit of bumping Adam's knees. Bringing out her major artillery, Sybil had borrowed from her mother the Nettlefield necklace, a double strand of pink pearls and diamonds that rested on her truly splendid bosom. The low décolletage of her dress, which bared her shoulders and as much of her breasts as she dared, had, to her satisfaction, attracted more than a few looks from the men in the room. Her shiny chestnut hair was parted in the middle, then swept back to a bun where it exploded in a burst of curls. She smelled alluringly of English Violet by Floris of London, the *only* perfume used by the upper class. She had intended to dazzle Adam. But, rather to her concern, the new heir to the Pontefract estates seemed disturbed and distracted. Adam Thorne's mind was obviously somewhere else, which only increased Sybil's determination to focus it on her. Lady Rockfern had said he was prone to Hamlet-like moodiness, and she was obviously correct. But the moodiness only made him that much more attractive to Sybil.

"What a handsome couple," purred Lady Rockfern, who was sitting on an opera chair at the side of the room between the Earl and Countess of Nettlefield. "Sybil is such a beauty."

"Ah, dear Sidonia, and your nephew is so dashing," replied Lady Nettlefield. "He is almost ostentatiously good-looking."

"Well, well, pure Norman blood, you know." Lady Rockfern smiled, blissfully unaware that her own blood was one-quarter Indian. "It does produce the best-looking people on earth."

"What a pity about Lord Augustus being blasted out of the water," said Lord Nettlefield, a red-faced man in his fifties whose daily consumption of two bottles of claret had left him fifty pounds overweight. "But it must have come as a pleasant surprise to Adam when he learned he was the new heir. What glittering prospects he has!" And what a blessing if Sybil can nab him, he thought. Of course, the de Veres are hopelessly nouveau, but a hundred thousand a year! I wonder how small a dowry I could get away with. . . .

"His father, I believe, is a hopeless drunkard?" said Caroline, Lady Nettlefield, a gaunt beauty in an amethyst velvet ball gown with two white plumes in her gray hair behind the Nettlefield tiara—one of the few pieces of family jewelry she had managed to prevent her husband from pawning. Lady Nettlefield also wore a heart-shaped beauty patch on her left cheek, a remnant of the fashion of her youth.

"I can't deny it," said Sidonia, a look of stern disapproval on her horsy face. "Sir Percival has, alas, no redeeming features at all that I am aware of. He is lazy, shiftless, impecunious, and drunk."

"Still and all, he's a gentleman," remarked Lord Nettlefield, uncomfortably aware that Lady Rockfern had also just described *him*. "As Christians, we must be charitable."

"Lady Rockfern tells me you are in love," Sybil said as Adam led her out on the terrace for some air. The ballroom, with its hundreds of candles and overheated dancers, had become unpleasantly hot. "Who is the lucky lady?"

"Her name is Elizabeth Desmond," replied Adam, escorting her to the stone balustrade overlooking the great fountain. "And if I seem a bit distracted this evening, it's because I received some terrible news about her yesterday."

"Nothing serious, I hope?"

"It's extremely serious. Lizzie's been accused of murdering her father."

"Murder?" Sybil's normally cool composure was shaken. "Is it possible?"

"No! I know Lizzie as I know myself. She hasn't a violent bone in her body. She's incapable of murdering anybody, much less her father. I went to Wykeham Rise yesterday to propose to her and found the town in an uproar. It's come as a great shock."

"I can imagine! Is she being held by the police?" Sybil was not a vicious woman, but she couldn't help but feel a twinge of relief that her rival was in serious trouble.

"No. She's disappeared, and the police are searching for her all over Yorkshire. She must be terrified. I . . ." He closed his eyes and clenched his fists, which were resting on the stone balustrade. Sybil began to realize the depth of his attachment to the vicar's daughter. Rather to her surprise, she felt jealousy seeping into her veins.

He opened his eyes and she saw tears in them.

"I must protect her," he said, softly. "You see, when I was a child, I vowed to become her knight. I know it sounds foolish, but I meant it then, and I still do."

"I don't think it sounds foolish," Sybil said. "I think it's charmingly medieval and romantic." I wish he'd vow to become *my* knight, she thought.

"I'm sorry," Adam said. "I didn't mean to burden you with my problems."

"*Au contraire*, Mr. Thorne, I am delighted you have seen fit to confide in me. I hope our friendship—if I may be so bold as to use that word—will deepen with time, and nothing enriches friendship more than an exchange of confidences."

"You're very kind, Lady Sybil, and very understanding."

"Please: Sybil."

He looked at her in the flickering moonlight. Whereas he had been so dazzled by Lizzie's beauty that all other women paled in comparison, he had to admit Sybil was gorgeous.

"And I'm Adam. At any rate, I tried to convince the sheriff there was a mistake, but apparently there's an eyewitness. I don't know what to do. The best thing I can think of is to stay here and hope Lizzie can contact me somehow—"

A shot rang out. Both Sybil and Adam turned to look out at the great park. It was a partially cloudy night, but the wind had pushed the clouds away from the moon so that there was enough illumination to see two figures running across the lawn.

"Excuse me," said Adam, running down the terrace toward one of the zigzag stairs. There was another shot, and Sybil gasped as she saw one of the men stumble and fall. Now two other men appeared around the side of the great mansion. It was the watchmen. They were both carrying rifles and firing.

"What is it?" asked Sybil's father, coming out on the terrace along with many of the guests.

"It must be poachers."

"Damned cheeky beggars!"

Adam reached the bottom of the steps and ran in the direction of the fallen figure. He could see that the man had something white on his head, but just then the moon became obscured by clouds again. The running watchmen fired two more times, but the second man had vanished into the woods surrounding three sides of the park.

Adam reached the fallen man at the same time as the watchmen.

"It's a bloody Indian!" exclaimed one of the men, pointing at the white turban.

Adam saw the bullet wound in the man's back. He knelt to turn him over.

"Careful, guvnor, them niggers is tricky," said the second watchman.

Adam looked at him. It was the second time he had heard the word used since he found out he had Indian blood in him, and he was beginning to hate it.

"He's an Indian," he said pointedly. "Go after the other man."

"Yes sir."

The two took off as Adam turned the Indian over. The man was dead. Something had fallen out of his right hand and was lying next to the corpse. Adam picked up the Idol's Eye diamond.

"Grandfather!" he whispered.

Getting up, he stuck the diamond in his pocket and raced back toward the house, where now the entire party had gathered on the terrace watching the drama. Adam fought panic as he ran. In just a few days he had come to care for the old man he had hated for most of his life. Adam knew that his grandfather had come to feel genuine remorse for the way he had treated Adam's mother (as well as his own) and as Lord Pontefract had said, he was paying for his sins by the murder of his son and family. Now, the discovery that the two Indians had obtained the great diamond made Adam fear the worst. He looked at the third floor windows of his grandfather's bedroom: they were dark. Lord Pontefract had been too weak to come downstairs for the ball. Normally, by now he would be asleep.

Miss Higgins, the nurse, slept in the next bedroom. Presumably she would have been awakened by any noise, but still . . .

He ran back up the zigzag stair to the front terrace where his aunt was standing with Lord Nettlefield.

"What's happened?" asked Lady Rockfern.

"Two Indians," he panted, not stopping.

"Indians?" snorted Lord Nettlefield. "The blackguards! What would Indians be doing *here*?"

Adam rushed into the great entrance hall, ran across the marble floor and started up the stairway. He rushed by the big Poussin hanging on the first landing, then on to the third floor of the house where a painting-lined gallery connected the principal bedrooms. Adam knew that if the Indians had been able to get to the roof of the mansion—and any reasonably agile man should be able to climb up one of the heavy lead gutter-drains—then access to the interior of the house would be merely a matter of breaking the lock on the roof door. From there, down the stairs to the servants' quarters on the top floor of the house, which were empty since all the servants were downstairs for the ball. And then . . .

He opened the door to Lord Pontefract's bedroom. "Grandfather?"

He lighted a candle and groaned. The room was a mess. It had been ransacked: drawers thrown on the floor, the *bureau à cylindre* jimmied open, pictures off the wall . . . He saw the Constable landscape swung out on its hinges and the safe door open.

Adam slowly approached the big bed, holding the silver candlestick high. As its light pierced the gloom, he saw the old man on the bed. He looked asleep.

"Grandfather?"

Silence. Adam was next to the bed. He winced.

There was a silk rag around the old man's neck. Adam could see a coin under the rag.

The Indians had strangled him in the manner of the *thuggees*.

On Lord Pontefract's chest was a note. Adam picked it up. It read: "Kali is avenged."

CHAPTER

4

The naked farmboy jumped off the rock and, holding his nose with one hand, cannonballed into the pond in the pine forest. He swam to the opposite side, then dog-paddled lazily to the middle, where he began floating on his back. It was a hot, late-summer afternoon three days after the terrible storm that had lashed the north of England. A slight breeze soughed through the stately pines, whose smell sweetened the air.

Lizzie, looking dirty and exhausted, peered from behind the trunk of a pine. She had hidden in the loft of a barn for two nights, both horrified by what she had done to her father and terrified of being found by the sheriff. Finally, the night before, she had decided she had no choice but to continue on her way to Pontefract Hall. Adam, she thought. My true knight. If *ever* I needed him, it's now.

She waited till dark, slipped out of the barn and started toward the pike. She was starving. Passing an orchard, she picked an unripened apple and devoured it, even though its tartness puckered her mouth. One thought pounded through her brain: Adam would know what to do.

Or would he? She slowed her pace. What could he do? If he didn't turn her over to the authorities, he would be abetting her in the crime.

This thought brought her to a halt. The realization that she might be involving her love in a criminal act was almost as horrifying to her as the knowledge that she had—however innocently—committed a criminal act herself.

It was then she sat down on a rock and weighed her options. If she didn't go to Adam, where could she go?

London. London, with its millions, its faceless crowds.

London was the safest place for her to hide. Then she could write to Adam and he could come to her there. In the anonymity of the great city they could be reunited safely. And then what?

One step at a time, she told herself as she started south. She had to get to London first, and that wouldn't be easy.

By dawn, she figured she had walked perhaps five miles. She was exhausted, her feet were sore, and she was dirty and hungry. It was then she saw the pine forest. The perfect cover to get through the day. She headed for its cool darkness. I've become a vampire, she thought. A creature of the night.

Amid the cool, sweet pines she began to feel better. The forest teemed with life: birds, chipmunks, squirrels. She even saw a distant deer which eyed her curiously then bounded out of sight. When she was a mile inside the forest, she lay down on a bed of pine needles and fell asleep.

When she awoke, feeling refreshed but still starving, she looked up through the tall pines and saw that the sun was high in the heavens. She got to her feet and continued on her way, deciding that as long as she was in the forest she could travel safely by day.

It was then she spotted the farmboy taking off his clothes to go for a swim.

As she peered around the tree trunk, her eyes stared at his pile of clothes.

She had just found the perfect disguise.

"*Arrêtez-vous! Arrêtez la diligence!* STOP!"

The young Frenchman banged his silver-tipped cane on the roof of the coach as he yelled out the window. The fat coachman rolled his eyes with annoyance and reined in the four horses. The coach bumped to a halt on the country road. Lucien Delorme, for such was the lone passenger's name, opened the door and hopped to the ground.

"You, boy!" he said to the dirty farmboy walking along the road. "Where are you going?"

"To London," Lizzie said, eying Lucien cautiously. The thirty-year-old Frenchman was dressed expensively in fawn trousers and a beautifully cut gray coat. A pearl stickpin held his perfectly tied cravat. His black beaver hat gleamed softly in the sun.

"I am going to London too," he said. "Would you like to ride with me?"

Lizzie had found a pocketknife in the boy's pants. Although it had almost killed her, she had used it to cut her long blond hair to complete her disguise. She had no idea why the stranger was being so accommodating, but he was the answer to her prayers.

"That's very kind of you, sir, and yes, I'd be delighted."

"Excellent. Climb in. You can keep me, uh, company."

Smiling, Lucien followed Lizzie into the heavy coach, yelling up to the coachman, "Drive on!"

Snap! went the whip, and the coach lumbered into motion.

"What is your name, young man?" Lucien said as he seated himself opposite Lizzie.

"Charlie," she replied, thinking fast.

"Charlie. Such a nice name. And how old are you?"

"Eighteen, sir."

"Are you hungry, Charlie?"

"Oh yes, sir," Lizzie replied truthfully.

"Here, help yourself." He opened a wicker hamper beside him on the leather seat. "*Jambon*—ham? Sausage? A . . . how you call it? Deviled egg? Help yourself, Charlie. And I pour you a nice glass of red wine, eh? You like some wine?"

Lizzie had practically dived into the hamper, stuffing two deviled eggs into her mouth so fast she almost choked. She nodded yes and grunted a sound that approximated "please." Lucien couldn't take his eyes off her as he uncorked a bottle of *Côtes du Rhone* and filled a short glass.

"*Tiens*, you certainly *are* hungry," he chuckled, holding out the glass. The coach hit a bump and the wine splashed out of the glass onto Lizzie's knee. "*Merde!* Your English roads are so *cahotant*. . . . bumpy. Here: I wipe the wine from your pants. . . ."

As Lizzie took the glass, he pulled a napkin from the hamper, reached over and began wiping her dirty black trousers. Lizzie gulped the remainder of the wine, wondering why in the world he was being so deucedly nice?

Then his hands began kneading her thigh.

"Um, sir, my pants are dirty anyway," she said, trying to pull away from him.

"I love your leg." His whisper was full of passion.

Lizzie was dumbfounded.

"Sir, please, I'm a . . . a man!"

"Yes, and I want to devour you with kisses. Ah, Charlie, you drive me *mad* with desire. . . . *MERDE!*" he almost screeched. He had run his hand up into her crotch. "You are a eunuch!"

"I am not!" she yelled back, grabbing a heavy sausage from the hamper and whacking his shoulder. "I'm a woman!"

"Stop!" he cried, pulling away from her and falling back into his seat as he dodged her sausage. "Stop hitting me! You'll ruin my jacket! And if you are a woman, why are you dressed like a boy? You have me all confused."

Lizzie put the sausage back in the hamper and tried to compose herself, her brain whirring.

"Well, I . . . I've run away from home," she said, not untruthfully.

Lucien was staring at her. After a moment he snickered. The snicker became a laugh. Then the laugh died away as he leaned forward, studying her face.

"You are a very pretty boy," he said softly, "but you must be a gorgeous woman. I would love to dress you. Yes, yes . . . I would design such beautiful dresses for you. . . ." He straightened and folded his arms over his chest. "Charlie," he said, "would you like to come with me to Paris?"

"Paris?" she repeated rather numbly. Lizzie didn't understand this curious young man at all.

"Paris, where I design clothes for the most exalted women in France, including the Empress herself. Unfortunately, most of them have bad figures. I will pay you well."

Lizzie stiffened at the mention of being paid.

"I am not talking about the world's oldest profession," he said. "I'm talking about the world's *newest* profession."

"His Lordship drew up this will only last week," said Mr. Bartlett, adjusting his gold-framed glasses on his eagle-beak nose. "Which, in the event, was fortunate."

Lady Rockfern dabbed her eyes with a handkerchief. She and Adam were seated in front of the desk in the paneled library of Pontefract Hall. The solicitor broke the red wax seal and unrolled the parchment. He cleared his throat and began reading: " 'I, Augustus Gascoigne Grimthorpe de Vere, second Earl of Pontefract, being of sound mind, do declare this my last will and testament. I bequeath to my beloved daughter, Sidonia, Lady Rockfern, the sum of two hundred and fifty thousand pounds. The rest of my estate I bequeath in its entirety to my grandson, Adam de Vere Thorne.' "

I'm rich, Adam thought. I'm the third Earl of Pontefract. It's incredible!

Twenty minutes later, after Mr. Bartlett had driven off, Mr. Hawkins, the butler, closed the front doors and turned to Adam.

"Milord," he said in his plummy voice, "may I extend my congratulations to you on the occasion of your accession?"

Milord. It sounded so strange.

"Thank you, Mr. Hawkins."

"Milord, if it may not be presumptuous to ask you at such an early time, but the staff is somewhat anxious . . ."

Adam looked confused. "About what?"

"If Milord has any intentions to change the staff in any way."

"Ah, I see." He thought a moment. "How many staff are there?"

"There are presently fifty-four persons employed at the Hall, including the groundskeepers."

It's like a private army, he thought, marveling at the number of his dependencies. "You may announce that I have no intentions of changing the staff at the present, and that I am giving everyone an extra ten pounds on the occasion of my inheriting."

The pompous butler in the white wig and blue-and-gold livery looked surprised. "Ten pounds, milord? Apiece? That is most extraordinarily generous, milord. On behalf of the staff, I offer our most heartfelt thanks."

He bowed. Adam's aunt, who was at his side, now took his arm and led him to the grand salon.

"You realize, my nephew, that ten pounds is what the scullery maids make in a full year?" said Lady Rockfern in a low voice. "You will spoil the servants, sir. It is generous, but it is a mistake."

"Aunt Sidonia, Fate, or whatever one wants to call it, has made me an extremely rich man. When I have so much, I can't believe it's a mistake to share with those who have so little."

She shot him a suspicious look. "I trust you do not endorse the radical views of the Socialists?"

He smiled. "I don't even know what their radical views are. Now, Aunt, we must discuss you. As you know, I am leaving soon for India. I don't know how long I'll be gone, but it may be as much as a year. I'm worried about your safety. Obviously, hiring the extra watchmen here wasn't enough."

"Dear Adam, I've already made up my mind," interrupted Lady Rockfern. "I have no desire to remain at Pontefract Hall after Father's tragic death. I have made arrangements to move in with Lady Hillsdale, my dearest friend, who has a charming house in London. I trust I will be safe from those despicable *thuggees* in Knightsbridge. Besides, you are now the master of Pontefract Hall and I'm sure a young man like yourself has no desire to be encumbered by an elderly aunt."

"That's not true," exclaimed Adam. "You know you are free to stay here as long as you like."

She smiled and patted his arm. "That's sweet of you, Adam, but it is time for me to move on. Besides, I enjoy London. But we have your future to think of. Now that Miss Desmond has so mysteriously vanished, what are your plans?"

"I have none, except to go to India."

"But Adam, you are embarking on a journey that you have admitted may be dangerous. Indeed, India itself can be dangerous, what with the ghastly heat and the many diseases we are susceptible to there. Dear Lady Hillsdale's niece, who was married to a Company official in Calcutta, only two years ago was carried off by the cholera and the poor thing was barely thirty. God forbid that another tragedy should befall us after the many terrible disasters that our family has recently suffered, but if something happened to you in India, the earldom would die out, there being no other male heirs."

Adam paused by the beautifully carved marble mantel. He had come to love Pontefract Hall. The possibility of losing all that had been thrust upon him so quickly was not pleasant, but he had promised his grandfather he would return the diamond.

"Aunt, what are you suggesting?" he said.

"I shan't be coy, since time is of the essence. Lady Sybil is a sweet woman of the utmost refinement. She also is related to some of the noblest families in the land, and I need hardly commend to you her beauty. You could do worse, Nephew. Much worse."

"But Aunt, aside from the fact that I'm not in love with her, my ship sails in five weeks—"

"It would be awkward, of course. And there is the fact that we are in mourning. But under these extraordinary circumstances, it could be arranged. Particularly if you did not require a dowry from Lord Nettlefield, who is more than usually hard-up these days."

Adam shook his head. "No. It's out of the question. I love Lizzie Desmond."

"And where," his aunt said in a cool voice, "*is* Lizzie Desmond?"

"I wish to God I knew," he sighed.

"Adam, your mother was mistreated by my father," his aunt continued. "But you are now the Earl of Pontefract, the head of this family. You owe it to me, as well as yourself, to try to secure the succession before you go to India. You may be in love with Miss Desmond, but in our position love has very little to do with marriage. Besides, she is a fugitive from the law and totally unsuitable to become your wife even if you could find her. I must urge you to reconsider about Sybil."

"But even if I did marry Sybil, there's no guarantee that in a few weeks I could father a child."

"At least there would be a chance. And you know, Sybil has many suitors. There's Sir Walter Musgrave's younger son, Edgar, who's madly in love with her. And Lord Dudley, who's immensely rich, has proposed to her twice already. Sybil told me she refused him because she's not in love with him, and she will only marry for love. But she's not going to remain single forever."

"Perhaps she doesn't love *me,*" he said.

"It would be rather difficult for her to love you, since all you think about is the Desmond woman. Furthermore, you haven't even had the courtesy to pay Sybil a call."

"All right, I'll think about it," he finally sighed. "But I'm not going to India on the *Eastern Star*, though I'll keep the booking till the last minute."

"I don't understand."

"I have an idea the *Eastern Star* may meet with an accident. I'm writing to the head of the shipping company suggesting he increase the guard at the India Docks when the ship comes in."

"Ah, I see. Yes, that is wise. Where are you going, Adam?"

He had started across the room toward the central hall.

"To pay a call on Sybil."

He was still in love with Lizzie. But he did have a responsibility to the family.

Fifteen minutes later, he dismounted from Grayling in front of Nettlefield Hall. The house, nowhere as imposing or grand as Pontefract Hall, nevertheless was a small Georgian gem. But the place looked rather rundown, which reminded Adam of Thorne Manor. A few sheep grazed on the front lawn, which was choked with weeds. As used as he had become to the beautifully maintained lawns and gardens of Pontefract Hall, Adam was suddenly rather ashamed of his own wealth and he felt sorry for Sybil and her family.

He spotted her walking around the side of the house, shading herself from the warm sun with a pale blue parasol that matched her dress. Adam started toward her, thinking how different she was from Lizzie. Lizzie had an earthiness to her, but Sybil was cool and composed, a Gainsborough compared to a Rubens.

"Mr. Thorne," she smiled as he came up to her. "Or rather, Lord Pontefract." She extended her gloved hand, which he kissed. "I haven't had the opportunity to tell you how distressed we all are over your grandfather's death. I read in the local paper that the police had not yet found the other Indian."

"No, and I doubt they will. I feel he's probably on his way back to India by now. May I walk with you, Sybil?"

"I would be enchanted. It's such a lovely day, though the flies have been a nuisance this summer. Perhaps we should walk to the lake. The views are so lovely. Have you heard any news of Miss Desmond?"

"Unfortunately, no."

They walked in silence for a while as they headed for a circular lake. Sybil thought Adam looked troubled, and he was. He was trying to make up his mind what to do, whether to give in to his aunt's pressure and, by so doing, betray Lizzie, or to remain loyal to her and by so doing betray his family. Sybil certainly had a lot in her favor, and he was attracted to her. Finally he said, "Sybil, I'm not very good at conversation. I'm not well-educated, and I suppose most people wouldn't even consider me a gentleman."

"Manners alone do not make a gentleman. As Lord Tennyson says, kind hearts are more important than coronets."

Adam looked at her, thinking that her classic profile was almost perfect. "Perhaps you're right," he said. "Or at least, I *hope* you are."

She smiled at him. "You have a coronet now, milord. Do you also have a kind heart?"

He frowned. "That's what I wanted to talk to you about.

You see, I have to go to India soon, and my aunt has been pressing me to find a wife before I go. I have a responsibility to the family . . ." He paused. "I'm not saying this very well, am I?"

"Dear Lord Pontefract—"

"Adam."

"Very well, Adam. I have no idea what you're trying to say. Look at our two swans. Aren't they beautiful? It's hard to believe they have such vicious tempers. But then, appearances are deceiving, aren't they?"

They had stopped at the edge of the lake. Adam waved a horsefly from his nose.

"What I'm trying to say is, would you consider being my wife?"

"But you're in love with Miss Desmond," she said. "And I could never consider marrying a man who was in love with someone else. Shall we start back? That cloud on the horizon looks somewhat ominous."

She turned back toward Nettlefield Hall, leaving Adam behind. A look of anger came over his face. Suddenly he bolted toward her. Grabbing her right hand, he turned her around so forcefully she dropped her parasol. He took her in his arms and kissed her. Immediately she pushed him away and slapped him, hard.

"I don't know how you treated your Miss Desmond," she said, "but you will treat me with respect, sir." She picked her parasol off the ground. "Under the circumstances, I will bid you good day."

She walked away from him. Adam watched her, surprise replacing the anger on his face.

"Damn," he muttered.

"I proposed to her, but she's impossible!" he shouted to his aunt that evening. "Impossible! I'm sorry to disappoint you, Aunt, but you have to admit I tried. The family will just have to take its chances I don't die of some horrible disease in India. The woman has an icicle for a heart."

Sidonia was seated by the fire in the library, working on

her needlepoint. "I don't believe that's true," she said. "What did you say to her?"

"Exactly what you've been saying. That I have a responsibility to marry, and would she consider being my wife?"

"That sounds so romantic, I'm surprised she didn't swoon with rapture."

Adam shot her a look.

"All right, I'll admit it wasn't very romantic. But I don't love her! Oh, the whole thing's impossible. Where's Lizzie, dammit? Everything would have been so simple if she . . ." He waved his hands in frustration, not finishing the sentence. Then he started toward the door. "I'm going to bed," he snorted. "Good night, Aunt."

After he had left the room, Sidonia put her needlepoint on her sewing table, got up and pulled the bellcord. A few minutes later, the butler appeared.

"Milady?"

"I realize it is late, Mr. Hawkins, but would you ask Chester to bring around a carriage? I wish to go to Nettlefield Hall."

"I won't marry him!" Sybil said hotly an hour later. "Why should I marry a man, no matter how attractive he is—and yes, I find him attractive—who's hopelessly infatuated with another woman?"

She was standing in front of the fireplace in the small drawing room of Nettlefield Hall. Her anxious-looking parents were sitting on a threadbare Hepplewhite sofa. Sidonia was seated opposite them in a chair whose chintz had faded.

"You must give him time, Sybil," Sidonia said. "He's headstrong and impetuous, and he's been in love with this Lizzie creature since they were children."

"It's like you and Edgar," said Lady Nettlefield to her daughter.

Sybil frowned. "Kindly leave Edgar Musgrave out of this conversation," she said. "I wouldn't marry *him*, either."

"It's damned well time you married *someone*," huffed

her father, taking a drink of port. "And if you ask me, you should jump at the chance to marry Adam. It seems to me he has everything a reasonable—or even an unreasonable—woman could want."

"But he doesn't love me," insisted his daughter.

"What's love?" snorted her father. "When you get to my age, love is nothing but a vague memory of an adolescent itch."

"I beg your pardon?" his wife snapped.

Lord Nettlefield stood up, his belly protruding beyond his open coat. "Sybil, you turned down Lord Dudley twice, and I begged you both times to accept him. Good Lord, the man's got twenty thousand acres—"

"Lord Dudley bores me," Sybil interrupted.

"Oh? Well, young lady, let me tell you that your intransigence is beginning to bore *me.* I have three daughters I have to marry off, and it's a damned expensive proposition. Sidonia tells me a dowry is not expected if you marry Adam, and I say you're a fool not to accept him. He's a fine young man, he's rich and he has a title. You're twenty now and getting to be a bit long in the tooth. How many plums like Adam are going to be dropped in your lap?"

Sybil's face turned icy at mention of her age. "Perhaps I prefer to be an unmarried spinster," she spat out.

"And live in back rooms, sponging off your relatives? Not a very attractive future, my dear," her father retorted. "No, Sybil, you're too damned proud. Always have been. Now, I'm not going to force you into any marriage. But if your foolish pride prevents you from accepting a man any other woman would jump through hoops for, I will be extremely displeased. Extremely. I have nothing more to say on the subject."

"Surely," Sidonia said in her gentlest tone, for Sybil looked on the verge of tears, "you have some feeling for Adam?"

"If you want to know the truth," she blurted, "I adore him." Everyone stared at her. "But can't you see how galling it is to me when all he thinks about is Miss Desmond?"

There was a silence.

"If that's the case," Sidonia said, "it seems perfectly clear to me that you should marry him and force him to fall in love with you. It's been done before."

"Yes," Lord Nettlefield said enthusiastically. "Sidonia is right. Make Adam fall in love with you. Seduce the man, dammit!"

"Shocking," murmured his wife.

"An interesting challenge," Sidonia said.

Sybil straightened. "Very well, I accept the challenge. I will marry Adam. And someday, I swear he's going to love me more than he loves Lizzie Desmond."

"You have a very good natural carriage, my dear," Lucien Delorme said to Lizzie, "but remember: you will be modeling for the Empress herself, so you must have *perfect* carriage, no?"

"I'm doing my best," said Lizzie, who was walking in a circle with a book on the blond wig Lucien had had made for her. They were in his atelier, or studio, on the second floor of his house in the Rue Cassette in Paris. Two of Lucien's assistants, one a middle-aged woman and the other a boy in his teens, were busily packing elaborate gowns into two huge leather trunks while Lucien watched Lizzie practicing her walk.

"The Empress is the most elegant woman in Europe, and if I can become her couturier it will make my fortune. Much depends on you, my dear: you'll be wearing my clothes. So think of yourself as an empress."

An empress on the run from the law, she thought.

"Henri! Imbécile! Prends garde!"

The boy had almost dropped one of the dresses on the floor.

"Pardon, Lucien."

"Everyone is so nervous!" groaned Lucien, wringing his hands. "It's a plot to make *me* nervous! Straighter, Adelaide. Straighter! You are an empress, you must walk like one! In two days we will be at Biarritz modeling for Eugénie—two days! Walk like an empress! Say: 'I am an empress.' "

"I am an empress," said Lizzie, who was walking so stiffly her back hurt.

"Your Majesty, Monsieur Delorme is here with his collection," said Mlle. Bouvert, reader to the Empress.

María Eugenia Ignacia Augustina, the former Countess de Montijo and now the Empress of the French, turned from her desk in her study at her villa at Biarritz and smiled.

"Good. Show Monsieur Delorme in."

The beautiful thirty-year-old wife of Emperor Napoleon III stood up. She was a stunning woman with regal bearing, tall and slim with a long neck. This daughter of a Grandee of Spain and sister-in-law of the Duke of Alba had innate style, a lively intelligence and flaming red hair. Her marriage in 1853 to the newly proclaimed French Emperor, the nephew of the great Napoleon, had surprised the courts of Europe. But luck was running with this pair of "adventurers," as they were still often called behind their backs. The French Second Empire was at the high noon of its glory; and just the previous spring, Eugénie had secured the dynasty by giving birth to a boy, the Prince Imperial, heir to his father's throne.

"Your Majesty," said Lucien Delorme, bowing as he came in the high-ceilinged room overlooking the Atlantic Ocean. Eugénie extended her hand, which the courturier kissed.

"Monsieur Delorme, I am prepared to be dazzled by your creations," said the Empress.

"Ah, Your Majesty, it is your beauty that dazzles," said Lucien, used to shameless flattery. "My poor dresses are eclipsed by your smile."

"Then perhaps I should continue with Madame Palmyre," Eugénie said, mischievously referring to one of the two official court dressmakers whose monopoly Lucien was hoping to destroy.

"But Your Majesty wishes to inspire the French fashion industry, not bore it to death," Lucien replied.

Eugénie laughed. "My dear Monsieur Delorme, I see you are a scorpion with a sting. But let's waste no more time: I'm eager to see what you've made. Where are your sketches?"

Lucien clapped his hands. "I have a surprise for Your Majesty. I'm calling them 'living sketches.' "

A beautiful girl in a black dress with a yellow jacket came into the room, which had open doors to a balcony over the ocean.

"This is Diane," Lucien announced. "She wears a day dress, perhaps suitable for Compiègne." He referred to the royal hunting château north of Paris.

Eugénie looked delighted. "What a clever idea, monsieur," she exclaimed. "To show the dresses on living people. I am overwhelmed. And I like the dress, too. How much?"

"Two thousand francs."

"Isn't that rather expensive?"

"Not for an Empress."

Eugénie laughed again as the model twirled in front of her, the huge black skirt billowing.

"My next model, Your Majesty, is a girl I hired in England last week. I came across her as I was returning from a buying trip to the mills in the north. Her name is Adelaide." Lizzie had told Lucien her name was Adelaide Markham after he hired her to model for him, the 'Charlie' disguise being replaced by a new pseudonym: Lizzie still was terrified of the police, even in France. After a minute, Lucien went to the door and looked out. What he saw alarmed him. Louis Napoleon, the Emperor of France whose amatory exploits were the dirty joke of Europe, was next to Lizzie talking to her in subdued tones as his right fingers toyed with the end of his mustache. The Emperor was shorter than Lizzie and was an unattractive man with a head too large for his potbellied body, but Lucien knew that if he lured his beautiful English model into bed and if Eugénie found out about it, his budding business with the Empress would be nipped.

"Adelaide," he said softly.

Lizzie, who was wearing a breathtaking white ball gown festooned with pink bows, looked at him. Then she curtsied to the Emperor and hurried to Lucien.

Louis Napoleon moved his fingers down to his goatee, which had been renamed an "imperial" in his honor. As Lizzie disappeared into Eugénie's study, the Emperor began plotting how to steer the English beauty into his imperial bed.

James Randolph Cavanagh III looked in his mirror and liked what he saw: this twenty-nine-year-old plantation owner from Virginia was good-looking and he knew it and delighted in it. He had naturally curly thick brown hair, steel-blue eyes, clean-cut features and a wide mustache that he liked to think gave him the dashing look of a bandit chief. Tonight he wanted to look especially dashing, because tonight he was going to a ball at the Tuileries Palace, an invitation he had secured through his fellow American, Dr. Harry Evans, who was the Emperor's dentist. Since Napoleon III had excruciatingly bad teeth, Dr. Evans' influence at the court was considerable.

Jack, as he was known, adjusted his white tie, took one final brush over the broad shoulders of his tailcoat, then picked up his top hat and white-silk-lined opera cloak. Putting them on, he left the bedroom of his twelve-franc-a-night suite at the Grand Hotel du Louvre, Paris's swankest new hotel, and headed for the staircase to the lobby. Jack Cavanagh owned five thousand acres of rich land in Virginia. He owned three hundred slaves. His main crop was tobacco, but it was his skill as a stock speculator that made him rich. He had made a fortune in railroad stocks, which brought him an income of over one hundred thousand dollars a year—a fortune in 1856, when the dollar's purchasing power was perhaps twenty times what it would later become. Jack was one of the richest men in the South, and he liked the high life. This was his first trip to Paris, a city with the "wickedest" reputation in the world, and Jack had high hopes of meeting one of the *grandes horizontales*, or beautiful courtesans, who were the talk of the town. Dr. Evans had warned him that the glamorous *haute bicherie* was not admitted at the court, but that the Emperor's new love, the gorgeous English girl named Adelaide Markham, would be at the Tuileries that night. Jack wanted to see it all. He was also itching to get laid.

He took a cab in front of the hotel and headed for the palace. Paris was in the process of being transformed under the energetic—some said despotic—direction of the Prefect of the Seine, Baron Georges Haussmann. Great sections of medieval Paris were being demolished, over fifty thousand dwellings had been torn down, and the wide modern boulevards constructed in their stead. The Parisians were howling with rage at this desecration of their city, although even the most outraged would admit that the new sewers and the destruction of the narrow, stinking streets which bred cholera was probably a good thing. To Jack Cavanagh, this new Paris that was rising was breathtakingly beautiful and exciting beyond belief. As his *fiacre* approached the Arc du Carrousel, the *entrée d'honneur* of the enormous Tuileries Palace—the Buckingham Palace of Paris, built by Catherine de' Medici—the young Virginia planter was drunk with Paris.

Lizzie Desmond picked up a copy of the London *Times* from a table in Lucien Delorme's front hall. After the burlesque attack on "Charlie" in the carriage, Lucien's physical interest in her had vanished, and when he invited her to stay in an extra bedroom of his studio house on the Left Bank, she had agreed for reasons of expediency. Lucien, whose father was a rich stockbroker, had family money, and his two-story house in the pleasant and aristocratic quarter of old town houses and convents was charming, overlooking a small private garden. It was here that he designed his dresses, gave the designs to seamstresses who worked for slave wages, then put the dresses on Lizzie for fittings. It was interesting work for her and, more to the point, it was safe. She had been away from England now almost three weeks, and her anxiety was beginning to subside. She enjoyed Lucien's never-never-land world of fashion and was coming to have a passion for his beautiful clothes. She also enjoyed the admiration of Parisian men—not to mention the Emperor—because she was only human and was becoming aware of her own beauty for the first time in her life.

But it was all soured by her remorse and guilt about the death of her father. Time and again she wondered about the wisdom of her fleeing. While she knew in her heart she was not guilty of murder, in the eyes of the law she probably was and her flight only compounded her apparent culpability. The fact that Lucien had paid for a forged passport for "Adelaide Markham" to get her out of the country made matters even worse (the designer suspected Lizzie was in trouble with the law, but in his eagerness to use her as a model he hadn't asked too many questions). And always the memory of her dear father's smoking corpse on the bed in the crofter's cottage: the man who had devoted his entire life to rightness, destroyed by his sinning daughter.

And now she was to learn that she had lost the *other* man in her life. As she turned the pages of the *Times* (Lucien, like many chic Parisians, was an Anglophile and subscribed to the London paper to look fashionable), a headline caught her eyes: "Lord Pontefract Weds Lady Sybil Hardwick." She began trembling as she read:

> The third Earl of Pontefract, who succeeded to the title two weeks ago after the sensational murder of his grandfather, the second earl, at Pontefract Hall in Yorkshire, surprised the county by his marriage to Lady Sybil Hardwick yesterday at Nettlefield Hall. The unseemly haste of the nuptials was necessitated by Lord Pontefract's departure for India on the *Eastern Star*. The new earl, who is the former Adam Thorne, has vowed to find the other Indian murderer of his grandfather and bring him to justice. It is believed the two men, one of whom was killed on the grounds of Pontefract Hall, are fanatics of a sect worshiping the Hindu goddess Kali. The new Countess of Pontefract is the daughter of the Earl and Countess of Nettlefield . . .

"Adelaide, are you ready?"

She turned to see her employer hurrying down the stairs from his bedroom. Lucien was a dainty man two inches shorter than Lizzie, but in his perfectly tailored evening clothes he looked elegant, and in Paris elegance forgave many sins. At the bottom of the stairs he stopped. "What's wrong? You're crying."

"It's . . . nothing." She put the *Times* back on the table and sank into a chair, sobbing. Adam, she thought. My love, my knight, my everything . . . and he's married someone else. And I'm carrying his child . . . what can I do?

"Stop crying! Stop it this instant! You'll ruin the dress!" Lucien was standing in front of her, stamping his feet.

"I don't care about the dress," she sobbed. "And I can't go to the ball. I just want to die."

She buried her face in her arms.

"Your tears will stain the silk!" Lucien was almost screaming. "Stop it!"

She looked up, anger in her eyes. "Oh be quiet, you horrid little man," she exclaimed. "My heart is broken, and I don't care about your silly dress."

"Silly?" he squealed. "You call this *éblouissante* creation *silly?* You're . . . what's the word? Fired! I fire you! Now, take off my dress and leave this house at once!"

Lizzie realized she had gone too far. She had created an alter ego in Adelaide Markham to protect herself from the police, and no matter how heartsick she felt, she had to placate Lucien and keep her job. She stood up, drying her eyes on her lace kerchief. In fact, the "silly" dress was sublime, a dream of pale blue silk, its huge skirt swagged with rose chiffon. She knew she looked fabulous. She gave him a cool stare, forcing the ache and guilt out of her heart.

"I don't think you'll fire me, Lucien," she said. "The Emperor will be terribly put out if I'm not at the Tuileries tonight. I apologize for my little display a moment ago, but I read some rather shocking news in the *Times*—"

"What news?" interrupted Lucien, his passion for gossip overruling everything else.

"Someone I know," she whispered sadly. "Someone I loved, but I fear I've lost him forever." No! she thought, straightening, determination coming into her face. Someday I'll find Adam. She looked at Lucien. "Shall we go to the palace?"

She wrapped her cashmere shawl around her shoulders and started for the door. Lucien thought he had never seen a woman look more magnificent.

"Do you, Lettice Winifred Desmond, take this man to be your lawfully wedded husband, to have and to hold . . ."

As the Reverend Bartholomew Cringall droned on, Lettice looked through her white wedding veil at Horace Belladon, the man she had almost lost, thanks to her sister. Horace Belladon had been so appalled by the notoriety of Reverend Desmond's murder that he had backed out of his engagement with Lettice. The murder had generated reams of publicity, and the headlines had been as lurid as Stringer MacDuff had predicted: "Murder on the Moors!" "Vicar's Daughter Kills Father!" "Suspect Vanishes, Believed Escaped from England!" A nation fascinated by violent crime devoured every morsel of the case, and the two remaining Desmond sisters cowered behind the ivied walls of the parsonage at Wykeham Rise until, two weeks after their father's remains were buried in the crypt of the Yorkshire church, they were evicted by the Church of England to make room for the family of Reverend Desmond's successor. Even hard-hearted Horace Belladon had been moved by the plight of Lettice and Minna, who had been left practically penniless, and he advanced Lettice a loan of two hundred pounds, urging them to come stay with him at the Priory, his home in the Manchester suburbs, until the storm of publicity died down. Lettice hardly needed urging: she was desperate. They left the parsonage with their few belongings and traveled to Manchester, moving into the spacious brick villa where Horace's widowed mother chaperoned. In time, Horace's middle-aged passion for the beautiful Lettice rekindled and he renewed his proposal, which she lost no time accepting.

But she would never forgive Lizzie for almost costing her the rich Mr. Belladon.

"I now pronounce you man and wife."

Tears of joy and relief filled her eyes as she lifted her veil and turned to her chubby, bewhiskered groom, who now kissed her. The Gothic Church of St. Stephen was half-filled with Manchester businessmen and their eminently respectable wives, many of whom had wanted to boycott the ceremony but were forced to attend by their husbands, who, after all, were in business with Horace. And the scandal *was* beginning to die down.

But as Lettice and her groom started up the aisle, the organ pealing Mendelssohn's Wedding March, the new Mrs. Horace Belladon swore to herself someday she would pay Lizzie back.

It was a Winterhalter world waltzing to Strauss. As Lucien's carriage drove into the Place de la Concorde, Lizzie gasped with pleasure as she saw the Tuileries Gardens, illuminated by thousands of gas lamps in white glass globes. The fountains and pools were lit by hundreds of colored lights, and the trees were lit by luminous balloons and Bengal lights.

"It's like a fairyland!" she exclaimed.

"The Emperor puts on a good show," Lucien agreed.

They waited in the Place du Carrousel as a long line of carriages disgorged their elaborately dressed passengers in front of the Pavillon d'Horloge, the central section of the massive stone palace. Finally, their door was opened by a pygmy in a green silk jacket and white turban, and Lizzie stepped out, followed by Lucien, who handed his crown-embossed invitation to a court chamberlain in a scarlet coat. Then they entered the palace, joining the crowd inching its way up the grand staircase with its high, arched ceiling. At both ends of each step stood one of the Emperor's elite Cent Gardes looking splendid in their sky-blue tunics, white breeches, black top boots, their helmets with flowing horsehair manes and their burnished steel breastplates.

"Aren't they gorgeous?" said Lucien, ogling the guards. "They're picked for their looks, you know. It doesn't matter whether they can fight. They have to be at least six feet tall."

Lucien couldn't take his eyes off the guards, but Lizzie was drinking everything in. At the top of the staircase they pushed into the Salle du Trône, then on to the Salon d'Apollon, the Salon du Premier Consul—great, high rooms, baroquely decorated, their walls swirling with gilt, their chandeliers dripping crystal, paintings of the imperial family hanging everywhere. A pantheon of Napoleons. The Emperor. His cousin, the heavyset Prince "Plon-Plon." The Princesse Mathilde. And, most prominent, a huge Winterhalter portrait of Eugénie.

But despite the glamour and excitement of the evening, two thoughts beat in Lizzie's brain like a drum: Adam and her child.

In the huge Salle des Marichaux, Jack Cavanagh gaped at the gilt caryatids holding up the elaborate ceiling and the portraits of Napoleon I's marshals of France. Mentally he compared this palatial extravaganza with the more humble republican rooms of the White House, where he had dined twice. Jack decided he liked this French palace better. As a Southern slave owner and a heavy contributor to the Democratic Party, Jack was becoming increasingly disenchanted with Washington. The damned Abolitionists were gaining power every day.

But he quickly forgot American politics when he saw the radiant blond in the pale blue dress with the dusty-rose chiffon trim come into the room on the arm of the little man with the curly hair.

"My God," he said, "that's the most beautiful woman I've ever seen!"

"It's Miss Markham," said Dr. Evans, joining Jack. The American dentist was a frumpy man with a beard. "The English 'model,' I think they're calling her. The Emperor is mad for her."

"Is she his mistress?" asked Jack, his eyes glued to Lizzie.

"Oh no. At least, not yet. Delorme, the little fellow with her, doesn't want the Empress furious at him, and Eugénie has a temper. Want to meet her?"

"Miss Markham? You bet!"

Dr. Evans led Jack through the crowd to Lizzie and Lucien, both of whom had just taken flutes of champagne from a passing footman. After the introductions, Jack asked Lizzie for a waltz, as the orchestra at the end of the room had begun playing. Lizzie quickly accepted.

"So you're an American?" she said as Jack twirled her around the parquet. "I've never met an American. I thought all Americans wore deerskin, like Daniel Boone."

"Well"—he smiled—"I guess we're not as slick as you Europeans, but we're not exactly savages."

"And where in America are you from, Mr. Cavanagh?"

"Virginia. I'm a tobacco planter, ma'am. May I say, Miss Markham, you are the most beautiful thing in this palace, and there are a lot of beautiful things in this palace."

Lizzie smiled. It occurred to her that she rather liked this good-looking American with the odd-sounding Virginia accent. It also occurred to her that since the love of her life had married someone else, she had better start looking for a new love.

And a father for her baby.

Adam awoke in the middle of the night to the sound of someone sobbing. He sat up in his bed in the room next to the master bedroom where his grandfather had been murdered. Pale moonlight filtered through the tall windows. He saw his wife standing before one window, looking out over the park. She was wearing a white nightgown.

"Sybil?"

Silence, except for the sobbing.

"What's wrong?"

He got out of the big bed and crossed the room to her side. He put his arms around her, but she shrugged him off.

"Go back to bed," she said.

"Not till you tell me what's wrong. Are you crying because I'm leaving for India tomorrow?"

She laughed slightly.

"Don't flatter yourself."

She put a handkerchief to her eyes to wipe them.

"It really *is* impossible for you to come with me," he said as she went to a table and lit an oil lamp. "The ship I'm taking is filthy, and it may be dangerous—"

"I'm not crying about India, although leaving a week after our marriage seems rather inconsiderate of my feelings. People must be having a good laugh at my expense. I'm sure they're saying, 'Lord Pontefract is so infatuated with his bride, he goes to the other side of the world on his honeymoon—*alone*.' "

"If they're foolish enough to say that, let them. I couldn't care less. You knew I had to go to India—"

"I'm telling you, it's *not* India!"

"Then what *is* it?"

"Tonight—and last night and the night before that—you tossed and turned in our bed so much you woke me up. You must have bad dreams, Adam. Or maybe they're sweet dreams. At any rate, you talk in your sleep. And you know what you say? 'Lizzie.' You keep repeating her name. Over and over and over. 'Lizzie, Lizzie, Lizzie.' It's not enough that you think of her when you're awake. You have to insult me by dreaming about her!"

Adam turned red. "I'm sorry, Sybil."

"Do you deny it?"

"No. I dream about her. I'm trying to put her out of my waking thoughts, but I have no control over my dreams."

"To my mind, there is nothing more tedious than a jealous wife, but I see no reason why I have to hear the woman's name repeated over and over in my bed. I'll spend the rest of the night in another room."

"Sybil, I'm sorry. I *am* trying. . . ."

"Perhaps by the time you get back from India, you'll have succeeded in ridding yourself of your obsession. In the meantime: good night."

She picked up the lamp and left the room. Alone, Adam went to the window and leaned his arm on the center sash. Squeezing his fist, he leaned his head on his arm, closing his eyes.

When he opened them, they were filled with tears.

When Sybil reached the bedroom next door, she was crying again.

"So you want to marry me?" Lizzie said a week later as Jack Cavanagh got down on one knee before her. They were having dinner in room number sixteen at the Café Anglais, arguably the best restaurant in the world. Lizzie had just finished some *écrevisses à la bordelaise* prepared by Adolphe Dugléré, arguably the best chef in the world.

"Adelaide, honey, you've just taken my breath away," Jack exclaimed, clasping his hands in a prayerful gesture. His eyes were bloodshot from a bottle of Château Lafite—the Café Anglais had a cellar of two hundred thousand bottles, and the wine could be passed from table to table on a miniature railway. "I suppose I fell for you when I first saw you, but this past week . . . well, I just can't think of anything or anyone but you. You dazzle me. Please say you'll be mine."

Silly or not, tight or not, she could see he meant it: Jack was madly in love. His proposal was tempting. He was nice-looking and rich, if a bit rough around the edges—but then, Adam had been rough around the edges. She got up from the lavishly set table and walked across the carpeted room to stare into a mirror. She knew this room was one of the most notorious in Europe. Number sixteen at the Café Anglais—'*le grand Seize*,' as it was known in Paris—was the scene of numerous seductions by the *gratin* of Paris. Jack had tried to seduce her more than once this past week, but she had held him off. But now she had to make a decision, because he had told her he had to return to America soon. America held obvious attractions for someone wanted by the English police, although the idea of marrying a slave owner gave her a certain uneasiness. However, he had assured her he was "easy" with his slaves, as he had put it. She wasn't in love with Jack. But the harsh fact was that her pregnancy was beginning to show. She desperately needed a father for that baby, and there was Jack, on his knee, offering her safety, legitimacy and wealth. She decided, in fairness to him, she should tell him *some* of the truth.

She turned to him. "I am flattered and honored, sir, by your proposal. But before I answer you, I feel I must tell you the truth about myself. My name isn't Adelaide Markham. I made that up when I ran away from my home in England."

He slowly got to his feet. "Why did you run away from home?" he asked.

"I found out that I am carrying a child."

He blinked. "Who's the man?" he asked hoarsely.

"An Englishman I probably will never see again. His name is unimportant."

She saw him clench his fists. She saw sweat appear on his brow. He didn't speak for almost a minute. Finally, he whispered, "Will you let me claim the child as my own?"

She hesitated, then said, "Yes." Why not?

"Will you keep it a secret?"

"Yes."

"Will you swear to me there'll never be another man in your life as long as I'm your husband?"

She stiffened. "Sir, I may not be pure," she said, "but I would never be deceitful. I would of course honor my marriage vows."

He hesitated, but only for a moment. He rushed across the room, taking her in his arms and planting his reechy-breathed lips against hers, kissing her passionately. Then he threw back his head and whooped, "Yahoo! Ya-HOO! I've got me the prettiest bride in the world! Oh honey, when my friends back in Virginny see you, they're gonna turn pea green with envy. Ya-*HOO!* This calls for champagne!"

He ran to tug at the bellcord.

"God damn!" He grinned at her. "Ain't this romantic?" She noticed that his speech got more "country" as the alcohol level in his blood rose. "You're gonna be the prettiest thing Gloucester County's ever seen! But hey, I don't even know your name! I can't marry you if I don't know your name, can I? What is it?"

"Elizabeth Desmond."

"Elizabeth. I like that."

"My friends call me Lizzie."

"Lizzie," he breathed softly. "Why, honey, I think that's the most beautiful name I ever heard. It's the most beautiful name in the world. Ya-HOO!"

I've made the right decision, she told herself. Yes, I'm sure it's right.

Then why am I already having second thoughts?

CHAPTER

5

Adam leaned on the rail of the freighter *Jupiter* and watched the bank of the Thames slide by, wondering what lay in store for him in India. Although he had told Sybil he thought the other Sikh assassin had returned to India, he had no proof of that. Nor, for that matter, did he know whether there weren't yet more *thuggees* in London after him and the Idol's Eye, which he had strapped around his waist beneath his shirt in a specially-designed belt. Over six weeks had passed since his grandfather's murder, but Scotland Yard, in the person of Inspector Sebastian Quaid who had been put in charge of the case, still had no idea who was behind the assassination. To throw the Sikhs off his trail, Adam was not only traveling under his own name of Thorne rather than the more attention-gathering title Lord Pontefract; he had also booked passage on the *Jupiter*, which had cheap quarters for a few passengers, instead of the luxury ship *Eastern Star*. Unfortunately, this was costing him time. *Eastern Star* sailed from London to Alexandria, Egypt, where the passengers took a newly finished railroad via Cairo to Suez, sailing from there to Bombay, the total time being two months. But the *Jupiter*, carrying freight, had to lumber all the way around Africa and thence across the Indian Ocean to Calcutta via Ceylon, and the total time, depending on the winds (for the *Jupiter* had no engines), could be as much as six months. Adam had brought along books on Indian history and the Hindu language, being determined to use the time to advantage by absorbing as much as possible of his Indian heritage.

"Take a last look at our green and pleasant land," said

a burly man with a fierce black beard who came up to the railing beside Adam. "You won't be seeing much green in India. My name's Bentley Brent, lad, and since we'll be seeing a good deal of each other the next few months, we should get acquainted."

"My name's Adam Thorne."

They shook hands, then Bentley leaned on the rail.

"And why are you going to India, if I might be so bold as to ask?"

"I'm writing a book about it," Adam replied with glib evasiveness. He had no intention of telling anyone about the diamond.

"Ah well, it will have to be a big book, because it's a big country. I've been out there over ten years and still could hardly qualify as an expert on the bloody place. I'm a captain in the Fifty-third Native Infantry, stationed at Cawnpore. I've been home in Shropshire on six months' leave, but I have to admit I rather miss India, dirty and hot as it is. I have a feeling the food on this tub is going to win few culinary prizes, eh? And the captain could pass as a pirate."

"Let's hope he isn't."

Adam was delighted to meet this hulking officer, who was traveling in mufti, because he felt certain that he would prove to be a goldmine of firsthand information about the Subcontinent. And this turned out to be true. In the next few days—and Bentley's prediction about the food turned out to be distressingly accurate—he filled Adam in on life in India, including an overview of the history of the East India Company, the charter of which had been signed by Queen Elizabeth I on the last day of the year 1599. During the next hundred years, English merchants vied with the Portuguese and French for the lucrative Indian trade while the power of the Mogul Emperors, who controlled the Subcontinent, slowly waned. When the last great emperor, Aurangzeb, died leaving seventeen descendants to fight over their inheritance, the Empire began to disintegrate, and as the central power waned in Delhi, new power centers sprang up elsewhere. Foreign invaders marched in to seize what land they could while the old princely states, such as Hyderabad, tried to extend their influence at Delhi's expense. The result was chaos. The English East India Company found itself forced to protect its trade militarily, and by the end of the eighteenth century, the Company's influence was so extended that the English government decided to absorb it. Those portions of India controlled by the Company now became in effect a colony of the British government under the charge of a governor-general appointed by London. British troops were brought in, and native troops were organized under the command of English officers like Bentley, the native infantrymen called *sepoys* and the cavalry *sowars.* British power grew, and the governor-general in Calcutta began to take over princely states whose rulers he did not approve of.

"India's a powder keg," Bentley told Adam after dinner the fourth night out. "Ever since the army started bringing out their wives, with their damned stuffy morals, treating the natives like niggers, the whites and the natives are at each other's throats. If you ask me, India is about to explode."

The explosion was to be set off by a curious new bullet and a very ordinary biscuit called a "chupatty."

"Lizzie," burped Jack Cavanagh, "I'm the happiest man in the world. No, I take that back. I'll be the happiest man in the world when you get out of that wedding dress, pretty as it is. I'm just *dyin'* to . . . well, you know what I mean."

He refilled his champagne glass. They were in the drawing room of his suite at the Hotel du Louvre, having come directly from the American Embassy in Paris, where they had celebrated their marriage in festive style. During the past ten days, Jack had lavished gifts on his bride-to-be: a complete wardrobe designed by Lucien Delorme, a magnificent diamond-and-ruby necklace with matching earrings from Lemonnier, Paris' leading jeweler, as well as an engagement ring of two perfect white diamonds that took her breath away. To the poor daughter of a Yorkshire parson, Jack's purse seemed bottomless. And while he had proven to be a heavy drinker, still his kindness and attentions to her were such that she had become convinced she was doing the right thing marrying him after all. Her heart would always belong to Adam, but as Mrs. James Randolph Cavanagh III, she and her unborn baby were American citizens beyond the reach of the English law—or, at least, so she assumed. Now she smiled prettily as she came to her husband, put her arms around him and kissed him.

"I'm very happy," she whispered.

Jack put down his champagne glass and started to pick her up. "Hell, I can't wait," he said. "I'll carry you over the threshold like a proper groom and plunk you down on the bed."

"No, Jack, it's going to take me a bit of doing to get out of this dress. Give me fifteen minutes."

He put her down. "You damned women put so much armor around you, it's a wonder any babies get born at all. All right, honey, I'll wait out here. You've got fifteen minutes."

She kissed him again, then hurried across the room and went through the double sliding doors to the bedroom, closing them behind her. She closed her eyes, thinking a moment of Adam. Then she started to get out of the elaborate wedding dress Lucien had designed for her. First, she removed the crescent headpiece with its train of delicate lace. Then she stepped out of the white dress, the crinolines, the underskirt and the frilled pantalets. She put on the white nightgown, also designed by Lucien, then climbed in the big bed to await her groom.

Precisely at the end of the fifteen minutes, the double doors slid open and Jack came in. He had removed his coat and cravat, and his face was flushed from the champagne. He slid the doors shut and came to the bed, staring at her. "You're so beautiful," he whispered as he began unbuttoning his shirt. "So beautiful. I'm the happiest man in the world."

When he was naked, he climbed in between the silk sheets and took her in his arms. "I better warn you, honey, I'm a very physical man," he said. "I sure hope you like it as much as I do, and I assume you do, since you got deflowered somewhere along the line. Which is one reason

I'm so crazy about you. You've got experience, not like those whey-faced professional virgins back home."

Lizzie reflected that it wasn't perhaps the most tactful remark to make on her wedding night, but she held her tongue. Jack didn't hold his, though. After kissing her, he opened her nightgown and began licking her nipples, his hungry hands kneading and exploring her flesh. Gently and expertly, he got her out of her nightclothes and mounted her, continuing to kiss and lick her body. "Your tits," he mumbled. "God, what tits you got! I love 'em!"

When it was over, he held her in his arms and whispered, "Did you like it, honey? Did you enjoy it? Was I good?"

"You were wonderful," she smiled, giving him a reassuring kiss because it was obvious he *wanted* to be reassured. And, in fact, he had been good.

"I've yet to hear you say, 'I love you.' Do you love me, Lizzie?"

"Yes, darling, I love you."

"You weren't thinking of that . . . that other man?"

"Of course not."

But she was lying.

Sybil cantered through the mist into the stableyard behind Pontefract Hall. Chester, her coachman-groom, came out of the stone stable to help her dismount.

"Milady," he said, "Mr. Musgrave arrived about twenty minutes ago."

Sybil looked a little surprised. Then she went inside the house where Mr. Hawkins told her Edgar was in the drawing room. She had mixed feelings as she went through the house. She had had a schoolgirl crush on Edgar Musgrave, who was the only man before Adam who had ever excited her. But she was fully aware that Edgar was selfish, heartless and tricky, coasting through life on his charm and considerable good looks. She had the odd feeling he was up to no good.

When she came into the great room, he was standing by the fireplace leafing through a book. He looked up and smiled, putting the book on a table. "Sybil. Or should I call you Lady Pontefract?"

"Don't be absurd. When did you get back from Tuscany?"

"Three days ago. And when I went through my mail, I found your wedding invitation. I was devastated to have missed being there. And now I hear the lucky groom has gone off to darkest India. How could he have torn himself from your side so quickly?"

He was impeccably dressed: she knew his tailor bills were enormous, and his tailor was lucky if he were paid within a year. Edgar was an expert at living beyond his means. But he was definitely good to look at. Tall, slender, with a long, narrow face, piercing blue eyes and thick, curly golden hair. She had always loved his hair.

"If you ever read anything besides your checkbook, Edgar, you might have noticed in the *Times* that my husband has gone to India to try to find his grandfather's murderer."

"Oh, I never read my checkbook. My bank balance depresses me so. Yes, I heard about the murder—or should I say 'murders'? Some sinister Indian seems intent on wiping out your husband's entire family. Happily, you now have me to protect you."

"How gallant of you. But I feel quite safe, thank you."

"Safe and lonely, I wager. Well, since you won't let me protect you, surely you'll let me amuse you. And yes, I'd be delighted to stay for lunch."

She laughed. "I see you've lost none of your outrageousness."

"On the contrary, six months in lovely Italy has made me more outrageous than ever. And totally, irresistibly charming."

He took her gloved hand and raised it to his lips, giving her a suggestive look with his blue eyes.

"Let me make one thing quite clear, Edgar," she said. "I am very much in love with my husband."

"Ah, but you were once very much in love with me."

"That was before I acquired better taste in men."

He released her hand. "But first love is always the strongest. I am told your husband had a first love: the notorious Miss Desmond. Does he ever speak to you about her?"

Sybil turned away.

"Dear me, I think I've hit a sore nerve." Edgar came up behind her and put his hands on her arms. "I shan't mention her name again."

She turned back to him, tears in her eyes.

"Oh Edgar," she whispered, "if only I could make him forget her!"

"If only," he said softly, "I could make you forget your husband."

The rain poured, the lightning sizzled, the thunder crashed, and Adam wondered if the *Jupiter* would make it through the storm.

"Does it always rain this hard?" he yelled to Bentley Brent who, like Adam, was hanging on to a line on the port side of the main deck as the three-masted *Jupiter* wallowed in the heavy seas of the Bay of Bengal.

"This is a gentle shower compared to the monsoon," Bentley yelled back. "When the monsoon comes, it's as if God tipped over the Indian Ocean. Nature tends to be melodramatic out here. When it's hot, you fry. And when it rains, you drown."

And yet, there was something exciting about the natural extravaganza, and neither Adam nor Bentley was about to go back in the cramped quarters of the ship, if for no other reason than that, for the first time in ten days, the withering heat had been broken and the rain-fresh air smelled sweet.

"Land ho!" yelled a lookout far above their heads. Adam projected his hand over his eyes, trying to keep the rain out as he squinted to see the coast. During his many conversations with Bentley the past seven months—it had taken an agonizingly long time to complete the voyage, thanks to a broken mast off South Africa and two weeks in the doldrums of the Indian Ocean's Horse Latitudes—there had been something else besides the fact that he was the Earl of Pontefract that Adam had concealed. Adam had never told anyone, including Sybil, that he had Indian blood in his veins. It agonized him that he couldn't bring himself to say it. Rationally, he told himself it was a ridiculous thing to keep secret. Only one-eighth of his blood was Indian, and he looked completely English, though his hair was jet black. Besides, what was there to be ashamed of? His great-grandmother had been a Brahmin, the second-highest caste; and he now knew enough Indian history and culture to realize that his English ancestors had been painting their bodies blue when his Indian ancestors had been enjoying the refinements of an exquisite civilization.

But he couldn't bring himself to say "I am part Indian." In his many conversations with Bentley, the latter, while professing a fondness for his *sepoys,* nevertheless let slip in little ways that he considered them somehow inferior because of their dark skin. He would make jokes about their laziness, their shiftiness, or their childlike attitudes. Sometimes, like the wives of the English officers he had criticized, he even called them "niggers." As much as it bothered him and even shamed him, Adam continued to pass as a lily-white Englishman.

But as he peered through the rain, he knew there was another reason besides returning the great diamond that he was coming to India. Somehow he had to make peace with himself. He had to come to terms with his Indian blood.

Suddenly the rain slackened and he saw a low-lying coast on the horizon.

"India," he said more to himself than Bentley. There was awe in his voice. But there was also fear.

The next morning, the *Jupiter* moved slowly up the Hooghly River toward Calcutta.

"Corpses," said Bentley, leaning on the rail and pointing at distant black objects floating downstream. "Poor Hindus can't afford firewood to burn their family corpses, so they just chuck them in the river. The vultures get them in the end. Or the fish. Fancy being so poor you can't afford firewood to burn your dead."

He spoke matter-of-factly, but Adam, leaning on the rail next to him, felt a twinge of repulsion. The morning was stiflingly hot under a slate-gray sky, and there was an odd smell in the air. At first Adam wondered if it were the smell of death, but later he would learn that it was the smell of India, an exotic blend of heat and dirt and spices.

"I know you're going to Lucknow," Bentley continued. "But you've come a long way and you should spend a few days in Calcutta. If you'd like, I could show you the sights. And since there's no hotel fit for a white man, why don't you stay with me at Sir Carlton McNair's house? He's made a fortune in the tea business and built himself one of the grandest houses in Calcutta. I'm sure he'd be pleased to put you up."

Adam thought Bentley was right; since he'd come so far, there was no great hurry to return the diamond. So by the time the *Jupiter* docked at the Chandpal Ghat, the city's main wharf, he told Bentley he'd be "delighted" to accept his invitation.

The nearly naked dhoti-wearing natives swarmed aboard the ship looking for tips to carry baggage ashore. One of them furtively strayed farther, and took note of the name "Adam Thorne" on the ship's passenger list.

"The Englishman has arrived in Calcutta aboard the *Jupiter*," said the rather sly-looking young Indian whose name was Azimullah. He had begun life a starving orphan in Cawnpore, a city on the River Ganges in central India. He had been taken into the Cawnpore Free School where he became first a *khansaman*, or cook, then a teacher, and finally the confidential agent of the Maharajah of Bithur, Dhondu Pant, who was known as Nana Sahib.

"This Adam Thorne is clever," replied thirty-two-year-old Nana Sahib as he lined up a billiard shot. The two men were in the billiard room of Nana Sahib's palace in Bithur, a town a few miles upriver from Cawnpore. "He eluded my men in London by pretending to sail on the *Eastern Star*. Well, he's in India now. It will take more than cleverness to escape me here. Is he staying in Calcutta?"

Nana Sahib hit the billiard ball. He was stout, with a sleekly elegant look. His pale-complexioned face had a thin black mustache which swooped over his small, sensuous mouth. He was richly dressed in a pink silk *achkan*;

three strings of enormous pearls hung around his neck, and he sported a huge diamond ring on the middle finger of his right hand.

"My man tells me he went with a certain Captain Brent to Sir Carlton McNair's mansion, where he's staying until McNair's dinner for the Governor-General, Lord Canning."

Nana Sahib was lining up another shot.

"Canning is an ass-kisser. All the bastard English are snobs, fawning over titles. A year ago, Adam Thorne was a nobody. Now—thanks to me!—he's Lord Pontefract, one of the richest men in England, and of course Lord Canning kisses his ass."

"Excuse me, Your Highness," said Azimullah, "but my man says no one knows he is Lord Pontefract. The Englishman is going only by the name Adam Thorne."

Nana Sahib shrugged. "Canning's still an ass-kisser. I'd like to kill every damned white-skinned *boorao*—and maybe I will." He winked at Azimullah. "So, my friend, how is our plan to retrieve the diamond progressing?"

Though Azimullah was fluent in English and had, in fact, charmed London society with his good looks and good English when Nana Sahib had sent him there the previous year, he spoke Hindi to his employer, as the Maharajah's English was feeble. The word Nana Sahib had used to describe the English—*boorao*—was one of the worst insults in the language. "*Boor*" meant "cunt."

"Very well, Your Highness," said Azimullah. "We will bring the Englishman to the Maharajah's palace at Raniganj and take the diamond from him. Then we will dispose of him."

Nana Sahib straightened. "Good," he said. "And don't kill him swiftly, as his grandfather was killed. Kill him slowly."

Azimullah bowed. "As you wish, Highness."

A frown came over Nana Sahib's face. Holding the billiard cue in both hands, he slowly bent it until it snapped. Then he threw the broken pieces across the room against the wall, frightening the *punkah-wallah*, or fan-waver, on the other side (a cord was tied to his big toe, went through a hole in the wall and was attached to the big wood and cloth fan, or *punkah,* hanging from the ceiling in the billiard room). "The English," Nana Sahib said, bitterly. "They dethroned my father. They took away his power and gave him in return a pittance of a pension. Then, when he died, they denied me the pension. The Governor-General told me I had no claim on Her Majesty's Government. Her Majesty is a *boor*!" His voice rose to a manic pitch. "I'll kill the English! I'll kill them *all*! And I'll begin with Adam Thorne, because the great diamond is going to be *mine*!"

PART II

CONFLICTS

CHAPTER 6

"Now, honey, I know you told me your daddy had been active in the movement to abolish slavery in the English colonies," Jack said to Lizzie as they traveled in one of his carriages from the Richmond, Virginia, train station to his plantation. It was November 1856, the month after Adam sailed for India. "But I think I'd better warn you that 'Abolitionist' is a dirty word around here, so I wouldn't go around advertisin' the fact. Now that we're home, in slave country, you'd better learn a few things about the nigra so you won't have any difficulty adaptin' to our 'peculiar institution,' as the Northerners like to call it. For instance, the first thing you have to learn about the nigra is that he is shiftless and lazy."

"Jack!" Lizzie cautioned, indicating the coachman in the olive-green greatcoat and black top hat who was sitting less than four feet in front of them. Even though it was a chilly November day, the carriage was open. Lizzie, who actually had never seen a Negro before in her life, still felt an instinctive sensitivity to their feelings.

"Don't worry about Moses," Jack said. "He knows what I say is true. Isn't that right, Moses?"

"Yes, massa," said the driver, not turning his head.

"You see, honey, it's so easy to make slavery out as a cruel institution. The Lord knows, the Northerners talk themselves cross-eyed about how awful the whole thing is, and that what's-her-name, Mrs. Stowe, wrote that dumb book that makes all us slave owners out to be a bunch of monsters, which just isn't true at all. Slavery is actually, in its way, a very humane institution. Isn't that right, Moses?"

"Yes, massa."

"You see, you have to remember the Africans haven't had the advantages we whites have had. After all, they're practically just out of the trees. Slavery gives them a decent home, it gives them security, it gives them work and three square meals a day. . . . There's a lot to be said for slavery. Isn't that right, Moses?"

Silence. Jack leaned forward. "I said, isn't that right?"

"Yes, massa."

Jack smiled and leaned back. Then he took her hand and squeezed it. "You'll see how smoothly it all works," he went on. "We all get along real well, like one big happy family."

She was wearing a magnificent sable coat he had bought her in New York, where they had spent ten days shopping after their passage across the Atlantic. Lizzie had given the idea of slavery hardly any thought at all as she light-heartedly spent her husband's huge income that was based on it. But now, she began to give slavery some very direct thoughts indeed as she started to see its actuality.

"Jack," she said, lowering her voice, "don't you find it—if nothing else—unChristian to own another human being?"

"Aw, honey, they're not human beings. Not like you and me, anyway. They're more like pets, or children. And of course, you have to whip pets every once in a while to keep them, you know, trained."

She sat up straight, staring at him. "Surely you don't allow whippings?" she said. "You told me in Paris you were easy with your slaves—and that's the exact word you used: 'easy.' "

"I *am* easy with them—isn't that right, Moses?"

"Yes, massa."

" 'Course, every once in a while Mr. Duncan—he's my overseer—Mr. Duncan has to use a little discipline, but that's only with the field hands. We never whip the house servants. That wouldn't be proper. Besides, the house servants are practically family. Take Charles, the butler, for instance. Why Lizzie, you wouldn't find a more dignified butler in a duke's palace in England, and he's black as the ace of spades. Then there's Aunt Lide, his wife. She's the cook, and when I was a boy, she was my mammy. She's like a mother to me, and wait till you taste her possum stew! Well, it's not exactly what Monsieur Dugléré whips up at the Café Anglais, but I guarantee you're gonna love it. And you'll love Dulcey—that's Charles and Aunt Lide's granddaughter—she's gonna be your personal maid. You'll see, honey. We do well by our nigras and we love them. And yes, they love us, too. I think if your daddy had ever come to Virginnie and seen how the system works first-hand, he might have changed his mind about slavery. 'Course, the system has faults—every system does. But it works. Our economy's boomin', and the price of slaves is goin' up every year. So don't you worry your pretty little head about whippin's. Once you've been a week or so at Elvira Plantation, you'll see that it's pretty darned close to heaven."

They were driving down a country road. Now the carriage hit a bad bump, almost knocking Jack's silk hat off. He leaned forward and jammed his walking stick into the back of the driver. "Hey! You—Moses! Slow down when you see a bump, you hear?"

Lizzie saw the broad-shouldered driver turn around to look at her husband. She had noticed at the Richmond train station that he was one of the most magnificent-looking men she had ever seen, his skin a light chocolate.

"Sorry, massa," he said.

The look on Moses' young face was not exactly what Lizzie would have called a look of love. Then he turned back. Jack smiled at his wife.

"You see, there are other ways to handle nigras besides whippin' 'em. Take Moses, for instance. Now, Moses is the best nigra I ever seen when it comes to handlin' horses. Besides, he looks good drivin' my carriages, and I like to put on a good show because I have a position to maintain here in Virginnie. But unfortunately, Moses knows he's good. He's a little . . . well, we got a word called 'uppity.' Plus, he stole some of my schoolbooks from the library a couple of years back and was actually tryin' to teach himself the alphabet—he wants to read. 'Course, we can't allow that to happen. So I had to put him in his place."

"What did you do?" asked Lizzie.

"I sold his wife and six-year-old son to a planter in Kentucky. Now, if Moses behaves himself, I've promised to buy his family back in a couple of years. It's worked real fine, hasn't it, Moses? You've been a good nigra, haven't you?"

"Yes, massa."

"And you're gonna continue to be a good nigra. See?" He turned to Lizzie. "You don't need to whip 'em. There's lots of ways to handle niggers."

Lizzie realized with a sinking feeling that she had married a monster.

By the time they reached Elvira Plantation, it was nearing sunset, for they had stopped at a tavern near the York River for a long and, in Jack's case, wine-filled lunch. But Lizzie was just as glad because the skies had cleared in the afternoon and now her first look at her new home was presented in the best possible light, the twilight of an autumn day.

"It was built by my great-granddaddy in 1743," Jack said as they drove up the long, tree-lined drive to the brick mansion. "He was so in love with my great-grandmomma, whose name was Elvira Randolph Cavanagh, that he named the place after her. I don't mean to brag, honey, but there's not many finer homes in Virginnie."

"It's beautiful," she said truthfully. The house, Georgian in style, was two stories high, with a pitched roof flanked by two tall chimneys. There were two slightly recessed wings on either side of the central structure, which was fronted by an imposing four-pillared white portico that housed both an upstairs and a downstairs porch, the banisters criss-crossed white wood which gave a pleasing effect of light elegance. To the right of the house, the drive wandered through yew hedges to a number of outbuildings and a walled garden. The brick was soft pink and the shutters were black. The house was surrounded by lawns, and tall, ancient trees loomed over the roof. "This is the west front," Jack said as Moses pulled the carriage up before the portico then jumped down to open the door. "Wait'll you see the east front."

Lizzie climbed out of the carriage. As her boots stepped on the gravel drive, her eyes looked into Moses'. He was staring at her with an intensity that rather frightened her.

"Welcome to Elvira Plantation, mistress," he said in a voice that was husky and, at the same time, velvety. "Us house servants will try our bess to please you."

"Thank you, Moses," she said. Her husband's revelation of what he had done to the coachman's family left her numb with guilt. What she wanted to say was: Oh God, I'm sorry! But that was out of the question.

Tearing her eyes away from his, she walked up the steps to the wide front door which was flanked by vertical lights and topped by a graceful fan window; on either side were handsome brass lanterns. Now the door was opened by a tall and ancient black-coated butler with grizzled white hair. His extremely black face struck her as rather sad.

"Welcome, welcome, miss," he mumbled as he came out and bowed to her.

"This is Charles, whom I told you about," said Jack, coming up beside Lizzie and putting his arm around her waist. "Well, Charles, what do you think? Isn't she the prettiest thing you've ever seen?"

"Yessah, de mistress sure am pretty, yessah," said the old man, forcing a smile. "Prettiest mistress in all Virginnie, no doubt about it."

Lizzie smiled at him. "Thank you, Charles," she said.

"Moses, take the luggage upstairs and tell Dulcey to unpack for the mistress," Jack said. "Tell her to prepare a bath for her."

"Yes, massa."

"Come on, honey. I want you to see the most beautiful view in America."

He led her inside the house, which was bisected by a wide central hall that had a handsome staircase. Jack hurried her down the hall, which had gleaming, wide-plank floors, toward a fan-topped door at the opposite end that was the twin of the front door. "Ta-da!" he exclaimed, flinging open the door.

Lizzie took a deep breath of pleasure. Past the east portico, the lawn sloped down to the Atlantic Ocean.

"What do you think?" he asked eagerly. "Do you love it?"

"Oh, yes! It's beautiful!"

He took her in his strong arms. "Do you love *me?*" he whispered, starting to kiss her.

She hesitated. "Jack, do me a favor," she whispered. "As a . . . as a wedding gift."

"Sure, honey. 'Course, I've already given you the moon, but hell, I'm so nuts about you, I'll toss in a planet or two. What do you want, you little witch?"

She gave him her prettiest smile. "I want you to buy back Moses' wife and son."

His eyes went cold. "No," he snapped.

"Please?"

She felt his fingers dig into her arms.

"No. And I don't want you interferin' with the nigras, you understand? They're mine. I know how to handle them. And another thing: if they get the idea you feel sorry for them, they'll take advantage of you every way they can. The only way to keep them down is through fear. No, I'll change that. Not fear: *terror.*" He released her. "Watch."

He strode down the hall to the front door, where Moses and two other house servants were carrying in the luggage. To her horror, Jack raised his walking stick and smashed it down on Moses' left shoulder. The big coachman dropped the valises, roaring with rage. He turned on Jack, who raised the stick again. For a moment Lizzie was certain the two men would attack each other. Then Moses backed down.

"Massa," he said quietly, "whaffo did you strike me? What did I do?"

An insolent smile came over Jack's face. He put the gold head of the walking stick under Moses' chin and pushed it slightly up.

"You were born black," he said softly. Then, shooting

his wife a look, he walked out of the hall yelling, "Charles, get me a whiskey."

"Mistress has such pretty white skin," said Dulcey a half-hour later as she poured another pitcher of hot water into the gray marble tub. It was a big tub with a drain, although Elvira Plantation had no running water. Lizzie sat in the water, suds up to her shoulders, the sweet smell of the bath salts she had brought from New York filling the room. She watched Dulcey curiously. The maid, who was in her teens, was pretty, but Lizzie thought her manner was rather odd, as if her thoughts were elsewhere. Dulcey set the pitcher on a table, then returned to the tub. "Mistress want Dulcey to sponge her back?"

"Yes, thank you, Dulcey." Lizzie handed her the big French sponge. Dulcey, who was wearing a black dress with a white apron, knelt by the tub and began slowly sponging Lizzie's shoulders. "Dis am de onliest bathroom in Virginnie," she said. "Massa, he put it in three year ago after he made all de money wid de railroad stock. He brought a man all de way from New Yawk town, a man call an architect. Dis marble, it come all de way from Italy he say. And dat funny wicker chair over dair wid de chamberpot inside?" She giggled. "Dat call sump'n lak a shayz pursee."

" '*Chaise percée,*' " corrected Lizzie. "It means a chair with a hole in it."

"Uh-huh, I knew dat. Well, anyways, I clean de pot out every mornin'. Dulcey keep everyting nice and tidy for mistress, you'll see. And for massa too. Massa got nice white skin too. I seen him in de summertime when he go swimmin' in de ocean. I seen him all over." Again she giggled. "Massa pretty too. Very pretty man."

Again, Lizzie eyed her. It was a curious thing to say.

Dulcey, smiling, held out her right arm in front of Lizzie. "Mistress see *my* skin?" she said softly. "My skin pretty too, because I'm half white, you know. My daddy was a white man."

Dulcey handed her the sponge and stood up. Lizzie

watched the strange girl as she walked across the bathroom to the door. She turned and curtsied. Then she left the room, softly closing the door.

Lizzie pressed the sponge against her neck and wondered if she had moved into a madhouse.

"My cousin just sent a note inviting us to lunch tomorrow," Jack said an hour later as he lifted a piece of ham from the silver tray held by Charles. "You'll like her. Her name's Clemmie DeVries, and her husband's my lawyer."

Lizzie, wearing a yellow taffeta dress, was seated at the opposite end of the mahogany dining-room table. The two eight-branched silver candelabra on the center of the table matched a display of some of the most magnificent silver plate on the sideboard that she had ever seen. The wallpaper above the dado represented hand-blocked views of the Hudson River Valley, circa 1810, and the windows, which looked out over the Atlantic, were hung with heavy scarlet brocade curtains, their valences great swooping swags. The room, like the entire house, was enchanting and kept in mint condition, though Jack had told her nothing had been altered since his mother had decorated it a quarter-century before.

"Where do the DeVrieses live?" Lizzie asked as one of the three black teenage waiters filled her crystal goblet with a ruby claret from a delicate decanter.

"In Yorktown, about eight miles from here. It's where you English finally lost the Revolution."

"I'm American now," corrected Lizzie.

"Yes, of course. I'm sorry, honey. At any rate, Billie and Clemmie have just built a new house which I think is hideous, but I keep my opinions to myself. Clemmie just had her fourth baby—I personally think Billie's wearing her out. Clemmie will introduce you to all the local ladies, who will probably bore you to distraction, at least they do me. Do you like the wine?"

"It's delicious. What is it?"

"A Château Bechevelle 1839. A very special year for a very special occasion: the first evening at Elvira Plantation of my very special wife."

He raised his glass and smiled at her. Well, she thought as she raised her glass, he may be horrid to his slaves, but he worships me. Maybe I can continue to work on him . . .

"You didn't say you loved me this afternoon when I asked," he remarked.

"I love you," she said, forcing her sweetest smile. But as she remembered the savage attack on the coachman, she knew she was lying.

He got drunk that night, which she was getting used to, and made love to her. When he was finished, he rolled over beside her in the big four-poster bed with its arched crocheted canopy and stuck his hands behind his head.

"Tell me about Dulcey," she said. "She seems a little peculiar."

"She is. She's a bit touched in the head, but she's harmless."

"She told me she has a white father."

There was a long silence.

"Jack?"

"Well, hell, I suppose you might as well know. I could kill her for tellin' you, but the fat's in the fire now. But I'd appreciate it if you didn't talk about it. You see, her daddy was my daddy."

Lizzie sat up. "You mean Dulcey's your sister?" she whispered.

"Half-sister. And that 'half' makes all the difference in the world. Yes, my daddy just couldn't keep it in his pants—pardon my language, honey—and he especially favored ladies of color. My mother was very moral, very religious, and it broke her heart, which is why she died young. And I guess he felt mighty guilty about it because the night of her funeral he locked himself up in the library and blew his brains out."

"How horrible for you!"

"It wasn't horrible. I was glad he did it. I hated his guts for what he did to my mother, who was the sweetest woman who ever lived. I hated his guts for makin' love to nigras."

Elvira Plantation might be a beautiful house, Lizzie reflected, but it is filled with ugly ghosts.

"When did this happen?" she asked.

"Last year. That's when I decided to go to Europe and get away from it all, at least for a while. And that's when I saw you, and my life changed because you brought beauty back into it. That's why you're so important to me."

She stared up at the canopy and said nothing.

The next day was rainy and cold, so they took the closed carriage into Yorktown—Jack had a total of four carriages in the carriage house. Lizzie sat in the comfortable leather seat opposite her husband, staring out at the flat fields of Virginia and wondering about poor Moses, seated outside with only an umbrella to protect him from the downpour.

"Clemmie's the brainy one in the family," Jack said. "Her mother, my Aunt Paula—my mother's elder sister—sent her to Paris to be educated, so she's a lot smarter than most of the women around here. She has 'views' on slavery, which is a polite way of sayin' she doesn't approve of it. She talked Billie into freein' all her house servants, which didn't go down too well for a while. But Clemmie gets away with it because she's got about the bluest blood in Virginnie and the women don't want to cross her."

"Jack, do *you* approve of slavery?" Lizzie asked, deciding to bring it out in the open. Jack, very dapper in a brown tweed suit under his mackintosh, looked at her, rather evasively, she thought.

"It's not a question of approvin' or disapprovin'," he said. "It's a question of economics. I grow tobacco. The average American male smokes or chews something like a hundred dollars' worth of tobacco every year. There's not an office, tavern, club or home in this country that doesn't have a spittoon. Raisin' tobacco takes a lot of labor no white man's ever going to do. I have about a hundred workin' slaves, plus their families, and their average price is, say, a thousand dollars—and goin' up. So I have a lot of capital invested."

"But you're talking about money," she persisted. "These people are flesh and blood—"

He grabbed her wrist, hard. "Listen," he said softly, "you're carryin' a bastard baby in your belly. So Lizzie, honey, don't start givin' me a lot of Abolitionist swill, 'cause you're in no position to moralize. Now, do we understand each other?"

"You're hurting me!"

He relaxed his grip. "You haven't answered. Do we understand each other?

"Yes."

"That's better."

Jack crossed his arms over his chest and sank back into the carriage seat. Lizzie said nothing more. She realized Jack was right: she was in no position to preach. But a sort of crusade was forming in her mind. She might not be able to bring her father back to life, but somehow she was going to help the lives of Jack's slaves, and in so doing she would carry on the Abolitionist work of Reverend Desmond and, perhaps, help pay for her sins in the eyes of heaven.

The DeVries' house was a three-story, red-brick building set on a spacious, treed lot on the main street of Yorktown. The mansard roof bristled with a wrought-iron balustrade which matched the exuberant wrought-iron fence that surrounded the property. The carriage drove up the brick drive and stopped under a porte cochere where a butler, a horse-boy and a handsome white couple in their early thirties awaited them. As Lizzie climbed out, the woman, who had luxuriant brown hair caught up in a double braid behind her neck, came forward, both hands outstretched and a smile on her pretty face. "I should have known Jack would wed a beauty," she said. "I'm Clementine. Welcome, dear Elizabeth."

The two women kissed. Then Lizzie was introduced to Billie, a strapping six-footer with curly brown hair who was beginning to flab into middle age. Billie kissed her gloved hand, then the four went into the mid-Victorian house while Moses, beside the carriage, watched, the rain dripping from his coachman's hat. Once the two couples disappeared inside, he went into the kitchen to eat with the servants.

After lunch, Clemmie led Lizzie out of the grim dining

room, leaving Jack and Billie to their cigars. Taking her to a small music room, Clemmie sat on a horsehair sofa and picked up her knitting.

"I'm making a sweater for Randolph," she said as Lizzie took a chair next to her. "He's my eldest son. They're all at school now, but I hope you and Jack can stay till they get home."

"Clemmie, may I ask you something rather personal?"

"Of course, dear."

"You see, I'm trying to adapt, to become American, but hearing about slavery is different from actually seeing it."

She hesitated. Clemmie looked up from her knitting with her strong brown eyes. "But you don't like it," she prompted.

"It's more than that. I think it's . . . Jack said yesterday that the only way to keep the slaves from turning on us is to terrorize them. Could that possibly be true?"

"Oh, it's true, all right. There's a lot of sentimental twaddle about the slaves loving their masters, and I suppose in some instances this is true, especially with the mammies. But the truth is, what keeps most of the slaves from slitting all our throats in the middle of the night is plain fear. Mind you, they have good reason to be afraid. An elaborate system has been set up to keep them in their place. There are the slave patrols who track down the runaways. But more than that, the slaves are chattel—legally *things*—and slave owners can do anything they like to them, including murder. True, I suppose under certain unusual circumstances a slaveowner could be brought to trial if he murdered one of his bondsmen, but no white jury would ever convict him, which everyone knows. But the masters don't have to resort to murder anyway. They have whippings, which are perfectly normal, and other means of punishment and terrorizing that no gentlewoman would ever repeat, though I've heard stories that would make you faint. Slavery brings out the most infernal instincts in the slave owners, which is one reason I hate it. Slavery is a brutal, unnatural system that's destroying the South. That's why I freed my bondsmen, though I had only a few. I didn't want to fear them, and I couldn't—or wouldn't—make them fear me."

"Then . . ."

"Then what, my dear?"

"At home, our servants are thought of as friends of a sort. But here . . . ?"

"You can never be a true friend to someone you own. Jack wouldn't let you, anyway. He hates the Africans, I think partially because of the way his father chased after his slaves."

"Then you know?"

"Oh yes, I know the whole sordid story. The irony is that Jack, who was a sweet and lovable boy, has become a sort of monster, so that you might even say he's another victim of the institution."

"But it's outrageous to have to live this way!"

"I totally agree, and I'm delighted to hear that you feel the same as I. However, don't fool yourself, dear Elizabeth: we are in the great minority here, so be careful what you say and do."

"You mean, if others think I hate the 'peculiar institution,' they'll turn on me?"

"Yes."

"Then I'm as much a slave as Charles or Aunt Lide or Dulcey?"

"In a way, we're *all* slaves to the institution, though needless to say it's more comfortable being a white slave than a black one. But in my opinion—which I don't advertise—some day the North is going to force us to free the slaves, and in my way of thinking, it will be a relief. But even that won't solve the problem."

"I don't understand."

"You see, my dear, when the first slaves were brought to this country in the early seventeenth century, a seed was planted that may ultimately destroy America. Because it's unnatural to have a nation that is part white and part black. Oh, perhaps in hundreds of years it will work itself out some way. But certainly not in my lifetime, and I doubt in the lifetime of my children or theirs."

"You're certainly pessimistic, aren't you?"

"Yes, because I've lived with slavery. Slavery is a curse on this country. The system is an infernal machine that someday will explode and may destroy us all—white and black alike."

"If I'd known . . ." Lizzie interrupted herself.

Clemmie looked up. "You'd what? Never have left England? I sometimes wish I'd never left France."

Lizzie frowned, but said nothing, although that had been her thought. Of course, she couldn't return to England now. But the conversation with Clemmie so depressed her that she pleaded a headache to cut short the visit, which was just as well, since Jack and Billie had drunk enough port to put themselves into a near-stupor, a fact that obviously displeased Clemmie.

"Courage," she whispered as she kissed Lizzie good-bye under the porte cochere. "And it's possible I'm entirely wrong about what we discussed. Let's hope so, at any rate."

Jack, who had been going on at drunken length about a Christmas ball he intended to give for his new bride, climbed in the carriage after her and promptly fell asleep, his snores providing Lizzie with an obbligato to her thoughts as the carriage rattled down the rain-slicked drive. Clemmie had struck her as a highly intelligent person whom she liked, and no doubt her estimate of the simmering racial situation in the South was partially true. But Lizzie couldn't bring herself to believe the outlook was as bleak as had been painted. Or if it were, that didn't mean she could evade her personal duty to forge some sort of human contact with her slaves other than sheer, bullying terror, whether Jack liked it or not.

By the time they had returned to Elvira Plantation, she had made up her mind she would start with Moses.

Jack woke up, understandably complaining that he felt rotten. Lizzie helped him upstairs to their bedroom, helped him out of his clothes and tucked him in bed where he promptly fell asleep again. Then she tiptoed out of the room, closed the door and went down the hall to the stairs. She was just getting to know the house, and as she went down the graceful staircase, she passed a life-size portrait of a lovely woman in a gray silk dress that she now knew was Jack's mother. The sad story he had told her the previous night about his parents explained the rather forlorn look on her face, and grotesque images of Jack's father haunting the slave quarters looking for new sexual thrills flashed through her mind. It was all barbaric and rather medieval. Virginia was a throwback to an earlier age.

She went into the elegant drawing room with its fine English furniture and pulled the bellcord. After a moment the ancient butler appeared.

"Yes, mistress?" he said.

"Charles, I would like to see the slave quarters."

The old man looked surprised. "Yes, mistress."

"Ask Moses to take me to them."

"Yes, mistress," he said, trying not to show his disapproval.

Minutes later, Moses came in from the entrance hall, wearing his slave clothes. Lizzie had seen that the numerous house servants were well-turned-out: Charles in his dignified black tail coat, Dulcey in her black dress with white apron and cap, the teenage footmen snappily dressed in blue and yellow livery, giving them the look of toy eighteenth-century lackeys. Moses, when he wore his coachman's uniform, looked spiffy in his black top hat, his olive-green greatcoat, brown trousers and shiny boots. It was obvious Jack wanted to present a good show, a *bella figura*, to the world, and he did. But now for the first time Lizzie saw the handsome coachman dressed like the few field hands she had glimpsed from the windows. He was wearing homespun trousers held up by a piece of rope, and a ratty shirt that was torn in several places. He wore no socks and his shoes were crude sandals. The rain had stopped and it had turned cold, but he had no coat to protect him from the elements. He held a tattered brown hat in his hands.

"Mistress wish to see de slave quarters?" he asked, staring at her in a way she didn't quite understand.

"Yes, please."

"Why?"

The question surprised her. "Because it's part of the place and I want to see it."

"Does massa know?"

She stiffened. "That's none of your business."

"Excuse me, mistress, but massa told me dis mornin' dat I was to report to him anything you axe me to do. You saw yesstiday how massa treat me. I hopes you doan wanna get me in trouble wid massa."

Her eyes flashed with annoyance. "My husband is presently asleep, as he has had too much to drink. Now, if you want to go upstairs and wake him up and tell him that I, who, after all, am now the mistress of this plantation, have asked you to show me the slave quarters, then I will wait here while you do so."

He looked surprised. Then he said, "Does mistress want me to be beat wif a stick again?"

She backed down. "No, of course not. And that was one thing I wanted to discuss with you. I want to apologize for what my husband did to you yesterday. In a way, I fear it was my fault."

"How is dat, mistress?"

"I . . . asked him to buy back your wife and son."

His eyes widened. "You *did*?" he whispered.

"Yes. You see, this is all a new world to me, and . . . well, I was shocked that he had broken up your family. I think it was an outrageous thing to do, and I want you to know that I'll do everything in my power to persuade my husband to reunite you with your family."

He stared at her for almost a full minute. Then came to her and took her right hand in his own. He raised it and touched it to his cheek for a moment. She felt his tears on her hand.

"Thass the first kind ting a white person done ever said to me," he whispered. Then he released her hand. Taking one last look at her, he turned and walked out of the room. She was so dazed by what he had done, for the time being she totally forgot about seeing the slave quarters. All she could think of was Adam. She remembered how her sister had always teased her about Adam's smell. But Adam had had two smells: a smell of sweaty passion when he made love to her, and the strong smell of lye soap when he put on clean clothes.

Moses had smelled of lye soap.

It was then that a tall and rather lugubrious man appeared in the doorway to the central hall. He had a very long face with several days' stubble of beard and two extremely beady eyes. He wore a black coat with brown pants, and he held a black hat in his left hand. His long black hair looked dirty. Lizzie judged he was about forty.

"Good afternoon, ma'am," he said in a soft drawl. "Charles told me you wanted to see the slave quarters. I'm Mr. Duncan, the overseer, ma'am, and I'd be glad to give you a tour. Begging your pardon, ma'am, but it's probably not a good idea for a white lady to go unescorted to the quarters, if you know what I mean."

"No, I don't know what you mean."

He smiled a dreary smile.

"We wouldn't want to give any of the nigras an opportunity to get into trouble, if you know what I mean."

She frowned with annoyance. There was a smarminess about the man that she instantly disliked, although she told herself overseers were hardly likely to be lovable. Suddenly the ugliness of the whole system struck her. She didn't want to see, or even think about slaves anymore.

"I'll have my husband give me a tour some other time," she said sharply.

"Very well, ma'am. And welcome to Elvira Plantation."

"Thank you." But as she tried to dismiss slavery from her mind, the feel of Moses' warm tears on her hand haunted her.

During the next week, Lizzie learned that there was a hierarchy among the slaves, with the house servants on top and the field hands on bottom. The house servants lived in small, attractive brick cottages on the other side of a brick-walled garden, out of sight of the main house but physically near. The field hands lived a half-mile away in the "quarter," their own village of shanties. Food for the quarter was meted out by Mr. Duncan, which was one of his methods of control, but the house servants were fed by Aunt Lide, Charles' wife and the cook at Elvira Plantation. As befitted their position at the top of the slave heap, Charles, Aunt Lide and Dulcey had the best cottage nearest the garden wall. And as befitted his second-best rank as coachman, Moses had the cottage next door, which Jack had graciously permitted him to continue living in alone after he sold his wife and son off to a Kentucky planter.

Lizzie was also learning that what Jack had said about the economic side of slavery was true: slavery was a tremendous boon economically, which was one reason most Southerners were so passionately attached to it. The fact that only a few, like Clemmie, saw the moral horror of the system made Lizzie despair of ever being able to improve the lot of Jack's slaves. Moreover, aside from Moses, who seethed with ill-concealed anger, the rest of the slaves seemed to accept their life with resignation, which baffled Lizzie until she thought of Mr. Duncan and the ever-present threat of physical punishment. She began to realize that to most bondspeople, now many generations into slavery, there wasn't any alternative to a brutal system. And since the owners took great care to prevent their slaves from learning to read, the only news they had of the growing strength of the Abolitionist movement in the North came by word of mouth, which was sketchy at best.

But even more insidious, Lizzie had to admit that a life of being waited on hand and foot by countless servants had its undeniable charms. And when Jack wasn't drunk or defending the "peculiar institution," he invariably treated her with deference and kindness: it was obvious he was still madly in love with her. Lizzie began to worry about her "crusade." After all, it was so easy just to drift along in a world that was so comfortable, in a world where even the slaves didn't seem too unhappy, at least from what she had seen.

But then, just before lunch on her eighth day at Elvira Plantation, Charles delivered the mail to Jack in the drawing room, and her comfortable world began to unravel.

"Samantha's dead," Jack said after opening a letter.

"Who's Samantha?" Lizzie asked, sitting on a sofa working on some needlepoint.

"Moses' wife. This is a letter from Carl Durkens, the Kentucky planter I sold her to. She died in childbirth. So you see, even if I'd bought them back the way you wanted me to, it wouldn't have done Moses much good."

Lizzie put down her embroidery, amazed as usual at Jack's insensitivity to his slaves. "How terrible! To lose his wife and child—"

"It wasn't Moses' child," said Jack, dropping the letter in a wastebasket. "Durkens had her bred."

"What do you mean?"

"Honey, you keep forgettin' slaves are worth money. A lot of owners breed their slaves so they can sell the children off when they're grown."

"How barbaric!" Lizzie exclaimed.

Jack shot her a dry look. "I keep forgettin' your delicate moral sensitivities, my dear. Anyway, we won't say anything about this. Especially to Moses."

"You're not going to tell him?"

"Why should I? Moses is a potential troublemaker, and as long as I have his family as a carrot, I can keep him in line. The moment he finds out his wife's dead, I've got only half a carrot to control him with."

"But Jack, that's so cruel."

Jack came to her and leaned down to kiss her forehead. Then he smiled. "Now, honey, we're not goin' to have another silly fight about the nigras, are we? I thought you were gettin' all that Abolitionist twaddle out of your pretty little head."

"It has nothing to do with Abolitionism. It's just common human decency to tell him."

He shook his head slowly. "Honey, you haven't caught on yet. They're not human. Now, let's go have lunch. I'm starved, and me and the Bensons are huntin' this afternoon."

He took her hand and led her into the dining room. The lunch was venison, which Aunt Lide cooked to perfection, but Lizzie had no appetite. She knew that she had come to a moral crossroads. If she were going to persist in her crusade to better the lives of the slaves, surely she had a duty to tell Moses about his wife. On the other hand, she had no illusions about how Jack would react if she did. Perhaps, she thought as she forked her food, it isn't any of my business. After all, Jack treats me well. Why should I defy him?

Then the memory of her father floated to her consciousness, and she knew that if she were to have any self-respect, she would have to defy her husband. If Moses wasn't a human, what in God's name was he? Hadn't his tears been human tears?

After lunch, Jack rode off on his horse, Avenger, to hunt with the Benson brothers, who owned Sweetwood, the plantation next door. When he was out of sight, Lizzie put on a cloak with a hood over her head and let herself out through one of the French doors in the ballroom. It was a bracing afternoon with the hint of snow in an oyster sky. She walked around to the side of the house, then through a wooden door into the brick-walled garden, where Aunt Lide grew vegetables in the warm months. She crossed the garden to the opposite door and opened it, looking out at the small cottages of the house servants. Each cottage had a front porch, and she saw Moses sitting on his, whittling a piece of wood. She motioned to him to come into the garden. Looking puzzled, he put down his knife and jumped off the porch. When he came through the door, Lizzie closed it.

"Is sumpn wrong, mistress?" he asked.

"Well, yes. Moses, can you keep a secret?"

"Yes'm."

"You have to swear you won't tell anyone what I'm about to tell you—especially my husband. You could get me into a lot of trouble if Mr. Cavanagh knew."

He looked confused. "I wouldn't want to get you in trouble, mistress. I swear to keep it a secret."

Lizzie hesitated. "It's your wife, Moses," she said softly. "Samantha. Word came today that she's dead."

His eyes widened. "Dead?" he whispered. "How? She was so young . . ."

"She died in childbirth. I'm so sorry."

He was breathing heavily. "They done bred her," he whispered. "Musta been that. She told me she'd remain true. They musta bred her."

Seeing the tears in his eyes, she reached out and put her hand on his sleeve. "I'm so sorry," she repeated. He nodded numbly. She started back to the house.

"Thank you, mistress," he said in a choking voice. "Thass twice you been kind to me. I won't forget."

She looked back, nodded, then hurried on. She knew she had done the right thing.

CHAPTER 7

The Indian in the *dhoti*, or loincloth, emerged from the jungle and ran toward the bungalow office of Mark Thornhill, the magistrate of Muttra, a small town in central India not far from the Taj Mahal at Agra. A *chowkidar*, or watchman, was dozing at the front gate. It was dawn. The Indian ran up to the *chowkidar* and tugged his sleeve.

"What do you want?" said the *chowkidar*, snapping out of his doze.

The Indian handed him four cakes of coarse flour, each about the size of a biscuit.

"Put these on the desk of the *Angrezi*," whispered the man, *Angrezi* meaning "Englishman." The *chowkidar* nodded, and the Indian ran back to the trees and disappeared into the jungle.

"A most mysterious thing is happening in India these days," said the Honorable Charles John Canning, first Viscount Canning of Kilbrahan and Governor-General of India. "No one seems to know the meaning of it, or who is behind it or where it originated. We don't know whether it's a sort of religious ceremony or whether it's some sort of secret society. It's called 'The Chupatty Movement.' "

Lord Canning was seated next to Lady Agatha McNair, his hostess for the evening and the wife of Calcutta's richest tea planter, Sir Carlton McNair. The setting for the dinner was splendid: Sir Carlton's dining room was a long hall lined by tall marble columns, between which great window-doors opened onto his verandah and gardens. Through the doors a slight breeze was flowing, much to the relief of the twelve guests seated at the long table. They were dressed in formal evening clothes, and the huge skirts of the women, billowing up and out because of the arms of the dining chairs, almost imprisoned them. To dress formally and uncomfortably in such heat did not strike the English as absurd, as it would their descendants. Part of the power of the British Raj, or rule, was its appearance of splendor, aimed at dazzling the Indians who, after all, were used to the splendor of their own Mogul Emperors and Maharajahs. Thus, even though it was over ninety in the dining hall, the men wore either uniforms or white tie and tailcoats, and the women suffered in yards of material, their damp bosoms nevertheless twinkling with diamonds. However, everyone silently blessed the two huge *punkahs* swishing over their heads. Two large crystal chandeliers, their candles protected by hurricane lamps, provided illumination.

"Do you mean the little cakes, milord?" asked Lady McNair, seated at the Governor-General's right.

"Yes," said Lord Canning, an imposing man in his forties who was the son of a former Prime Minister. "Four chupatties—sometimes five—have been appearing in the strangest places. For instance, I received a report from Thornhill at Muttra that four chupatties appeared on his desk, and he has no idea how they got there or what they mean. And this has been happening all over the country. It's as if the Indians are sending out some sort of message."

Adam, who was seated on the opposite side of the table, was as fascinated as the other guests.

"I'll tell you what it means, milord," boomed Sir Carlton McNair, a huge walrus of a man with a red face and a Scottish accent. "I get reports from my plantation overseers. The natives are afraid of these blasted missionaries who are swarmin' all over the country, wavin' their Bibles under the natives' noses and tryin' to convert them to become Methodists or whatever. I say send the missionaries packin' back to England and we'll have peace in India."

"But surely, Sir Carlton," said the beautiful Lady Canning, born the Honorable Charlotte Elizabeth Stuart, the daughter of an earl and great-granddaughter of another Prime Minister, the Third Earl of Bute, "the natives could only benefit by conversion to Christianity. It is, after all, such a *nicer* religion. Hinduism can be so terribly emotional."

A titter ran around the table as Sir Carlton's dozen native servants stood at attention behind the Europeans, their arms crossed over their chests (one servant stamped on a huge cockroach that was racing gaily for Lady Canning's left foot).

"Aye, but it's *their* religion," rumbled Sir Carlton, "and we'd be fools to meddle with it. The natives are terrified they'll be forced to convert and lose caste. You know they all believe in reincarnation, and if they lose caste in this life, they'll come back in the next life as Untouchables. If you'll pardon my blunt words, milord, I'd say you could spare us all a lot of trouble if you'd issue a statement reassuring the natives that we don't agree with the missionaries."

Adam's eyes turned to Lord Canning.

"I fear it would be difficult for Her Majesty's Government not to support Christian missionaries," said the Governor-General. "We can't forget that the Queen is head of the Church of England."

"But surely it's more than that," said his wife, who had shiny brown hair. "Surely it is our obligation as Christians—and as members of a superior civilization—to try and convert these poor heathens to the one true faith."

"Beggin' your pardon, ma'am," said Sir Carlton, "but we can't forget that they think *theirs* is the one true faith. If you consider the millions of lives that have been lost over the centuries in religious wars, you have to think twice before attackin' anyone else's religion. I've heard that a slogan has been painted on the sides of buildings: '*Sub lal hogea hai*,' which means 'Everything will be red.' Not to shock the ladies, but I venture to suggest that has an ominous ring to it."

"And there are the bullets," said Bentley Brent, who was in his dress uniform. "I hear the natives are raising an absolute stink about having to bite the new bullets for the Enfield rifles. The Muslims say the bullets are greased with pork fat, which they can't eat. And the Hindus say they're greased with beef fat, which *they* can't eat. They're *all* saying the bullets are part of a plot to force them to convert to Christianity."

"Yes, I've gotten reports about the bullet problem from several regiments," said Lord Canning, flicking a large black ant off his wine goblet. "The officers are instructing the *sepoys* and *sowars* that the grease is actually lamb fat and not harmful to either religion. But we must remain calm and not become alarmist. I am absolutely confident that our native troops are loyal to the Queen. And despite certain inevitable grumbling on the part of the native population, surely every sensible Indian is cognizant of the many blessings we English have brought to the Subcontinent."

Adam Thorne had been in India only four days, but so far he would be hard put to spell out what these mysterious blessings actually were. But he held his tongue. And after the passing of the "jaggery board"—a selection of six different varieties of sweets made from date palms and served much like a cheese board in Europe, along with deep-fried bread called *loochi*—the ladies retired, leaving the men to light up their cigars or begin smoking their gurgle-gurgling hookahs, a practice the *Angrezi-log* had taken to with considerable zeal. Adam, who had an allergy to cigar smoke, excused himself and went out on the verandah. By now the temperature had cooled a bit, and the black sky arched above him with a melon-slice of a moon floating in it. Adam had taken an instant liking to this lovely walled garden with its many exotic palms and trees and its delightful circular fountain with a stone plinth in the center, topped by a comical stone frog, his mouth open to the skies, water squirting from his eyes in two jets. Here in Sir Carlton's garden the air was sweet. But Adam had seen enough of Calcutta to realize the jolting discrepancies between the rich and the poor. Millionaires like Sir Carlton lived in minor palaces, great white buildings of classic design like this one, fronted by pillars. But Adam had explored Calcutta in the past few days, and what he had seen had shocked him. He knew that a hundred feet away from Sir Carlton's mansion one was suddenly plunged into a vastly different world, a world of dark alleys and squalid mud huts teeming with bugs and rats and children, a world dominated by the stench of open sewers and burning corpses on the ghats. Adam wondered if the bejeweled Memsahibs inside the house chewing the latest gossip from Europe felt any affinity at all with this other world to which they and their husbands were bringing the "blessings" of English civilization and Christianity.

"Mr. Thorne!"

He turned to see Sir Carlton's daughter, Emily, coming out of the house onto the verandah. She was a pretty girl of eighteen with bright red hair and a lightly freckled face. She was wearing a becoming white dress with the usual wide skirt. She came up to him, a frown on her face. "I do believe you have deceived us, sir," she said.

"I have? How?"

"Lady Canning swears that you must be the Mr. Thorne who is the new Earl of Pontefract, and indeed now that we ladies have all considered the matter, remembering what we read in the newspapers about your grandfather's murder, we've come to the conclusion that Lady Canning is right. Is she?"

"And what if she is?"

"Then, sir, you are guilty of a most wicked deception. For an attractive member of the male sex such as yourself to pass himself off as a bachelor and thus ignite interest, if not even hope, in the breasts of Calcutta's unmarried females such as myself is cruel beyond belief. Because if you are Lord Pontefract, then you are already married, is this not so?"

Adam smiled. He liked Emily McNair. There was an impishness to her that somehow reminded him of Lizzie.

"I must confess, you have pierced my disguise," he said, making a mocking bow. "Yes, I am married, though to be fair, I never said I wasn't."

"Then, sir, you have also deceived us as to your reason for being in India. You told Captain Brent and my father that you were out here to research a book. But the truth is that you have come to India to avenge your grandfather's murder, which is an infinitely more thrilling reason. We read all about it in the papers. How do you intend to do it?"

"That's a good question, Miss McNair."

"Oh please, milord, call me Emily. I feel that social intercourse in our modern society has become far too formal."

"Very well, I'll call you Emily if you call me Adam instead of 'milord.' "

"Oh, Adam! I love that name! It has such a romantically primitive sound to it, like Adam and Eve in the Garden."

He smiled. "You're a very romantic young lady, aren't you?"

"*Wildly* romantic. I devour romantic novels, the more lurid the better. Actually, there's not much else to do in India."

"If your father's correct, India may be anything but boring soon."

"You mean the chupatties and the bullets? Yes, that's all very queer, isn't it? What do you think it means?"

"I'm too new to India to set myself up as an expert. You know, Emily, you're a very pretty girl. But in the moonlight, you're . . ." He stopped.

"Oh, *please* go on," she exclaimed.

He laughed. "I almost forgot I'm an old married man."

She sighed. "I suppose you're madly in love with your wife."

His face became sad. "Well, no," he said, "I don't think 'madly in love' exactly describes it."

Emily thought that, in the moonlight, this sad and remarkably handsome young man was the lover of her teenage dreams.

"Emily!"

Lady McNair came out on the terrace. Her daughter looked disappointed.

"Emily, dear, are you bothering Mr. Thorne?" said Lady McNair, coming up to the couple.

"Of course not, Mama. I was fascinating him, wasn't I, Adam?"

"Adam?" Her mother looked shocked. "I'm sure Mr. Thorne has not given you permission to use his Christian name."

"Oh, yes he has." She smiled triumphantly. "Moreover, I know Adam's dark secret. He really is the Earl of Pontefract."

Lady McNair, a handsome woman in her forties, looked at her young houseguest with new interest. "So Lady Canning was right?" she cooed. "*Dear* Lord Pontefract, why were you being so mysterious, you naughty man? If I'd known . . . Well, we must entertain you in a proper fashion. I must give a ball . . . yes, next week . . . I'll send out the invitations in the morning . . . and I'm sure the Governor-General will want to entertain you at Government House—"

"Please, Lady McNair," interrupted Adam, "you're very kind, but I really would prefer that people not know who I am, although I suppose it's too late for total secrecy. At any rate, as you know, I'm leaving for Lucknow in the morning, and I really can't change my plans."

Lady McNair's expression of excited hope turned to cool disappointment. "Well, of course, milord, although Calcutta society will be disappointed. However, I suppose we will survive. Come, Emily. It is past your bedtime."

"Oh, Mama, you treat me like a child."

"I was under the impression you *are* a child," said her mother frostily. "Now, come: we mustn't waste any more of Lord Pontefract's valuable time."

As she took her daughter's hand, Emily turned to Adam. "I *will* see you in the morning before you leave, won't I?" she asked wistfully.

Adam smiled. "Of course. Good night, Emily."

"Good night . . . Adam." She whispered his name dreamily as her mother dragged her back into the house.

"You behaved shockingly!" Adam heard Lady McNair hiss at her daughter as they disappeared, leaving him alone on the terrace. He turned around and leaned on the balustrade, looking at the moon and the stars. He had described his marriage to Emily in disparaging terms only because she had reminded him of Lizzie. Actually, he liked

Sybil and ever since leaving her, his guilt about her had weighed on him. Speaking Lizzie's name in his sleep had been damned rotten luck. But then, the whole thing had been damned rotten luck, ever since Lizzie had disappeared. . . .

It was then he felt the sting on the side of his neck. He threw up his hand to swat what he assumed was a wasp or bee, but felt instead a small dart. By the time he had pulled it out, his consciousness was already swimming. He tried to steady himself by holding the balustrade. Then his knees buckled, and he fell sideways onto the terrace, unconscious.

Three Indians hurried out of the dark garden and silently ran toward his body.

He didn't awake abruptly, as was his morning custom, but rather, consciousness returned to him gradually. During a period that might have been minutes or hours—he had no idea—the real world began to make itself evident. He saw he was in a white room, lying on a bed piled with ornate cushions, a pointed, open window above him blowing a hot breeze over him. Groggily, he sat up, remembering the dart in his neck. He put his hand on the wound, but felt only a slight swelling. He realized from his growth of beard, as well as his empty stomach, that he must have been unconscious for at least a day.

It was then the wooden door opened and one of the most beautiful girls he had ever seen entered the room. She carried a silver bowl filled with fruit which she brought to the bed. She had smooth skin, light sepia in color, a large voluptuous mouth, and her kohl-rimmed eyes were lustrous brown. A caste mark was in the middle of her forehead. She wore a beautiful pale green sari and had a gauze veil over her black hair.

"You are awake." She smiled. "You must be hungry. I have brought you something to eat."

"Where am I?" he asked, taking a peach and hungrily biting into it.

"In the palace of His Highness, the Maharajah of Raniganj, who is the cousin of Nana Sahib. We are northwest of Calcutta. You were brought here by servants of His Highness, Nana Sahib."

" 'Brought'? You mean 'kidnapped.' And who is Nana Sahib?"

She set the silver bowl on an inlaid octagonal table and passed her cool hand slowly over Adam's cheek. "All will be explained in time. You are tired and dirty. Let me lead you to one of His Highness's *gussalkhanas* and I will bathe you."

She smiled seductively, took his hand and raised him to his feet. He realized he was still in his dress clothes, although someone had removed his tailcoat and white tie, and though he was burning with curiosity, he found that, despite his wooziness, he was burning with something else. It had, after all, been over six months since he had had a woman.

She led him across the room and out the door to a long white marble corridor. The palace seemed eerily empty, and it occurred to Adam that if, in fact, he had been kidnapped, it was a strange sort of prison. At the end of the corridor, she opened two pierced marble-lattice doors, which looked like delicate screens. Beyond was a flight of steps leading down to a square pool. The room had open windows on three sides, and several brightly colored parrots squatted on the sills.

"His Highness has provided you with clean clothes," said the woman, whose English was excellent, although marked by the musical intonation of the Indian. "That is, if you don't object to wearing native clothes."

She pointed to a marble bench on which had been placed an Indian suit. Adam stared at the ivory *achkan* coat, feeling an odd sensation. The Indian box flashed through his mind, with the miniature inside of the beautiful Brahmin girl, his great-grandmother. . . .

"Come, Mr. Thorne."

He turned to see that the woman had removed her sari and was standing on the step leading into the water. She was totally nude.

"If this is an example of native hospitality," said Adam, letting down his braces from his shoulders, "I like it."

He stepped out of his shoes and trousers, then took off his white dress shirt, which stank. When he, too, was naked, he walked down the steps into the pool. The water, which had lilies floating on it, was wonderfully cool.

"Nana Sahib buys the finest English soaps in Calcutta," said the woman, indicating a soap dish at one side of the pool. "Nana Sahib likes many English things. Unfortunately, he does not like the English."

"Is that why he kidnapped me?"

Again she smiled. "Thorne Sahib must not ask too many questions."

Adam swam across the pool to the soap dish. Climbing halfway out of the water, he took the cake of soap and began lathering his arms and chest.

"May I ask one more question? What's your name?"

"Lakshmi. I am a *nautch* girl."

Adam had learned enough in India to know that the *nautch* girls were professional dancing girls who were often courtesans as well. He lowered himself into the water to wash off the soapsuds, then swam lazily toward Lakshmi, although the pool was shallow enough for him to walk. For the wild young Adam Thorne of the Yorkshire moors, this was an incredibly exotic setting. He felt as rutty as he ever had in his young life. Standing in front of Lakshmi, he put his hands on her smooth shoulders.

"You smell better," she said, bluntly enough.

"There was room for improvement. What is your game, Lakshmi? Do you work for this Nana Sahib, or his cousin, the Maharajah of Raniganj? Or both?"

"Perhaps I work for both."

"The Maharajah of Raniganj seems rich, judging from this place. Is the mysterious Nana Sahib rich as well?"

"His father, the Peshwa of Bithur, was rich. But when he died, the English refused to continue to pay Nana Sahib his father's pension."

"Which is why Nana Sahib hates the English?" He ran his hands down her full breasts. "What happens next?" he whispered.

"That is up to you, Thorne Sahib. Do you have any diseases, like syphilis?"

Adam was taken aback. "No."

"Nor do I. Good. In India, one must be careful. So many of the *Angrezi* soldiers are infected."

"And on that romantic note . . ."

He pulled her gently to him and kissed her mouth, wrapping his arms around her. Her breasts pressed into his chest, filling him with lust. He felt her fingers gently grasp his erection and insert it in her.

"You know a few tricks," he whispered.

"Love is my living."

He had never made love standing waist-deep in a pool, but he found that the slickness of her wet skin was maddeningly erotic. She put her arms around his neck and wrapped her legs around his thighs so that she was half-floating as, at the same time, being half-carried by Adam. He was kissing her hotly.

He gasped after a lovely while. As he shot into her, he almost lost his balance. Lakshmi let out a shriek of pleasure, then let go of his neck and floated backward on the water away from him.

"You make love like an Indian," she said, standing again. "Full of fire and passion, not like the *Angrezi* soldiers who have to get drunk first. I think *Angrezi* like beer better than *boor.*"

"What's *boor*?"

She pointed in the water to her vagina. "Now, Thorne Sahib, since you have given me such pleasure, I will give you a word of advice. As I told you, Nana Sahib hates the *Angrezi-log.* I have heard rumors in the palace that he is toying with the idea of killing you, although he may not have the nerve to do it."

"Why me? What does he have against *me*?" Adam said angrily.

"Beyond the fact that you are an *Angrezi*, I do not know. But Nana Sahib is like a child in many ways, and he is enormously swayed by what he sees. I have brought you Indian clothes. If you permit me to darken your skin with stain so that you look like an Indian instead of an *Angrezi*, I believe Nana Sahib would find it impossible to kill you."

He stared at her. How bizarre! he thought. I *am* Indian,

or at least part Indian and ashamed to admit it. Now she wants to save my life by having me pretend to be all Indian. Nonetheless, the idea appealed to him. If he had traveled to India to come to grips with his identity, what better way than to look like an Indian? After all, wasn't so much of the anti-Indian prejudice on the part of the English based on skin color? Suddenly a submerged longing that had been growing in him since he found out the truth about his mixed ancestry blossomed into excitement.

"Yes," he whispered, eagerness in his dark eyes. "Make me an Indian."

"Good. Follow me, Thorne Sahib."

She stepped out of the pool, picked up a white robe off a bench and put it on. Then she handed another robe to Adam, who followed her to the end of the pool. "Use the robe to dry your body," said Lakshmi, "and then I will apply the stain."

Adam obeyed, following her into a small vestibule off the pool room. She opened a cabinet and removed a porcelain jar. "Sit," she said, pointing to a bench. He obeyed. She opened the jar, smeared her fingers with dark brown stain and began rubbing it onto his forehead. "It will take perhaps a month to wear off," she said, working with expert fingers. "You will not be able simply to wash it off. I suggest you grow a beard, as shaving might take it off the lower part of your face, leaving you with two colors, which might be odd."

"I see your point."

After she had done his face and ears, she told him to take off his robe.

"Why?" he asked.

"I must stain your entire body," she said matter-of-factly. "Nana Sahib is not a rational man. He consumes enough *ganja* and *bangh* for ten men, and who can tell where his mind will light next? What's more, he is a cruel man. He might take it into his head to torture you, and if he saw that your body was white and we had deceived him, he would go mad with rage and no one could control him. My life would be forfeit too."

Her reasoning sounded as crazy as she claimed Nana

Sahib was, but he decided that he might as well be Indian all the way. He stood up from the bench and removed his robe. After she had darkened his torso, she knelt behind him and began applying the stain to his buttocks and the backs of his thighs, which he found a curiously sensual experience. When she had finished his legs, she came around to his front and began working on his groin.

"*There*, too?" he said curiously.

"With the Indian, this is the blackest part of his body. I speak from experience."

After she had finished, which took over an hour, she led him back to the pool, where he put on the Indian clothes.

"It's astonishing," she exclaimed when he was dressed. "You could pass as a Hindu."

"Is there a mirror?"

"Yes, in here."

She led him to another anteroom, where there was a full-length mirror. Adam stepped before it and stared at his reflection.

"My God," he whispered. "I *do* look like an Indian!"

Curiously, he also *felt* like an Indian. He wondered if the ghost of his Brahmin great-grandmother was watching and, if so, what she was thinking.

"Come, Thorne Sahib," said Lakshmi. "I will take you to Nana Sahib."

She led him through more corridors of the palace until they came to two doors guarded by a pair of fierce-looking Indians in white *dhotis*. Adam was rather surprised to see that the guards carried the recently issued Enfield rifles that had been discussed at Sir Carlton McNair's house in Calcutta. The guards opened the doors and Lakshmi led him into a large room dominated by an immense hurricane-lamp chandelier. The windows were pierced screens outside of which were hung *tatties*, screens of sweet-scented grass which were kept wet to cool the wind. The furniture of the room, which Adam guessed was a sort of throne room, was gilt chairs in the French style whose upholstery was tattered in places, the target of hungry insects. A *punkah* swayed lazily from the ceiling, which was festooned with spiderwebs.

Nana Sahib was sitting on one of the gilt sofas, with Azimullah standing next to him. He took one look at Adam, burst into laughter, and clapped his hands with glee. "It's wonderful!" he exclaimed in Hindi. "He looks just like an Indian. You have done well, Lakshmi."

"Thank you, Your Highness. I did not tell him *why* you want him to look like an Indian."

"No, of course not. I would have beaten you if you had. Speak to the *Angrezi*, Azimullah. Tell him my plans for him."

"Yes, Highness." The suave Indian turned to Adam and switched to English. "His Highness, the Peshwa of Bithur, demands to know why you have had the effrontery to threaten his life."

Adam looked confused. "Are you mad? I'd never even *heard* of Nana Sahib before an hour ago!"

"You stated to the English newspapers months ago that you were coming to India to find the murderer of your grandfather, the late Earl of Pontefract. You said that you would bring him to justice. Well, Thorne Sahib, you are looking at the murderer of your grandfather—or should I say 'murderers'? Nana Sahib sent me to London a year ago to try to redress the injustices of the English Government toward him and also to avenge the defiling of one of our holy places by your ancestor, the first Lord Pontefract. It was I who arranged for the explosion on Lord Fane's yacht, and it was I who sent the *thuggees* to Pontefract Hall. So, sir, we admit freely to what you consider a crime, although we consider it entirely justifiable revenge for the crimes your family has committed against Holy India."

"My family may have committed crimes—I won't deny that," said Adam, "but that doesn't justify murder of innocent people—"

"No white man is innocent!" Azimullah interrupted hotly. "The white man is trying to rule this planet by enslaving people with darker skins, whom you consider inferior, but the day will soon come when the tables will turn. What you do not know is that the great uprising against the English infidels predicted a century ago has already begun. It will spread all over India until the white man's blood has drenched our fields."

"You seem sure of yourself," said Adam, telling himself to appear cool even though he was appalled at what he was hearing. He was thinking of sweet Emily McNair. Whatever the injustices of the English in India, *she* surely was not to blame. Was she in danger?

"I am sure because our cause is just," said Azimullah, lowering his voice to its usual silky timbre.

"Did he leave the diamond in England?" said Nana Sahib in Hindi. "If he did, tell him we'll hold him hostage until he arranges for me to get it. It wasn't on him—Lakshmi searched him while he was drugged. Where is it?"

"I am getting to that, Highness," replied Azimullah in patient Hindi. Then back to English: "His Highness has empowered me to deliver your sentence of death . . ."

"Wait a minute! Sentence of death for what? And don't I get a trial?"

"You have had your trial already."

"I didn't see a jury."

"A jury?" Azimullah laughed contemptuously. "What a ridiculous system you *Angrezi* have tried to impose on us. What is the wisdom of twelve stupid men compared to the divine wisdom of one great man like Nana Sahib? You have been tried by him and found guilty. This, then, is your punishment: you have foolishly allowed the *nautch* girl to dye your skin brown. You now look like an Indian, even though you cannot speak our language. We will take you to Delhi, where already the mutineers from Meerut are attacking the English garrison. There we will turn you loose. Either the English will kill you, thinking you are an Indian. Or the Indians will kill you, thinking you are trying to escape their wrath by disguising yourself as one of them—which has already happened in Meerut. Either way, you face certain death."

A mutiny in Meerut? thought Adam. And now Delhi? Was this possible, or were they bluffing him? But if they weren't bluffing, he had to admit it was a clever way to kill him.

"Why does he not look afraid?" said Nana Sahib in Hindi. "The *boorao* shows no fear, but he must be acting. I want him to look afraid! If we are to get the diamond, we must put the fear of Kali in him. Threaten him with torture."

"Yes, Sire." Azimullah turned back to Adam. "You have one hope, thanks to the magnanimous nature of Nana Sahib. But if you do not accept his offer, be warned that he may turn you over to his torturers, who are skilled in the art of pain. There is also the Pit of Snakes, which can drive a man mad."

They might be bluffing, but Adam's skin crawled at the idea of a snakepit.

"It worked," chortled Nana Sahib in Hindi. "He looks afraid! Good! Now, the diamond."

"Where is the great diamond?" Azimullah asked. "If you return the great diamond to Nana Sahib, he is prepared to offer you clemency and remove the punishment of death."

So they *are* bluffing! thought Adam. This whole scheme is a ploy to scare me into giving them the diamond. The bastards.

"The great diamond is in the vault of the Bank of Calcutta," he said. "I put it there the day I arrived. Only I can remove it. I'll remind you that your *thuggees* tried to steal it once—"

"Not 'steal'!" shouted Azimullah. "We tried to 'retrieve' it for India. It was your great-grandfather who stole it!"

"Agreed. And I came to India to return it to the temple at Lucknow. Which, in fact, I was going to do the day after you kidnapped me. If Nana Sahib wants the diamond, all he has to do is go to the temple and take it—after I put it there. But if he kills me, he's never going to get the diamond because I've written in my will that the diamond is to be sold in case of any . . . shall we say 'accident'? occurring to me. Tell that to the great Pooh-Bah, and see how quickly he wants to kill me."

Azimullah, looking a bit uncomfortable, translated to

Nana Sahib, who in turn looked confused. "*Bhainchute!*" he muttered, calling Adam a "sister-violator," one of the worst insults in the language. Then his scowl was replaced by an oleaginous smile. "Tell him it was all a joke. Tell him he is our honored guest. Tell him we will feast tonight and send him back to Calcutta tomorrow. Tell him I will personally guarantee his safety as he takes the diamond to Lucknow." His smile increased. "But don't tell him that the moment the diamond is in Kali's hand, he is a dead *Angrezi.*"

"Yes, Your Highness." Azimullah bowed, then turned to Adam.

What Nana Sahib didn't know was that while he spoke, Adam had privately vowed to kill the fat, smiling murderer of his grandfather.

CHAPTER 8

The three teenagers riding alongside the snowy bank of the Rappahannock River in central Virginia had known each other all their lives. The two brothers, Clayton and Zachary Carr, lived on Carr Farm next door to Fairview Plantation, which was the home of the girl, Charlotte Whitney.

"Were you invited to Mr. Cavanagh's Christmas ball to meet his new wife?" asked Charlotte, who was eighteen. She had a good figure and looked quite elegant in her riding habit, her black hat on top of her brown hair.

"Yes, but Pa says he doesn't want to go," replied Clayton, who was the elder of the two brothers, being Charlotte's age. "He says it's too far."

"It's only three hours. And you gave in to him?" exclaimed Charlotte.

"Well, you know Pa, once he makes up his mind."

"Clayton Carr, I declare, you just don't have any gumption. You're an old fuddy-duddy. Why, it's going to be the ball of the season and everyone's dying to meet Mrs. Cavanagh, who's supposed to be *so* beautiful, and they say she has a wicked past. . . . What'll you and Zack do? Sit home and play with your mangy hound dogs?"

"Guess so," sighed Zack glumly. He was fourteen. The two brothers resembled each other in many ways, although Clayton's hair was sandy while Zack's was dark brown, and Clayton's face was liberally sprinkled with freckles. They were both strapping, good-looking boys who had grown up riding and hunting. Zack was at a boarding school in Richmond, while Clayton was in his first year at Princeton, where he had taken with him his personal slave, as was the custom with Southern students. Brandon Carr, their widower father, was well-to-do but nowhere as rich as Charlotte's father, Senator Phineas Thurlow Whitney, the senior senator from Virginia. The Carrs had fifty slaves, while Senator Whitney had over three hundred.

"I just don't understand you two," Charlotte said, shaking her head. "You're so spineless. You won't stand up for your rights, and it's your right to have a good time during Christmas vacation. Well, I suppose I'll have to dance with someone else. Guess *that* won't be a great sacrifice, the way you step on toes." This last was shot at Clayton, who looked annoyed. She dug her heels into her horse and galloped off.

"She stepped on *my* toes once," growled Clayton.

"Yes, but she's right, Clayton," Zack said. "I think it was mean of Pa not to let us go."

"Yeah, I know." Clayton was watching Charlotte gallop toward her home, Fairview Plantation, which was visible in the distance overlooking the Rappahannock River.

"You always say you're in love with Charlotte," Zack said. "Well, you gotta fight for her. And I wouldn't mind having a good time and meeting some girls. Damned school's like a monastery."

"Come on," Clayton said, turning his horse. "We're going home and lay down the law to Pa. We're going to that party."

"That's more like it," yipped Zack. The two boys spurred their horses and galloped down the riverbank, letting out enthusiastic Ee-HAHS!

"Isn't she beautiful?" said Ellie May Whitney, Charlotte's mother, as she watched Jack and Lizzie Cavanagh waltz by in the ballroom of Elvira Plantation. "I just thank heaven I'm not the jealous type, or I'd be pea green with envy."

Clemmie DeVries gave her a look. The wife of Senator Phineas Thurlow Whitney was, by even charitable standards, no beauty, with prominent buck teeth and bony shoulders. The two women were standing beside each other next to the big Christmas tree in one corner of the room. "Don't be silly, Ellie May," she said. "You're as jealous of Lizzie Cavanagh as I am, like every woman in this room. And the men would all like to strangle Jack so they could start courting his widow. Don't think I don't have my eyes on *my* husband."

"Oh Clemmie, Billie DeVries would never dream of looking at another woman, he's so madly in love with you."

"He'd dream, all right. Did you ever see such jewels? Jack has spent a *fortune* on her. He's *wildly* in love. I think it's so romantic."

"Well, I think it's flashy and vulgar, and if I didn't know Jack was a Randolph and FFV, I'd think he was some nouveau riverboat gambler. But my Aunt Minnie heard from her cousin in New York, who was in Paris a while ago that the new Mrs. Cavanagh was the"—she lowered her voice to a whisper—"mistress of the French Emperor."

Clemmie, who was looking handsome in a pale green dress with black fringe, rolled her eyes. "Ellie, I do wish you'd stop spreading that terrible rumor, which is nothing but gossip and you know it. I think Lizzie is a sweet woman. After all, her father was a clergyman."

"Uh-huh. Idabelle Clarkson's father was a clergyman, and you know what happened to *her*. And in her father's church!"

"Ellie May, that was never proved."

"I'd like to know why they sent her off to Tennessee for six months. Clemmie, you're just too goodie-goodie for words. Her Dulcey told my Delia that Lizzie Cavanagh is well into her fourth month, and if you start counting days, it makes it *mighty* close, if you ask me. Wouldn't surprise me a bit if Mrs. Cavanagh with her la-di-da English accent wasn't all she was supposed to be on her wedding night."

"Ellie May, you are not being Christian. In fact, you're being extremely mean. Give the poor woman a chance."

"Well, it's what *everyone* is saying."

"That doesn't make it true. Oh heavens, here comes Billie and I think he's gotten tipsy again."

The pale green ballroom was packed with dancers as Mr. McIlhenney's Cotillion Orchestra (advertised as

"Eight of the Most Refined and Expert Musicians in Dixie") sat at one end of the big room serving up the latest musical confection from Europe, their brass music stands lit by candles. It was *the* social event of the Christmas season in Gloucester County, and those wretches who had failed to receive invitations to the Cavanaghs' Christmas ball disguised their chagrin by announcing they would never be in the same room with "that woman," meaning Lizzie. The beautiful Mrs. Cavanagh, with whom Jack was obviously besotted, had caused a firestorm of gossip that was almost more than the locals could handle. Virginia society was one of the most aristocratic in America, but still it was suffocatingly provincial and narrow-minded. Lizzie's clothes, her jewels, her supposedly racy past, had divided the locals into two camps: pro-Lizzie and anti. But Clemmie liked Lizzie. She liked her much more than Ellie May Whitney, who she thought had a poisonous mind and whose husband, the eminent Senator, had a reputation for treating his slaves badly.

Now Billie DeVries, stirrup cup in hand, weaved his way around the side of the room where the older women were sitting on gilt chairs indulging in orgies of gossip and approached his wife and Ellie May.

"Billie DeVries, I *told* you to go easy on the liquor," said Clemmie in a low voice. "You're half-seas over and the buffet isn't for another hour. If you make a fool of yourself. . . ."

Billie, a bleary smile on his face, put his finger to his lips. "Sshhh, Clemmie. No sermons."

"Then put down that cup and dance with me. A little exercise will clear your head."

"Of course, my love. Hello, Ellie May. You're lookin' very pretty tonight."

Ellie May smiled, displaying her buck teeth. "Why, thank you, Billie," she said in a Mississippi accent that was infinitely more "Southern" than the Virginia accent.

"And you can finish my drink." Billie stuck his cup in her hand, then waltzed his wife rather uncertainly onto the floor.

"Your breath is simply awful," said Clemmie, wrinkling her nose.

"Doesn't Lizzie look beautiful?" Billie quickly changed the subject. They both looked across the room to where their host and hostess were waltzing, Lizzie in a Prussian-blue velvet dress that exposed what the primmer Virginia ladies thought was an indecent amount of her spectacular shoulders and breasts, even though by Paris standards the dress was unexceptional. Her diamonds flashed as she twirled in the candlelight.

"I must say I'm impressed," Charlotte Whitney said as she danced with Clayton Carr. "You got your father to change his mind. But where's Zack?"

"I made a deal with Pa. I'd go if Zack stayed to keep him company. You know he gets lonely since Ma died."

"I declare, that seems rather cruel to poor Zack. I know he wanted to come."

"He's only fourteen. He has to sacrifice to me."

"You heartless person!"

"Well, Zack was catching a cold anyway. I'm sure glad I came, though. You're looking beautiful, Charlotte."

Charlotte resembled her mother, albeit without the buck teeth, but her youth gave her angular face a softness, if not beauty. And her skin, her hazel eyes and her silky brown hair were enviable. Now she smiled.

"Why, thank you, Clayton," she said. "I didn't think you were interested in girls. I didn't think you were interested in anything except shooting squirrels."

"You know that's not true, Charlotte," he said with teenage ardor. "Why, I'm crazy about girls! And I'm especially crazy about one girl in particular."

"And who could that be, pray?"

"You know who I'm talking about. It's you."

"Why, that's sweet, Clayton Carr. And I do think that you might be sincere. Of course, a girl has to be careful. So many boys are apt to be deceitful."

"Oh, I'm sincere, Charlotte—honest. And I mean it so much that . . . well . . ." He gulped and his freckled face looked in torment. ". . . I'd like to think that someday, maybe when I'm out of Princeton. . . ."

His declaration of love was interrupted by the clanging of a distant bell. The orchestra's music died down and the dancers slowed to a halt. Everyone in the room knew that it was an alarm bell. Jack, a frown on his face, said, "Excuse me, honey," to his wife and hurried to one of the French doors at the side of the room. He opened it and ran outside. It was a cold, snowy night, and eddies of flakes whirled into the room on a strong wind, creating a magical effect until one of the footmen closed the door. The room, momentarily so silent, began buzzing with rumor.

Then Jack appeared in the door again. He raised his arms for silence. "Gentlemen," he announced, "I will ask those of you who are members of the patrol to join me, and bring your guns. Moses, my coachman, has escaped."

The statement created an electric effect in the room. The young men began whooping "Ya-HOO! Ya-HOO!" as they pushed through the crowd to the central hall for their coats and guns.

"It's as if they're going to a picnic," Lizzie exclaimed, coming over to Clemmie.

"More like a fox hunt," Clemmie replied grimly. "There's nothing they like better than hunting down a runaway."

"Clayton," Charlotte said, "why are you standing here? Why aren't you going with the patrol?"

He looked at her. "I'm not a member of the patrol."

"But a slave has escaped. You should go with the others and help find him."

"I'd rather stay here with you."

"I declare, Clayton Carr, are you a man or a mouse? Every red-blooded young Southerner has a duty to help hunt down runaways. What if one of *your* slaves ran away? Wouldn't you want all the help you could get? We have to stick together!"

Clayton hesitated. He didn't want to tell her that a semester in the Northern university town of Princeton had sown serious seeds of doubt in his mind about the "peculiar institution." Two of his roommates were Northern boys, and one of them was a rabid Abolitionist. Many a New Jersey night had been spent in heated argument about the issue that was slowly ripping the nation apart, and Clayton had to admit that increasingly he was finding it difficult to defend slavery. All the same, he knew that if Charlotte ever got a hint of his apostasy from the religion of slavery—and he knew that for the entire Whitney family, slavery was a religion—any hope of a romance was dead. So he said with notable lack of enthusiasm, "I guess you're right. If you'll excuse me . . ."

He walked toward the central hall. The room was meanwhile filling with talk and laughter again, as the women returned to their gossip and the remaining men to their drinks. Lizzie went to one of the French doors at the side of the room and wiped the frosting off one of the panes with her finger. Outside, the men, many of them drunk, were mounting their horses as slaves stood by holding torches for illumination. Jack was already mounted on Avenger and was shouting at Mr. Duncan, who was holding a pack of yapping bloodhounds on a multiple leash. At least two dozen of the younger guests, including Clayton, were joining the patrol. As Clemmie came to the window, Lizzie asked quietly, "What will they do to Moses if they catch him?"

"Maybe they won't catch him. The snow will make it difficult for the bloodhounds to track his scent. On the other hand, if they can find his footprints . . ."

"Does he have a chance?"

"Not much, I fear."

"What will they do to him?" she repeated. "Tell me. I'm not squeamish."

Clemmie sighed. "In most cases, they let the hounds attack the runaway for a while."

Lizzie looked at her. "What do you mean?"

"When they catch the runaway, they point their guns at his head and tell him that if he moves, they'll blow his brains out. Then they let the hounds attack him for as much as five minutes . . . Lizzie! Are you all right?"

Lizzie had leaned against the wall, her face drained of color. Then she straightened and nodded. "It's incredible to think that . . . that so-called civilized people could . . ."

She was interrupted by Mr. McIlhenney, the orchestra

leader, tapping his baton on his brass music stand. "Ladies and gentlemen," he announced, "kindly take your positions for the reel."

To Lizzie's amazement, the older gentlemen began forming a line on the dance floor as the chattering ladies lined up in front of them. Then, as the orchestra broke into a merry reel, the guests began skipping in circles, do-si-do-ing as the onlookers around the room clapped in time to the music.

"They're going on with the party," Lizzie exclaimed.

"Well, of course," said Clemmie. "Runaways aren't that unusual."

"But that's shocking! I won't allow it!"

Anger in her eyes, she started away from the French door. Clemmie took her arm.

"Lizzie, don't do anything rash," she said in a low voice. "Remember what I told you: you may not like the system—I don't either. But these people have staked their lives on it. If they think you're against them, they'll turn on you and make you a pariah."

Lizzie looked at her a moment, then tore her arm away and hurried onto the dance floor.

"Stop it!" she cried to Mr. McIlhenney. "Stop the music!"

The bandleader, a look of confusion on his face, tapped his baton and the band ground to a halt, as did the dancers. All were staring at Lizzie.

"How can you dance?" she exclaimed. "Don't you realize what's going on outside? A man is being hunted down like an animal!"

Ellie May Whitney said, "Well, my dear, it's only a slave."

"But he's a human being, like you and me!"

There were a few titters as well as a few gasps. Senator Phineas Thurlow Whitney, Ellie May's husband who was twenty years her senior, stepped forward. He was a tall gentleman, perfectly tailored in an immaculate swallowtail coat, with long white hair that hung to his shoulders and a sweeping white mustache. Somewhat of a dandy, he wore an elegant white cravat which he knew, from having been

Ambassador to the Court of St. James during the Administration of President Franklin Pierce, had become *de rigueur* in London after dark (most of the men in the ballroom wore colored cravats, because Americans had not yet begun to differentiate between daytime and nighttime clothing). When the other guests saw Senator Whitney, a respectful hush fell over the room. The senior senator from Virginia was one of the most powerful Democrats in Washington, a city that was then still dominated by Southerners and the slaveholders' interests.

"Madam, we all understand that you are a foreigner," he said in a paternal manner, his Virginia accent cultivated and musical. "And of course we are all so pleased that our dear friend and neighbor Jack Cavanagh has brought to us from Europe such a radiant jewel of feminine charm and pulchritude as yourself. But dear lady, in Virginia by no stretch of the imagination could a nigra be called 'a human being like you or me.' With all due respect, ma'am, and realizing that you are unused to our customs here in the South, I would ask you to retract that unhappy remark. And I believe I speak for all the ladies and gentlemen here. Am I correct?"

He looked around the room. The other guests nodded and mumbled accord. Ellie May came to her husband, linked her arm in his and smiled her sweetest smile at Lizzie.

"Of course, we all want to be friendly and neighborly here in Gloucester County," she said. "And you *know,* Lizzie, that all of us have just closed our ears to all those silly rumors about your life in France when you were . . . I believe they call it 'modeling' gowns? . . . for the Emperor Napoleon's wife. We *all* need to stand together here in the South, because we know we have so many enemies up North, and the last thing we need is another enemy right here in our very bosom, you might say. So I know you're going to do what my dear husband has asked you to do, and retract that . . . that silly remark you made about the nigra."

Lizzie looked around the room, the expression on her face cool. Clemmie watched her, impressed by her courage but praying she would back down. Clemmie knew these people. But how magnificent she looks! she thought, eying with envy her truly stunning face, her superb figure, her gorgeous blue dress, the blazing diamonds and rubies around her neck and at her ears. My stars, she thought, she may be a clergyman's daughter, but she could pass for an empress. Lucien Delorme's coaching had worked.

"I will not retract one syllable of what I said," Lizzie finally exclaimed in ringing tones. "Mr. McIlhenney, send your musicians home. The ball is over."

Picking up her long skirt, she strode through her guests, who parted before her, staring at her as if she were a leper.

Which she had just become.

"Oh, mistress, dey discover Mose had tuck off an hour ago," Dulcey said twenty minutes later as she removed the pins from Lizzie's elaborate pile of curls on top of her head (it was actually an expensive fall Lizzie had bought in New York: her own hair had grown back only halfway). "I was in de kitchen eatin' my kush and collards—you know Aunt Lide make de bestest kush in de whole wide worl'—an' in runs Broward, all excited, an' he say Mose done disappear." Dulcey removed the fall and put it in a black leather box. Lizzie had told her she cut her hair short because it was the fashion in France. "Mistress want me to brush her hair? She have such purty hair, lak honey almos'. Purty soon it gonna be all grown back in, lookin' real nice."

Dulcey picked up a silver brush and began to work on Lizzie's hair. Lizzie had changed into an ivory peignoir after coming upstairs to her bedroom. The guests had all left by now, and the wind was whistling around the house, rustling the gold brocade curtains that had been pulled across the leaky, recessed windows. A fire sputtered in the brick chimney, providing the only heat in the chilly room. As Dulcey brushed her hair, Lizzie wondered if there were some connection between her telling Moses of his wife's death and his attempted escape. If so, had she been wrong to tell him after all? She didn't know, but the thought of the bloodhounds attacking him made her blood run cold.

"Aunt Lide gonna start makin' de Christmas pies tomorrow," Dulcey was rambling on. "I sure loves Christmas, don't you, mistress?"

"Yes. That's enough, Dulcey. It's chilly in here and I'm going to bed."

"Yes'm, mistress."

"I seem to have dropped my handkerchief somewhere," Lizzie added as she got up from the dresser. "If you see it downstairs . . ."

"Yes, mistress, I takes a look aroun'."

"Good night, Dulcey."

"Good night, mistress."

The girl curtsied, then left the room as Lizzie snuffed out the eight candles of the round crystal holders. Then she went to the canopied bed, which Dulcey had turned down. A gust of wind whooshed down the chimney, blowing a puff of smoke into the room. The gold curtains rustled slightly. Lizzie shuddered, then took off the slippers she had bought in Paris and climbed into the bed, which had been warmed by a long-handled metal pan filled with hot coals. A silk-shaded oil lamp on the bed table cast dark shadows around the bedroom. Lizzie picked up a novel from under the lamp and opened it to the bookmark. It was Charles Reade's *It Is Never Too Late to Mend,* the sensational English best-seller of the previous year, which dealt with a young English thief who was transported to Australia. Lizzie started reading where she had left off, a chilling account of the brutal treatment of prisoners in Birmingham Gaol—Reade was one of the first 'documentary' novelists who dramatized contemporary abuses—but she quickly put it down. She had had enough brutality for the evening. It seemed that half the world had nothing better to do than brutalize the other half.

She leaned over to turn down the lamp when she saw the sandaled feet beneath the gold curtains over one of the windows. She froze. The skin on the feet was mocha.

Silence except for the moaning of the wind. Lizzie's right hand reached for the bed-table drawer, her eyes on the feet. Jack kept a revolver in the drawer. Slowly she opened it and pulled out the gun. Then, holding it with both trembling hands, she aimed it at the curtains.

"Whoever you are," she said in a hoarse whisper, "come out. I see your feet. I have a gun, and I'm not afraid to shoot."

Two hands opened the curtains and Moses stepped out.

"Mistress, put de gun down," he whispered. "I ain't gonna harm you none, honest."

Baffled, she lowered the gun. "Moses! What are you doing *here*?"

"I figure dey would never tink I come here, mistress. While dey out wif de hounds lookin' all over de county for Moses, he right here at Elvira Plantation."

"That was rather clever. But it won't be so clever if my husband catches you here. You're in great danger."

"I knows, mistress," he said, coming closer to the bed. He was wearing his slave clothes, a wool shirt and pants. She wondered why she wasn't frightened, but she sensed she was in no danger from him. "You see, when you tole me Samantha had died, I had to escape on account of my son. He's a fine boy, mistress, he really is, but he only seven year ole and now he got no daddy or momma, no nothin', and I tole myself I gotta go find him an' take him North so he can be free an' have a life that's worth livin'. An' then I thought of you. You been so kind to me twice an' I feel it in my bones that you're different from the other white folks an' . . . well, I was hopin' maybe you'd help me a third time."

"Help you? How?" she whispered.

"Dey's a fisherman name Stanley at Stingray Point on de Chesapeake Bay dat will take slaves by boat to free territory for one hunnerd dollars gold. I heerd about him in de quarter. If mistress could help me get to Stingray Point an' loan me de money, I could get to free territory an' find my boy. An' I swear, mistress, someday I'd pay you back de money. I *swear*."

She stared at him. "But helping slaves escape is a crime."

He looked at her, his face expressionless. He said nothing. She hesitated, thinking. Then she put the gun back in the drawer. "Of course I'll lend you the money," she went on, thinking out loud. "And maybe there would be some way . . . I mean, if my husband didn't find out . . ." She closed the drawer and looked at Moses again. "Christmas!" she said. "I was thinking of going into Yorktown tomorrow to do my Christmas shopping. I could take you to Stingray Point instead. Yes, that's it! Go to the carriage house and hide in one of the carriages—"

"De brougham! I'll hide in de luggage space! Oh mistress, if you do dis for me, de good Lord gonna make a special place in heaven for you."

"And if my husband finds out, God knows what he'll do. We must be careful, Moses, but I think this is a workable idea. Now, go. I have no idea when Mr. Cavanagh will come back."

He came to the bed and took her right hand in his. He squeezed it. "If only," he whispered, "we could have been friends."

The remark took her by surprise.

"Perhaps we *are* friends," she said.

A frown came over his face. He released her hand.

"No," he said, "we can never be friends. Not as long as you married to Massa Jack. He been behavin' himself ever since you come to Elvira Plantation, but before, he had Mr. Duncan and his two stupid sons lay onto me wid de whip." He turned and raised his wool shirt. She gasped at what she saw. His broad back was crisscrossed with dozens of hideous welts, many an inch thick, the welts bumping up over the skin as if moles had burrowed all over his body. "You want to know pain, mistress? If I could write, I'd write a big, fat book on pain."

She stared at the welts and realized she was looking at a summation of all the horror of two and a half centuries of American slavery. She didn't know what to say. Moses lowered his shirt and turned back to her. "Someday dey's gonna be a settlement, mistress," he whispered. "Someday de white man gonna pay for what he done to us. But you done prove to me dat all white folk aren't bad, mistress. An' for dat, God bless you."

"Hurry, Moses," she said.

He went to the bedroom door and opened it. But just

before leaving, he turned back to her and whispered, "You de most beautiful lady I ever saw: beautiful inside an' out."

Then he left the room, closing the door softly behind him. Lizzie was amazed at the risk she was taking helping the slave.

But she was glad she was taking it.

Aunt Lide was a tall, gaunt woman with a hatchet face. The next morning she stood over the coal stove in the kitchen of Elvira Plantation, wearing a white kerchief over her gray hair and a spotless white apron over her gingham dress as she broke eggs into a skillet. The kitchen was a big, cheerful room overlooking the kitchen garden, now covered with snow. The hulking black stove was a recent addition; Jack prided himself on keeping up with all the modern conveniences of the day. Aunt Lide had grown used to it, but it had taken her months to be weaned from the huge brick fireplace where she had cooked most of her life.

"Massa comin' downstairs," said Charles, coming in from the butler's pantry. "He look tired an' cross, 'cause de patrols didn't get back till almos' fo' dis mornin' an' dey didn't catch Moses."

"De coffee's ready. Get some coffee in him, he'll feel better. I swear dat Moses nuffin' but a troublemaker. Can't leave well enough alone, oh no. He gotta try to larn hisself to read. Huh! Niggers lak dat end up jes where he be: on de run wid de bloodhouns yappin' at his heels. Go on, Charles, take de coffee in."

"I's goin', I's goin'."

The old man picked up the silver tray with the coffeepot and headed back to the butler's pantry, then into the dining room. Jack was seating himself at the end of the table.

"Nice hot coffee for you, massa, an' Aunt Lide fryin' you some eggs. I knows you'se weary."

"Thanks, Charles. Since I need a new coachman, what do you think of Broward?"

"Oh Broward, he one fine boy, yessuh. He make a good coachman."

"And he's about Moses' size. Tell him to take Moses'

livery, get dressed and then prepare the brougham. My wife is going to Yorktown to do some Christmas shopping. She'll be down in twenty minutes or so."

"Yes, massa. Broward, he gonna make you one fine coachman, yessuh."

Charles poured the coffee, then left the room as Jack unfolded the Yorktown newspaper, which he arranged to have delivered at what to others would seem an extravagant expense. Five minutes later, he was cutting into his eggs and bacon when Dulcey wandered into the room from the central hall. She was carrying a rag doll in her arms. She came up to the table.

"Massa lak to meet Marcy?" she said.

"Don't bother me, Dulcey. I'm tired."

"Oh massa, please. Jes take a look. Marcy's my favorite doll."

Jack sighed. "Mm. It's pretty, though you're getting a little old to be playin' with dolls."

"Shrimpboat gave it to me," she went on, mentioning one of Mr. Duncan's two sons. "He tuck me into Yawktown de udder day an' oh, dey was such pretty tings in de windows! Dresses an' hats an' fine tings for de ladies to wear. Now if massa gave me some money, I could buy some of dose fine tings. Maybe a dress for Marcy. Maybe even a dress for . . . me."

Jack's look of impatience turned to curiosity. He knew Dulcey had a maddening way of beating around the bush.

"Why would I give you money?" he asked.

"Oh, to get me to tell massa tings I seen an' heard."

Jack chewed his bacon, studying her. Then he reached into his pocket, pulled out a gold piece and placed it on the table.

"And what have you seen and heard, Dulcey?"

"Well, lass night after de mistress send de guests home—"

"*Sent* them?"

"Yes, massa. Mistress tell all de guests to go home after you tuck off wid de patrols."

"Why?"

"I dunno."

"Before they *ate*?"

"Yes, massa, an' Aunt Lide she say to all de house servants she warn't gonna have all dat good food wasted, so all de hams an' chickens was tuck out to de icehouse. An' dat's when I found mistress' hankie, de pretty lace one wid her initials what you done bought her in Paris, France? It was on one of de stairs an' I tuck it back up to mistress, cep when I got to her door I heard voices. Yes, massa, she was talkin' to someone in her bedroom." She paused, a sly smile coming over her face. "She was talkin' to a man."

Silence. Dulcey's eyes went from Jack's face to the gold coin. Slowly, Jack pushed it toward her.

"Who was the man?" he whispered.

Dulcey picked up the coin and put it in the pocket of her apron. "It was Mose."

Jack went into a coughing fit. After he subdued the cough, he grabbed Dulcey's wrist. "Are you *sure*?" he whispered.

"Oh yes, massa. I seen him. An' you're hurtin' me. I doan lak to be hurt."

Slowly, Jack released her wrist as she watched him coolly. For the first time he realized that this girl he had always dismissed as a half-wit, perhaps defensively because of her blood relationship to him, was actually rather cunning.

"I'm sorry, Dulcey," he said softly. "So you saw Moses?"

"Yes, massa."

"Well? Go on."

She hugged her doll, continuing to look at him.

"You know, massa," she finally said, "since I'se related to you, it strikes me I should be treated a little better dan de udder slaves."

Jack controlled his temper. "In what way?"

"Well, seems to me a pretty gal lak me should have pretty clothes an' be treated pretty, wif kisses an' tings lak dat." She smiled slightly. "Massa so handsome," she added suggestively.

He was no fool. He got it. But she's my half-sister! he

thought. And goddamn, I won't turn into a pig like my father.

But she *is* good-looking . . .

"Perhaps you're right, Dulcey," he said. "Perhaps I haven't treated you as . . . as prettily as I should. Well, that will change from now on."

"Promise?"

"Yes, I promise. Now: you saw Moses?"

"Uh-huh. Well, first I heard him, 'cause I listen at de door. Den she tell him to go, fast, an' he come to de door an' I hide m'self in de shadow. An' he open de door an he say to mistress, 'You de mos' beautiful lady I done ever seen. Outside an' inside.' Dass what he say."

Jack's face had turned red. He was clenching and unclenching his fist. "Did mistress cry out for help?" he whispered.

Dulcey smiled. "Oh no, massa. She didn't say nuffin' at all."

"I see. And then what happened?"

"Well, Mose he hurry down de stairs an' into de ballroom, which was empty 'cause everone done gone home. I run down de steps an' watch him while he goes out one of de ballroom doors into de night . . . you see, all de house servants was in de kitchen cleanin' up. So I hurry to de door an' look out. An' guess where he went?"

"Where?"

She paused, hugging Marcy, the doll. "You cross your heart 'bout your promise to treat Dulcey real nice?"

"Dammit, where did he go?"

Dulcey's face became ice. "You not treatin' Dulcey *nice*," she whispered.

Jack bit his lip. "I'm sorry."

"Give Dulcey a kiss. You've never, *never* kissed me."

Slowly he took her free hand and raised it to his mouth.

She smiled. "Dat feel real good," she purred.

"Now, where did he go?"

She was hugging the doll again. "He went in de carriage house an' he never cum out. I speck he still dere. I heerd mistress say he to hide in de luggage space of de big carriage."

Jack's eyes widened. Then he got to his feet.

"Thank you, Dulcey," he whispered. "I won't forget this. If you want, you can move into Moses' house and live there alone."

Her face lit up. "Oh massa, tank you! Tank you! An' maybe you come pay Dulcey a visit some night?"

"That's extremely possible. Now, you run up and ask mistress to come downstairs. And don't breathe a word of what you told me."

"Oh no, massa, I keep my mouf shut."

She hurried out of the room as Jack went into the butler's pantry and then the kitchen. Broward, the teenage slave Jack had appointed his new coachman, was sitting at the wooden table with Charles, drinking coffee.

"Broward, go get Mr. Duncan," Jack ordered. "Fast. Tell him to bring his boys and his guns."

"Yes, massa."

As Broward jumped up, Jack returned to the dining room. He picked up his cup to finish his coffee, then went into the central hall. Lizzie was coming down the stairs, followed by Dulcey. She wore a white Empress Eugénie hat with a great feather that swooped over and down the side of her face. Over her traveling dress she had put on an ermine-lined gray velvet cloak that had been designed by Lucien Delorme. As Jack stood at the bottom of the stairs watching her, he told himself he was now seeing this ravishing creature in a new and infuriating light.

"You asked for some shopping money," he said. "Just how much did you want?"

"Oh, I think two hundred dollars should do. In gold."

"Two hundred dollars? I'm aware that my lovely wife is developing a passion for shopping, but that does seem like a lot of money."

"Well, I wanted to buy something especially nice for Clemmie and Billie. And then there are all their children. And of course"—she gave him her prettiest smile as she reached the bottom step—"there's you."

"Uh-huh. Well, it sure is nice to have a thoughtful wife. And a faithful one too."

She gave him a curious look.

"Broward will drive you. He'll be back in a few minutes. I sent him on an errand. Meanwhile, you wait here, honey, and I'll go get your money."

"Thank you, dear."

As Dulcey vanished into the kitchen, Jack went to his paneled office at the rear of the house, opened a wall safe, and took out a steel box. He put it on his desk and opened it. Inside was a thick band of paper money, tied by a string, and several thousand dollars in gold coins. He removed two hundred dollars in gold, put it in his pocket, returned the box to the safe and then took out a revolver, which he tucked into his leather belt. Closing and locking the safe, he went back to the central hall where Lizzie was waiting.

"Open your purse," he said. Lizzie obeyed. He put the gold coins in.

"I feel rich." She smiled, closing the purse.

"Broward should be back now. Shall we go to the carriage house?"

"You don't have to accompany me. I know you're tired."

"But I'm a gentleman, honey, and a gentleman always escorts a lady. You *are* a lady?"

He took her arm and led her out the front door. It was another cold, windy day. Lizzie knew something was wrong, but she told herself the best defense was to maintain her unruffled facade. The truth was, she was nervous as a cat. She realized the stakes were high. Abetting a slave's escape was a crime. Once again she was breaking the law, although this time she was doing it intentionally. But she could not bring herself not to help Moses escape, and she knew that ultimately he would be caught if he weren't given assistance. Virginia was not the Deep South, like Alabama or Mississippi, but it was still a long way from the free territories. His chances of making it on his own were minimal.

The carriage house, icehouse, and stables were contained in a long, low brick building near the walled garden and the quarters of the house servants. As Jack and Lizzie approached the building, Broward galloped up, followed by Mr. Duncan and his two sons, Shrimpboat and Pee-Wee. The men dismounted as Jack and Lizzie joined them.

"Broward, bring out the carriage for mistress," Jack ordered.

"Yes, massa."

He hurried to the carriage house, where he had already hitched two horses to the closed carriage. Jack signaled Mr. Duncan and his sons to stand ready. The overseer looked a bit confused, but the three men unslung their rifles. Broward climbed on the driver's seat and shook the reins. The carriage rumbled out into the snowy drive. Jack went to it and opened the door. He made a mocking bow to Lizzie.

"Your carriage awaits, milady," he said, adopting a hammy tone. "Aha, but wait! Did something just move?" He pulled the gun from his belt and turned toward the carriage. "Could it be some vile thing has hidden itself in the luggage compartment beneath the rear seat? Could there be a nigger in this woodpile? Alas, I must protect my sweet, helpless wife from this menace. I will count to three and if by then the nigger beneath the back seat hasn't climbed out, I shall fire bullets into the luggage space. You hear that, nigger? One." He aimed the gun. "Two."

"Jack!" cried Lizzie. "You can't do this!"

He looked at her. "Oh? Why not?"

"Put that gun down. Moses, come out before you get hurt."

The leather seat pushed up and a terrified Moses appeared.

"Well, well." Jack smiled. "Our runaway is back. Welcome home, Moses. Now, climb out of that carriage, boy. We've got a reception committee waitin' for you, and a real warm welcome. Real warm. Shrimpboat, put the shackles on this nigger."

"Yes sir, Mr. Cavanagh."

"Chain his ankles first. This boy's *never* gonna run away again."

"Yes *sir*!"

Shrimpboat looked happy as he took two iron shackles from his saddlebag. Jack came over to Lizzie.

"That nigger was in your bedroom last night," he said in a voice too low to be heard by the others. "Do you deny it?"

"Who told you this?"

"That's my business. Do you deny it?"

She hesitated. "No."

"Did he try to violate you?"

"Of course not."

"Uh-huh. That's your story now. Listen, Lizzie: I don't want to have to hurt you. After all, you're my wife. I don't *think* you'd stoop so low as to fool around with a nigra, and I choose to believe that Moses, somehow or another, got into your bedroom last night to hide. I may be a horse's ass to believe that, but I'm willin' to give you the benefit of the doubt. But what you're gonna *say* is that he tried to rape you. And you're gonna stick with that story like grim death, because otherwise, honey, you're in a lot of trouble with the law for helpin' this boy escape. So, are you gonna do what I tell you?"

Lizzie looked past him at Moses, standing by the carriage, watching them. Shrimpboat, a tall, acned boy of eighteen, was stooping in front of him, attaching the shackles to his ankles.

"What are you going to do to Moses?" she whispered as the wind fluttered the feather in her hat.

"I'm gonna do what I'd do to any black man who tried to rape my wife. I'm gonna castrate him."

"No!" The cry burst from her. "Jack, you can't! That's inhuman—grotesque!"

"Damn you—"

"I won't let you do it. I'll tell the truth!"

"Shut UP!"

He slapped her so hard, she fell sideways to the ground.

"BAS-*TARD!*" roared Moses, grabbing Shrimpboat's rifle, which he had stupidly leaned against the carriage as he attached the shackles. "WHITE BAS-*TARD!* Don't you touch dat woman!"

He aimed the rifle at Jack's back and fired. As Lizzie screamed, Jack jerked forward, then pitched facedown on the ground. He twitched a moment, then lay still.

"Shrimpboat, duck!" yelled Mr. Duncan, aiming for Moses. He fired. Moses, hit in the stomach, flew back against the carriage and slumped to the ground. Lizzie, screaming, got to her feet and hurried to Jack. Kneeling, she felt his wrist. He was dead. Straightening, she ran to the carriage, where Mr. Duncan was about to blow Moses' face off with the rifle.

"Wait!" she cried. Mr. Duncan, scowling at her, lowered the rifle as Lizzie knelt besides Moses. She knew he was dying. The shirt over his stomach was matted with blood, and his chest was heaving, his breathing difficult. His eyes were half-closed. She put her hand on his cheek.

"Moses."

His eyes turned toward her. "Mistress," he whispered. "So kind . . ."

"Dear Moses, I'm so sorry . . ."

"Mistress find my son an' help him lak you try to help me?"

"Yes, I swear."

"His name is Gabriel . . . from de Bible. He's a fine boy . . . maybe he have a better chance . . ."

He tried to lift his hand. She took it and squeezed it. There were tears in her eyes.

"Mistress so . . . beautiful. Most beautiful ting I ever see . . ." He was gasping for air, his eyeballs rolling up. "Wish we coulda been . . . friends."

There was a soft rattle in his throat as his life passed out of him. The strength in his hand relaxed as he let go.

Slowly, Lizzie rose to her feet, letting go his hand. Mr. Duncan and his two sons, Shrimpboat and Pee-Wee, watched her. Their faces were dark with suspicion.

CHAPTER 9

As Adam galloped toward Calcutta on his white Arabian accompanied by Azimullah and a dozen *badmashes*—as murderous a crew as he had ever seen—he marveled at the gullibility of Nana Sahib to swallow his lie about the great diamond being in a bank vault. On his first night in Calcutta, Adam had hidden the huge jewel in what he thought was a clever and unusual spot. As events were turning out, he had no doubt that his foresight might save his life, for Adam had no illusions about his "security guard." The *badmashes* galloping on either side of him—dirty men in ragged *dhotis* and *puggrees*, turbans, who were armed to the teeth with daggers, swords and rifles—shot him looks that only a blind man or a fool could have failed to interpret. Although Azimullah was being solicitous and had agreed to Adam's request to spend the night in Calcutta at Sir Carlton McNair's house, Adam knew that once he took the diamond out of the "bank," he was a dead man. But of course the diamond wasn't in a bank.

The horses they were riding had been provided by the Maharajah of Raniganj, who had a famous stable of Arabians. They were magnificent-looking animals, although Adam was interested to find that the fabled steeds were not particularly fast. The country they were riding through was sere, a dusty, red-brown flat landscape punctuated by rocks, scrub and *kikar* and *peepul* trees, the latter large fig trees sacred to the Hindus. Adam saw occasional brown monkeys in the trees, and when they stopped in a mud village for *tiffin,* or lunch, he could hear the chirrup of tree rats, *saht-bai*, and weaver birds. Adam was filling his canteen at the village well when Azimullah came up to him.

"I have just been to the village telegraph station," he said. "You know that the mutiny began in the town of Meerut, when the *sepoys* refused to use the infidel bullets. Now they are on their way to Delhi to beseech Bahadur Shah to lead them in the great rebellion against the English. It is not a good time to be an Englishman in India."

Adam took a drink of water from his canteen.

"I take it the chupatties that were appearing so mysteriously in the English houses were a warning?"

"Exactly. A warning to you English to get out of India before the whirlwind struck. The whirlwind is now striking. But the mutineers are making a mistake going to Bahadur Shah. He may be the last legitimate heir of the Mogul Emperors, but he is eighty-two years old, a crazy man who thinks he can transform himself into a flea. Besides, he is a puppet of the English. The true leader of the rebellion will be Nana Sahib."

"You seem confident."

Azimullah smiled. "I know what the mutineers are doing to you English. The Englishwomen in Meerut tried to disguise themselves as Indians to escape the wrath of the mutineers, but they were all found out and destroyed. You are also disguised as an Indian, but remember, Thorne Sahib: without our protection, you also would be found out and destroyed."

Adam looked around at his "bodyguards." Then he smiled at Azimullah. "I can't tell you how safe I feel in your hands," he said.

Azimullah was not amused by his irony.

Emily McNair was miserably hot and bored. Her family normally moved to their hill station at the beginning of the hot weather, usually toward the end of April. Their tea plantation in Darjeeling was three hundred miles due north of Calcutta in the mountains near the Sikkim border where the climate was blissfully cool, ideal for the tea bushes. Lady McNair, the daughter of a Manchester surgeon, could plant her roses and pretend she was back in England. Emily loved Darjeeling. Her life in Calcutta was much more restricted, because Calcutta was the seat of the Governor-General, Lord Canning, and official protocol dominated everything. But in Darjeeling she was much freer. A tomboy, she loved riding, climbing trees and in general horrifying her strict mother with her antics.

But this year, because of the uncertainties caused by the spreading mutiny, her father had decided they should stay in Calcutta until at least the worst excesses of the mutineers had been curbed. But when news of the massacres at Meerut and the march on Delhi reached Calcutta, the English community began to panic. There were only 23,000 men in Queen's Regiments, as the all-European regiments were called, and only 14,000 English officers in the 300,000-man Indian Army: in other words, in all India there were fewer than 40,000 soldiers they could count on to protect them from a native population of 150 million. Suddenly, Calcutta seemed wonderfully safe, and the rest of India a death trap.

But Calcutta was fiercely hot. By the middle of May, the temperature had soared to 138 degrees in the shade, and the humidity turned the city into a steambath. Out came the *koels*, or cuckoos, the brain-fever bird with its weird calls ascending the scale, and the tin-pot bird, whose hammering sound could be maddening. The heat also brought out mosquitoes and a multitude of insects, such as the stinkbug, which had a nasty habit of appearing in people's soups. And of course the heat brought out the snakes: deadly kraits, cobras and hamadryads that could crawl out of bathroom drains or hide in the "thunderboxes," or privies, with unfortunate results for the unwary. Emily hated the hot weather, and as she paced around in the drawing room of her parents' house, its many windows closed off by screens to keep out the searing heat, she thought she would scream.

"I think I'm getting prickly heat," she said to her mother, who was sitting in a chair beneath the slowly waving *punkah*.

"Emily, *do* stop pacing around. And if you get prickly heat, we'll put some ointment on it. It can't be helped."

The door opened and Ranjit, Lady McNair's *khidmatgar*, or butler, came in and salaamed.

"Memsahib," he said, "there is an Indian gentleman asking to be presented."

"An Indian gentleman?" repeated Lady McNair, as if the two words were oxymoronic. "Who is he?"

"He gave his name as Lord Pontefract."

"Adam!" exclaimed Emily. Not the least of her frustrations was being deprived of the young officers who summered in Darjeeling, and the mutiny and heat had canceled all social activities in Calcutta.

"Emily, behave yourself," ordered her mother. "Surely there is some mistake, Ranjit? Lord Pontefract is no Indian."

"Nevertheless, Memsahib, that is the name the Indian gentleman gave. He is attended by a number of horsemen who look to me like *dacoits*."

"Robbers?" breathed Emily. "Adam has fallen in with a pack of thieves. How wonderfully romantic!"

"Emily, you will hold your tongue or I shall report your behavior to your father. Ranjit, has this . . . this Indian gentleman threatened you?"

"Oh no, Memsahib, he looks very peaceful. It just the others who . . ." He shrugged.

"Well, show him in. But if the others try to come in too, bar the door."

"Yes, Memsahib."

Ranjit bowed his way out as Emily hurried to one of the windows to open the screens.

"Emily, what *are* you doing?"

"Oh Mama, if it *is* Adam, I want to see how my hair looks."

"Impossible child! You let the sun in and this room will be an oven in minutes. And if it is Lord Pontefract, which I can hardly believe, I will not have you throwing yourself at him. I'll remind you he is a married man."

Emily had gone to a mirror and was smoothing her red hair.

"He's not in love with his wife."

"How in the world would you know that?"

"You can just tell. Oh Mama, he has this sadness about him that makes him absolutely irresistible."

"I'll remind you that young ladies are supposed to be retiring and demure—two words, alas, that I fear are not in your vocabulary."

"Good afternoon, Lady McNair."

The voice was familiar, but the man it belonged to, when Emily turned to look at the door, was not. The Indian gentleman with the short dark beard, wearing the ivory *achkan*, white trousers, and white turban, looked like a prince from the *Arabian Nights*. Emily, who had devoured these stories as a child, had met a number of Indian princes during her fifteen years' residency in the Subcontinent, but the majority of them had been either grossly fat, doddering, senile idiots like Bahadur Shah, or drunkards or *ganja* addicts. But here, standing in the door, was as romantically handsome a prince as she had ever imagined. She came toward the door.

"Adam?" she said softly, recognizing him as she came closer. "Is it you?"

He smiled. "Yes, it is I—or rather a darker version of myself. Some interesting things have happened to me."

"We thought you'd run away, or perhaps been kidnapped or even *murdered*! We didn't know *what* to think!"

"Actually, I was kidnapped. Lady McNair, I was accompanied here by a rather disreputable-looking escort—"

" 'Disreputable'?" snorted Lady Agatha. "My butler said they look like a gang of thieves!"

Adam smiled. "Well, yes, they do, but actually they're gentle souls who wouldn't harm a flea. I'm going to meet them tomorrow at the Bank of Calcutta—they're going to help me make a withdrawal. Meanwhile, I wondered if I could impose on your hospitality yet again by asking if I could spend the night?"

"Oh Adam, of course."

"A moment, Emily," interrupted her mother, rising grandly to her feet. "I can indeed see that it is you, Lord Pontefract. However, I cannot for the life of me see why you are indulging in this bizarre charade of painting yourself to look like a nigger."

Adam was getting used to hearing the Indian natives described this way, even though he still disliked the word intensely. However, he needed to spend the night in this house, so he maintained his *sang-froid.* "It was a sort of trick, ma'am," he said unctuously. "Or perhaps more accurately, a joke."

"Well, sir, it's a poor sort of joke, if you ask me. For a proper Englishman to paint his skin black for no good reason strikes me as tampering with God's natural order of things. It is particularly unfortunate at such a trying time as the present. However, sir, you of course are welcome to stay the night. Ranjit." She addressed the *khidmatgar*, who had appeared in the doorway behind Adam. "Show Lord Pontefract to the east guest room."

"Yes, Memsahib," said the bowing butler, looking at Adam with ill-concealed bewilderment.

The butler wasn't the only one bewildered by Adam. Emily was fascinated by his mysterious reappearance dressed as an Indian. Throughout dinner that night she peppered him with questions about his mysterious disguise, but he remained maddeningly elusive. Her parents were as flabbergasted as Emily. Yet such were the rules of the colonial English in the high noon of "the stiff upper lip" that neither Sir Carlton nor his wife asked any further questions. Adam was an immensely rich nobleman, and the English nobility were known for their eccentricities.

In any case, the mutiny was much more on Sir Carlton's mind. As they plowed their way through the enormous dinner in the furnacelike dining room, he thundered about the pusillanimity and vacillation of Lord Canning in the face of what was rapidly becoming the worst crisis in British India for a century. Adam was surprised at how Sir Carlton—who at the previous dinner with Lord Canning had seemed to feel the English were at fault for their lack of sensitivity to the native Indian religions—was now laying the blame for the massacres at Meerut on the "bloodiness and wretched ingratitude" of the native *sepoys*.

"Canning should be hanging the brutes from trees," Sir

Carlton said as his servants filled his wineglass from the "petticoated" bottles—i.e., bottles wrapped in wetted cloths to keep them cool. "Mind you, there's more to come. And it's going to be worse before it gets better. Far worse. I hear reports that no one is safe anymore, that the brutes are murdering us English everywhere."

He cut into his *mangsho jhol*, marinated goat cooked in mustard oil with potatoes and onions. Adam thought that perhaps Sir Carlton was overreacting, part of the general panic that was sweeping the European community in India, but nevertheless his alarm was not unfounded. What was disturbing was that the mutiny was shaping up as an "us-against-them" situation, with little room left for moderates between the literally black and white extremes.

And where, Adam wondered, did that leave him?

That night, as Emily tossed and turned in her bed in her awesomely hot bedroom, she couldn't understand why her body ached with such longing for Adam—even more now, oddly enough, that his skin was dark than before, when it was white. She told herself over and over that she must be in love with him. But the fierce passions coursing through her young body seemed far removed from the pale, soulful lovers of the pre-Raphaelite paintings she had seen in museums in England. If this was love, then it had a mysterious power infinitely stronger than anything she had ever imagined before.

She couldn't sleep. She was drenched with sweat in the bedroom that even at midnight was still a murderous hundred degrees. Finally, at two in the morning, when the first hint of coolness brought some relief, she was starting to doze off from sheer exhaustion when she heard a noise in the garden outside her window.

She sat up. Silence. The garden surrounding her parents' mansion was walled off from Calcutta's squalor, but in these dangerous times it was certainly possible someone might have scaled the six-foot brick wall. What's more, she knew that the two native watchmen generally dozed through the night. Raising the mosquito net, she took her slippers off the bed table (no one in India left shoes on the floor for fear of scorpions), put them on and got out of bed to hurry to the open window. Though she was on the second floor, she easily spotted the man in the turban who was standing in the frog fountain—in fact, it was the noise of his stepping into the water that had alerted her. Standing on his toes, the man was reaching up, putting his hand in the upturned mouth of the frog statue atop its stone plinth in the center of the fountain.

The man was Adam.

She ran to her wardrobe, threw on a bathrobe, then hurried into the dark and silent upstairs hall and ran down the stairs. Hurrying into the grand salon, she went out one of the doors onto the rear terrace. Adam, his trousers rolled up and his bare feet wet from the fountain, had just walked onto the terrace. When he saw Emily, he looked startled.

"What are you doing?" she whispered, hurrying to his side. "What did you take out of the frog's mouth?"

He hesitated, wondering whether to show her. Then he slowly opened his right fist. She stared at the huge diamond which, even in the darkness of the starry night, seemed to flash pale fire.

"It's the Idol's Eye," he whispered. "I took the liberty of using your fountain as a bank vault."

She was stunned by the size of the jewel.

"But what is it?"

"It was taken from the temple at Lucknow. I'm probably the only man in history who's trying to return a diamond instead of stealing it, but I'm having a devil of a time doing it."

"You mean, you're trying to take it back to Lucknow?"

"Yes. I promised my grandfather I'd do it, just before he was murdered. But a certain pudgy villain named Nana Sahib is trying to murder *me* before I can return the diamond. That's why I'm leaving now. Thank your parents for their hospitality. With any luck, I'll be back in a few weeks."

"But you can't travel through India by yourself," she whispered. "You don't speak the language . . . you're certain to be killed, especially with the mutiny on. You heard Papa at dinner: the mutiny is spreading, and English people everywhere are being attacked. You wouldn't stand a chance."

"That's what Nana Sahib thought. That's why he had my skin dyed, so he could throw me to the wolves. But I have a pistol and—"

"Wait, please! Let me go with you!"

"Emily, don't be ridiculous."

"But I speak the language! I've lived here all my life—I can even speak the Bengali dialect. Just give me a half-hour. I have lampblack in my room and I can borrow some clothes from the servants. I'll disguise myself as your *syce,* or groom—every Indian gentleman travels with a *syce*—and if we're stopped, I'll do the talking and say you have laryngitis and have lost your voice."

He restrained a laugh. "That's a wild, lovely idea. My congratulations on your imagination, but—"

She snatched the diamond out of his hand and ran back to the door of the house.

"Emily!"

"You can't leave without the diamond," she said at the door. "So you'll *have* to wait for me. And I wouldn't miss this for the world!"

"Emily, there are a dozen armed men outside these walls," Adam said, hurrying after her. "My only hope is to climb over the wall in the dark and try to sneak through them. Now, give me the diamond: two people sneaking out are going to make it that much easier for them to spot, and they'll shoot to kill."

Emily hesitated. "Then we shouldn't sneak," she said. "You told me you were riding an Arabian. They're slow horses. My father's got the fastest horses in India in the stable here. We'll take two and they'll never catch us. Wait for me."

As she vanished inside the dark house, Adam groaned. "Damn." But even though the journey would be dangerous and he would be responsible for her safety, still he had to admit that having the Hindi-speaking Emily along would be an enormous advantage. He had taught himself some Hindi on the voyage out from England, but he was far from fluent and it would hardly suffice in a tight spot.

As Emily ran up the great stair, breathless with excitement, she told herself that by running away with Adam she was breaching every known code of ladylike deportment. She would shock her parents, she might even be putting herself in danger, but she didn't care. She was embarking on the greatest adventure of her young life, and she was wildly in love.

Adam hurried across the garden and jumped up, grabbing the top of the wall. Hoisting himself up, he looked out at the street, where he could see Azimullah standing beside his horse across the way. The other *badmashes* had also dismounted and were squatting on the pavement, most of them asleep.

"At least we'll have the advantage of surprise," Adam whispered a half-hour later when Emily reemerged from the house. She had darkened her face with lampblack and was wearing a dirty turban and equally dirty pants and shirt. "Most of them out there are asleep. Where did you get the clothes?"

"I borrowed them from my own *syce*. I hid the diamond in my turban. Do I look convincing?"

"You could fool me. But I'm warning you again, this could be dangerous."

"Oh Adam, don't be such a fuddy-duddy. I'm not afraid, and I can take care of myself."

"I'll go out first and draw them off. Then when they're gone, you come out. Where can we meet?"

She thought a moment. "Barrackpore," she said. "It's fourteen miles north of Calcutta. It's where the Governor-General has his country home, and it's well-guarded with English troops. They'd think twice before going to Barrackpore. I'll meet you there at dawn, in front of Lord Canning's estate."

"All right." He pulled a pistol from his belt. "I borrowed this from your father's desk. I hope he doesn't mind."

"He'll be furious!"

"Yes, and I don't think he's going to be very happy when he finds you've gone with me, either. Where are the horses?"

"Back here."

She led him around to the rear of the house where there was an eight-stall stable next to a carriage house. Emily opened one of the stable doors. Inside, a horse snorted in the dark. "We'll take Cinnamon and Zanzibar," she whispered to Adam. "Cinnamon is my horse, and Zanzibar is Papa's. They're both champions. Papa wants to race them in the Governor's Cup."

Quickly they saddled the two magnificent animals, then led them around the house to the wooden gate leading to the street. Adam mounted Zanzibar, holding his pistol in his right hand.

"All right," he whispered. "Open the gate. And we'll meet at Barrackpore at dawn."

"Turn right and go to the river. You'll see signs. Good luck."

"We'll both need it. And I still think you're crazy to do this."

"I've never had more fun in my life."

She went to the wooden gates and pushed up the thick bar that locked them. Then she swung one inward. Adam dug his heels into Zanzibar. The horse shot forward, clattering out onto the street. Adam knew he had only one shot in his pistol, and he hoped to kill Azimullah with it. As he galloped past the startled Indian, he fired at him, missing his chest but hitting his shoulder.

Azimullah yelped in Hindi, clutching his shoulder. Shots rang out. Adam ducked low as he raced down the street. He remembered racing across the Yorkshire moors as a boy, but there he hadn't been chased by a band of murderous Indians. He looked back. The *badmashes* had all mounted except for Azimullah and were hot in pursuit, firing their rifles. Adam raced around a corner and galloped as fast as he had ever gone in his life. Zanzibar was indeed a champion: Adam thought that if he came out of this alive, he'd like to buy this wonderful steed.

In the hours before dawn, Calcutta was just beginning to awaken. Adam, galloping toward a square, saw merchants setting up their booths in a bazaar. He galloped through the booths, scattering baskets and knocking over tables. The merchants shouted in rage, jumping up and down, shaking their fists. Adam thought the resultant mess might slow the *badmashes*. He raced down narrow streets, finally coming to the Hooghly River and the main road heading north. Seeing a sign reading "Barrackpore," he dug his heels into Zanzibar and flew like the wind.

In the east, the dawn was igniting the sky.

CHAPTER 10

"I want you to prepare articles of manumission for all my slaves," Lizzie said, standing in front of the marble mantel in the drawing room of Elvira Plantation. "I'm freeing all my bondspeople. If they want to continue working for me here, I'll pay them an honest day's wage. But there will be no more slavery at Elvira Plantation."

Billie and Clemmie DeVries both looked startled. It was two days after Jack Cavanagh's funeral. Lizzie looked magnificent in black mourning. Now Clemmie, also in mourning for her cousin, stood up, came to her and hugged her.

"What a wonderful gesture," she said, smiling.

"I hope it's more than a gesture," Lizzie said. "I've given it a lot of thought, and I've come to the conclusion that if I can make this plantation work successfully with freed labor, perhaps some of the other slave owners will see that there is an alternative to this horrible institution."

"I have to remind you, Lizzie," said Billie, who had been Jack's lawyer and was now his widow's, "that you're talking about giving away a lot of capital assets—maybe a half-million dollars, which is a lot of money."

"The money's not important," said Lizzie, who had been astonished when Billie read her Jack's will after the funeral to discover that he had left her over three million dollars, a staggering fortune at the time. "And I refuse to think of human beings as capital assets."

"Oh Lizzie, I can't tell you how happy it makes me to hear you say that," exclaimed Clemmie. "It's such a noble thing to do."

"Well, you gave me the idea in a way, when you freed your slaves."

"Yes, but I only freed a handful. You're freeing over three hundred."

"And that's the problem," said Billie, who got up from his chair and went to one of the tall, triple-hung windows to look out at the drizzle.

"What's the problem?" Lizzie asked.

"You're freeing so many." Billie turned to her. "You're going to frighten the other slaveholders. Look, Lizzie, you're entitled to your political opinions, as we all are. But Jack was one of the most important slave owners in the South, and now you are. If you free that many slaves, it's goin' to scare the livin' daylights out of the other slave owners."

"Why?"

"You'll be startin' a free-labor market, which means you'll be rockin' the boat, perhaps givin' ideas to not only the slave owners but also the slaves. If a lot of people start manumittin' their slaves, the monetary value of the other slaves is goin' to go down. You may not care about the money your slaves are worth, but the other slave owners sure do, and they're goin' to hate you."

"They hate me already, after what I said at the ball. Let them hate me more, the narrow-minded idiots. If they liked me, I'd feel ashamed."

"But your reputation as a lady—"

"Hah! As if I had any. Don't think I don't know what they say about me—that I was Napoleon's mistress and God knows what else. The silly cats."

"They say more than that."

Silence.

"What do you mean?"

Billie looked at his wife. "Tell her, Clemmie."

She frowned, giving him a slight "no" signal.

Lizzie caught it.

"What is it? Tell me, Clemmie."

"I won't repeat such filth."

"Honey, she has to know the truth," exclaimed Billie.

"It's for her own good. Lizzie, they're sayin' that you and Moses were—"

"Billie DeVries, shut your mouth!" his wife snapped.

"Let him talk," Lizzie said. "What are they saying? That Moses was my lover?"

"Lizzie, only the most craven minds would ever believe it," Clemmie said, taking her hand. "You see, Mr. Duncan and his two bratty sons told everybody that when they shot Moses, you ran to him and . . . and held his hand."

"Yes, I did," Lizzie said. "I'm not ashamed of it. But he wasn't my lover. If anything, we were trying to be friends, though I suppose I was foolish to try even *that.*"

"What I'm tryin' to tell you, Lizzie," said Billie, "is that you've made powerful enemies. Senator Whitney is one of the most powerful men in Washington, and you defied him and Ellie May at your Christmas ball, and believe me, Ellie May is spreadin' poison about you all over Gloucester County. Now, honey, if you free all your slaves, God knows what they might do to you."

"But *why*?" she almost shouted.

"Don't you see? It's a club down here, it's all or nothin', and you're a traitor to the noble cause."

"The noble cause of *slavery*?"

"Yes!"

"But what could they do to me? It's not against the law to free slaves."

"But it's against the law for a white woman to sleep with a black man."

She stared at him.

"But I didn't," she said softly.

"I know that, honey. But a white jury down here might just say you did, particularly if all the important slave owners in Virginia were pressurin' the jury, which they would be. Things could get real nasty. As your lawyer and friend, my advice to you is to lay real low. Maybe free a couple of your slaves as a gesture for Christmas, and then free a couple more next year. But if you free three hundred slaves all at once, you're just askin' for trouble. *Big* trouble."

Frowning, Lizzie considered this. As much as she hated to admit it, she thought Billie was probably right.

"I assume," she finally said, "that there's no law against making life comfortable for slaves? For treating them decently?"

"Well, no, of course not. In fact, a lot of slave owners do."

"All right, I'll take your advice because I fear you're probably correct, unfortunately. But tell that loathsome Mr. Duncan he's fired as of today. He and his two sons had better get off this plantation by sunset or I'll have them thrown off. Then prepare manumissions for Charles, Aunt Lide and Dulcey. I'm freeing them, at least, for Christmas. By the way, I hope you all will share Christmas with me?"

"We'd love to, dear, and we'll all try to make it a happy one despite the tragedy," said Clemmie.

Lizzie grimaced at this reference to her late husband. The truth was, she couldn't bring herself to grieve for his loss.

"Do you like this dress?" Lettice Belladon was standing in front of a pier mirror in her suite at Willard's Hotel in Washington, D.C. She was wearing a beautiful periwinkle silk ball gown trimmed with maribou, the dress showing a good deal of her voluptuous bosom. Her husband, Horace, looked up from checking his gold watch.

"It's quite lovely, my dear, but we must be on our way. I don't want to be late for Senator Whitney's reception. Everyone is going to be there—perhaps even the President, Mr. Buchanan."

Lettice picked her shawl off a chair and put it around her shoulders. "Oh, I'm sure it will be quite fashionable," she said, "if anything in this filthy town could be called fashionable."

"We must be charitable, dear. We can hardly compare Washington to London or Paris."

Lettice laughed as she went to the door. "Well, hardly. It's nothing but a backwater village with pretensions, if you ask me. And I've never seen such a collection of dreary frumps as these Washington wives."

"We must bear in mind that America is one of Belladon Textiles' fastest-growing markets. And of course we must not offend our hostess, Mrs. Whitney. Her brother raises some of the finest cotton in Mississippi and sells it to me at a very favorable price."

"Her brother also made an indecent suggestion to me," Lettice said, assuming a look of wounded virtue, although at the time she had been amused by the tipsy planter's invitation to join him in the gazebo for a little "frolic."

"Well, we won't mention that tonight," Horace said, opening the door. Horace and Lettice Belladon were in America touring the major clothing stores of the eastern seaboard, as well as visiting some of the biggest cotton plantations. Now they went down to the lobby of the hotel and climbed in a taxi. "Senator Whitney's house on H Street," Horace said to the coachman. As the taxi lurched into motion, Lettice noticed the crowds of blacks loitering in front of the hotel. "Do you suppose they're slaves?" she asked her husband.

"Very likely," Horace replied, brushing his graying muttonchop whiskers with his gloved fingers. "As I understand the situation, the Southern interests control the Senate and the Supreme Court, and the President, of course, is a Democrat and partial to the slave owners. This is a very Southern town."

In their two days in the capital of the young American republic, Lettice had seen enough to have formed a very unfavorable opinion of the place. She had toured the Capitol, where the original dome was being removed to be replaced by a grander version. The Senate chamber and the ornate red-and-gold Hall of Representatives had been finished, and the great marble Extension, in the works for seven years, was proceeding toward completion. Lettice had thought all this was rather impressive, although the effect of grandeur was diminished by the fact that the Capitol grounds were strewn with blocks of marble, columns and capitals, lumber, iron plates and keystones as well as workmen's sheds and privies. She had driven past the Post

Office and Patent Office, diagonally across from each other at Seventh and F Streets. She had seen the enormous Treasury Department on Fifteenth Street, which was still under construction. She had been amused by the little brick State Department which was as insignificant as the Army and Navy Departments, installed in old-fashioned houses west of the Executive Mansion. And she had found the White House itself devoid of taste or splendor when compared, for instance, to Buckingham Palace. She had heard that parties in the White House were considered so "stiff," the budget so niggardly, that there weren't even flowers on the dinner tables, that people dreaded receiving invitations. The President, Mr. Buchanan of Pennsylvania, was a bachelor and his niece, the young Miss Harriet Lane, presided over the Executive Mansion. Though the public liked her (the new song, "Listen to the Mocking Bird," had been dedicated to her) Washington society thought she was a prude and a bore. What a capital! thought Lettice. What a country!

Their taxi pulled into the driveway of the pretentious pillared mansion that Senator Whitney had built three years before, and Horace and Lettice stepped out. The brightly lighted house was already filled with partygoers, and as Lettice climbed up on the porch she heard from inside Scala's Marine Band playing a lively rendition of "Dixie," leaving little doubt as to the sympathies of the host and hostess. The Belladons had been in Washington only two days, but they were already aware of the strains between the Northern politicians and the pro-slavery Southerners, strains that were invading even social relationships: there was an increasing number of hostesses who would invite only Northerners or Southerners, as the case might be. However, despite his obvious pro-slavery bias, Senator Whitney and his Mississippi-born wife were still straddling both worlds, at least socially.

The Belladons were admitted to the central hall by a dignified black butler, and they joined the guests moving through the receiving line. Lettice thought that Ellie May Whitney was certainly plain with her protruding nose and more than a hint of buck teeth, but a good maid had made her look as presentable as possible and her voluminous green satin gown with the pale pink stripes was, in Lettice's opinion, attractive although it showed more than it should of Ellie May's bony shoulders and flat chest. Her husband, on the other hand, was the very picture of senatorial dignity with his shoulder-length silver hair and beautifully tailored swallowtail coat—Lettice thought he was one of the best-turned-out men she had met in America. As she observed him working the receiving line, she also thought he possessed the professional politician's gift of being able to make whomever he was talking to think he or she was the only person on earth the Senator was interested in—at least for fifteen seconds. Charm oozed from every patrician pore as the Senator squeezed hands, smiled, and spoke in his musical Virginia tones to the well-heeled and well-connected guests inching past him and his wife.

"Mr. Justice Campbell of the Soo-*preem* Court and Mrs. Campbell!" warbled a young black footman at the top of his lungs, obviously having the time of his life as he held out a silver salver to receive the large invitations (which, however, he couldn't read: the guests had to whisper their names in his ear). "Senator and Mrs. Slidell of *Loos*-iana! Mr. and Mrs. Horace Belladon of Manchester, England!"

When Ellie May Whitney, a smile on her thin lips, turned to Lettice, she blinked in surprise.

"Mrs. Belladon!" she exclaimed in her deep Southern accent. "My brother wrote me how lovely you are, and how right he was. But you must forgive me, dear lady: I do declare I thought you were someone else. Why yes, you look so much like her . . . do you have any relatives in Virginia?"

Lettice looked confused. "No . . ."

Ellie May turned to her husband.

"Phineas, look: isn't Mrs. Belladon the spittin' image of Lizzie Cavanagh?"

Lettice's eyes widened. "Lizzie?" she said. "You know someone named Lizzie who looks like me?"

"Why yes. The notorious Mrs. Jack Cavanagh of Elvira Plantation in Gloucester County. It's an amazing resemblance . . . Are you all right?"

Lettice, who had turned quite pale, was leaning on her husband's arm. "I had a sister named Lizzie. She disappeared last year . . . none of us knew where she went. She murdered my father."

Ellie May's eyes widened. "Murdered?" she whispered.

Horace whispered something in his wife's ear, but Lettice straightened, shaking her head. "My husband says I shouldn't mention it, but it's certainly no secret."

"We must talk," said Ellie May quickly. "Wait till after the receivin' line is over, then meet me in the coffee room. Our guests can amuse themselves—this is *far* too good to wait for. Murder! Who would imagine?"

Twenty minutes later, Ellie May, the Senator, Horace and Lettice closeted themselves in the small coffee room off the formal dining room. Ellie May shut the double doors, then turned to the Belladons, her huge green skirt swishing. "Tell me *all,*" she said, her green eyes blazing with gossip-mania.

"Lettice, I'm not sure this is wise," said Horace, who looked nervous. "We shouldn't be airing your family's dirty linen . . ."

"My family?" snapped Lettice. "It's now *your* family too. And if Lizzie is hiding out in America, she should be brought to justice. After all, there's no doubt she did kill Papa."

"How?" asked Senator Whitney.

"She was on her way to see the man who had put her in the family way—"

"Shocking," murmured Ellie May, devouring each word as she sat on a velvet sofa.

"Oh, Lizzie has the morals of a tomcat and always did."

"Then the stories of her and the French Emperor must be true."

"The French Emperor?" Lettice looked confused.

"Please, let's stick to the subject," said Senator Whitney. "How did she murder your father?"

"Well, it was a stormy night and she stopped in a crofter's cottage owned by a man named Stringer MacDuff. According to him, he offered to put her up for the night, but shortly afterward my father appeared at the cottage.

He had been warned by the local midwife that Lizzie was with child, and he knew right off who the father was—"

"Who?" interrupted Ellie May.

"No one knows for sure, but I'm certain it was that alleycat, Adam Thorne, who's now the Earl of Pontefract."

"An *earl*?" Ellie May felt faint. Like most upper-class Americans, she had a passion for English titles.

"Father guessed that Lizzie was on her way to Pontefract Hall and went after her. When he saw the lights in the cottage, he stopped to ask Stringer MacDuff if Lizzie had stopped there, which she had. Lizzie threw an oil lamp at him, which burned him to death. Then she vanished, and no one's heard of her since until tonight. You say she's now Mrs. Jack Cavanagh? Who's he?"

"Jack *was* one of the richest plantation owners in the South, and he met your sister in Paris. He was murdered by a slave who . . ." Ellie May pursed her lips primly and looked at her husband.

Phineas lowered his voice. "It is said—though it's never been proved—that the slave was your sister's lover."

Lettice gasped. "Lizzie and a . . . a slave?"

"Yes. It's the scandal of Virginia," said the Senator. "Happily, the slave was killed. But your sister bought back his young son from a Kentucky slave owner, freed him and has put him in a private school near Boston. She's also building new homes for her slaves as well as a small infirmary for them. She's spoiling them rotten, and the other slave owners—including myself, I might add—are fed up to the teeth with her. Of course, until tonight there wasn't much we could do about it, except try to prosecute her for miscegenation with the slave—which we were reluctant to do because of the obvious aspersions it casts on our fair sex and the shock it undoubtedly would cause amongst our children. But if she's wanted in England for murder . . ."

"She is," said Lettice firmly. "I never particularly liked Lizzie, but after the things she's done, I would not be unhappy to see her sent to prison, and I don't care if that does sound unsisterly. But can she be extradited to England to stand trial? She must be an American citizen now, isn't she?"

"Yes, but I'm under the impression we have a treaty with Great Britain that makes murder an extraditable crime," said the Senator. "But if not, anything can be arranged in Washington. Lord Lyons, the English Minister, happens to be here tonight. I think I'll go have a word with him. If you will excuse me?"

Bowing slightly, he let himself out of the room. Not the least of the reasons he wanted to get rid of Lizzie was that he had found out she had been sending money north to the Abolitionists.

When Lizzie realized she had become one of the wealthiest widows in America, she was anything but displeased. She was not an overly greedy person and was as passionate a shopper as any other red-blooded woman, but she also had come to appreciate the enormous power of money to do good or evil. Lizzie decided to revolutionize the lives of her three hundred or so slaves whose names, ages, weights, and prices, she discovered, were all recorded in a ledger, like animals. The first thing she did, much to the delight of a Richmond shoe store, was to order six hundred pairs of men's and women's shoes in various sizes and distribute them to the slaves. This was met by dumbfounded amazement on their part, many of them not knowing how to tie the laces. She next dispatched Billie DeVries to Kentucky to buy back Moses' son, as she had sworn to do. The seven-year-old Gabriel was a healthy, bright child. Billie paid eight hundred dollars for him, manumitted him and took him to Boston to put him in a small school in Gloucester that had been started by Abolitionists to educate the children of slaves who managed to escape the South by the Underground Railroad or other means. These things done, she launched her construction scheme.

Now, as Broward drove her through the new slave quarter in the open carriage, she told herself she had reason to be pleased with what she had accomplished so far, even though there was still an enormous amount to be done. Ten brick cottages had been finished and six more were under construction. These new cottages had been modeled on the house-servant cottages near Elvira Plantation, and while they were far from palatial, they were neat, warm and comfortable. Moreover, privy facilities had been built, and Lizzie had insisted to the slaves that they keep their new grounds neat. This had been an alien idea to men and women who had lived in filth all their lives, but Lizzie had been firm and she was winning the trash battle. The new quarter, which was a half-mile from the old, looked almost tidy.

Still, Lizzie had no illusions about the enormity of the task she had undertaken. Trying to uplift the slaves from a near-animal existence to a stage where they would be mentally fit for eventual freedom wasn't going to be easy. After firing Mr. Duncan, she had eliminated the physical horrors of slavery—the whippings and terrorizing. She had installed one of the slaves as overseer, an intelligent young man named Roscoe who seemed to be a natural leader the slaves obeyed. But if terror had been eliminated, the habits of more than two centuries of forced servitude still existed. She found that the majority of her slaves were devoid of self-direction. They had to be told what to do, sometimes over and over. It irritated her that this reality fit so well with the Southern whites' condescending stereotype of the slaves as children, but she had to admit that most of her people would not become independent and able to direct their own lives in a rational way anytime soon.

But one thing she had accomplished, she told herself as the carriage started back to the plantation. She could ride unarmed to the slave quarter without danger. And the slaves were beginning, some grudgingly, to trust her. Given their general terror when she had appeared as Jack's bride the previous fall, that was no mean accomplishment.

It was a warm April day and spring was in the air as she rode back to the house she had come to love. Now that Jack and Mr. Duncan were gone, the natural beauty of the place had come to enchant her, although she had to admit her life was increasingly lonely. The only whites who would even talk to her were Dr. Lockwood, her personal physician, and the DeVrieses; she had noticed that lately even their visits were becoming less frequent. Although Clemmie always had an excuse for canceling a dinner invitation, Lizzie wondered if the other whites weren't bringing more and more pressure to bear on them, pressure that even Clemmie couldn't resist. Lizzie knew she was hated for what she was doing with her slaves; and while she had no intention of changing her ways, it was definitely lonely being a pariah. As she lay in bed at night, her young body aching for caresses, her thoughts returned over and over again to Adam. How she longed for him; yet Adam seemed so long ago and far away, it was almost like loving a phantom. But as she placed her hands on her extended belly, she knew that at least his child would soon be hers. Dr. Lockwood from Yorktown had told her that she would be going into labor any day now. Adam might have married someone else—she had long since forgiven him for that, given the circumstances—but his blood and hers were united, and that was precious to her.

"Broward, who's that?" she called as they came up the driveway. A closed black carriage was parked in front of the west portico. Leaning against it were two men in dark suits and black hats.

"I doan rightly know, mistress."

He slowed the carriage, then stopped. The two men came over to Lizzie.

"Mrs. Cavanagh?" said the elder, who had a thick black beard.

"Yes?"

"I'm Mark Channon, a U.S. marshal, ma'am. Here's my badge. This gentleman is Mr. Edgar Downing, who's legal attaché to the British Ministry in Washington. I've taken the liberty of telling your colored folk to pack you some things in a valise, ma'am. You'll be coming with us to Washington City."

Lizzie stiffened, staring at him. "Why?"

"You're being extradited to England, Mrs. Cavanagh," said Edgar Downing, "to stand trial for the murder of your father, the Reverend Hugh Desmond."

CHAPTER 11

Nana Sahib, the self-styled Maharajah of Bithur, was lying on a divan spooning James Keiller & Sons Dundee marmalade from a jar while watching Lakshmi, the *nautch* girl, do a languid belly dance. For all his hatred of the English, Nana Sahib had a passion for many English products, including marmalade. His rundown palace was situated in the small town of Bithur, which was a few miles up the Ganges River from the central Indian city of Cawnpore.

Now, Nana Sahib's *khidmatgar* came into the room, put his palms together in the traditional bow and said, "Your Highness, Lord Azimullah has arrived and requests an audience."

Nana Sahib sat up, wiping the marmalade from his lips as Lakshmi modestly covered her nakedness with a veil. Since Nana Sahib insisted he was the Maharajah of Bithur—a title the English did not formally recognize, although they humored him along to shut him up—he had made Azimullah a "lord" to dress up his tatty court.

"Send him in."

"Yes, Highness."

Nana Sahib got off the divan, buttoning his *achkan* over his bulbous belly. Moments later, Azimullah came in the room and bowed. His left arm was in a sling. Nana Sahib sensed that his normally suave factotum was nervous.

"Well?" he said. "Do you have the diamond?"

"Master, I am a miserable dog who no longer deserves the radiance of your benevolence. I am lower than a worm—"

"What happened?" shouted Nana Sahib.

Azimullah ran to his fat master, threw himself on his knees, and banged his head on the floor. Azimullah knew how to appease Nana Sahib. He also knew he was in grave trouble.

"Oh Divinity, the dog of an Englishman tricked us all. The diamond was not in the Bank of Calcutta—"

Nana Sahib grabbed a bamboo cane. "Where was it?"

"He must have hidden it at Sir Carlton McNair's mansion, where he spent the night—"

"You let him out of your sight?" roared Nana Sahib, beginning to whack his back with the cane.

"No, no, Highness, we watched the house through the night. But in the second hour before the dawn, the gates flew open and Thorne Sahib galloped out—"

"You didn't stop him?" yelled Nana Sahib, striking Azimullah even more fiercely.

"We gave chase, Highness, naturally, but the Arabian horses are slow and Thorne Sahib's steed was fast as a shooting star. He outdistanced us and vanished."

"Cur! Dog!" Nana Sahib's cane bit into his servant's back. "Did you go to Lucknow? You know that's where he's taking the diamond."

"Such is the state of the country now with the mutiny that we were told we would be refused entry into Lucknow. Only the English are allowed in. So I decided it wiser to come back here. If I may suggest, Radiant One, the capture of the great jewel is not so important now as perhaps the capture of India."

Nana Sahib was panting from his exertions, sweat pouring down his round face. Now he stopped the caning. "What do you mean?"

"I have news, sire. Bahadur Shah has agreed to lead the rebels, but as you know, he is old and feebleminded and cannot inspire the *sepoys* as you could."

Nana Sahib wiped his face with his sleeve. "So? What are you suggesting?"

Azimullah turned his face from the floor to look up at Nana Sahib. Blood was seeping through his thin white shirt from the caning.

"There are four native regiments stationed at Cawnpore," Azimullah began. "The First, Fifty-third, and Fifty-sixth Native Infantry and the Second Cavalry—in all, about three thousand troops, the Indians outnumber the Europeans ten to one . . ."

"Yes, yes, I know all this," Nana Sahib interrupted. "They're all under the command of Major General Wheeler."

"True, Radiant One. But I hear that General Wheeler is afraid. All the *Angrezi* are afraid, because they are so outnumbered. But General Wheeler trusts you. If you go to Cawnpore and offer your assistance, pretending to be his friend, we could gain entrance to the heart of the city and direct the mutiny. And once we have Cawnpore, then we can take Lucknow and Delhi. And then India will be yours."

A smile crawled over Nana Sahib's face. Azimullah might have failed him with Adam and the diamond, but the wily lieutenant had just shown him how to take over direction of the great mutiny.

"Yes," he said softly, "that's the way to do it. We will become the worm in the *Angrezi* apple. And then—India! Mine!" His left hand clenched into a fist. "Rise, Lord Azimullah. We will start for Cawnpore at dawn."

Azimullah was getting to his feet.

"What happened to your shoulder?"

"It is where Thorne Sahib shot me."

"We will deal with Thorne Sahib later. You are right: India is more important than the great diamond. But I will soon have both."

Adam reined in Zanzibar. Ahead of him and Emily, a cloud of red dust was rising into the burning sky.

"Someone's coming," he said, shading his eyes with his hand. The sun was high in the heavens, burning fiercely, sending the thermometer soaring past 120. "It looks like about two dozen natives."

"This may be our first real test," Emily said, looking around. They were in the middle of a blasted plain almost devoid of vegetation. "There's certainly no place to hide out here. Remember: you've lost your voice."

They continued riding on the fifteen-hundred-mile-long Grand Trunk Road that slashed diagonally across India like a cartridge belt from Calcutta in the southeast all the way up to Peshawar near the northwest frontier of Afghanistan. So far their plan had worked reasonably well. Emily had met Adam at Barrackpore as planned. But they found the garrison deserted and the Governor-General's country house boarded up. When Emily asked one of the local children what had happened, she was told that because of the spreading mutiny, Lord Canning had decided to remain in Calcutta to supervise the resistance to the uprising and had taken all his guards with him. Although Adam had originally thought to take the diamond to Lord Canning in order to protect Emily, he now found he had no choice but to press on toward Lucknow. For all he knew, Azimullah and his *badmashes* might show up at any moment, so for the rest of the day they traveled as fast as they could on the Grand Trunk Road, resting only after sunset in a slight depression off the road where several *peepul* trees gave them concealment. Shortly after ten that night, they heard hoofbeats. A party of horsemen galloped by. "It's Azimullah," Adam whispered to Emily. In fact, it had been Azimullah on his way to Bithur.

With the removal of the threat of Nana Sahib's thugs, Adam's concern for Emily's safety began to abate. Whatever awkwardness, in terms of propriety (that cherished word), he might have felt traveling alone with a teenage girl vanished as they rode across India. Emily's parents were undoubtedly sick with worry about their daughter's reputation, but Adam had no intention of taking advantage of her. Ironically, he thought, while he had made love to Lakshmi, the *nautch* girl, without thinking twice, Emily, the young English lady, was the true Untouchable.

Adam shook off his thoughts as the band of natives approached them. "Let's get off the road and let them pass," Adam said. They moved to the right off the dirt road, but when the band galloped up, a bearded man, evidently the leader, raised his hand and reined in his horse. The entire party halted, sending up more dust. Adam saw they were heavily armed with guns and swords.

Several of them wore uniforms of native regiments, although they had torn off their insignia, and Adam knew they were mutinous *sepoys*.

The leader spoke to him in Hindi, but Adam pointed to his throat, then to Emily. She spoke in Hindi. There was a moment of silence as the leader glared suspiciously at Adam, who coughed several times. Then the man rode over, pulling his sword from a scabbard. He put the point of the sword on Adam's chest, speaking to him again in Hindi. Emily spoke back, her voice rising angrily. The man leaned forward and rubbed his finger hard across Adam's left cheek. He squinted at the cheek, obviously trying to see if the skin was dyed. Then he grabbed Adam's collar and ripped it open, exposing part of his chest. He squinted at the skin, and Adam thanked God for Lakshmi's foresight in dyeing his entire body.

The man broke into a grin. He turned to the others and shouted as he dug his spurs into his horse. The band galloped off, leaving Emily and Adam in their dust.

"He thought you were an *Angrezi* because you wouldn't speak," Emily said. "If your dye hadn't stuck, we'd both be dead."

Adam wiped the sweat from his forehead. "I owe you my life," he said.

She looked at him and said, "I won't let you forget it."

"Tell me about your wife," Emily said the next night as she hungrily finished a delicious *dahi bara* they had bought from a *khomcha-wallah*, or street vendor, in the nearby town of Sultanpore in the central Indian state of Uttar Pradesh. Emily and Adam were sitting in a grove of *chenar* trees eating their supper by the light of the moon. It was almost ten in the evening; their horses were tethered to one of the trees.

"My wife," Adam repeated, finishing his *dahi bara*, a mango-flavored combination of peas, yogurt and spices wrapped in large dried leaves. "Why would you be interested in my wife?"

"Because, obviously, I'm interested in you. Is she pretty?"

"Sybil? Yes, she's a beauty."

"Do you love her?"

"Well, Emily, I think that's a rather personal question."

"Under these circumstances, I can't imagine a question that wouldn't be personal."

"You have a point. Let me say this: I think my wife is a great lady, a woman of refinement and honesty."

"You haven't answered my question. Do you *love* her?"

Adam sighed. "I admire her," he finally said. "I respect her. I'm even attracted to her."

"But do you love her?" she repeated insistently.

"I . . . No," he finally admitted. "No, I suppose I don't love her."

"Then why did you marry her?"

"The woman I actually loved had vanished. I suppose I've lost her for the rest of my life."

"Who is she?"

"Someone I've known since I was a child. Someone very dear and precious. Believe me, Emily, I'm not proud of what I've done. I married Sybil dishonestly, and she knows it. I think she is terribly hurt by it, and I'm to blame for that. The only thing I can try to do, when I get back to England, is somehow make it up to her."

Emily felt a sense of satisfaction. If Adam weren't in love with his wife, which she had suspected, then he was fair game.

And there was nothing in this world that Emily McNair wanted more than the love of Adam Thorne.

The next dawn, they started again on the road to Lucknow, trying to make as much time as possible during the relatively cool hours. They were on the road less than forty minutes when they encountered a grisly indication of what might have happened to them the previous day. They were riding through the hot, dusty plains of Uttar Pradesh when they saw vultures circling in the sky. As they approached a carriage which had been turned on its side, Adam cautioned, "This may not be pleasant."

Emily's lampblacked face became unusually solemn. They came even closer and could see the bodies sprawled on the ground next to the carriage. The horses had been stolen.

"Don't look," Adam said.

"No, I want to see."

Two vultures that had been feeding on one of the corpses now spread their huge wings and flapped into the air. Adam became aware of a sickening stench. They were close enough to see there were four bodies, all swarming with a mass of black flies. An Englishwoman, perhaps in her thirties, sprawled on her back, her eyes staring lifelessly at the sun, her throat slit, the blood clotted to a black stain. Beside her a younger woman, possibly a sister or a neighbor fleeing the violence: her nose, ears and breasts had all been slashed off. And next to her, two children, a boy and a girl perhaps seven or eight years old, their bodies clad in the sweet clothes of Victorian childhood. Both children's blond heads had been decapitated.

"Dear God!" whispered Emily.

"I wouldn't be surprised," Adam said, "if our friends from yesterday hadn't done this." He remembered the look on the man's face as he had rubbed his finger over his cheek.

"Yes," Emily said. "We might have been . . . like this."

The vultures circled above them silently.

"The filthy beggars," muttered Captain Bentley Brent of the Fifty-third Native Infantry. The burly, bearded career officer who had come out to India with Adam on the *Jupiter* was standing on the roof of one of the army barracks, or cantonments, (pronounced can*toon*ments) watching through binoculars the flames and smoke roiling up from Cawnpore a mile away. "They're burning the European houses."

"Aye, and God knows what they're doin' to the Europeans, Captain," said Lieutenant Angus Ogilvie, a fair-haired Glaswegian standing next to him, also watching through binoculars.

"Damn Wheeler!" said Brent. "He was a fool to trust Nana Sahib. To let him and his damned beggars take over the protection of the Treasury just because we're low on men . . . I told him he was letting the cancer right into the guts of Cawnpore. But it's too late now."

Word had come an hour before that Nana Sahib had joined the mutineers in Cawnpore, betraying General Wheeler and the English to whom he had falsely vowed allegiance. The cantonment, or entrenchment as it was called locally, consisted of two main red-brick, plaster-coated buildings, each capable of holding a hundred men, one with a thatched roof, the other on which Brent and Oglivie were standing with a *pukka*, or standard tile, roof. Aside from a few outbuildings, there were also several half-finished barracks in the entrenchment girdled with flimsy bamboo scaffolding. The whole compound was surrounded by a trench and a four-foot-high mud wall, both only half-completed. The entrenchment stood on an exposed position on the sandy plain to the east of Cawnpore, about a mile from the Ganges. Even though by early June there were few Europeans in Cawnpore who didn't know that the city was on the verge of mutiny, the entrenchment—exposed and half-finished as it was—was considered the safest place for Europeans, and for several days the *firinghis* had been streaming out of Cawnpore, seeking whatever safety the military barracks provided. Men, women and children, carrying as many provisions as they could, were now crowding into the barracks hoping to sit out the mutiny under the protection of the Indian Army—or what remnants of it that were still loyal. As one of the senior officers present, Bentley Brent had watched the sea of confused and frightened humanity pour across the dun plains in the overwhelming heat, and in his heart he feared the worst. He knew that General Wheeler, astoundingly complacent, had not only handed over the Treasury to Nana Sahib, but had laid in enough stores in the entrenchment for a mere twenty-five days. He was convinced, he told Brent, that the "unpleasantness" would last no longer than that. Granting that the General's native wife might have given him a false sense of security, Bentley Brent still thought that Wheeler was a blind fool.

In Cawnpore, on the Chandni Chowk, or main street, Nana Sahib was being hailed by hundreds of natives as a hero. "Nana Sahib! Nana Sahib!" they chanted over and over as they swarmed around his horse, raising their fists or, in many instances, their rifles and swords. Murder was in the air in the hot, crowded street; the silk and silver merchants whose shops lined the Chandni Chowk stood in their doorways or under their awnings shouting with the others. Nana Sahib, his pudgy, sweating face alight with excitement, waved his arms for silence. After a moment the noise died down enough for him to be heard.

"It is time," he shouted, "for us to reclaim Holy India as our own!" A roar of approval. "It is time," he continued, "to send the jackals back to England or to their ancestors!"

"To their ancestors!" roared the crowd, many of whom were still wearing the uniforms of the Indian Army, although most had torn off their infantry or cavalry insignia, their chevrons and medals. A former sergeant with a fierce mustache ran out of a shop holding a terrified Portuguese merchant, who was struggling unsuccessfully to free himself from the *sepoy*'s grip.

"Nana Sahib!" cried the merchant who looked in his forties and was as fat as the self-styled Maharajah of Bithur. "You know me, Nana Sahib! I have sold you the English marmalade you love! Save me, great one!"

Nana Sahib, on his horse, squinted at the man. "Yes, I know you," he cried. "And yes, I confess I love English marmalade. But from this moment on, I swear to the great goddess Kali that I will never touch English marmalade again, or use English soap, or buy any English product until the last Englishman in India is dead—and I include Englishwomen and children. Let them all die! And as for you, Portuguese dog: farewell!"

He ran his finger across his double chin. The crowd laughed and cheered as the *sepoy* pulled out his *tulwar,* or sword, and drew it swiftly across the merchant's throat. As blood squirted over the *sepoy*'s khaki jacket, the merchant stumbled into eternity.

"Death!" screamed Nana Sahib, raising his right fist to the sultry sky. "Death to all *firinghis*!"

"Death to all *firinghis*!" echoed the crowd.

"Now, let us ride out to the entrenchment and kill the English jackals!"

"Nana Sahib! Nana Sahib! Nana Sahib!"

The chanting crowd surged forward, a flood of dark humanity spilling down the Chandni Chowk like a raging river roaring to its rendezvous with death.

Unlike Cawnpore, which had developed at the end of the previous century as an East India Company garrison and had no history or architecture of distinction, the great city of Lucknow, some eighty miles to the east, was rich in both. As Adam and Emily sat on their horses viewing the city of over 600,000 that sprawled across twelve square miles beside the River Gumti, they were both dazzled by the beauty of the place, the hills of which were crowned by splendid palaces, temples, and mosques, a vision of gold and azure domes, cupolas, colonnades, and minarets.

"Papa says Lucknow is the cradle of the *sepoys*," Emily said, "because so many of them come from Oudh."

"What's Oudh?" Adam asked, waving a fly from his nose.

"It was a kingdom—the Kingdom of Oudh—and Lucknow was its capital. But we annexed it last year and kicked the King, or Nawab, and the royal family out of his palace, which Papa said the King did not like at all."

"I can imagine."

"Now it's the capital of Uttar Pradesh. Look at the beautiful gate."

She pointed to a great ocher gate built in an imposingly delicate style. Its central arch, flanked by slender minarets, soaring some sixty feet, the whole set in the reddish crenelated wall that surrounded the city. It was the *Rumi Darvaza*, or Roman Gate, which had been copied from a similar structure in Istanbul.

"You say the Chief Commissioner is Sir Henry Lawrence," Adam said. "Is he to be trusted?"

"Oh, I'm sure he is. Papa says he's a very strict Christian."

"There are a lot of strict Christians I wouldn't trust."

Emily looked at him with surprise. "You surely don't mean that?"

"I surely do. Who's causing all this trouble out here? Your father said it was the Christian missionaries, and I think he's right. We English are wrong to try to impose our religion on the Indians. They have plenty of fine religions of their own, and most of them are a lot older than Christianity."

"But surely *you* are a Christian?"

He hesitated. "I don't know *what* I am," he finally said rather sourly. "But let's go see if we can meet Sir Henry. It might be wise to have his help when we return the diamond."

They rode down a slope toward the gate of the city. The Great Trunk Road was normally thronged with caravans, merchants, soldiers and travelers, but today the dirt road was strangely empty. Adam rode in silence, struck by the shimmering beauty of Lucknow. The brief glimpse he had had of London before embarking for the Orient had impressed him, but nothing he had seen there could compare with Lucknow.

The gate was guarded by a dozen English soldiers, half of them mounted. As Adam and Emily approached, one of them raised his rifle and shouted, "Halt! No natives are allowed in or out of the city unless they have papers signed by the Commissioner."

"We're not natives," Adam said. "I am the Earl of Pontefract, and I request an audience with Sir Henry Lawrence."

The soldiers laughed.

"This nigger thinks 'e's a bloody earl," guffawed one private. "Talk about cheek!"

"Go on," shouted another. "You might as well try for a dukedom, eh? 'Is grace, the bleedin' Duke of Wog. 'Ow's that?"

"He *is* an earl," Emily cried angrily, removing her turban and letting her red hair tumble out. "And I'm the daughter of Sir Carlton McNair of Calcutta and Darjeeling. Now, kindly display some proper manners."

The soldiers stared at her red hair and the grins vanished from their faces.

"Then why are you dressed like natives?" asked a sergeant who was obviously in command.

"That's what we want to explain to Sir Henry," Adam said. "And I *am* the Earl of Pontefract."

He was amused by the way the English soldiers' attitudes reversed. Like weather vanes before a changing wind, their class-ridden souls almost genuflected before a title. The sergeant signaled for the gun to be lowered, then executed a snappy salute. "Sorry, milord," he said, "but things are a bit edgy here. We have to take precautions. However, I've heard the Earl of Pontefract was in India, so welcome to Lucknow. Sudbury!"

"Sir!"

"Escort His Lordship to the Residency."

"Sir!"

One of the mounted soldiers saluted and spurred his horse. "If you'll follow me, Your Lordship," Sudbury said, starting through the gate. Emily recovered her hair with her turban and she and Adam followed Sudbury through the gate into the city. Inside the walls, the native life reasserted itself with its customary bustle, but Emily quickly noticed the angry looks Sudbury attracted. A shopkeeper came out of his stall and yelled something in Hindi.

"What did he say?" asked Adam.

"He told the soldier he'd be dead in a week," Emily replied.

"It's ugly here," Sudbury said. "There's no doubt about that. They say that if Nana Sahib can take the entrenchment at Cawnpore, he'll come here next."

"Nana Sahib?" asked Adam. "He's at Cawnpore?"

"That's what I hear, milord. The bloody beggar—beggin' your pardon, miss—the beggar betrayed General Wheeler and went over to the mutineers. Now he and his *badmashes* are besieging the entrenchment where the English civilians are hiding out. They say it's terrible, what with the heat and very little water and they're running out of food. Our people are dying like flies, and they're stuffing the corpses down wells since there's no other place to put 'em and corpses go bad fast in this bloody climate—beggin' your pardon again, miss."

Adam reflected that Nana Sahib was carving out a niche for himself as one of the prime ogres of English history. But at the same time, it occurred to him that, to the Indian natives, Nana Sahib must look like a hero.

They passed the beautiful *Bara Imambara*, the great tomb built by the eighteenth-century King of Oudh, Nawab Asaf-ud-Daula. Then the lovely royal palace called the Heart's Delight, or Dil Kusha, in whose gardens peacocks roamed. But as they neared the Residency, it occurred to Adam there were no white faces visible. "Where are the Europeans?" he asked Sudbury.

"Hiding," was the terse reply.

The Residency, which had been built in 1780, was an imposing building overlooking the Gumti River and surrounded by a banqueting hall for the British officials and soldiers as well as a church, offices, stores, stables, and private houses. The enclave—in effect, a city within a city—was entered through an archway and guardhouse known as the Baillie Guard Gate. As they approached the gate, Adam saw dozens of shackled prisoners digging a trench around the walls of the Residency, which bristled with cannon. Adam didn't need to ask why the trench was being dug.

Once inside the walls of the Residency, it was the reverse of Lucknow in that now Adam saw nothing but white faces, with the exception of a few servants. In fact, aside from the sweltering heat, he thought himself back in England, for everything was European with a vengeance, with flowerpots neatly lined on verandahs and lace curtains over bungalow windows. Sudbury took them to the central building, where he turned them over to a lieutenant. The young officer led them through the high-ceilinged rooms, filled with clerks who gave the "Indians" curious and hostile glances, to the reception room of the Commissioner, where they were greeted by a Colonel Perkins. Perkins stepped into his superior's office for a moment, then returned to signal them to enter. "Sir Henry," he announced, "the Earl of Pontefract and Miss Emily McNair."

Sir Henry rose from his imposing desk, behind which hung a full-length portrait of Queen Victoria, and came around to shake Adam's hand. Though the recently promoted brigadier general was only fifty-one, he looked much older, thanks to a craggy face, burned by years of the brutal Indian sun, and a long black, almost patriarchal beard. "My lord, welcome," he said to Adam. Then he looked rather curiously at Emily. "And this is my friend Sir Carlton's daughter?" he said. "Is he aware that you are running around India disguised as a native?"

"Oh no. And if he knew, I think he'd be apoplectic. But you see, Lord Pontefract can't speak Hindi and I can. And when you hear why we came to Lucknow, I think you'll agree it was important I help him."

Moments later, Sir Henry was staring at the huge diamond Adam had produced from his belt. "The Idol's Eye," he whispered as the jewel flashed its fire in his palm. "Of course I know the story of your great-grandfather—who doesn't? And you're returning it to the temple?"

"Exactly. Although with the mutiny, perhaps my timing is a bit off."

"On the contrary. It would be a powerful piece of propaganda for us. Of course, as a Christian I deplore these pagan religions. But there can be no doubt that the news of an Englishman returning a valuable icon to India would do a great deal to reverse the anti-English sentiment that's running so high now. If you'll permit me, milord, I will send a wire to Lord Canning asking him to release this story all over India. Meanwhile, I'll place a special guard at the temple to protect the jewel, although few Indians would risk the wrath of Kali by defiling her temple. But this is quite, quite extraordinary. You and Miss McNair will be my guests?"

"Thank you. And if possible I would like to return the diamond to the temple personally. It would bring my family's tradition full circle, so to speak."

"Perfectly understandable. We'll go to the temple at midnight, when most of the natives are asleep. No point in asking for trouble."

* * *

In later years, Adam would remember it as one of the high points of his eventful life, combining as it did all the beauty, mystery and sinister glamour of India. First, there had been the swift procession through the dark streets of Lucknow: Adam, Emily and Sir Henry in the Commissioner's carriage, surrounded by a dozen mounted officers of the Thirty-second Foot, the only European regiment stationed at Lucknow (Adam had learned that this "safe" regiment was, for some mysterious bureaucratic reason, actually barracked a mile and a half outside the walls of the city, while the much less "safe" native regiments were stationed closer to the Residency). Then the arrival at the dark Temple of Kali, lighted only by the torches carried by four of the red-coated English officers and Sir Henry's carriage lanterns. They emerged from the carriage, and Adam looked up at the temple's dark walls and towers. In the flickering torchlight, the many carved figures on the temple's facade seemed to move, creating an eerie effect.

Sir Henry led the party into the temple, the interior of which was a forest of stone columns, all heavily carved with scenes from the life of Vishnu and other Hindu deities. Adam had learned that Hinduism was the most eclectic of all major religions, in that Hindus could believe in any or all or none of the myriad gods in the Hindu pantheon. It was also the only major religion that had no single founder, such as Jesus or Buddha, or any "holy book" like the Bible, although a Hindu could regard the *Rig Veda* or the *Upanishads* or the *Bhagavad Gita* as "Bibles." Perhaps the religion's enormous diversity accounted for its vast popularity in India: one could practice Hinduism almost any way one chose. Be that as it may, the religion's passion manifested itself in the exuberant carvings on the columns, some of which Adam noticed were extremely erotic, if not bordering on the pornographic. He glanced at Emily, who didn't seem particularly shocked because she didn't understand what the copulating carvings were actually doing.

But when they approached the huge statue of the Goddess Kali, Emily clearly understood what emotion it was conveying. Both she and Adam were startled by the hideousness of the stone woman who loomed above them, her red tongue protruding from her mouth in a hideous grimace. Her body was black, her breasts bare. Two of her four hands carried a sword and a severed head, the other two were extended palm upward in gestures of blessing and protection, for Kali was not only the death-goddess, she was also the mother goddess who could be gentle.

"According to legend," said Sir Henry, "the diamond was held in her lower-left hand."

The base of the statue had four stone steps. Now Adam slowly climbed them, his upturned eyes on the eyes of the goddess above him. Emily, Sir Henry and the English officers watched the strange ceremony in silence. When Adam reached the top step, he held up the huge diamond, iridescent in the torchlight.

"A century ago," Adam said, his firm voice echoing in the stone chamber, "my great-grandfather stole this diamond from this sacred place. I now return it to its rightful place and beg forgiveness from the great goddess Kali for my ancestor's sacrilege."

He set the diamond in the goddess's hand, holding on to it for a moment. Silence. Then he released it and climbed back down the steps.

"Well done, milord," said Sir Henry. "Now, let's go back to the Residency for some supper. By the way, you said that business about the 'great goddess Kali' with real conviction. You almost made me think you believe it."

"Maybe I do," said Adam softly.

Sir Henry looked startled. Then he laughed rather nervously.

"Look!" cried Emily, pointing to the base of Kali's statue.

A large snake slithered past their feet and around the statue to disappear into the darkness of the temple.

"A wire from Cawnpore, Sir Henry." The subaltern handed the telegram to the Commissioner, saluted smartly, then about-faced to march out of the Officers' Banquet Hall in the Residency. It was half an hour later, and even though it was almost one in the morning, Emily and Adam both were so keyed up by the return of the diamond that neither felt sleepy. The heat had abated and they were hungrily attacking the cool *sev ka raita*, a mixture of yogurt, spices and apple slices. The banquet hall could seat two hundred at long wooden tables, but it now was empty except for the party that had gone to the temple. The dozen young English officers were attacking their food with gusto, drinking quantities of ale from silver tankards. Along the Jacobean sideboards, the regimental plate was proudly displayed: silver chargers, polo cups, elaborate candelabra, silver tureens, silver punch bowls—all beautifully polished, gleaming in the candlelight as if the British Empire and all of its regal accoutrements would last forever.

"A massacre!" said Sir Henry, looking up from the telegram. "There's been a massacre at Cawnpore! This telegram is from the senior officer left alive, Captain Brent—"

"Bentley!" exclaimed Adam.

"Exactly. Nana Sahib's troops had besieged the entrenchment, as you know, and almost starved them out. There are terrible casualties, including women and children. General Wheeler—whose son, I am sad to report, had his head blown off by a cannonball—was finally convinced to make a truce and Nana Sahib agreed to release the civilians unharmed. As the women, children and wounded were led down to the Ganges to put them in boats to take them to safety downstream at Allahabad, Nana Sahib—the beast!—ordered his men to attack. They fired on the English, chopped at them with swords, drowned them in the river . . ." The normally phlegmatic Sir Henry's voice began to crack. "General Wheeler was most foully murdered, as was Chaplain Moncrieff while he was reading prayers from the Bible. The Ganges runs red with English blood. Gentlemen, I will lead us in a moment of silent prayer for the noble dead."

Sir Henry closed his eyes, which were teary, as did Emily and the officers. Adam left his eyes open, trying to absorb this new horror. When Sir Henry was finished, he looked up. His face was filled with fury.

"Gentlemen," he said, "I swear to you that for every drop of English blood that has been spilled, a gallon of Indian blood will flow in revenge!"

"Revenge!" cried one young officer, jumping to his feet. "Revenge the massacre!"

"Revenge! Revenge Cawnpore!" All the officers were now on their feet, banging their tankards on the table.

"Kill the niggers!"

"Revenge!"

"Avenge Cawnpore!"

"Kill the niggers!"

As the room filled with hate, Adam's face filled with pain—for both the English who had been slaughtered and the Indians who were about to be. Then, suddenly, he saw what had to be done. He got to his feet and held up his hands for silence.

"Sir Henry," he said, "I think I have a way to smoke Nana Sahib out. Do you have any *sepoys* you still trust?"

"Yes, a few."

"If I can have ten men, I think in a few days I can bring you Nana Sahib—dead or alive—and perhaps this mutiny can be stopped before others are hurt."

"Well, milord, I suppose I can find you ten. But how do you propose doing this?"

"I'll tell you after it succeeds."

He felt a tug at his right sleeve and turned to see Emily at his side.

"Dear Adam, may I come?"

There were a few snickers from the English officers at the sight of the blackfaced *syce* calling Adam "dear." But Emily was not the type of girl to let snickers go unanswered. Turning on them, she said hotly, "I'd like to know what so amuses you gentlemen? Adam *is* dear to me! I love him, and . . ." She stopped, shocked by what she had let slip out. Adam put his hands on her shoulders.

"Emily, I've endangered your life as it is. No, you can't come with me. We have to get you safely back to your parents—"

"There's a caravan of married women leaving for Calcutta tomorrow," Sir Henry said. "They'll be properly guarded. Miss McNair can go with them."

"No!" she cried. "I want to be with Adam!" She took off her turban and shook out her glorious red hair. The officers, who hadn't realized her beauty, became silent. She looked up at Adam with poignant eyes. "I suppose I've made a fool of myself saying I love you," she said softly, "and Mama would faint if she knew, but it's true, and I'm not ashamed of it. So please, dearest Adam, don't send me away. I'd rather die with you than live without you."

Adam suddenly took her in his arms and kissed her on the mouth. The kiss became a long and passionate one. The officers began tapping their tankards on the table, muttering, "Well done!" "Bravo!"

Sir Henry, looking shocked, cleared his throat. "Lord Pontefract," he exclaimed, "this is neither the time nor the place . . ."

Adam released her, smiled at her and whispered, "Now, go home. Before your father puts out a death warrant on me, and before you get hurt. It's very important to me that you don't get hurt."

Emily stared at him, stunned. "That was my first kiss," she whispered.

The officers smiled and clapped politely. "Bravo!" they murmured again. "Well done!" "Bravo!"

"Say, lads," cried one young lieutenant, picking up his tankard and raising it high, "isn't that what we're fighting for? A sweet English girl's first kiss? I say we drink to that!"

"Hear, hear!"

As they all drank, Adam reflected that this side of the English coin was so preferable to the other side that cried, "Kill the niggers!"

CHAPTER 12

The baby's lusty wail filled the high-ceilinged room on the third floor of Willard's Hotel.

"It's a girl!" Clemmie DeVries smiled.

"A girl," whispered Lizzie, who had just been delivered of the bawling seven-pound baby.

"And a very healthy girl, it seems."

"Adam's daughter."

"Adam?" Clemmie looked confused.

"I'll call her Amanda."

"Amanda Cavanagh. Yes, that's a lovely name."

Clemmie wondered who in the world Adam was, but decided Lizzie was still a bit delirious from the delivery.

"Let me hold her," Lizzie said.

The doctor brought the baby to her, and the mother took her in her arms.

"Oh, she's beautiful." She kissed the top of her head, which was covered with light fuzz. And someday, Lizzie thought, her father is going to be proud of her.

Willard's Hotel on Pennsylvania Avenue at Fourteenth Street had become the most popular hotel in Washington, D.C., after its main rival, the National Hotel on Sixth Street, managed to kill a number of its guests, including the nephew of President Buchanan, with a mysterious malady imaginatively dubbed the National Hotel Disease. Guests from all over the country mingled with politicians and diplomats in the public rooms of Willard's, and deal-making and politicking were the favorite sports in the smoke-filled bar, where the capital's young bucks spent many happy hours gulping down a "pernicious" new invention called cocktails. Lizzie had rented a suite at Willard's (ironically, only three days after the Belladons checked out to return to Europe), and her arrival was just in time since she quickly went into labor.

The DeVrieses had come with her, for Billie, as her lawyer, was contesting Lizzie's extradition to England, even though an extradition treaty between the United States and England had existed since 1843. But the day after Amanda's birth, which was April 15, 1857, a somber-looking Billie came into Lizzie's bedroom, where Clemmie was gently rocking the baby's new cradle.

"Lizzie, I hate to bring you bad news so soon after your lyin'-in," Billie said, "but the Attorney General has told me he will definitely not block your extradition."

Lizzie, who was sitting up in bed, tried to appear calm. "Then, this means I'm going to have to stand trial?" she said.

"I'm afraid so. I was hoping the Abolitionists in Congress would support me, but Senator Whitney is just too damned powerful, and he's out to get you. He knows you've been sending money North to the Abolitionists."

"What chance do I have of acquittal?"

Billie pulled up a chair by her bed and sat down.

"Well, of course I don't know what kind of a case the Crown has against you. I've been following the Madelaine Smith trial in Scotland . . ."

"Who's Madelaine Smith?"

"She's a well-bred young lady from Glasgow who was accused of poisoning her lover."

"Apparently she wasn't that well-bred."

"Uh, no, I suppose not. At any rate, English law has a peculiar rule that the defendant cannot testify. It turns out that this worked well for Madelaine Smith: because she couldn't testify in her own defense, the jury came in with a verdict of 'not proved,' so she was let go. The same rule may work for you."

"The whole case would turn on Stringer MacDuff's testimony, then, because he was the eyewitness."

"How do you think he will testify?"

She remembered that horrible night in the cottage, remembered how quickly MacDuff had acted to save his own skin by going to the police. She looked across the room at the cradle.

"I think," she said slowly, "that perhaps I'd better get out of the country." She turned to Billie. "Do you think you can arrange to get me and Amanda to Mexico?"

Billie stood up. "I'm afraid that's impossible," he said.

"Why?"

He went to the door of the suite and opened it. She saw two armed guards standing outside.

"Senator Whitney," Billie said, closing the door again. "He's convinced the Attorney General to make you a prisoner."

For the first time Lizzie began to feel panic-stricken.

"Lizzie Cavanagh must be screaming!" crowed Ellie May Whitney as she came out on the porch of Fairview Plantation. "Listen to this headline in the *Evening Star*: 'Mrs. Cavanagh Extradited to England Under Armed Guard!' " She handed the copy of the Washington scandal sheet to her husband, who was sitting in a rocking chair.

"Yes, the publisher told me he was really going to roast her in print," Phineas said as he took out his gold-rimmed spectacles so he could read the article. "I expect Mrs. Cavanagh will be swinging from a hangman's noose before very long, and it couldn't happen to a more deserving woman."

"Clemmie DeVries keeps insisting there was nothing going on between Lizzie and that slave, but if you ask me, that's *exactly* what the story is. Her own sister says she has no morals. I wonder if Jack Cavanagh knew she was carrying someone else's baby? Poor Jack! If he'd married a decent, honest Virginia girl instead of some trash from Europe, he'd be alive and happy today."

She looked down the beautiful lawn to the Rappahannock River, which flowed past Fairview Plantation, some ten miles to the southeast of Fredericksburg. Fairview was generally considered to be one of the most beautiful plantation houses in Virginia, on a par with Elvira Plantation,

Berkeley Plantation, Shirley, Stratford Hall—the birthplace of Robert E. Lee—and Montpelier, the estate of James Madison. Like Elvira Plantation, Fairview was mostly planted in tobacco. But unlike Jack, Senator Whitney had also built a factory on his land, where slaves, under the supervision of white workers, turned the cured tobacco into cigars, snuff, "twists" of chewing tobacco and, increasingly, cigarettes. Over two hundred slaves worked the flat fields, planting, topping, weeding, cutting, harvesting and prizing the cured tobacco leaves into hogsheads. But Phineas was, through his wife, also married to the other great cash crop of the South, King Cotton. Both were labor-intensive, so the Whitneys were fanatical proponents of slavery; and when Lizzie began championing the Abolitionists, they naturally became fanatical opponents of her.

"The article sizzles her fine," Phineas said, putting the newspaper down.

"Do you expect she really will hang?" Ellie May asked.

"I'm going to make sure she does," Phineas said. "Mrs. Cavanagh gives us slave owners a beautiful opportunity to discredit the Abolitionists. I've come up with a way to guarantee her conviction for murder. I'm going over to Carr Farm tomorrow to talk to Brandon about it. No use leaving things to chance."

"No, I suppose not," said Ellie May, not quite sure what he meant. "By the way, Charlotte writes me from school that she's getting some pretty poetic letters from Clayton Carr up at Princeton. It sounds to me as if he's working himself up to a proposal. What would you say about Charlotte marrying him?"

"Why, I'd be tickled pink. You know I like the Carr boys—always have. Clayton and Zack are fine stock. They come from good breeding and they're solid Southerners. I couldn't be more pleased if Charlotte fell in love with Clayton. They're not talking about doing anything sudden, though, are they?"

"Oh, no. They'd wait till Clayton graduates. I'm fond of the Carrs, too, though they don't have much money. . . ."

"Money isn't everything, Ellie May. Breeding's the important thing. Breeding and loyalty to our way of life."

Mr. McNally, a fat, bearded man on a gray horse, rode up in front of the house and the overseer dismounted. He walked up the steps to the porch and tipped his hat to Ellie May.

"Good day, Mrs. Whitney," he said. "Lovely weather we're having, isn't it?"

"Good day, Mr. McNally. Yes, it's been such a nice spring so far."

"Excuse me, Senator, but we're having a little trouble over in the quarter."

"What trouble?"

"The boy Tucker has been caught stealing again. Another chicken."

"Tucker has a record of petty thefts, I believe?"

"That's right, sir. The boy's light-fingered. Last month we caught him stealing some turnips from the great house. I gave him a whipping then, but he don't seem to learn."

"Well then, you'll just have to whip him until he does learn, wouldn't you say?" The Senator smiled. "Give him a hundred lashes, then salt him. Let him hang for a day. That should teach him."

"Isn't Tucker Sarah's boy?" Ellie May asked.

"Yes, ma'am."

"She's one of my best laundresses, Phineas. I wouldn't want to upset her."

"If she gets upset, that's too bad," said her husband shortly. "She should teach him Christian morals, though God knows it's hard enough to teach them *anything*. Go ahead, Mr. McNally. Give the boy his punishment."

"Yes, sir."

Tipping his hat again, the hulking overseer went back down the steps of the verandah and mounted his horse. As he rode off, Ellie May went back inside the house, leaving the Senator alone in his wicker rocking chair. It was a lovely April afternoon and the sweeping lawns of Fairview were lushly green, thanks to heavy spring rains. Tall oaks shaded clumps of azaleas, fiery in their exuberant red and purple blossoms. The red brick great house was something of an architectural cliché with its white-columned porch, but the house was nonetheless impressive and its view down a slope to the lazy Rappahannock River was spectacular. With his power in Washington at its zenith and his tobacco business bringing in a fortune, Phineas had reason to be pleased with himself; and railroading Lizzie to the hangman's noose was the cherry on top of the sundae. He was just dozing off, a fly buzzing around his head, when he was jolted awake by a distant scream. He sat up to see a black woman running toward the house. She wore a polka-dot bandanna over her hair and had on a black dress and white apron. "Massa! Massa!" she was screaming.

"What in thunder?" muttered the Senator. Ellie May came out of the house.

"It's Sarah," she said.

"Massa, please—dey killin' mah boy! Please, massa, stop de whuppin'—dey killin' Tucker! Oh God, please massa . . . Tucker a good boy . . . please!"

She was standing at the side of the verandah, holding up her clasped hands, weeping hysterically.

"I told you she'd get upset," sighed Ellie May.

"Stop this noise!" ordered Phineas, getting out of his rocker and going to the rail of the verandah.

"Oh please, dey's blood all over his back! Tucker only seventeen. . . . Mr. McNally gonna kill him!"

"Silence!" roared Phineas. "Dammit, woman, stop making this infernal racket! Your son is a thief and deserves punishment."

"He jes stole one chicken, massa . . . he so hungry. . . ."

Ellie May came up beside her husband, a frown on her face. "Sarah," she said, "you're getting hysterical over nothing."

"Nothin'?" wailed the woman. "Mah son's bein' whupped to death! Oh please, mistress, you'se a mother . . . please . . ."

Ellie May squirmed. She turned to her husband. "We don't want the boy hurt permanently," she said.

Phineas looked annoyed. "You womenfolk are too

damned soft," he muttered. "You'll spoil these darkies. All right, woman," he said to Sarah. "I'll ride to the quarter and stop the whipping. But see to it your son behaves from now on."

"Oh yes, massa. Thank you, massa. You a good man, massa, a kind man."

"I'm a fool. Now, get back to your work."

"Yes, massa."

Wiping her eyes on her apron, Sarah hurried away from the house. Muttering, "Damned hysterical wench," the Senator left the porch and walked around to the stables, where he mounted his horse, Calhoun, and took off at a gallop. The slave quarter was a half-mile from the great house. Set in a field beside a ravine were three rows of squalid one-room shacks. They were built of logs and mud reinforced with horsehair, and their tilting chimneys were made of sticks and pitch. The roofs were wood shingles or, in some cases, tin. Chickens, dogs and cats wandered around at liberty and the unseeded ground was littered with trash and garbage. The place stank, for there weren't even privies. A crowd of frightened slaves was standing silently watching as Mr. McNally flayed the naked, bleeding back of a teenage black with a bullwhip. Two other white men stood guard, holding shotguns.

The Senator dismounted.

"All right, Mr. McNally, that's enough," he said, coming to the whipping post, a thick stake with leather wristholds attached to the top.

Mr. McNally, who was sweating, put down his whip. "Well, sir, you said give him a hundred lashes, and I'm only up to seventy-four."

"I know, but I think Tucker here has learned his lesson." Whitney walked around the young man to the other side of the post so he could see his face. "You learned your lesson, boy?" he said. "You gonna be a good nigger and stop this thieving?"

Tucker, whose jet-black face glistened with sweat, looked up at the kindly white face of his well-dressed owner. The white mustache and shoulder-length hair under the broad-brimmed black hat. The immaculate brown coat and fawn trousers. The avuncular smile.

Tucker spat in his face.

Senator Whitney stiffened. Then he pulled a handkerchief from his breast pocket and wiped the spittle from his cheek.

"This nigger is beyond redemption," he said softly. "Put him in the rain barrel."

He walked away as the crowd of slaves moaned. Quickly Mr. McNally loosened the wrist straps. Tucker, who had been brutalized to near-unconsciousness, slumped to the ground.

"Take him to the rain barrel," McNally ordered, and one of the white guards came over and grabbed the boy's left arm, jerking him to his feet.

Sarah, who had just run up from the great house, cried out, "What you doin' to mah son?"

"Your son spat in my face, woman," said the Senator, who had gone back to his horse and was remounting. "In all my sixty years, I've never been treated with such disrespect by a nigra, and by God, I won't stand for it—especially one of my own nigras. Your son's going in the rain barrel."

Sarah started screaming. "Oh no, massa—please! Please! Doan do dat—please! Oh Lordie, please. . . ."

She had run to the horse and was hugging the Senator's left boot as she sobbed and screamed.

"Let go my boot, woman!"

"You can't do dis, massa! Tucker a good boy—please! Oh God . . . !"

Savagely the senior Senator from Virginia whipped her face with his riding crop. Screaming, she fell to the ground, narrowly averting being kicked by one of Calhoun's hooves, for the horse was prancing nervously from the commotion. The slaves watched in silent terror as the two guards dragged a bleeding Tucker across the ground to a six-foot-high wooden barrel standing on a stone slab at the edge of a hill that sloped down to a small stream. The first guard dropped Tucker on the ground and the second pulled off his ragged linsey-woolsey trousers. When the bloody slave was naked, the two men picked him up and lowered him into the barrel. The inside of the barrel staves were studded with four-inch nails pointing inward.

The guards clamped a wooden cover on top of the barrel. When Phineas gave the signal, Mr. McNally pushed the barrel over on its side. It landed with a thump. Horrible screams emitted from inside the barrel. The two guards kicked it, and it rolled over the edge of the slope.

As Sarah and the other slaves watched in horror, the barrel bounced down the incline until it rolled to a stop next to the stream almost forty feet below.

"I'd advise you not to look," said the Senator to Sarah as he spurred his horse. "And don't bother to hope he's alive."

He rode off. Sarah, kneeling in the dust, her cheek slashed by the riding crop, slowly raised her fists to heaven.

Brandon Carr, a man in his forties, was much more a scholar than a businessman and had spent the past ten years of his life writing a ponderous biography of James Madison. Brandon was balding and, superficially, mild-mannered, though as his two sons, Zack and Clayton, were aware, he had a tough streak of tenacity and could, on occasion, display a mean temper. Carr Farm was a very minor moon compared to its neighboring planet, Fairview Plantation. Brandon raised some tobacco, but mostly his slaves raised crops like corn and tomatoes. It was a sleepy farm, and Brandon, while a firm believer in the "peculiar institution," was known to be humane with his slaves: if there was such a thing as a "good" slaveowner, Brandon was it. Brandon, Class of 1834 at Princeton, was a Virginia gentleman, proud of his state's courtly traditions. But his house had none of the pretensions of either Elvira or Fairview Plantation, and was as rundown as the latter was beautifully maintained. It wasn't that Brandon wouldn't have liked to give the place a new coat of paint. It was simply that he was perennially short of cash.

The morning after the murder of the slave Tucker, Senator Phineas Thurlow Whitney's carriage pulled up in front of Carr Farm. Elton, Phineas' aging driver, climbed down to hold the door for his master. Phineas stepped out and walked up the path to the two-story farmhouse with the front porch that sagged a bit to the left. It was another lovely spring day, and Brandon, dressed in a white coat and white hat, was sitting on a rocking chair on the porch, smoking a cigar. As Phineas climbed up onto the porch, Brandon rose, removed his hat, and offered his hand.

"Brandon . . ." The Senator smiled, shaking hands. "Isn't this splendid weather we're enjoying?"

"Indeed it is, Phineas. Shall we stay out here, or would you prefer to go inside?"

"No, here would be fine."

The two men sat down next to each other.

"Ellie May tells me that Clayton's been writing Charlotte some pretty flowery letters." The Senator chuckled as he pulled out a leather cigar case. "I think that boy of yours has got a real crush on my daughter. I'll speak the plain truth with you, Brandon. It would give me great pleasure if our two families, who have been neighbors for so many years, would be united by marriage."

Brandon leaned over to light Phineas' cigar with a lucifer match. "It would please me too," he said, "except for one thing. I heard what you did to one of your slaves yesterday. You know how thoroughly I disapprove of excess severity to our servants. It's not Christian, Phineas."

Phineas sat back in his rocker, inhaling on his cigar, his sharp eyes watching Brandon.

"I'll take my chances with God," he finally said. "The boy spat in my face. I felt I had no alternative to what I did."

"But murder . . . ?"

"Brandon, you run your place your way, and I'll run my plantation my way. I didn't come over here to be lectured about a damned insolent darkie."

"Phineas, we both believe in slavery. It's the very basis of our economy. Slaves were brought over here because the white man couldn't work in the heat: without the slaves, no cotton would be picked, no rice grown, no tobacco raised. We have no fundamental difference on that score. But by God, sir, we have a responsibility to these people."

Phineas leaned forward. "Now you listen to me, Brandon Carr. You sit here, writing your history books, lost in a dream world. I'm in the thick of the battle. I'm up in Washington trying to keep our Southern dominance of the Government, and I can tell you, the moment we lose that dominance, the South is in serious trouble. So don't lecture me about treating the slaves humanely! I'm trying to save the institution, and it's not an easy job. *My* efforts are making it possible for you to sit here on your tail end in safety and comfort. And as an old friend and neighbor, I take your criticism very badly, sir. Very badly indeed."

Brandon sighed. "I won't apologize, Phineas. But I'll say nothing more on the subject. Now, you said in your note you wanted to talk to me about going to England. For what reason?"

"It's about the trial of the Cavanagh woman. A number of us have put together a common purse to defray your expenses."

"But what do you want me to do?"

When Phineas told him, Brandon scowled. "I'm sorry, Phineas, but I could not have on my Christian conscience what you propose. You will be sending her to the hangman's noose."

Phineas told himself that there was no dealing with Brandon. The man was totally impractical, a wool-gatherer who didn't understand how high the stakes were for the South.

"Elizabeth Desmond Cavanagh, you are charged with the crime of murder. How do you plead, guilty or not guilty?" The bewigged judge, Mr. Justice Molyneux, looked splendid in his rich scarlet-and-ermine robes. He sat on the bench at the Central Criminal Court, known as the Old Bailey, on Newgate Street in the City of London. The gaslit courtroom was thronged, for murder trials were regarded as theatre in London, and the trial of the beautiful Yorkshire-born American widow had generated reams of publicity. It was September 1857, almost five months since Lizzie and her baby had set sail from New

York. Now she stood in the dock, dressed simply in a dark blue dress and bonnet. She eyed the judge and said firmly, "I plead not guilty, my lord."

She was anxious. No human being could not feel anxiety standing in the dock being tried for murder, and her fears had not abated when her solicitor, Sir Edmund Carter, confirmed that the rules of English law prevented her from testifying in her own behalf.

But her nervousness increased almost to panic when she heard the Prosecution call as its first witness, the Parisian couturier Lucien Delorme. Sir Edmund had warned her that the probable thrust of the Crown's case would be that her fleeing England was evidence of guilt.

And that, added to the testimony of Stringer MacDuff, might hang her.

CHAPTER 13

"Cawnpore is ours!" cried Nana Sahib to the huge crowd as fireworks lit up the hot sky. Dressed in his most gorgeous ivory silks, with five strands of huge pearls around his fat neck and the Peshwa Diamond in his turban, he was seated on top of one of his elephants in a gold *howdah*, or canopied seat. "By the kindness of God, all the Christians who had been here and at Delhi and Meerut have been destroyed and sent to hell by the pious and wise troops of the faithful, firm in their religion. The yellow-haired *firinghis* are being chased from Mother India, and it is now the duty of all citizens to obey my new government. Today I am the Maharajah of Bithur. But soon I will be proclaimed emperor of all India!"

"Nana Sahib, Nana Sahib!" chanted the ecstatic mob of several thousand natives.

"Our cause is on the march to victory! And now, my friends, come with me to my palace at Bithur for a great victory *nautch*! All you can eat and drink! You are the guests of Nana Sahib!"

"Nana Sahib, Nana Sahib!" screamed the ragged mob, which had found a new hero.

Six *nautch* girls, led by Lakshmi, danced sensuous belly dances in the throne room of Nana Sahib's palace at Bithur. It was the night following his public victory party, which had filled the palace with his celebrating subjects, and tonight Nana Sahib was holding a more private *nautch* with just his closest friends. The chubby maharajah was sitting on his gilt throne smoking *ganja* as he watched the *nautch* girls. Lakshmi, who had gossamer purple veils attached to her shoulders and wrists, ran the veils slowly over his face as she danced past him, causing him to smile woozily. On cushions at one side of the room sat five musicians strumming sitars, while behind them were four guards armed with Enfield rifles. The guests—all male—were also seated on cushions around the room, drinking wine and arrack from silver goblets and helping themselves to fruit and sweetmeats passed on gold trays by Nana Sahib's servants. The languor of the guests and the sultriness of the air combined with the hashish made Nana Sahib feel he was floating in a dream. His eyes drifted from Lakshmi's undulating navel upward past her jiggling breasts to the ceiling where the punkahs lazily swayed and the round stained-glass ceiling that his father had had copied from a skylight he had seen in a Paris hotel glittered in the candlelight. Through a large round hole in the center of the glass ceiling a heavy chain dropped, holding a huge green glass chandelier with over fifty lights in red glass hurricane lamps which the late Peshwa had ordered from Baccarat in France. Nana Sahib's father had had a passion for everything French, as his son until recently had had a passion for English soap and marmalade.

Lord Azimullah hurried into the room just as three jugglers began a routine with wooden pins. Making his way around the guests, he came to the throne and said, "Your Highness, a miracle has occurred. The Englishman is here to present you with the great diamond."

Nana Sahib looked at him with eyes dulled by hashish and wine. "The Englishman? Adam Thorne? He's *here*?"

"Yes, sire. He requests an audience to present you with the diamond."

"But I don't understand. He's done everything to keep it from me."

"He says that he now understands that you represent the people of India, and therefore it is only fitting that he return the diamond to you."

"How marvelous . . ." Nana Sahib frowned. "Is he alone?"

"Yes, sire."

"The man must be a fool." He laughed and slapped his

knee. "The idiot! The *Angrezi* idiot! You're sure it's not a trick?"

"Since he is alone, sire, I fail to see what he could do. But I will instruct the guards to watch him."

"Yes, of course. But we shall have some fine sport, eh? Bring him to me. We will let him make his pretty little speech and give me the diamond. Then we shall have some fun putting the dog to as slow and painful a death as we can imagine. It will be fine entertainment for my guests, eh? What could be more pleasant than watching an Englishman die?"

"Your Highness is, as always, inspired."

Azimullah bowed, then made his way back to the double doors of the room and left. Nana Sahib got to his feet, steadying himself for a moment by leaning on one arm of his throne. Then he raised his other arm for silence. The musicians put down their instruments and the *nautch* girls stopped twirling.

"My friends, I have a surprise for you—one that should enliven our festivities this evening. The blaspheming Christian missionaries have come to our country and fouled our ears with stories of the bravery of the so-called Christian martyrs. Well, we are about to welcome a Christian martyr, and we shall see how brave this white *Angrezi* Christian is. Servants, more wine! More arrack!"

Clapping his hands, he sank back on his throne while the servants passed among the guests refilling the goblets. Three tumblers had joined the jugglers and were doing hand-flips around the room, to which the audience applauded. Then Azimullah led Adam in. The Englishman who looked like an Indian followed Azimullah through the guests, who watched hungrily. Adam carried an ivory box in both hands.

The dancers, jugglers and tumblers stopped and silence shrouded the room. Adam stood in front of Nana Sahib's throne and bowed.

"Bid him welcome," the maharajah told Azimullah.

"The mighty potentate Nana Sahib, Maharajah of Bithur, bids you welcome, Englishman," announced Azimullah.

"Tell Nana Sahib," said Adam, "that I bring him the great diamond not only because he now represents the Indian people but also because I fear the English may steal it from the temple at Lucknow and give it to Queen Victoria to put with her crown jewels."

Azimullah translated.

"Yes, yes," Nana Sahib said impatiently. "Tell him to give me the box."

"The Maharajah says, do not waste his time. Give him the box."

"Of course."

Adam stepped up to the throne and placed the ivory box in Nana Sahib's hands. Eagerly the Maharajah lifted the lid. Then he glared at Adam. "It's empty!" he yelled.

A volley of shots rang out from above, shattering the stained-glass ceiling and killing the four guards at the side of the room instantly. As Nana Sahib screamed, Adam pulled a long dagger from his coat, leaned forward and plunged it into the Maharajah's heart.

"My grandfather is avenged!" said Adam as Nana Sahib sprawled back in his throne, blood gushing over his silk jacket, a look of amazement on his face. As shots continued firing from above the glass ceiling, a rope was dropped through the hole. Adam raced through the screaming guests, tumblers, jugglers and *nautch* girls. He jumped, grabbed the rope with both hands, and began climbing toward the ceiling.

"Hurry!" yelled Bentley Brent from above him. Bentley, whose skin was blackened and who was dressed like an Indian, was standing on the thick wooden beam above the glass ceiling that held the enormous chandelier. He saw Azimullah aiming a pistol up at Adam, who was now almost to the ceiling. Bentley fired, killing Azimullah, who fell back on top of Nana Sahib's corpse.

The guests were pushing each other into a mass at the doors as they tried to get out of the throne room. They also were preventing more of Nana Sahib's soldiers from getting in. Another face-blackened English soldier and one of the four *sepoys* Adam had recruited for the expedition now grabbed his arms and hoisted him up onto the beam.

The men, ten in all, ran down the beam into the attic of the palace, then to a door leading to the roof. Bentley had known an English architect in Lucknow who had done some repair work for Nana Sahib's father five years before. When Adam had revealed his plan to use the diamond to gain access to the palace in order to assassinate Nana Sahib, Bentley had contacted the architect who had diagrams of the building.

Bentley emerged on the dark roof, followed by Adam and the others. They ran to the edge and looked over. The palace was situated in the center of Bithur, surrounded by a small walled park which was half-filled with the horses, carriages, *dholis* (sedan chairs) and *gharries* (carts) of Nana Sahib's guests, as well as their *syces*, most of whom were asleep. Bentley started climbing down the *peepul* tree by the side of the palace which they had used to get to the roof. Within minutes, the invaders were on their horses, galloping out the main gate just as Nana Sahib's confused guards began pouring out of the palace, seeking their lord's assassins. But they were too late.

As Adam galloped through the hot night, he felt an exhilaration he had never before in his life experienced. He felt no remorse for killing Nana Sahib. Far from it: the danger and excitement had been keen fun.

What he couldn't know was that by assassinating the greatest villain in the British Empire, he was going to become its greatest hero.

Extract from a letter from Queen Victoria to Lord Palmerston, her Prime Minister, dated August 26, 1857.

Balmoral

The Queen has received with *great* pleasure the news of the death of that Fiend, Nana Sahib, the self-styled Maharajah of Bithur. Ld. Palmerston is aware of the horror and shame we *all* felt when news of the atrocities Nana Sahib committed at Cawnpore reached us. Every outrage which women most dread was inflicted on those poor but brave Englishwomen by this beast, and it was perhaps a great mercy *all* were killed. But now the Fiend has been dispatched by this *most* clever and brave man, Ld. Pontefract, and the Queen can hardly convey the emotions she feels, of such happiness and pride that England has produced *such* a gallant hero. Alas, it is *such* a great pity that Ld. Pontefract's *folie d'amour* was made public at the trial of that wretched Mrs. Cavanagh, but the Queen is all too aware of the dark side of the masculine soul—as is Ld. Palmerston—and it is sad, but only human, that the young man sowed his wild oats. If it weren't for that unfortunate incident, the Queen would be pleased to bestow the Garter on Ld. Pontefract. But under the circumstances, that might be construed as the Crown rewarding vice, which is most assuredly *not* the impression the Queen wishes to convey. Nevertheless, it will give the Queen the *greatest* pleasure to elevate Ld. Pontefract to the rank of marquess. Oh, it is *such* a joy to be Queen of a nation that breeds noble, brave men like this *remarkable* Ld. Pontefract!

Signed,
V.R. (Victoria Regina)

"Milady, Mr. Musgrave is in the drawing room," Mr. Hawkins said to Sybil, who was reading the letter the Queen had written her in the library of Pontefract Hall. Now she put the letter down, a startled look on her face. Edgar? she thought. What in the world is he doing here?

"Tell him I will be there shortly," she instructed the butler, who bowed and left the room. Then she got up from her desk and went to a mirror. She mustn't let him see how nervous she was, she told herself. She pinched her cheeks to return some color to them, since they had gone totally pale. Then she smoothed her lustrous hair. Edgar! What a fool she had been, but she had been so terribly hurt by Adam. The affair had lasted less than a month and then Edgar had gone off again to Italy, which was his first love, she thought. She had assumed she had seen the last of him, but now here he was again. Keep calm, keep calm . . . What in God's name does he want?

Appearing as composed as she could, she walked through the house to the drawing room. There he was, as natty as always, his face burned slightly red from the Italian sun.

"Edgar," she said, forcing a smile as she crossed the room to him, extending her hand. "What a surprise. When did you get back from Italy?"

"Last week. I decided to take a vacation from my Italian creditors, who are getting just as unpleasantly persistent as my English ones. How lovely you look, Sybil. Have you missed me?"

He smiled as he raised her hand to his lips.

"Not particularly. And since you never wrote, I assumed you didn't miss me."

"Ah, but I did. You never were out of my thoughts. Nor was that pleasant idyll we enjoyed when Adam took off for India. And now he's coming home, the great hero! Isn't life full of surprises?"

"Yes, I just received a letter from the Queen. She's to make Adam a marquess."

"How very grand! So you're to be a marchioness. Fancy that. And someday the son and heir, Lord Henry, will be the second Marquess of Pontefract. By the way, might I see Lord Henry?"

"He's in the nursery, asleep. I'd rather not wake him."

"I hear he's a beautiful baby, with beautiful blond hair. Hair like mine, I'm told."

"Most babies have blond hair," she said, tensing.

"Perhaps. But since your hair is a lovely chestnut color and Adam's hair is black, if the boy grows up blond, it's going to look rather queer, isn't it? The fact is, dear Sybil, in your heart you're not quite sure who the father is. And if the father is me, it puts you in a rather . . . shall we say awkward? . . . position. While England's greatest hero is risking his life for the Empire in India, his wife back home is posting with considerable dexterity, as Hamlet puts it, to her adulterous sheets with her boyhood chum and neighbor. To wit: me. Oh no, it won't look good, Sybil. In fact, it will look quite bad. And think how embarrassed the Queen would be! The scandal might rock the Empire."

Sybil was rubbing her hands tensely. "All the years I've known you," she whispered, "I thought at *least* you were a gentleman. What a fool I was."

Edgar laughed as he stuck his hands in his pockets. "Yes, my dear, you were a fool. I'm too poor to be a gentleman. As the younger son of an impoverished country gentleman, I've had to live on my wits and charm all these years. But suddenly I think I'm sensing a definite sea change in my fortunes."

Her eyes narrowed. "What do you mean?"

"I'll drop by my bills in the morning. What terrible nuisances bills are, and tradesmen do have this tedious *idée fixe* about being paid. But you'll pay them for me, won't you, my darling? How kind and thoughtful of you. I've always believed you were a generous woman, but then you have so much to be generous with, don't you? I mean, you *are* one of the richest women in England. I think a settlement of twenty thousand pounds ought to make me feel comfortable. And then, you'll invest an additional fifty thousand pounds in the Funds for me—"

"You blackmailer!"

"Such an ugly word. But consider the alternatives."

"I won't pay it. Adam would find out—"

He grabbed her wrist, hard. "You *will* pay it," he whispered. "Or by God, I'll tell every newspaper in England that the beautiful Lady Pontefract is nothing but a whore!"

"I let you make love to me only because Adam had hurt me so. . . ."

"You seemed to enjoy it at the time."

"But I love Adam."

"You have an odd way of showing it."

"Let go my wrist!"

"The money. Seventy thousand pounds. It's nothing to your precious Adam, who's a millionaire many times over, but it will change *my* life. Are you going to get it?"

She was almost sobbing. "Yes," she whispered. "Now please, let me go."

Edgar released her.

"I thought you'd be reasonable," he said. "I'm going to London tomorrow and will be staying at my club. I'll expect twenty thousand pounds by next week and the rest by the end of the year. Good-bye, Sybil. It's been so delightful seeing you again."

Bowing, he walked out of the room.

Sybil put her hands to her face. Blackmail!

And the worst part was it had been her fault.

The square black cloth was placed on the white wig of Mr. Justice Molyneux. The crowded courtroom at the Old Bailey fell silent as the people who had thronged the room during the week-long trial now waited for the dreaded words that would be the trial's culmination.

"Elizabeth Desmond Cavanagh," intoned the judge, "you have been found guilty of the crime of murder. It is the judgment of this court that you be taken to a place of execution where you will be hanged until dead. And may the Lord have mercy on your soul."

"Lizzie!" sobbed Minna Desmond, her younger sister who had come to London to take care of Baby Amanda during the trial. Now she fainted. Lizzie, almost in a daze, was led by the two stern matrons down a concealed stair to the cold stone cells below the court. Death. The end of time. She had expected it, but its reality was numbing.

Oh, Adam, she thought. I'll never see you again.

Adam watched as the three English soldiers lashed the Indian to the mouth of the cannon, the small of his back against the muzzle.

"For the Hindu, this is the most horrible of all ways to die," said Bentley Brent, who was standing next to Adam smoking a cigarette. They were in a field outside the town of Arrah, which had been besieged by the mutineers in late July and then relieved by Major Vincent Eyre. Eyre was now punishing twenty of the mutinous *sepoys* by blowing them from the mouths of twenty cannon. "As you can see, our men are smearing blood and fat on their bodies. The blood is their victims'—English blood—and the fat is beef fat. Thus, they are defiled, they lose their caste and the poor brutes will never make Hindu heaven. It's part of their religion, you know."

"It's disgusting," said Adam. "Why can't they just hang them?"

"Too easy, my boy. After what they've seen at Cawnpore, our lads are out for blood. Revenge, they say. I've heard men say—perfectly normal, religious men—that they'd like to hang every nigger in India."

"But you don't approve of that, do you?" Adam asked.

Bentley inhaled, then blew out the smoke. It was fiercely hot, and both men protected their heads from the blazing sun with pith helmets.

"No," he finally said, "I don't approve. I think the mutineers who committed atrocities must be punished, but if we English are to have any future in India, we have to make some sort of accommodation with the natives. Ah, they're about to fire the guns. Better put a handkerchief over your nose. In a few minutes it's going to stink here like the very devil."

He pulled out a handkerchief, as did Adam. There were about fifty English officers and men gathered on the flat field which had formerly been used by the English as a polo ground. A smaller crowd of natives lingered on the edge of the English, watching in sullen silence. The twenty cannon were in a line, facing south, with the twenty near-naked *sepoys* tied to the muzzles, their bodies sweating in the sun.

"God knows," Adam muttered, "what they must be thinking."

Major Eyre, who was an artillery officer, raised his saber, then lowered it swiftly. The cannoneers touched their flames to the firing holes and the twenty guns belched. Adam, wincing, saw the bodies blown apart, heads and limbs flying everywhere, the Indian torsos blasting into bloody bits, spattering some of the onlookers.

And then silence. Smoke. And gathering vultures.

Adam, holding his kerchief over his nose, turned to go back to his horse. He had seen the atrocities the mutineers had inflicted on the English and was aware of the repulsive details of the massacres at Cawnpore and the horrors being suffered by the English at the siege of Lucknow, now in its eighth week. The English were saying the punishment must fit the crime. But Adam was beginning to wonder if the punishment weren't a crime in itself.

He mounted his horse to continue his journey to Calcutta. He had seen enough of India. It was time to go home. He had accomplished his purposes: he had returned the diamond and avenged his grandfather's murder.

The only thing left unresolved was his attitude toward the Indian blood in his veins. About that, he was still confused. And at the height of the hysteria over the massacres at Cawnpore and Delhi, an Englishman faced ostracism if he admitted he had mixed blood.

"I'm a father?" he said four days later in Sir Carlton McNair's mansion in Calcutta. Lady Agatha and Emily were with him in the drawing room.

"Yes," Lady Agatha said. "A son was born to you on the twenty-third of July, making him a Leo—such a promising sign, I believe. The notice was in the London *Times*, which just arrived a few days ago. Your dear wife, Lady Pontefract, has named him Henry Algernon Marmaduke, after her father."

"Henry?" Adam took the paper and read the announcement Lady Agatha had circled. "Henry's not a bad name, though I detest 'Algernon.' However, my wife obviously didn't feel it necessary to consult me."

"But of course, you are here in India, and she had no address for you."

"Yes, I suppose. A son!" A smile came over his face, which was beginning to lighten as Lakshmi's dye wore off. He had shaved his beard and was beginning to look more English by the day. He had even changed out of his Indian clothes into Western mufti he had bought in Benares. "A son and heir. This calls for a celebration . . ."

He stopped. Emily, bursting into tears, had turned and run out of the room. Adam looked at her mother. "Was it something I said?"

Lady Agatha smiled and patted his arm. "Dear Lord Pontefract, I must apologize for Emily. She's behaving like a lovesick schoolgirl, which I suppose describes her rather aptly. The fact is, she is quite smitten by you. Of course, when I realized she had run off with you, I feared the worst. But with her safe return and her assurances that you behaved like a true gentleman . . . well, all is forgiven now, and we here in India owe you so much—so *very* much. I can't tell you what an honor it is for us to have you under our roof, if only for a few days. But Emily . . ." She sighed. "Alas, I fear her emotions have betrayed her breeding. The very mention of your wife sends her into fits of pouting. I have spoken to her several times, but it does no good." Again she sighed. Then she brightened. "Lord Canning is giving a ball in your honor at Government House tomorrow night, and this time you can hardly refuse. I suppose this is indelicate of me, but if you could see your way to having a dance with Emily, I think it would mean so *very* much to her."

Adam smiled. "Emily is the sweetest girl in the world," he said. "Not only will I ask her to dance, I would be honored if she'd be my escort."

"Oh! But milord, you are a married man!"

"And, as you pointed out, I am in India and my wife is in England. There surely can be no harm in it."

Lady Agatha hesitated. "Yes, I suppose you're right," she said. "I'll go tell the child. She'll be thrilled—thrilled!" She hurried off.

A son, Adam mused. He remembered his wedding night. Sybil had surprised him: the cool, elegant Gainsborough had turned out to have a Rubenesque enjoyment of the flesh after all. The marriage had started out promisingly, and then he had soured everything by speaking Lizzie's name in his sleep. He couldn't blame Sybil for being hurt. And now that she had given him an heir, his feelings for her took on new warmth. Now he was more eager than ever to get home.

However, he couldn't help wondering what had happened to Lizzie.

"This is the happiest evening of my life," said Emily the next night. Then she added wistfully, "And it's also the saddest."

She and Adam were standing alone in the drawing room

of Government House, a huge white pile of a building copied from Robert Adam's design for Kedleston Hall. The building, with its central portico and dome, was imposing. Set in a six-acre park in Calcutta, it represented British power in India. Emily, looking lovely in a pale turquoise dress, her red hair set in fashionable thick curls that brushed her bare shoulders, ran a gloved finger over one of the tables in the room while, above her, the huge punkahs, decorated with white silk ruffles, slowly swayed.

"How can anyone as young and pretty as you be sad?" Adam asked.

"Surely you must have guessed. Tomorrow you go back to England." She looked at him. "Why did you kiss me that night in Lucknow?"

"Because I wanted to. I hope you weren't offended?"

"Far from it." She hesitated. "Mother has scolded me for throwing myself at you, and I suppose she's right: I have. But since I've gone this far, I might as well go all the way. Do you love me, Adam?"

He looked surprised. "I like you," he said.

"That's not the same thing. I want a grand passion out of life! I want a love that will make what they write in novels seem pale and feeble by comparison. I have that feeling for you, Adam: I don't have enough time to be demure about it. I love you with all my heart."

"You'd be better off finding someone more available, Emily. When it comes to romance, I'm not very lucky."

She straightened slightly. "I saved your life in Uttar Pradesh," she said softly. "And I told you I'd never let you forget it. Well, I shan't. You owe me, Adam Thorne. And someday I'm going to make you love me the way I love you."

"You make that sound almost a threat."

"Perhaps it is."

They looked at each other a moment, almost like sparring partners. Then Lord Canning, their host, came into the room.

"Ah, here you are, Adam," said the Governor-General. "I have just received a dispatch from Her Majesty, the

Queen. When you return to England, it will give her the greatest pleasure to elevate you to the rank of marquess. May I offer my congratulations?" He extended his hand. Adam shook it, rather dazed.

He had barely become used to being an earl.

CHAPTER 14

My dear Sybil," said Sidonia, Lady Rockfern, as she looked around the drawing room of Pontefract House in London, "you have done a superb job. My poor, late father hadn't set foot in this house for years, and the last time I was here, it almost broke my heart to see how the place had deteriorated. But you have restored it so beautifully! And with such perfect taste. I'm sure Adam will be pleased."

"He may not be pleased at what it cost," Sybil said, "but I thought he would want it done. And now that he's coming home so much in the public eye, I think it's even more important that we have a London home we can be proud of."

Sidonia smiled as she patted Sybil's arm. "How well everything has turned out," she said. "And how pleased I am that you and Adam are wed. Such a perfectly matched pair. And how fortunate he didn't marry . . ." she lowered her voice and frowned ". . . that other one."

"I have to confess, Aunt Sidonia, it's been painful for me these past weeks having to read all the publicity of Mrs. Cavanagh's trial. I fear all of London must be snickering about me. To think that my beloved husband is the father of that wicked woman's child! It is such a terrible embarrassment."

"There, there, Sybil: I understand your sensitive feelings, but we women must face the facts. It is sad but true that men can get away with conduct that would banish a woman from polite society forever." Sybil, thinking of Edgar, felt a twinge of guilt and apprehension. "But happily for all of us, Mrs. Cavanagh will cease to be a problem as of tomorrow at dawn."

"Yes. As a Christian, I feel sorry for her, and I will say a prayer for her soul. But I would be a hypocrite if I didn't admit to a certain relief that the law is—how shall I put it?—eliminating a serious domestic problem for me."

"Indeed." Sidonia checked her lapel watch. "We must be on our way. Adam's ship will dock in two hours, and we mustn't be late. Such an honor to have the Prince Consort himself there! It is a splendid day for our family—splendid." Again, she lowered her voice. "A word of advice, my dear. I assume Adam doesn't know about Mrs. Cavanagh. Perhaps it would be wise if we didn't mention her until tomorrow. We know Adam is impetuous. And to be perfectly candid, although the wretched woman richly deserves her fate, hanging is an unpleasant subject. It might spoil the sweetness of Adam's moment of triumph."

Sybil frowned. "No, Aunt Sidonia. I thought of that, but I believe it would be wrong. I realize the depth of Adam's attachment to the woman—believe me, it is a burden I have carried for over a year now. But if I didn't tell him, I think he would hold it against me. Let him say good-bye to Mrs. Cavanagh if he wants. After all, I have won, and it is only fair for me to be generous in victory."

"You are right. Ah, dear Sybil, what a noble character you have. Come, we mustn't dawdle any longer. To be late today, of all days, would be inexpressibly vulgar."

The London Adam was returning to in the fall of 1857 was the *caput mundi*, the head of the world, as Rome had been two thousand years before. Despite the Victorians' prudish attitude toward sex (which the Queen euphemized as the "shadow side" of marriage, although she managed to produce nine children and had a keen appreciation of the male sex), the population of England had tripled in the past century and London then had almost five million souls, making it the largest metropolis the world had ever seen. It was the greatest port in the world, and although its slums, like Wapping, appalled foreigners with their near naked, starving homeless steeped in vice and squalor, in the vaults of the Bank of England lay gold bars worth the staggering sum of eleven billion pounds. The British Empire, the biggest in the world, was growing so fast, its colonies multiplying so rapidly, that even Lord Palmerston, the Prime Minister, "had to keep looking the damned places up on the map." And even though the average Englishman obtained few practical benefits from the Empire—and considerable hardships if one were in the Army or Navy with their severe discipline, bad pay, primitive medical care and the risk of death in battle—still the Empire thrilled the English, filled them with jingoistic pride, and they kept sending their sons out to die for it.

The accounts of the Indian Mutiny that had come back to England—especially the massacre of women and children at Cawnpore at the hands of Nana Sahib, exaggerated as the accounts became in the retellings with the gratuitous additions of numerous rapes of Englishwomen by the Indians, which had so shocked the Queen—had fired the public imagination. Never before had England become so bloodthirsty. And in Adam, the dashing young nobleman who had managed to kill the "Fiend," as Nana Sahib had come to be known, the English had the perfect hero.

When his steamship tied up at the India Dock on a blustery autumn day, Adam was surprised to see a crowd of over a thousand on the dock, cheering wildly and waving dozens of Union Jacks while an army band played "Rule, Britannia!" A huge banner had been stretched across one of the warehouses proclaiming: "Welcome Home and God Bless You, Lord Pontefract!" A number of carriages were lined up at the wharf. Standing beside one, bearing the royal coat of arms on its door, was a tall man in a black fur-lined coat and tall silk hat, whom Adam recognized as Prince Albert, the Queen's thirty-eight-year-old German husband. The Prince Consort was surrounded by dignitaries, including a number of generals in their brilliant red uniforms. Adam also saw his Aunt Sidonia and, between her and the Prince Consort, Sybil, looking beautiful in a lynx coat and hat.

"Did you see who's here? It's the bloody Prince Consort!" said Bentley Brent, coming up to join Adam at the rail. Bentley had been brought home on special leave to be presented the Victoria Cross by the Queen herself, an honor Adam wasn't eligible for since he wasn't in the army.

"Yes, I recognize him. What does one call him if we're presented?"

" 'Sir.' And the Queen is 'Ma'am.' Who's that stunner next to the Prince?"

"My wife."

"Well, you're to be congratulated."

The band segued to "Soldiers of the Queen" as the gangway was put in place. Captain Norcross, the ship's commanding officer, accompanied Adam and Bentley down the gangway to the dock, where they were met by Prince Albert.

"We are so very proud of you both," said the Prince Consort in his thick German accent. "A capital job! Capital!"

Both men bowed, then shook hands with the Prince. Then Adam hurried to Sybil, put his arms around her and kissed her.

"My darling Adam," she said. "How very proud I am of you!"

She meant it. If only, she thought, it weren't for Edgar, this would be the happiest moment of my life.

"Remember Cawnpore!" yelled the crowd. "Remember Cawnpore!"

An hour later, their carriage pulled into Pontefract Square, the lovely Georgian square Adam's grandfather had built thirty years before when the West End of London was being developed by the Grosvenor and Cadogan families, as well as builder Thomas Cubitt. It was early evening, and a top-hatted lamplighter was turning on the gas lamps, revealing the first flakes of a snowfall. The garden in the center of the square was small, like so many in London, but it gave the square a focus as well as a good place for nannies to stroll their babies. *My* baby is strolled there, Adam thought as the carriage pulled up in front of a cream-colored mansion that dominated one corner of the square. Four stories high, with a pedimented cornice and a classical frieze around the house above the first floor, Pontefract House had dignity and style. Adam had spent only one night there before sailing to India the previous year, so seeing this part of his splendid inheritance the second time was almost as new an experience as the first. Leaving the carriage, Adam accompanied Sybil through the wrought-iron gate up a short walk to the pillared portico. "The house was in a shocking state," Sybil said. "I had workmen in. It took almost a year, and I'm afraid a considerable amount of money."

"I remember how run-down the house was. I'm glad you did the work, particularly now, with Henry. I'm very eager to see him."

"I don't think you'll be disappointed," Sybil said with a smile. But she was thinking, dear God! The blond hair! Edgar . . .

The door was opened by Mr. Ridley, the balding butler Sybil had hired.

"This is Mr. Ridley," she said as she went inside. "I had to engage an entire staff."

"Welcome home, milord," said the butler.

"Thank you, Mr. Ridley."

Footmen took their coats. Then Sybil led him up the stair to the second floor where, at the end of the hall, she opened the door to the nursery.

"Mrs. Leeds, this is my husband, Lord Pontefract," Sybil said. "Mrs. Leeds is the nanny. And here is your son."

Adam came up to the cradle, which swung between two iron stands and was wrapped in blue bunting. He looked down at the chubby baby, who was asleep.

"May I?" he asked, pointing.

"Of course."

Adam gently lifted the baby out of the cradle and held it to his shoulder.

"Waa! Waa!"

"I woke him up." Adam smiled. "I'm sorry, Henry. Hello, young fellow. I'm your papa. Are you glad to see me?"

"Waa! Waa!"

Adam kissed him, then put him back in the cradle.

"He's wonderful," he said as he rejoined Sybil. "And he's the spitting image of you."

"It's too early to tell," Sybil said, diplomatically, praying that Henry Algernon Marmaduke de Vere, the future Marquess of Pontefract, wouldn't grow up looking like Edgar Musgrave.

When they returned to the hall, Sybil put her hand on her husband's arm.

"Adam, I have unpleasant news," she said, "which I wouldn't tell you except that . . . well, her time is very short. It's about your friend, Lizzie Desmond."

Adam's eyes widened as he heard the news.

Note dispatched by courier from Buckingham Palace to No. 10 Downing Street:

> To: Lord Palmerston
> From: H.M. the Queen
>
> 20 November 1857
>
> An extraordinary thing happened this evening. As she was dining *en famille*, the Queen was advised that Ld. Pontefract was at the Palace begging for an interview, saying it was a matter of life and death. Under the circumstances, he could hardly be refused, and the Queen withdrew to the Bow Room, where young Ld. Pontefract was soon admitted. He was in a state of extreme agitation and, after brief formalities, begged the queen to stay the execution of Mrs. Cavanagh. He pleaded with the Queen to allow him time to prove her innocence, saying he was certain something had gone wrong at her trial for he knew her soul and would swear she was incapable of such a vile crime as murder. Oh, the Queen has never seen such ardor! She was quite taken off her feet! Ld. Pontefract, whose physical presence is so splendid, moved the Queen almost to tears by his protestations of Mrs. Cavanagh's innocence. Surely we must give this brave man, to whom England owes so much, the chance he requests, for if there is even

a shadow of a doubt about Mrs. Cavanagh's guilt, the honour of English Law demands the doubt be removed before the supreme penalty is exacted. Therefore, the Queen has instructed the Home Secretary to reschedule Mrs. Cavanagh's execution for the morning of Dec. 5th, which will give Ld. Pontefract two weeks to try to save her. Oh, if Ld. Palmerston could have seen and heard this young man's plea, I feel sure he would feel in his heart, as does the Queen in hers, that perhaps this is one of the rare instances where the Law has erred and Mrs. Cavanagh is, after all, innocent!

Signed,
V.R. (Victoria Regina)

"Lizzie, there's a man to see you," said the matron in the black dress. "Says his name is Adam Thorne."

Lizzie, who was sitting on her plank bed in her cell in the women's wing of Pentonville Prison, whispered, "Adam!"

"Dressed like a toff, he is. Come along now. You only have twenty minutes."

Lizzie stood up. The brick walls of the seven-foot-wide, thirteen-foot-long cell were whitewashed with lime. The single window, which consisted of fourteen small panes of glass, afforded dim illumination. A tin bucket was the toilet. Lizzie, who wore a plain, dark gray dress, came to the steel door and followed the matron out into the corridor. Adam. When the Governor of the prison located in the north London district of Islington had told her that morning that Queen Victoria had granted her a stay of execution, she had had the first faint glimmer of hope since her disastrous trial at the Old Bailey. And now Adam! She wanted to cry out with joy.

When she was brought into the visitors' room, Adam at first barely recognized her. She seemed so thin and fragile. She came to the grille that bisected the room and put her hands against it. There were tears in her eyes.

"Lizzie," he whispered, putting his hands on the grille

opposite hers. "My darling Lizzie. Your own true knight has come to save you."

She remembered the moors, the ruined Newfield Abbey, lying in the wildflowers with Adam, her knight. How long ago and far away that seemed now.

"Oh, Adam, I thought I'd never see you again . . ."

"Don't cry, my darling. Everything's going to be all right. And I've been to see Minna and Amanda. They're fine, too. Now, we haven't much time, so listen to me. I spoke to the Queen last night. She's granted you a stay of execution—"

"So it was *you* who arranged it?"

"Yes. I have two weeks to find out what went wrong at the trial. This morning I went to your solicitor, Sir Edmund Carter, and I read the transcript of the testimony. Sir Edmund told me that Stringer MacDuff was what swayed the jury, that your barrister couldn't get him to change his story on cross-examination, and of course he couldn't put you in the witness box. What did you think of MacDuff's testimony?"

She was wiping her eyes.

"He lied. My father attacked me. He was beating me with his whip, screaming at me . . . he threw me halfway across the room, and I was terrified he'd kill our baby. That was when I threw the lamp at him, but MacDuff didn't say that on the stand."

"He said your father came in the room and you threw the lamp at him, which set him on fire."

"I know! That's how he lied! He left out father's attacking me, and since he was the only witness and I couldn't testify, there was no way to break his story. So naturally, the jury convicted me."

"Do you have any idea why he did that?"

"Yes. Sir Edmund thinks someone had pressured MacDuff to change his story, or perhaps even paid him. He was terribly well-dressed at the trial—I mean, for a crofter."

"Who do you think might have paid him?"

"I've thought about it for weeks, needless to say, and there's only one person I can think of. He's an American, a Senator from Virginia. You see, when I was in America I was sending thousands of dollars to the Abolitionists in the North. Senator Whitney, who's the leader of the pro-slavery forces in the Senate, found out about it. He'd have a motive, because if I'm guilty of murder it discredits the Abolitionists. I'm almost certain it was Senator Whitney."

Slaves! thought Adam. Niggers in India, slaves in America . . . the Indian blood in his own veins, which was his still-guilty secret . . . He had enjoyed being a hero to the English, but having seen the Indians blown from the mouths of the cannons, having encountered the bloodthirsty howls for revenge from the English, his ambivalence about the English Raj had resurfaced. How curious that Lizzie had been involved in a similar fight in America, halfway around the world from India. And if anything, American slavery was far uglier than what the British were doing in the Subcontinent.

"I'll go to Yorkshire tomorrow and see MacDuff," he said. "I'll get the truth out of him. In any event, I'll get you out of here. I know you've gone through hell, but it's soon going to be over and we'll be together again."

"But your wife . . ."

"Don't worry about Sybil."

"Do you love her?"

The question was almost pathetic. Adam wasn't sure *what* his feelings about his wife were, although he thought it had been damned decent of her, under the circumstances, to tell him about Lizzie's plight. And of course, there was Henry. But Lizzie needed all the support he could give her now.

"I love *you*," he said. "There's never been anyone but you, and there never will be."

For the first time in weeks she smiled. "My own true knight," she whispered.

"Time's up!" barked the matron.

"You're going to Yorkshire?" Sybil exclaimed an hour later. Adam had just returned to Pontefract House. "But why?"

"There's reason to believe the chief witness against Lizzie perjured himself. I'm going to get the truth out of him."

He started up the great staircase two steps at a time. Sybil watched him, her anger rising. After all, she hadn't told him about Lizzie so he could *save* the woman! His first day back from India, and he had been gone almost the whole time. It was obvious—painfully so—that he was interested in Lizzie much more than her. She had put on her most seductive dress, a low-cut black velvet gown, and he hadn't given her so much as a glance, tearing into the house and up the stairs.

She waited till Mr. Ridley had gone to the servants' quarters; then she started up the stairs lined with family portraits and the masterpieces of art the de Veres had accumulated over the past century. Sybil was not a mercenary woman, but she enjoyed the fortune she had married into and had gone to great pains to make Pontefract House a splendid residence. Adam had hardly even noticed. The one thing he had said to her that morning was that he enjoyed the indoor plumbing she had installed. Bathrooms! She wanted love, and she was getting compliments on the new Thomas Thirkill's Improved Patented Water Closets. And the showers—an eighteenth-century invention that was catching on.

At the top of the stairs, she went down the hall. As was the common practice with the upper classes, she and Adam kept separate bedrooms. She had expected him to come to her room the night before, but when he got back from Buckingham Palace he told her he had a headache and went to his own room, locking himself in for the night. This after a year!

Reaching his door, she let herself in without knocking. Adam was in a robe, on his way to take a shower.

"How can you do this to me?" Sybil said quietly, closing the door. "How can you humiliate me further by becoming involved with this wretched woman again?"

"I'm not becoming 'involved.' I'm trying to save an innocent woman's life."

"How do you know she's innocent? She was convicted by an English jury. Besides, you could show a little consideration for me. You've been away for a year, and your first day home, I've barely seen you. And last night, I wanted you to come to my room so much, but you ran off to Buckingham Palace and came home with a headache! Really, Adam, I think I deserve better than that."

"I'm sorry, Sybil. I truly am. It's just that the news of Lizzie shocked me so—"

"That woman!" Sybil clenched her fists. "I thought I was through with hearing about her, and now she's back in my life, ruining my marriage again."

"Nothing's being ruined."

"Adam, let's keep pretense at a minimum. Don't you think I know what you want? You want to save her so you can go back to making love to her again. It's so galling to me, your wife, the mother of your child. It's so unfair. I do love you, but you make it so difficult for me!"

"Sybil, I'm sorry if you think I'm unfair. And I know it's been awkward for you because my involvement with Lizzie has become publicly known. But you must understand I intend to do everything in my power to save Lizzie—"

"Oh, I hate her name!" she cried out. "This vile woman, this slut . . . do you know what her sister told the press?"

"All I know is that Mrs. Belladon turned her in to the British minister in Washington, which is a vile thing to do to one's own flesh and blood."

"She had good reason. After all, her sister *did* murder her father!"

"That's a lie!" Adam shouted. "And I'll prove it's a lie!"

"Do you know what her sister said? That she had as a lover one of her nigger slaves! And this is the woman you wish to champion?"

A look of fury came over his face.

"Don't ever use that word in front of me," he said hoarsely.

"What word?" she gasped.

"Nigger. It's a word I hate."

"I don't understand you," she spat out. "But I'll tell you one thing, Adam Thorne: you're destroying this marriage, and turning a woman who loves you into a woman who is beginning to detest you." She went to the door and put her hand on the knob. "Tonight it will be *I* who will lock the bedroom door."

She went out into the hall, slamming the door behind her. Alone, Adam sank onto his bed and buried his face in his hands. He knew he was behaving like a brute, but his anxiety for Lizzie's life was frazzling his nerves. What if he *couldn't* shake Stringer MacDuff's story? He had less than two weeks, and the shadow of the gallows loomed larger over Lizzie every minute that ticked by.

CHAPTER 15

My son a hero! Capital, absolutely capital! Adam, my boy, I'm proud of you. Let's drink to your return to Thorne Manor."

Sir Percival Thorne, who hadn't shaved in several days, weaved across the filthy kitchen and almost collapsed on a bench at the food-littered table. Adam, who hadn't seen his father for a year, was shocked by his deterioration. Sir Percival had been a hard drinker for as long as Adam could remember, but he now realized he had become a drunk. He watched as his father's trembling hands uncorked a bottle of whiskey and filled three glasses. Then Adam looked at Jethro, the gray-bearded servant who had worked for his father ever since Adam was a boy.

"I read in the paper how thee disguised thyself as an Indian," said Jethro, who spoke with a broad Yorkshire accent. "That was clever, Adam. We're all proud of thee."

"My son killed that damned heathen, Nana Sa . . ." Sir Percival burped. "Nana Sahib. Come here, Adam. Have a drink. You too, Jethro."

The old servant put another log on the fire in the enormous stone hearth, then followed Adam to the table and picked up his glass.

"Lord Pontefract," hiccoughed Sir Percival as his son sat opposite him. "The lord of the manor . . . and what a manor, eh?" He laughed. "Well, well, life is strange. The de Veres . . . so haughty . . . always treated me like dirt, and now . . . the last laugh . . . the last . . ."

His eyes closed and he slowly fell forward onto the table.

"It's just past ten in the morning," Adam said with alarm. "When did he start drinking?"

"Start?" Jethro said. "He never stopped. The master's far gone, lad. Thee might as well face the fact Sir Percival may not last the winter."

"And he's not even fifty," Adam said, shaking his head. "What a pity. And what a waste. Well, let's get him to bed, Jethro."

"Ain't very often he gets *out* of bed, lad. He only did it for thee."

Adam picked his father up and carried him to the central hall, then up the stairs to his bedroom, which was not only predictably dirty, its floor strewn with empty bottles, but cold. It was snowing and Thorne Manor was icy. Adam remembered countless nights he had shivered through as a child. He leaned over and kissed his father's forehead. For all Sir Percival's weaknesses and faults, Adam loved him. And he knew Jethro was right: his father wasn't long for this cold world.

"Jethro, were there any Americans in the neighborhood this past year?" Adam asked five minutes later after he had returned to the kitchen."

"Americans?" said the old man, as if Adam had said "Hottentots." "Nay, lad, what American in his right mind would come to Yorkshire . . ." He frowned and hesitated. "Wait. There *was* an American. . . ."

"Yes? When?"

Jethro scratched his head.

"Aye, I heard about it . . . last summer, it was. There was a man who came to Wykeham Rise. He stayed at the Swan Inn, I think. Caused a bit of a stir, he did."

"Did he meet with Stringer MacDuff?"

"Ah, lad, that I don't know. Thou must ask at the Swan. Is it Lizzie Desmond thou'rt tryin' to save?"

"Yes, it's Lizzie."

"I never believed she murdered her pa, and not many folks around here do either. They say it was her sister what betrayed her."

"And they're right. Jethro, when was the last time my father paid you?"

The old man sighed. "Ah, lad, I don't take no money

from Sir Percival. He's been good to me many a long year. I pop in every day to make sure he's all right, and for that I wouldn't take his money."

Adam pulled his purse from his pocket. "Here's twenty guineas. I want you to hire someone to keep this house clean, and I want to find a nurse who'll take care of Father."

"There's Jane Carlton at Wykeham Rise. She's a good nurse, and a fine, honest girl."

"Then hire her. I had no idea Father had gotten so bad. He'll need care."

"Thou'rt a good son, Adam."

But not a very good husband, Adam thought as he remembered his row with Sybil. He went to a sagging walnut dresser at one side of the kitchen, opened a drawer and pulled out a small pistol which he stuck in the pocket of his coat.

That afternoon, two men galloped across the snowy moor toward the thatched cottage. One was Adam, the other a short, squinty man in a houndstooth cloak.

"Stringer MacDuff!" Adam yelled as he reined his horse in front of the cottage. MacDuff, who was coming out of his barn, looked in his direction as he pushed the door closed. "I want to talk to you!"

Adam and the other man dismounted and tethered their horses.

"Adam Thorne," said MacDuff as he came up, glancing curiously at the second man. "I mean, Lord Pontefract," he added, rather snidely. "And what would your lordship be wanting with me?"

"MacDuff, last June, on the fourteenth to be exact, an American named Roger Ward came to Wykeham Rise, renting a room at the Swan Inn."

"So?"

"On the fifteenth of June, you deposited one thousand pounds at the Yorkshire Bank and Trust Company on High Street."

MacDuff frowned. "How do you know that?" he said, softly.

"Let me introduce myself," said the second man. "I'm Inspector Sebastian Quaid of Scotland Yard. The manager of the bank showed me the record of the deposit."

MacDuff began to look nervous.

"Did the American give you the money?" Adam asked.

"That's none of your damned business."

"But it's Her Majesty's Government's business," said Inspector Quaid. "Roger Ward owns a plantation in Virginia. We believe Ward was sent to England by a cabal of Virginia slave owners to bribe you to change your testimony so Mrs. Cavanagh would be convicted, thus discrediting her and the Abolitionists. Thanks to Lord Pontefract's detective work. . . ."

MacDuff, who was wearing a heavy sheepskin coat, pulled a gun from his right pocket. "Get off my land," he said.

"It's not yours anymore," Adam said, pulling a deed from his pocket and holding it up in front of MacDuff's astonished eyes. "I bought this farm today from Mr. Gilpatrick. Now Stringer, you have two choices. You can cooperate with us and tell the truth to the authorities, in which case you'll be tried for perjury and go to jail for several years. At the end of which time, you could come back here and I'd give you a lifetime lease on this farm at less rent than you're paying now. Your other option is not to cooperate with us, in which case you'll go to jail anyway and I'll never let you set foot on this farm again. Think about it." He returned the deed to his pocket. "We'll give you two minutes."

MacDuff's gun was shaking. For almost a minute he held it aimed at Adam's heart. Then he lowered it.

"I'll cooperate," he said.

Letter from Queen Victoria to her Prime Minister:

Buckingham Palace
25 November 1857

It has given the Queen the *greatest* pleasure to grant a crown pardon to Mrs. Cavanagh, who was released from prison today. Again, that most admirable Ld. Pontefract has proved himself so clever, brave and resourceful, and the Queen is filled with admiration for him. And yet, a cloud lies over her happiness because she knows that this young man of so many accomplishments lacks the one quality that would make him a true Christian hero: to wit, fidelity to his wife.

The Queen has received Ld. Pontefract at the palace this afternoon where, in a private ceremony, she elevated him to the rank of Marquess in the English peerage, with the courtesy title of Earl of Castleford for his heir. Afterward, the Queen spoke to him briefly about his personal interest in Mrs. Cavanagh. The Queen spoke, she feels, *eloquently* on the joys of married life and the vast importance of the family and home. The Queen is all too keenly aware that not every home in her realm is a happy and moral one—indeed, the memory of her own wicked uncles is all too vividly alive in her breast—but she tried to convince young Ld. Pontefract that his own true happiness is to be found in the arms of his wife and wife *alone*. The fact that Lady Pontefract declined to attend the ceremony on grounds of ill health suggests to the Queen that that poor woman resents *strongly* her husband's championing of Mrs. Cavanagh, and she pointed this out to Ld. Pontefract in the most delicate terms she could find. Ld. Pontefract vowed that he would do his very best to be a model husband, and the Queen hopes and prays that he is sincere in his determination. The Queen reminded him that the example he sets to other Englishmen could be so very important in establishing a high moral tone for the country and the Empire and, though Ld. Pontefract said, with becoming modesty, that the Queen was perhaps exaggerating his influence, he repeated that he would try to live up to her expectations. Oh, how the Queen hopes he succeeds! For Ld. Pontefract is so *very* dashing, and the Queen is so *very* proud to be his sovereign that she would like nothing better than that Ld. Pontefract become as *perfect* a husband, enjoying the sweet pleasures of domestic bliss, as the Queen's own flawless treasure, Prince Albert.

Signed,
V.R. (Victoria Regina)

"Good morning, Mr. Ridley," said Sidonia, Lady Rockfern, as the butler opened the front door of Pontefract House. "Is my nephew at home?"

"Yes, milady. He's in his study."

"Pray ask him to attend me in the drawing room."

"Yes, milady."

She gave her fur wrap and bonnet to a footman, then went into the drawing room. She was wearing a sable-colored dress with white lace ribbons in her gray hair, heavily curled at the sides of her head. Sidonia could not get over the miracles that Sybil had wrought in the town house, a house Sidonia loved especially because she had grown up in it. Not only had Sybil's army of workmen installed all the modern conveniences—bathrooms, gas lighting, and an up-to-date kitchen—but she had lovingly restored the elaborate plasterwork, carvings, and moldings. The drawing room, which had a magnificent neoclassical plaster ceiling, Sybil had had painted a pale lilac, with the plaster swags, surrounds and cornucopias that festooned the walls painted white. Over the classic marble mantel hung a huge Romney portrait of Adam's grandmother, looking bewitching against a late-eighteenth-century landscape (portraits of Adam's Brahmin great-grandmother were conspicuously absent). The magnificent Chippendale sofa Sidonia was seated on was upholstered in pale yellow striped silk.

"Aunt Sidonia!" Adam exclaimed, coming into the room and crossing to kiss her. "How good to see you. You look in the best of health."

"As you know, I've had a wretched cold," she said, "which is why I couldn't receive you when you paid a call last week. Happily, that seems to have gone at last."

"And how is Lady Hillsdale?"

"Quite well, except for touches of rheumatism. Now,

my nephew, I have been so proud of you and the wonderful things you accomplished in India. Dear Father's terrible murder has been avenged at last. But I received a letter from Sybil yesterday that has caused me grave concern. All is not well with your marriage, Adam, and I fear much of it is your fault."

"I hope you're not going to lecture me, as the Queen did?"

"If the Queen lectured you, then I say more power to her. You need lecturing, Adam. You need it desperately."

He sighed and sank into a sofa. "Aunt Sidonia, I'm not going to try to evade responsibility. I know much of this is my fault, but I never loved Sybil—"

"Love?" interrupted his aunt sternly. "What about honor? What about duty to the family? What about your son? You are an important man now. All England looks up to you, and what is the example you set for them? This tawdry love nest in St. John's Wood—"

"You know about that?" he asked, surprised.

"Indeed I do. Sybil knows about it, and she wrote me the disturbing news from Yorkshire."

"But how does she know?"

"She hired a private detective to find out where you spend your long, sinful afternoons. For shame, Nephew! After bringing such glory to our family, to bring it such ignominy."

He buried his face in his hands a moment. Then he looked up in agony. "It's not shameful," he whispered. "I love Lizzie, and I love little Amanda. They can't go back to America: I have to help them."

"Help them if you wish: that's one thing. But you don't have to live with them. Oh Adam, don't think I'm being too harsh with you. I know what goes on—you're certainly not the only nobleman with a mistress in St. John's Wood. I know about Lord Hartington—it's the talk of London, he with that wicked creature they call Skittles. But you're different. You're England's hero. You must set an example."

"But what can I do? They need me! Senator Whitney almost got Lizzie hanged in London. If she goes back to

Virginia, who knows what he might try? And I need them."

"If nothing else, get her out of London. You can't have two families in one town. It's ostentatious."

Adam laughed, got out of his seat and hurried across the room to hug his aunt.

"Of course, that's it. You've given me a wonderful idea. Thank you, Aunt!"

She frowned. "I detect no indications of moral reform in you, Nephew."

"I'll get them out of town. That should make everyone happy."

"I doubt it will make Sybil happy." She stood up, looking at him sternly. "You don't seem to understand, Adam. Sybil loves you. She is a good wife to you, and mother to your son."

Adam sighed. "I admit it, Aunt. I've behaved abominably to Sybil."

"Please try to rectify your behavior in the future. Sybil is a woman of the highest moral character, and deserves the respect and love of her husband. Now I must go. Lady Hillsdale and I are attending a meeting of the Missionary Society for the Improvement of Morals in Heathen Lands. The meeting promises to be stimulating, though in light of your conduct, I believe some of our missionaries might find equally stimulating challenges closer to home."

Giving Adam a reproving look, she headed for the door of the drawing room under full sail.

"Oh Lizzie, Lizzie," he said that night as he kissed her, "they're all trying so hard to keep us apart. But they can't."

They were in bed on the second floor of the brick house in the London suburb of St. John's Wood that Adam had rented for Lizzie, their daughter and the nanny who had replaced Minna after Lizzie's release from prison. Now Lizzie sat up, holding the sheet over her naked breasts.

"I know," she sighed. "I feel so weak and wicked, and yet . . ." She looked at him, tears in her eyes. "And yet I love you more than life itself. If it weren't for you, they'd have hanged me. But still, your aunt is right."

He sat up and kissed her shoulder. "She's right for anyone but us, my darling. We're special. In my eyes, you're my wife, and I don't give a damn what other people say."

"But you must."

"Don't *you* lecture me. At any rate, I've given it a great deal of thought, and I think I have the answer. The best plan is to get you and Amanda out of London. I own a villa in Scotland—it's on the coast of the Irish Sea, just south of Ayr. I checked with my London agent today, and the house is empty and furnished. He says the view of the sea is beautiful. Why don't you and Amanda and Mrs. Parker go up there, and I can come to be with you . . . well, perhaps half the time, perhaps more. We could make up names and pretend I'm your husband. I fear the rest of the time I'd have to be with Sybil to keep up appearances, and of course I have my son to consider. But this way I could be with you and Amanda too. What do you think of that?"

"A double life," she mused.

"As they say, half a loaf . . ."

"Oh Adam, don't give me clichés. This is too important a decision." She got out of bed and put on a peignoir. "Of course, I still own Elvira Plantation in Virginia . . ."

"You can't go back there. We discussed it. It's far too dangerous."

"You're right, but . . ." She thought a moment. Then her face lit up. "This way there's nothing to stop me from freeing all my slaves. Oh Adam, maybe it would work out for the best. I could have Billie DeVries manumit all my bondspeople, which might be the strongest blow I could strike against Senator Whitney and his gang of bloodthirsty slave owners." She was smiling as she came back to the bed. "Let's do it. And we'd be together." She hugged him. "Oh yes, dearest Adam: I'll be your half-wife."

"You have all my heart," he said, kissing her. "And that's what's important."

"And perhaps someday . . ."

"Perhaps we'll get lucky and Sybil will die."

"Oh Adam, don't say that."

"Why not?" For a moment his face became murderous.

"Meanwhile," he added, "I have a few things to discuss with my wife. She's gone to Pontefract Hall—why, I'm not sure, though I think she's up to something. Anyway, I'll be leaving for there in the morning."

Adam was met at the train station in York by his chief coachman, Albert, who then proceeded to drive him the two hours to Pontefract Hall. It was another cold, blustery day, but Adam still felt a surge of warmth as he approached his ancestral seat. How much has happened since I first saw it last year with Aunt Sidonia, he thought. But the vast, sprawling pile still excited him. He was not yet quite used to the fact that this magnificent house was actually his.

Mr. Hawkins, the butler, and six footmen were lined up by the front entrance, as was the custom when the lord of the manor arrived. As Adam climbed down, Mr. Hawkins said, "Welcome home, milord."

"Thank you, Mr. Hawkins. Kindly tell Lady Pontefract I would like to see her in the library immediately."

He went into the house, removing his hat and cloak and giving them to yet another footman. Then he went with what the young footman thought of as "angry strides" across the entrance hall, his boots clicking on the marble floor, to the paneled library at the rear of the house. There he went to a window and looked out, waiting impatiently for his wife. When she came into the room, she was wearing her green velvet riding outfit, a smart black hat on her head, a riding crop under her arm.

"You wished to see me?" she said in a cool tone.

He turned on her. "You're damned right I do," he said.

"I see no reason why you should speak to me like a common farmhand."

"Maybe I am a common farmhand, but at least I'm an honest one—which is more than I can say about you, Sybil."

"What are you talking about? And why are you in such a fury?"

"The other day, I spent several hours going over the estate accounts with Mr. Lowery, my London agent. He told me that shortly before I returned from India, you had withdrawn seventy thousand pounds from the Funds. Might I ask why you withdrew such an enormous sum of money, and what you did with it?"

Sybil hesitated, becoming nervous. "Redoing Pontefract House was expensive. In case you're not aware, plumbers and carpenters don't come cheap."

"You're lying! Mr. Lowery showed me the bills for that: he paid them. Now tell me the truth, dammit!"

"Don't shout at me! The servants will hear."

"Let them hear, I don't care. I want the truth, Sybil."

"I . . . I had some debts."

"What kind of debts? Seventy thousand pounds is more than most people make in a lifetime."

She turned away. "Don't bully me."

He hurried across the room to her, grabbed her arm and turned her around. "What kind of debts?" he repeated, biting off each syllable.

"What do you care?" she said, bursting into tears. "You don't love me. All you care about is that awful Lizzie woman. . . . Why begrudge me because I ran up some debts?"

"What does Lizzie have to do with it?"

"She has *everything* to do with it," Sybil said, angrily pushing his hands off her. "Why do you think I turned to Edgar when you left for India? Because you had hurt me so deeply, because I knew you didn't love me."

"Edgar?" he said, softly. "Who's Edgar?"

"Edgar Musgrave. I've known him all my life, and I used to be quite fond of him until . . . well, until I found out what kind of a blackguard he is."

Adam looked confused. "You mean, you and this . . . this Edgar had an affair?"

"I certainly hope you're not going to preach a sermon on marital fidelity?"

"But what does this have to do with the seventy thousand pounds?"

"He's blackmailing me," she burst out. "He threatened to tell everyone in London. Edgar has no money, but he's well-connected socially. He could have ruined you and me . . . and most importantly, Henry. So I paid him off."

"Seventy thousand pounds?"

"Seventy thousand pounds. I didn't want to, obviously, but you were coming home the great hero and there had been so much odious publicity with Mrs. Cavanagh." She shrugged. "I paid him to keep his mouth shut. I'm not saying I'm blameless in this matter—I'm hardly that. But before you accuse me of anything, Adam, consider the reason why I let him make love to me. And the reason is your precious Lizzie. Last week—and I still don't understand why one word could make you so furious—I told you I was coming to hate you. I don't want to hate you, Adam. I want to love you. But in your heart you're married to Lizzie Cavanagh, and don't try to deny it. So where does that leave me? I made love to Edgar. At least he paid attention to me."

Adam looked into her green eyes a long while. Then he said, "At least we're finally being honest with each other."

"Yes, at least that. Neither of us turns out to be exactly a paragon, do we?"

"Far from it. But in a way, I'm glad this has happened." He hesitated. "I'm not going to blame you, Sybil. As you pointed out, I'm hardly the one for sermons. But you've been honest with me. I think it's time I be honest with you. If we have even a prayer of making this marriage work, I think you must know the family secret. Wait here. I'll be back in five minutes."

He went out of the room, leaving Sybil totally confused. When he returned, he was holding a box painted with Indian characters. He opened it and pulled out the miniature of Kamala Shah, which he handed to her. Sybil looked at it.

"She's lovely," she said. "Who is she?"

"My great-grandmother."

Sybil stared at him.

"That's right," Adam said. "The great Lord Pontefract, the hero of Cawnpore, the murderer of Nana Sahib, is part wog. I'm a chi-chi, which is what they call half-breeds in India."

"So that's why you were so furious at me when I said 'nigger,' " she whispered.

"Yes."

"Does it bother you?"

"It has in the past. But now I'm beginning to think it really doesn't matter to me so much. However, you're my wife and the mother of my son. I think it's important for you to know because someday we'll have to tell Henry that there's Indian blood in his veins. I can only hope that it won't bother him, either. But I suppose the important thing right now is: does it bother you?"

She handed the picture back to him, aware she had a new weapon. "And what about Mrs. Cavanagh?" she asked.

"You haven't answered my question."

"You haven't answered mine. I'm going up to my bedroom."

She smiled suggestively and walked out of the room.

An hour later, Adam knocked on Sybil's bedroom door.

"Come in."

He opened the door. Sybil had created for herself an extremely feminine bedroom. The walls and curtains were all in lavender and white, and there was a big four-poster *lit à la polonaise*, or bed in the Polish style, which had a canopy of great folds of lavender silk over it. She was sitting at her dresser putting some gold rings on her fingers. She had changed into a pale blue tea gown that made her look softly beautiful. She turned to look at her husband.

"May we declare a truce?" he said, closing the door. He crossed the room to stand beside her. "You're right: I've destroyed our marriage because of Lizzie, and I've been unfair to you. Now it turns out you've been unfair to me. But we're supposed to be civilized people. I can't believe we can't work out some solution that will make us all *reasonably* content."

"Us 'all'?" she said. "That sounds as if you're including Mrs. Cavanagh. She's nonnegotiable."

"Sybil, I'm sending Lizzie and Amanda to Scotland. They'll be away from London, and there'll be no more gossip or scandal. I swear I'll do my best to make you happy. I swear I'll be the best father in England to Henry. I'm so happy and proud to be his father, and I owe so much to you for giving him to me. All I ask is that I be able to spend a few days each month with Lizzie—"

"No!"

"Please be reasonable. Amanda's my daughter. All right, I was wrong to have fallen in love with Lizzie, I was wrong to have fathered Amanda, but it's happened! It can't be changed. God knows, it happens all the time, it's happened before and will happen again. But there's no reason why we can't adjust to the situation."

"In other words, you want two families?"

"I suppose . . . yes."

She turned to the mirror, looking at her reflection. Tears were in her eyes. He put his hand on the back of her neck and rubbed it tenderly.

"Please," he whispered. "If it's true you love me, then I'll come to love you. I already do in a way, because you gave me Henry."

Slowly she reached up and put her hand on his wrist.

"Oh Adam," she said, "all I *really* want is for you to love me. If only it could come true."

He reached down, put his hands under her arms and pulled her to her feet. Then he put his arms around her and pulled her into his strong, hard body. He kissed her passionately.

"And what," he whispered, "about my Indian blood?"

She smiled slightly. "I've always been passionately fond of curry."

He picked her up in his arms and carried her to the bed.

PART III

WAR

CHAPTER 16

"Ee-yow! It's war! Ee-YOW!"

Eighteen-year-old Zack Carr was galloping down the tree-lined drive of Fairview Plantation, waving his hat and yelling like a banshee. Charlotte Whitney, hearing the noise, hurried out onto the white verandah.

"It's war, Charlotte!" Zack yelled. "General Beauregard fired on Fort Sumter! We're gonna beat those trashy Yankees and make 'em beg for mercy!"

"Yes, I heard."

It was Friday, April 12, 1861. Zack dismounted and ran up the stairs to the porch.

"What's wrong?" he said. "You don't look very excited."

"It's Clayton. I wonder if he'll fight, now that the war's actually here."

"Clayton? Of course he'll fight."

"Don't be too sure. You haven't read his letters. Those Northern boys at Princeton have put all sorts of ideas in his head and gotten him all confused. Why, he even wrote me he wasn't at all convinced slavery was worth fighting for. Can you imagine a Southern boy saying *that*? Of course, I haven't dared tell Daddy that Clayton was wavering in his devotion to our great cause—if Daddy knew that, he'd have a fit for sure and make me break off my engagement to Clayton. And Zack, now I'm *so* in love. . . . Oh, it's all so confusing!"

Zack took his future sister-in-law's hand. "Charlotte, honey, don't you worry your pretty head about Clayton. I know my brother. When Pa calls him home, he'll get all this Northern nonsense out of his head and fight for Virginia. Why, our family's been here since 1691. He's not going to turn against that. You'll see: Clayton's true-blue and brave as they come."

Charlotte smiled wistfully. "I certainly hope you're right."

It had been the election to the Presidency of the relatively unknown Abraham Lincoln the previous November that had precipitated the crisis. Even though Lincoln personally hated slavery, he had so far been circumspect in attacking the institution for fear of alienating the slave states into secession. Nevertheless, he had come to represent to the slave owners the leadership of Northern antislave sentiment as well as everything they hated about the North; and realizing that control of the Federal Government had now slipped out of the hands of the Southern interests, probably for good, South Carolina soon after the election passed a bill of secession from the Federal Union. Because of the great distances involved in national elections at a time of slow transportation, there was a five-month hiatus between the election of a new president and his actual inauguration. Thus for five precious months, the country drifted under the vacillating, pro-Southern Buchanan. But when, on March 4, 1861, Lincoln was sworn in, events began rushing to a head. There was Federal property in the Southern states. Fort Sumter, on an island in Charleston harbor, was one such property. When Washington attempted to send supplies to Sumter, General Beauregard demanded surrender of the fort to the South. When the commander, Major Anderson, refused, Beauregard fired his batteries at the fort and the bloodiest war in American history was on. One out of every four men who fought in it never lived to learn the outcome.

"Senator Whitney—I should say General Whitney—has offered me a commission," said Clayton as he sat with Zack and their father at the dinner table at Carr Farm. Clayton had returned from Princeton three days before, having been forced to take a boat to Norfolk, then a train to Richmond, where his father had picked him up in their carriage and driven him north to home. In these early days of the war, both sides were teeming with confusion, but that a war was nevertheless on had been brought home to Clayton by the circuitous route he had been forced to take. The United States was now two separate nations. "The general wants me to be his aide, and he's offered me a captaincy."

"Are you going to take it?" asked Zack, anxiously watching his older brother. He remembered what Charlotte had told him only a week earlier about Clayton's uncertainty over the slavery question.

Clayton put down his chicken leg and wiped his mouth. The interior of the old farmhouse was furnished with some fine old pieces that had been in the Carr family for generations. An oil portrait of the boys' mother hung over the fireplace. Clayton remembered the almost endless college arguments about slavery. Up at Princeton, he had had serious doubts. But now, back on Carr Farm on this hot spring night, did he really have any choice?

"Yes," he said without much enthusiasm.

"Hooray!" Zack exclaimed. "I knew you would. I told Charlotte you were true-blue."

"Was there ever any suggestion you wouldn't fight?" asked Brandon Carr as he filled a glass with claret from a crystal decanter.

"Well, at college there were a lot of arguments about slavery. But no, I guess I never *really* considered not fighting if it came to war."

"I too have doubts about certain aspects of slavery," his father said, replacing the stopper in the decanter. "I've made it plain to your future father-in-law that I disapprove of his harsh treatment of his slaves. And a while back when Phineas wanted me to go to England and bribe the chief witness in Mrs. Cavanagh's case to perjure himself, I told Phineas I wouldn't do his dirty business for him, so they sent Roger Ward instead. But without slavery, the South would be reduced to chaos, so we have no choice but to fight." He turned to his second son on his left. "However,

Zachary, since Clayton is joining the colors, you'll have to stay home."

"Aw, Pa—"

"I want no arguments, son. I'm getting old, and I can't run this place by myself. Clayton will fight and uphold our family honor. There'll be no reflection on your manhood, Zachary, if you stay home. We all know you're no coward."

A coward, thought Clayton. That's what they would have called me if I hadn't fought. Goddammit, they all may be crazy fighting this war, but I'll show them I'm no coward.

"Hey, Clayton," Zack exclaimed, "now you'll be able to get married in a uniform. Won't that be grand?"

"We'll have to go to a tailor in Fredericksburg in the morning," Brandon said. "I read that a manual of uniforms for the Confederate Army has been issued. Its color is supposed to be cadet gray, though I hear the dye is making some of the cloth come out a yellowish-brown color, like butternut. I believe you'll look quite handsome in whatever color it is, Clayton. I'm sure Charlotte will be as proud of her groom as I am of my son."

Though speculation was rife that Lincoln would try to blockade the Southern ports, so far this had not occurred and for rich Southerners like the Whitneys, life was still abundant. So the marriage of Captain Clayton Carr and Charlotte Whitney was an extravaganza and, in fact, one of the last great social events of the antebellum South. God favored the occasion with balmy weather and cloudless skies, and as the carriages of the Virginia aristocracy disgorged their elaborately dressed occupants in front of the stately mansion on the Rappahannock, only the most pessimistic would have imagined that all this beauty was about to be blasted away by one of the worst hurricanes of history.

Clayton looked dashing in his new gray uniform with the swirls of gold braid on the sleeves. Charlotte looked lovely in an off-the-shoulder wedding gown festooned with sprigs of violets, its enormous skirt almost six feet in diameter at the hem, its train trailing another eight feet, her wedding veil cascading in waves of lace from a flowered cap on her head—all this meticulously copied from a woodcut of the wedding gown of the English Princess Royal that Ellie May had found in *Godey's Ladies' Book*. When the nuptial vows were finished and the groom kissed the bride, there was not a dry female eye in the house.

Then a copious buffet was served along with endless bottles of French champagne from Phineas' well-stocked cellar, and the nearly hundred guests addressed themselves with gusto to a long afternoon of gorging, drinking and dancing. Most of the young bucks, including Zack, got themselves thoroughly "spiffed," to use the latest of many American euphemisms for "drunk." But Clayton, anticipating his wedding night in a Fredericksburg hotel, remained sober. He and Charlotte were spending a ten-day honeymoon at Hot Springs, Virginia, after which he would report to his father-in-law for active duty.

"Clayton," Phineas said, taking the captain aside, "when you get back, I have a job for you."

"What's that, sir?"

"You recall Mrs. Cavanagh of Elvira Plantation?"

"Very well."

"As you know, she sent instructions from Scotland to Billie DeVries to manumit all her slaves, which he did, much to the strenuous objections of the other slave owners. There wasn't much we could do about it then, but now it's a different story. I've discussed her case with the authorities in Richmond, and we have decided to confiscate Elvira Plantation and turn it into a hospital for the army."

"Is that legal, sir?"

"The new government has decided to treat Mrs. Cavanagh as a traitor to the Confederacy because of her past donations to the Abolitionists. Yes, it's legal. Of course, we hope we won't need too many hospitals, but I fear we'll need more than we have now. Elvira Plantation will be useful. My staff is making a list of her former slaves. We're going to round up as many of them as we can find and put them to work for the Confederacy. The house servants we'll return to Elvira Plantation, where they can work as hospital staff. When you return from Hot Springs, your first job will be to round up the house servants."

"Very good, sir."

"Meanwhile, I want to tell you again how pleased I am to have you in the family, and I want you to have a wonderful honeymoon. But"—he lowered his voice—"be gentle with Charlotte. Her mother and I tried to explain to her what to expect tonight, but I fear neither of us did a very good job of it. I don't think she'll understand what you're up to. I, uh, assume you've had a woman before?"

Clayton reddened sheepishly. "Yes, sir."

"Um, yes. Well, that's good. When I was a young man, it was assumed that a gentleman would have had some experience. But now, with all this damned prudery, can't even call a piano leg a 'leg' anymore, it's getting so ridiculous. Well, you run along now and enjoy yourself. But be careful with Charlotte."

"I will, sir. And thank you, sir."

Clayton rejoined the merrymakers, marveling at Phineas' dogged persistence. He had tried to have Lizzie Cavanagh hanged. Failing that, now he was confiscating her property. His father-in-law looked so dignified and genial. But underneath, Clayton realized, Phineas was a pit bull.

"I don't have no darkie whores in my establishment," exclaimed an angry Miss Rose, the three-hundred-pound proprietor of Yorktown's leading bordello. "What do you think I am, trash? This establishment caters to white gentlemen only."

"But there are certain white gentlemen who take a fancy to an occasional piece of dark meat," said Clayton. It was a hot evening three nights after his return from his honeymoon. "My information is that you have in your employ a female by the name of Dulcey, formerly slave to Mrs. Jack Cavanagh of Elvira Plantation. I have here an army order for the return of all Mrs. Cavanagh's former slaves to army jurisdiction."

Clayton handed the steaming Miss Rose the order. As she read it, he looked around the gaudy bordello with its flaming-red flocked wallpaper and round-globed gas lights.

A number of attractive white girls in various stages of undress were lolling around the parlor, two lounging on a round leather banquette in the center of the room. One redhead blew a kiss at the handsome captain. Another discreetly raised her underskirt to show her private parts. Clayton stared hungrily.

"All right," growled Miss Rose, handing back the order and lowering her voice. "But I ask you as an officer and a gentleman not to let it out that I had a darkie on the staff. I only took her in because she's so attractive and needed work *des*perately. It was an act of charity on my part, Captain. Surely you understand that?"

"Oh yes. Of course."

Miss Rose, who was wearing a green silk tent dress stained under the arms with sweat, noticed Clayton's wandering eyes. She smiled lightly.

"Want a little action, Captain?" she whispered. "It'll be on the house. My contribution to the Glorious Cause."

Clayton hesitated. "I'm a married man," he said.

"Ain't they all?"

Clayton thought of Charlotte, who had been so frigid their wedding night, although by the end of the honeymoon, she had begun to warm up a bit. He couldn't start cheating on her. He was an officer, not a cad, and he loved his new wife.

"Please bring me the woman called Dulcey."

"You're the boss. But you're passing up some of the best poontang in Dixie. Lotte!" she called to one voluptuous blond. "Go fetch Dulcey. Tell her to pack her things. She's going to work for the army."

"She's already been sleeping with half the army," Lotte said, and the other girls guffawed.

A few minutes later, one of the most gorgeous Negro girls Clayton had ever seen emerged from a rear hall, although to call her Negro was an obvious mislabeling since her café-au-lait skin proclaimed much white blood in her. She looked about eighteen, and in her tight-fitting red silk dress with a flounced skirt cut just below the knee, her lush figure was sensational. Clayton felt his pants begin to bulge embarrassingly as she came up to him.

"Wot's all dis bout me bein' taken back as a slave?" she said angrily. "I ain't no slave no mo'! I done been legally freed by Miss Lizzie, an' I got the papers to prove it!"

"Sorry, honey, but you've just been *un*freed by the Confederate Army," said Miss Rose. "Here's the order. It's all legal. The rules just been changed."

Dulcey glared at Clayton. "Where you takin' me?" she asked.

"To Elvira Plantation, by order of General Whitney. It's been turned into a hospital. You're to work there as a floor nurse."

"A nurse? I doan wanna be no nurse aroun' sick men, no sir! You tell General Whitney to go to hell! I's free!"

"As Miss Rose explained, you've been *un*freed," replied Clayton patiently. "You'll have to come with me. I've got a dozen soldiers downstairs, so don't make me force you."

Dulcey was staring at him.

"Wait a minute," she said. "I knows you. Ain't you Massa Clayton wot done come to Miss Lizzie's ball at Elvira Plantation wid Miss Charlotte Whitney?"

"That's right. She's my wife now."

"Huh. So you an' she got married. Huh."

Dulcey's eyes roved up and down Clayton's six-foot frame. She noticed the bulge in his pants.

"Come on, Dulcey. Get your things."

She smiled slightly. "Guess I ain't got no choice, have I?"

She turned and walked back to the hall, wiggling her hips ever so suggestively.

Miss Rose noticed the sweat emerging on Clayton's brow.

"Ain't she something?" she whispered.

"Is Papa coming home today?" asked four-year-old Amanda Cavanagh as her mother knelt beside the tub and sponged her back.

"Not till Saturday, darling," said Lizzie. "You know he always comes on Saturdays."

"Oh, I wish he'd come sooner. I miss him so when he's not here."

"We all miss him."

"Why can't he be here all the time, like a proper papa?"

"You know why, Amanda. I've told you a hundred times, he has business in London." This was the excuse Lizzie had been using to explain Adam's appearance at her Scottish home only one week a month. She was acutely aware the excuse was beginning to wear thin: Amanda was asking too many questions.

"Is Papa going to bring me a present from London?"

"I'm sure he will. He always does, doesn't he? He spoils you something dreadful."

"Oh Mama, I'm not spoiled. I'm the sweetest little girl in the world. Papa told me I am!"

Lizzie laughed as she stood up to kiss the top of her daughter's blond head. "And that, my sweet Amanda, is why you're spoiled."

Amanda sneezed, and Lizzie frowned.

"That's the fifth time you've sneezed. I think you're catching cold. Mrs. Parker, we'd better get her to bed and give her some medicine."

"We should never have let her play on the beach today," said the sweet-faced, gray-haired nanny, coming over to pick Amanda out of the tub. "It was too damp."

"Yes, I fear you may be right. I'll be downstairs. Good night, darling."

She gave Amanda another kiss, then left the nursery with its delightful wallpaper depicting scenes from fairy tales and went downstairs. The eight-room stone cottage, which Lizzie in a burst of mid-Victorian sentimentality had named Heart's Repose, was bright and charming, and from its bay windows in the large drawing room and dining room it had splendid views of the sandy beaches of the Firth of Clyde, the great arm of the Irish Sea on the west coast of Scotland. In the eighteenth century, the place had been much smaller and ruder, a fisherman's cottage. Adam's grandfather had fallen in love with the wild and beautiful area and had expanded the cottage for use as a summer seaside villa. Since Lizzie had moved in four years before, Adam had lavished another small fortune on the place, installing modern plumbing and a new kitchen. Lizzie had planted a walled kitchen garden that reminded her of her garden at Wykeham Rise, and surrounded the house with flowers, which thrived in the rainy climate despite a lack of adequate sunshine.

Lizzie had come to love the cottage and the place. Her notoriety and Adam's fame had made it a waste of time to try and adopt pseudonyms: the locals found out who they were before Lizzie had unpacked. Their first year, they had attracted hostile stares and even a few ugly anonymous notes. But time wore down the locals' distrust. Lizzie came to be perceived as a beautiful mother whose romance with Adam was star-crossed. Eventually, they came to be accepted by most; to many of the younger Scots, as glamorous celebrities.

But Lizzie knew, in her heart, that time was running out. Happy as she was, even with Adam only a part-time lover, there was Amanda. Amanda asking more and more questions. Amanda wanting to know why she couldn't have a "proper papa." And as if Lizzie weren't sufficiently aware of the precariousness of her position, that night Amanda developed a fever and a doctor was sent for. It was nothing but a bad cold; but Amanda began crying in her bed for her papa. What, Lizzie thought, if Amanda developed a serious illness? What if, God forbid, she were hurt in an accident? What if she died and Adam weren't there? Was her own personal happiness worth depriving her child of a 'proper papa'? As much as she adored Adam, she had often toyed with the idea of returning to Virginia with Amanda, reclaiming her property and perhaps trying to find a new husband. But the outbreak of the Civil War had blocked that. So for the time being, she decided she had no recourse but to drift on.

But as she sat next to Amanda's bed, listening to her child cry for her papa, Lizzie knew that sometime soon she would have to change her life.

"I received a letter from my lawyer, Billie DeVries," Lizzie said to Adam the following Saturday as they walked along the beautiful beach in front of the cottage. "He tells me that Senator Whitney has now become a general in the

Confederate Army, and he's taken over Elvira Plantation to use as a hospital for wounded soldiers."

"Is that legal?" Adam asked.

"Billie says there's nothing I can do. Whitney is close to Jefferson Davis and is one of the most influential men in the Confederacy, so he can do pretty well what he pleases. But what really infuriates me is that he's rounded up most of my former slaves and forced them into work gangs for the rebel army. And he's made Aunt Lide, Charles and Dulcey work at the hospital for no pay."

"In other words, he's enslaved them again."

"Exactly."

It was a beautiful June day and a brisk breeze was blowing off the Firth of Clyde. But even though the water looked inviting, the beach was deserted because the Scots viewed ocean bathing as something fit only for lunatics. Lizzie hesitated to tell Adam the other news in Billie's letter because it threatened something fundamental to their relationship, or at least she feared it might. The Civil War, now in its second month, was already affecting the lives of thousands, including Lizzie's.

"The other problem," she went on, deciding she had to bite the bullet, "is that they've also cut off my income."

Adam looked surprised. "How?"

"General Whitney again. Billie says he got the Confederacy to confiscate all my stocks and bonds, which were in a Richmond bank, and replace them with Confederate bonds, which probably won't pay any interest until the South can win. So I have no income. And it's especially galling that my money is helping the South when I could have invested in Federal bonds."

"Of all the damnable tricks! Of course, I'll give you all the money you need. . . ."

"No!" She stopped, holding her blond hair which was blowing in the wind. "We've had four years of such wonderful happiness, even with Sybil claiming you most of the time, but one reason I've been happy was because I was financially independent. I wasn't being 'kept' like a mistress. I know that's putting a fine point on what most people would consider our 'immoral' relationship, but it's important to me. Now I don't know what to do. Oh, this Whitney creature, this monster of a man! He *hounds* my life! And then there's Gabriel. He's doing so well at his school, but now I have no money to pay his tuition."

She had told Adam the story of Moses and how she was raising his son at a Quaker school in Gloucester, Massachusetts.

"You know," Adam said, "for four years we haven't had a fight. We haven't even bickered, have we?"

"It's been paradise."

"Well, I think we're about to have our first fight."

"Not about money!"

"Yes, about money. You're like a wife to me, and you're the mother of my daughter. Why shouldn't you accept my money willingly?"

"Because I don't want to. I'm not trying to be especially noble, it's just that I . . . well, I prize my independence, even if I'm not exactly independent."

"I know what you mean, and I love you for it. But the fact remains, you have to have money, and if you won't take it from me as a gift, take it as a loan to tide you over. This war can't last much longer, and from what I read and hear, it looks as if the Southerners may win, unfortunately. When they do, you can pay me back. What's unreasonable about that?"

She sighed. "I suppose you're right. I'll take a loan. Oh Adam, you marvelous man, is it any wonder I love you?"

He took her in his arms and kissed her. "Now that dreary subject is settled, we can move on to more pleasant things. Let's go for a swim."

"Are you mad? The water's freezing."

"I know how to warm you up afterward."

"No. There's something else."

He released her. "*Now* what?"

They continued walking down the beach. "It's Amanda," Lizzie said. "We're not being fair to her. She only has a part-time father, and even though the local people have come to accept us as . . . well, whatever they accept us as, it's still not a proper way to raise a child. You know that as well as I."

"I love Amanda! I adore her!"

"But that's not the point. How do I explain to her where you spend most of your time? How do I explain to her that you have another family, that you now have *two* sons who are her half-brothers but she doesn't even know exist? How do I explain to her what *I* am? And someday she'll have to know."

"You're making trouble," he said sourly.

"Of course I'm making trouble. I have to think of Amanda, and you have to think of Henry and Arthur."

He stopped and took her in his arms again. Again, he kissed her. The wind blew and entwined their hair as he held her on the empty beach.

"We'll work something out," he finally whispered. "But I'm not going to let you go. You and I are one."

She was too desperately in love with him to say anything more. At least, for the moment.

On the steamy hot night of July 15, 1861, a young man in a dark suit and black hat galloped down the Virginia shore of the Potomac River. Shortly before midnight, he saw a light blink twice from a clump of trees by the river. The young man, Captain Clayton Carr of the Army of Virginia, headed toward the trees. The night was dark, although occasional heat lightning in the distance afforded some dim illumination. Clayton saw the man step out of the trees. He held a rifle. Clayton reined his horse.

"Palmetto," he said softly.

"Rattlesnake," said the man, lowering his gun. "Leave your horse with me. The boat's down there."

Clayton quickly dismounted, giving "Rattlesnake" the reins of his horse. Then he ran into the bushes, almost stumbling down the dirt embankment to the rowboat in which an oarsman sat.

"Climb in," whispered the oarsman. "Give us a shove first."

Clayton did as he was told, pushing the boat into the Potomac as he jumped in one end.

"Sit down, you jackass, or you'll tip us over," said the man. Clayton obeyed, and the stranger began rowing them across the river. Clayton, who had studied classics at Princeton, imagined the dark oarsman as Charon ferrying him across the River Styx. It was not as fanciful a comparison as it sounded, since death possibly awaited him on the Washington side of the Potomac.

"I can wait here till dawn," whispered the oarsman as the boat bumped ashore. "If you're not back by then, you're on your own."

"I'll be back," Clayton said nervously. If he got caught, the Yankees would probably consider him a spy and hang him. Once ashore, he found another horse tethered to a tree. Untying it, he mounted and headed for Washington.

Clayton had volunteered for this mission. His father-in-law, General Phineas Whitney, had disapproved of Clayton's volunteering as "foolishly risky," but General Beauregard had insisted the information Clayton might get in Washington could possibly win the war for the South, and this argument had carried the day. Clayton might have his doubts about slavery, but he was determined to prove that he was no coward.

As he galloped through the dark night, he reviewed the situation in his mind. The war was now in its fourth month, thousands of troops had poured into Washington from the North, but so far they hadn't done much except render the dirty, smelly city ever dirtier and smellier—some regiments taking up residence in the Capitol itself. Meanwhile, Richmond had been declared the capital of the Confederacy, and since it was just over one hundred miles south of Washington, pressure was mounting on the North to have the Federal forces move south, destroy or capture Richmond and put an end to the rebellion. Adding to the pressure was the fact that most of the militiamen in Washington had volunteered for only three months' service, and their time was almost up. If the Federals didn't move quickly, the militia would go home, leaving Washington wide open for attack by the Confederates, whose army was encamped south of Washington at two towns named Centreville and Manassas along a sluggish stream called Bull Run.

The Creole General Beauregard was getting information

from a number of sources in Washington, but his main source was an elegant widow named Mrs. Rose O'Neal Greenhow, who lived in a house "within easy rifle range of the White House," as Beauregard had suggestively described it to Clayton. Five days before, on July 10, Beauregard had received an encoded message from Mrs. Greenhow, delivered by a beautiful, dark-haired Washington girl named Miss Bettie Duvall, saying that the new commander of the Federal forces in Washington, General Irvin McDowell, had drawn up a plan to attack Beauregard at Manassas, and that she would be able to furnish the disposition of his forces and his route of advance on the night of July 17.

Which is when Clayton made his bid for a niche in history by volunteering to go to Washington and get the information.

One would have thought, with such enormous stakes at risk, that Washington would have been a sealed fortress, but in fact the opposite was the case. The Northern volunteers, while eager to "whip the Rebs," were mostly farmboys with the traditional American dislike of, and distrust of, discipline. The few trained officers on hand were graduates of West Point, an institution Americans disliked because of its overtones of European militarism, and the West Pointers had been decimated by defections to the Southern cause: both opposing commanders, McDowell and Beauregard, had been classmates at the Point. The result was that the Federal troops spent little time training and a lot of time drinking and whoring in Washington's seedier districts. The correspondent of the London *Times*, William Howard Russell, who had covered the Crimean War and the Indian Mutiny and knew what good soldiering was all about, was appalled by the slovenly hoodlums calling themselves Federal Soldiers. On one visit to Fort Corcoran in the capital, he saw one soldier almost walk into an unguarded powder magazine with a lighted corncob pipe!

So as Clayton galloped into the sweltering city, he found empty, unpaved streets, dark houses and no challenge to his progress. Clayton knew Washington—he had spent many days at Senator Whitney's mansion on H Street, now closed and shuttered—and he made his way without difficulty to Mrs. Greenhow's house where the eminent hostess entertained, despite her well-known Southern sympathies, such prominent Northern politicians as Secretary of State Seward even *after* the commencement of hostilities.

Clayton dismounted in front of the dark house and hurried to the front door, where he knocked, looking anxiously around to see if he was being watched. The street seemed empty. After a minute the door was opened on a chain. Inside, he could just barely make out a handsome middle-aged woman with dark hair.

"Mrs. Greenhow?" he whispered.

"Yes?"

Clayton handed through the door a folded piece of paper on which had been written in cipher, "Trust bearer." She took it and closed the door. He saw candlelight flicker in the transom. Then the door reopened. "Come in. Hurry!"

"My dear Sybil, difficult as it may be to believe, I am down to my last farthing. Something really *must* be done."

Sybil stared at her onetime lover, Edgar Musgrave. They were in the drawing room of Pontefract House in London.

"But I gave you seventy thousand pounds," she exclaimed.

"Ah, but that was a number of years ago," Edgar said. As always, he was dressed in the height of fashion, though she noticed that his good looks were beginning to fade and his blond hair was not as thick as it once had been. "It's amazing how money can melt away, like spring snow. Bills, bills, bills! It's deucedly expensive living these days, you know—I really have no idea how the poor survive. I mean, the really poor—like me. It's so tedious. I really have no knack for keeping money."

Sybil, who was wearing a pale green dress on this warm July day, almost snorted with rage. "If you think I'm going to allow myself to be blackmailed by you *again*. . . ."

"Please, can't we be spared your *obvious* theatrics? I happen to have spent a very pleasant afternoon yesterday sitting in that charming park across the street. Such a lovely day it was. And I saw your nanny come out of the house with your heir and the spare: young Lord Castleford and his baby brother you bore Adam last year. Lord Arthur is too young to bear a family resemblance to anyone, but Lord Castleford, who is now going on five, is still quite blond and I flatter myself that his resemblance to me now makes his parentage a matter quite beyond dispute. Such delicious bonbons, Sybil, but then you always had the best chocolates. I have no idea how you keep your figure."

He had opened a porcelain dish and popped a chocolate ball in his mouth.

"Has Adam noticed anything yet?" he went on.

"No. Or if he has, he hasn't said anything about it." How damnably annoying, she thought. Of course, she had been afraid all along that Edgar would show up and ruin everything for her. The maddening thing was that the truce Adam had proposed four years before had actually worked. He had been a loving husband to her and a good father to the boys. She even thought that he had come to love her in his way, which was perhaps not the consuming passion he had for Lizzie but was still enough to keep Sybil satisfied. True, there were the monthly departures for Scotland which irked her, but it certainly could have been worse. And now, this: the time bomb. If Adam learned the truth about Henry, their marriage could once again become a battlefield, which she certainly didn't want. She had to keep Edgar quiet.

She took a deep breath. "How much?" she said, softly.

"Mmm. Well, I think ten thousand should do, for the moment. And perhaps another ten next year. In fact, we might make it a sort of permanent arrangement. You pay me ten thousand a year, and I keep my distance. It's rather a good bargain for you, after all. It's much cheaper than our last arrangement."

"I'll make the arrangements with Mr. Lowery," she said. "Now please leave."

Edgar, smiling, stood.

"I hear Adam is up in Scotland again," he drawled. "I'm well aware Scotland is fashionable in August, but your husband goes up even in February. What *does* he find there to amuse him so? Has he taken up the bagpipe?"

"He fishes."

"Hmm. How very fishy. Well, well: I'm off. I'll wait to hear from your Mr. Lowery. And then I think I foresee a very pleasant autumn in Tuscany. Do you know Tuscany? So colorful, and the Italians are such wonderfully sensual people. It's also marvelously cheap."

Bowing, he left the room. She went to the window overlooking Pontefract Square and watched as he left the house and climbed in a cab. She had no idea how she would explain the ten thousand pounds to Adam.

She decided it was time to pay a visit to Sidonia, Lady Rockfern, at the town house she shared with Lady Hillsdale in Knightsbridge.

"Politics," said Sidonia with her usual firmness. It was the next afternoon. Sybil was taking tea with Sidonia in the drawing room of her house in Cadogan Square. "Adam has been idle far too long, and idle hands are the Devil's tools. It's time he had a profession. He tells me he's been tutoring to improve his spelling."

"Yes. In that, he hasn't been idle. His writing has become quite grammatical."

"Excellent. If he can write a proper English sentence, there's no reason he can't write a proper English law. And, my dear, if you can get him interested in politics, he will have to curtail his trips to Scotland, if you see what I mean. When I was a child, people expected Members of Parliament to be rascals and have lurid affairs. But the climate is changing—has already changed, for that matter. Politicians have to be respectable nowadays—or at least *appear* respectable. Get Adam into politics and he'll have no choice but to be respectable. More tea?"

"Yes, thank you. Of course, he has his seat in the House of Lords, but he's never even gone to see the place. How can I get him interested?"

"Send money. To the head of either party, though I

think the Tories might be the better bet. Send Mr. Disraeli a check for a thousand pounds, and you will launch my nephew on a dazzling political career."

Sybil smiled. "Dear Aunt Sidonia," she said, "I think you have hit upon an excellent scheme."

CHAPTER 17

Captain Clayton Carr stood on the bluff overlooking Manassas Junction and watched the first great battle of the Civil War. What was driving him crazy was that he had to watch. Being an aide to General Phineas Thurlow Whitney necessitated staying close to his father-in-law who, with General Pierre G. T. Beauregard, was outside the command tent also watching the action through binoculars. And there was plenty of action. A half-mile north of them, the Confederates had encountered the Federals and the boom of cannon and the pop! pop! pop! of rifles assaulted Clayton's ears while smoke roiled up from the thickly wooded plains and cornfields into the hot summer sky.

Clayton's daring ride into Washington to get the Federal plans from Mrs. Greenhow had been a brilliant success. General Beauregard had been impressed, saying he would recommend Clayton for a citation and a medal as soon as the Confederate government got around to striking medals. At least now there was no question of Clayton's bravery, and now no one could say that he had pulled strings to get a safe job as an aide to his father-in-law, though he was overly sensitive on this point. The Confederates, like the Federals, were woefully short of trained officers, and Clayton wasn't the only Southerner given a commission before he even knew how to execute an about-face.

In these first months of the war, the Confederate government had not only not struck medals, they had a very faulty distribution system for uniforms, and both Clayton's and Phineas' uniforms had been made by private tailors which they paid for out of their own pockets. Clayton had

had his daguerreotype taken by a photographer, who made up a dozen "cartes de visite" which Clayton had distributed to his friends and relatives. Even if I die, he thought, Charlotte will always have my picture to remember me by. It was a sentiment shared by thousands of soldiers on both sides of the conflict, the "carte de visite" being as popular as snapshots would be to a later generation.

Mrs. Greenhow's information about the movements of the Federal troops under General McDowell had proven correct, but even with this enormous advantage the going had been rough throughout the morning and casualties were high on both sides. The battle had been a bonanza for Washington caterers and carriage-rental services. The staggeringly sloppy intelligence of the Federals had allowed word to go all over the city that all the troops were moving south (although, to be fair, there was little way to keep it a secret once the troops began moving) and that the battle was expected on Sunday, July 21. Thus, dozens of Washingtonians, Congressmen and Senators, their wives and friends, and society belles had all packed or ordered picnic lunches replete with hams and champagne and driven south to watch the great battle that everyone assumed would send Johnny Reb running home and crush the great rebellion. Congressman Alfred Ely of New York, who wanted to watch the Thirteenth New York Regiment from his home district, Rochester, set out for Centreville with a party of friends in a fine double carriage with two horses, which rental cost him twenty-five dollars for the day.

"I hear," General Whitney said to General Beauregard, "the damn fool picnickers have had to run out of the way of their own troops."

The general nodded, still watching the battle through his binoculars. Beauregard was anxious for good news. He had been appointed Superintendent of West Point just before the War and had resigned to join the Confederacy, taking command at Charleston and ordering the salvo against Fort Sumter that started the conflict. He had great respect for the professional abilities of his opponent and former classmate, McDowell. But he knew that McDowell lacked "dash" and that he was commanding thirty thousand raw recruits, most of whom had never been under fire before. The same could be said of the Rebs. But Beauregard had an enormous advantage. All he had to do was hold his own, defending the Orange and Alexandria Railroad at Manassas Junction, which was McDowell's first target. McDowell had to break through the Rebel lines, capture the railroad and continue south through enemy territory to take the heart of the Confederacy, Richmond. Beauregard's hunch was that McDowell was not up to such a tall order.

He was about to be proven right.

Back in Washington, which seemed nearly deserted, so many people had gone out to watch the battle, a quiet group of people stood all day in front of the Treasury anxiously listening to the distant guns rumbling less than thirty miles to the southwest. After church, President Lincoln studied the unofficial telegrams that were coming in from the battlefield. Then he drove to Cruchet's Hotel at Sixth and D Streets to pay a call on the commanding general of the United States Army, General Winfield Scott. The young Winfield Scott had been victorious over the British in 1814. The aging Winfield Scott had defeated the Mexicans in 1848.

But in July of 1861 the fat, dropsical, gouty Winfield Scott could no longer even sit on a horse. However, he was still a hero to the North, and most Americans assumed that he was superior to any of the Southern officers.

When the President arrived at Cruchet's—Cruchet, a French caterer, was one of the best cooks in Washington, which was why General Scott made his headquarters there: the old man had refined his palate at the best restaurants in Paris, and he could hold forth for hours on the correct way to cook terrapin—the general was asleep.

When Mr. Lincoln awoke his commander-in-chief, General Scott told him the battle was "going well."

Then he went back to sleep.

* * *

"They're running, sir!" the messenger yelled, galloping up to Beauregard's headquarters at five that afternoon. "The Yanks have turned tail and are running back to Washington!"

"Ee-yow!" yelled Clayton.

Generals Beauregard and Whitney beamed.

"Is it a retreat?" asked Beauregard.

"No, sir, it's a *rout*!"

"God-*damn*!"

"Sir!" Clayton saluted his father-in-law. "Permission to ride out and see the rout?"

General Whitney hesitated. If something happened to Clayton, Charlotte would never forgive him, nor would his wife, Ellie May.

"Well . . ."

"*Please*, sir! This may be the last battle of the war! I *have* to see it!"

"All right, you young rascal. But watch yourself! You catch a Yankee bullet, and Charlotte's going to be real unhappy."

Clayton grinned. "There's no Yankee bullet fast enough to catch Clayton Carr. Ee-*YOW*!"

Grabbing his Enfield rifle—the same rifle that had set off the Indian Mutiny four years earlier was the favorite rifle of the Confederacy, making a fortune for the English manufacturers—he ran to his horse, mounted and galloped down the hill into the fields heading for Bull Run.

Ahead of him, one of the great traffic jams of history was occurring as the carriages of the sightseers and Congressmen vied with the fleeing Federal artillery, infantry and cavalry to make it back to the safety of Washington on the narrow dirt road. But Clayton was not destined to see that.

What he saw were bodies, Confederate bodies and Federal bodies, young bodies sprawled under the July sun in the grotesque positions of sudden death, draped over wooden post and rail fences, lying face-upward in ditches and face-downward in fields, booted feet akimbo, arms flung out, frozen as the bullets struck them into a macabre ballet of death.

What Clayton didn't see was the half-dead Yankee sniper in the tree ahead of him who had one bullet left and was damned if he wouldn't take one more Johnny Reb with him before he went to meet God. He aimed at Clayton and fired.

A fast Yankee bullet *did* catch Clayton. It hit him in his left thigh. Howling with pain, he fell off his horse onto the hot ground next to a cornfield. He thought for a moment he was dead, the pain was so terrible. Then, realizing he was still alive, he sat up with difficulty and looked at his leg. The gray trousers he was so proud of were matting with blood. Clayton didn't realize it, but the Minié ball had shattered his thigh bone into six pieces.

It was then that the pain and the heat caused him to faint.

The smartest politician in England watched Sybil pour tea from an embossed silver teapot, and Benjamin Disraeli wondered what she was after. They were in the drawing room of Pontefract House in London, three days after the disastrous Battle of Bull Run at Manassas.

"I am most grateful for your generous contribution," Disraeli said after Sybil handed him the teacup. "The Tories are supposed to be the party of the great landowning magnates, but it can be extremely difficult to extract contributions from millionaires. But your check, coming, as it were, from out of the blue, was doubly welcome because it has permitted me to meet one of the loveliest ladies in London."

"You flatter me, Mr. Disraeli," Sybil said, looking at the thin, rather hunched-over man with the black goatee and oily black curls dangling from his balding pate onto his forehead. "But it is the kind of flattery any woman likes to hear."

"I have found that flattery, even if insincere, is a useful tool in life and an indispensable tool for politicians. In your case, my flattery is, believe me, sincere. But I have also found . . ." He paused to sip his tea, searching her face with his intense dark eyes. ". . . that beautiful marchionesses do not generally send thousand-pound checks to political parties for purely altruistic reasons."

Sybil smiled. The fifty-seven-year-old Disraeli had a reputation for being crafty, even slippery. He was considered to be not very "English," which was a polite way of saying that he was Jewish. Until three years before, non-Christians had been refused entry into the House of Commons, which had not affected Disraeli because he had been baptized into the Church of England as a boy. Later in his career, however, he repeatedly voted against his party, at great political risk, to have the ban on non-Christians lifted so that his friend, Baron Lionel de Rothschild, could be admitted to the House of Commons—the first religious Jew to do so. All of this, plus the fact that he wrote novels, had earned him his "slippery" reputation—it was also considered "un-English" to write novels.

"It is true, Mr. Disraeli," she said. "I have ulterior motives. Since your time is valuable, let me explain them to you." She paused. "I believe it was Cardinal de Retz who said, '*Il n'y a rien dans le monde qui n'ait son moment décisif . . .*' "

" '*. . . et le chef d'oeuvre de la bonne conduite est de connaître et de prendre ce moment,*' " Disraeli completed the quotation. They both looked pleased at their mutual erudition. "It is a motto that I have guided my life by."

"I believe this is such a 'decisive moment' for me and my husband. To be brief, I wish my husband to enter politics. True, he has drawbacks, which I am sure you are aware of. Being a poor relative of the de Vere family, he never received a proper education, although he has tutored for the past several years to correct this fault."

"Education can be a handicap in politics. Ignorance has a certain basic appeal to the voters."

"Yes, I suppose. But my husband has several assets. He is quite well-known—even famous, to be immodest. He is loved by the English public. He is young and most presentable. He is a vast landowner and he is immensely rich. It seems to me he should take part in the governing of this nation, but he needs guidance—a political tutor, so to speak. Dare I say he needs someone like you, Mr. Disraeli?"

"Now it is you that flatter, Lady Pontefract. But I must remind you that I lead Her Majesty's loyal opposition. You would be better advised to approach Lord Palmerston, who would be in a position to reward your husband with some suitable public office."

"But my husband likes *you*, Mr. Disraeli. He has often spoken so highly of you, and he admires your concept of 'romantic Toryism': an England led by its nobility, but a nobility that cares for the poor and downtrodden, a nobility with a soul."

He put down his teacup. "You fascinate me, Lady Pontefract, and I am now more eager than ever to meet your distinguished husband. However, his frequent trips to Scotland would make it difficult for him to hope for a *serious* political career."

"It is his frequent trips to Scotland I am trying to stop," she said dryly.

He looked at her for a moment. Then he began to laugh. It was a quiet laugh at first, but one that built to a near-guffaw. Finally he pulled a white kerchief from his pocket and wiped his eyes.

"Oh, my dear Lady Pontefract," he wheezed, "I think I like you a great deal—a *great* deal."

"Please, Mr. Disraeli. Call me Sybil."

"And you, dear Sybil, must call me Dizzy."

"I have bad news, son," said the surgeon. "Your thigh bone's been shattered by the Minié ball, and if we don't get that leg off soon, gangrene's going to set in."

Clayton was lying on a cot in the crowded hospital tent that had been set up by the Confederates near the battlefield at Manassas. The heat and stench in the tent would have made him nauseous even if the pain in his leg hadn't been excruciating. Now, sweat pouring off his naked torso, he tried to sit up.

"No," he whispered. "Please, Doc, not my leg . . ."

"We don't have any choice, son. Take him to the operating tent," he said to his assistant. "Give him enough whiskey to get him drunk. We'll amputate in an hour."

"Yes sir."

The doctor moved to the next cot as his assistant signaled two orderlies to come over. Clayton, sobbing, was staring at his left thigh, which had swollen and turned almost purple where the blood had been washed away. "Oh Jesus," he mumbled. "I'm gonna be a cripple . . . oh Jesus, what will Charlotte think?"

He lay back down, his flesh crawling at the ordeal he was about to undergo. The orderlies transferred him to a litter, causing him to scream from the pain. Then they carried him out into the blazing sun.

He was hunting in a Virginia wood with his dog, Treat, his father and Senator Whitney. He was ten years old. It was a chilly autumn day and the foliage was a gorgeous explosion of yellows and reds. He saw a deer and raised his rifle. His father and Senator Whitney had been discussing the price of slaves, but now they fell silent and watched Clayton aiming his gun. He fired.

"Good shot, boy!" exclaimed his father.

Clayton, bursting with pride, ran toward the fallen deer.

"Hold him down," said the doctor.

"Please . . . please don't do it . . . don't . . . don't . . ." Clayton was screaming. The orderlies pressed down hard on his arms, pinioning him to the wooden operating table. Two other orderlies pressed on his ankles, spreading his legs apart. The doctor held the saw up for a moment.

"I don't want to be a cripple! Please . . . oh, Jesus . . ."

"We have no choice, son. We have to save your life. I'm afraid this is going to hurt."

"Jesus . . . oh, Jesus . . ."

The doctor placed the saw blade on his left thigh. The teeth touched the hairy, purple flesh. Then he began sawing.

Blood squirted as Clayton's screams slowly faded into drunken oblivion.

"Charlotte, Charlotte," he whispered.

Clayton was making love to his bride, kissing her skinny breasts.

"Oh Clayton, I *do* love you," she whispered. "Am I getting any better at this?"

"Yes. Really." It was only a half-lie. Charlotte was warming up to lovemaking, though her heart really wasn't in it. He inserted himself in her. She began moaning softly as he lay on top of her, his buttocks squeezing slowly. Then a strange pain began climbing up his left leg. He stopped making love as the pain filled his entire body. He screamed as he looked down at Charlotte.

She had turned into a hideous, grinning corpse.

He opened his eyes to see the beautiful girl with the café-au-lait skin. After a moment he recognized her as Dulcey, the girl from Miss Rose's whorehouse.

"Dulcey," he whispered.

"Dass me."

"Where am I?"

"You at Elvira Plantation. You in de bestest room in de house 'cause yo' father-in-law am Senator Whitney. You is in Miss Lizzie's room. I used to brush her hair here."

Clayton looked around at the beautiful room with the gold brocade curtains over the recessed windows. The windows were open, and a sultry breeze was blowing through.

"How . . . how did I get here?" Clayton asked, trying to probe the black hole that was the last several days. All he could remember was hunting with his father as a boy and making love to a corpse.

"You was brought here after yo' operation. You been asleep fo' several days."

"My operation. . . ."

Suddenly it flooded back to him. The saw. The pain. The screams. Sitting up, he threw off the sheet. He was wearing a white cotton nightshirt that hung to his knees.

Except he saw, with horror, that it hung only to his right knee. His left knee was gone.

"Oh no . . ."

He started to pull up his nightshirt, then looked at Dulcey, who was watching him impassively.

"Please go away. I want to look. . . ."

"I seen plenty a naked gempm'n in mah life," she said matter-of-factly. "An' I already seen *you.* I'm yo' nurse. I already washed you off twice, naked as a baby. I already seen yo' stump."

He winced. Slowly he raised the gown.

"Oh Jesus . . ."

His leg had been sawn off just below the pelvis. The stump was bandaged.

"De doctor, he say you can still have babies," Dulcey said. "You just ain't gonna be doin' much runnin' aroun' or dancin' no reel or nuffin'. I'm gonna go get you yo' lunch now, Cap'n Clayton."

She smiled at him suggestively. Then she turned to leave the bedroom.

Clayton took another look at where his left leg should have been. Then he lowered his nightshirt, leaned back in his pillows and wept.

"It's Papa! Papa!" squealed Amanda excitedly as she looked out one of the bay windows of Heart's Repose. Her mother's carriage had just pulled up in front of the cottage by the sea and her father was stepping out.

"Yes it is, darling," Lizzie said, going to open the front door, as always filled with as much excitement as her daughter when Adam arrived. She opened the door. It was a windy day, and Adam held on to his top hat as he made his way up the walk to the house. He was followed by Angus, Lizzie's driver, who was carrying Adam's bag.

"Welcome home, darling." Lizzie smiled as he came in the house and took her in his arms.

"Papa! Papa!" Amanda almost pushed her mother away to get at her father.

"Here's my pretty flower!" Adam laughed as he picked her up to kiss her.

"What did you bring me from London this time?"

"Well now, Miss Amanda, you're exhibiting definite signs of a greedy nature, which shocks me."

"Did you bring me a doll or a kitten?"

"I brought you a doll, you little witch. It's in the valise."

Angus had just brought in Adam's bag.

"Angus!" Amanda cried, running to him. "Open Papa's valise—*please*!"

Adam shook his head. "You're spoiling her," he said to Lizzie, who rolled her eyes.

"What's wrong?" Lizzie said that night as she lay in Adam's naked arms. The cloudy day had turned stormy, and the wind was howling around the cottage while down the long beach an angry surf pounded.

"Nothing's wrong," he said tersely.

"Oh my darling, don't pretend. I've felt it all evening: you're worried about something. Don't try to hide anything from me, who knows you like the palm of my hand. What's happened?"

He was silent for a moment. Then he sighed. "All right. I've been offered a position in the Government. Naturally, I turned it down, but Sybil's raising a storm that makes the one outside look like a spring drizzle."

Lizzie sat up and turned on the oil lamp next to their bed. She was no fool. She knew this was serious trouble.

"*What* position in the Government?" she asked.

"To be one of the Crown appointments to the council that advises the Secretary of State for India, which was set up three years ago when the Crown took over the administration of India from the old East India Company. Lord Palmerston was very flattering and kind, and said that my knowledge of India would be invaluable to Lord Cranborne, who's the Secretary for India, but I know it's all a trick on Sybil's part."

"What do you mean?"

"She's gotten very friendly with Mr. Disraeli by the simple device of giving money to the Tories. Of course, Disraeli has a lot of power in Commons, and he arranged to trade a few favors with Lord Palmerston, who then invites me to sit on the Council. It's all been engineered very elegantly, but I don't want any part of it."

"Is it because you'd have to give me up?"

He didn't say anything. She got out of bed, put on a peignoir and went to the window looking out over the raging sea.

"We've been living in a fool's paradise," she finally said. "Not that one can't be happy in a fool's paradise. I've been wonderfully, sublimely happy with you, my darling, and I think you've been happy with me. But I've known all along that someday it would have to end."

"It's *not* ending!" he exclaimed, sitting up.

"Yes it is. Because you're going to accept that appointment."

"Lizzie, maybe you didn't hear me: I've already turned it down."

"You'll go back to London and tell them you've changed your mind."

"No!"

He threw back the sheets, jumped out of bed and ran across the room to her, taking her in his arms and kissing her fiercely. As the rain beat against the windowpanes, he said, "You're mine, Lizzie. You're part of my body and part of my soul. I'll never give you up."

"Oh Adam, my sweetest Adam," she said, her resolve almost melting at the feel of his strong arms, "don't you know you are part of *my* soul? But what we have been doing is wrong . . ."

"It's not, dammit!"

"I know it's right for us, but to the rest of the world it's wrong. We've lived this beautiful dream for four years, but now the dream is over and we have to face reality—for our children, if for nothing else." She felt his embracing arms relax a bit. "You know I'm right," she went on. "And Sybil's right. She's thinking of your son and heir. . . ."

"He may be my heir, but I'm not so sure he's my son."

"What do you mean?"

He went back to the bed, sat on its edge and buried his face in his hands, his fingers digging into his thick black hair. When he looked up, she saw there were tears in his dark eyes.

"I'm almost convinced Henry is somebody else's son," he said. "I found out from my agent that Sybil transferred an extraordinary amount of money—seventy thousand pounds—to a young n'er-do-well cad named Edgar Musgrave, with whom she had had a close relationship. Sybil was a virgin when I married her, but I left for India shortly after the wedding. It's much more likely Henry was conceived after I left England. But I'm . . . I'm afraid to ask her. Sybil and I have managed to patch up our marriage, and I don't want to know the truth, because I'm afraid it will ruin everything if it *is* true. And I love Henry."

"Would it make a difference to you if he weren't your son?"

"Of course it would! No man wants to think his son and heir is really somebody's *else's*. The irony is, I married Sybil to try and safeguard the family inheritance, and here she's blown it right out the window! If Henry isn't my son, how can he legitimately inherit the de Vere money and my title? It should all rightly go to Arthur, who *is* my son. But if I disinherit Henry, it would ruin his life and cause a first-class scandal. Oh, the whole thing's a bloody mess. And now this."

Lizzie's heart went out to him. She knew how much he loved his sons.

"Don't politics appeal to you at all?" she asked.

He hesitated.

"Actually, they do. I'd like to be doing something useful. God knows, I've been so incredibly lucky, I owe some sort of service to people less fortunate than I." His face hardened. "But I won't give you up!"

She came to the bed and took his head in her hands, pressing it against her heart. "You *must* give me up," she whispered. "Whether Henry is or isn't your son doesn't matter. I know you love him like a son, and his future is important. You must go home, Adam."

"*This* is my home."

"No it isn't. You're not just Adam Thorne. You're the

Marquess of Pontefract, the nation's hero, and the father of the future Marquess. . . ."

"Whoever he is."

"Your home is Pontefract Hall and Pontefract House. Don't you realize it breaks my heart to say this, my darling? Don't you realize you've always been the most important thing in my life? But there comes a time when we have to accept the fact that there are other things more important than ourselves. We have to face the fact we have no future. You must give me up for your son's future."

He was looking up at her, tears streaming down his cheeks.

"But what would happen to you and Amanda?" he said.

"I'll arrange for you to see Amanda from time to time. But as for me, sweet Adam, to say good-bye to you once will kill me. I couldn't stand saying it twice."

"You mean, we're never going to see each other again? We've been inseparable since childhood!"

"It's better we don't. Otherwise, we'd inevitably fall back into the same routine we're in now: the double marriage that will destroy us."

"NO!" Adam shouted. "I'll divorce Sybil . . ."

"You know divorce is out of the question. Even if it could be arranged, which is practically impossible, you'd ruin your children's lives. They could never live down the scandal."

He closed his eyes. For a long time he was silent. Then he looked up at her again. "When?" he whispered.

"We'll say nothing to Amanda or Mrs. Parker. We'll pretend everything is as usual. You'll stay your usual week. And then . . ." She swallowed with difficulty. "And then, my sweetest love, you'll leave me."

He stared at her a moment. Then he took her hand and pressed it to his mouth.

"We'll pack a lifetime of happiness into this week," he whispered. "A lifetime. I swear it."

The open carriage pulled up in front of Fairview Plantation, and Phineas stepped out as his driver got his valise from the rear. The Senator walked up to the front porch of his home where Ellie May came out to kiss him.

"Welcome home, dear," she said. "Are they dancing in the streets in Richmond?"

"Well, not quite. There's a good deal of jubilation over the great victory. But if you ask me, we've thrown the victory away."

Ellie May, looking surprised, followed her husband inside. In the great hall, five generations of slave-owning Whitneys looked down from the walls, their portraits reflecting the happy tranquillity of their luxurious antebellum lives.

"Thrown it away?" Ellie May said. "How so?"

"Lincoln's reputation is zero, and that old gasbag General Scott's reputation is zero minus ten. The Northern newspapers are howling over the Federal defeat at Bull Run—they're even saying that General McDowell was drunk during the battle. He's been sacked, at any event. Lincoln's appointed a new general, a young man named McClellan. But the point is, when we had the Yankees on the run, we should have marched into Washington and hanged Abe Lincoln from a lamppost. But we didn't. We didn't do *anything*, dammit, and I'm afraid it may cost us the war."

"Father!" exclaimed Charlotte, who was hurrying down the gracefully curved stair. "Is there any news from Clayton?"

"He's regained consciousness," said Phineas, who was wearing a white suit. "I received a dispatch from Elvira Plantation. The doctors say he's going to be all right. Of course, he's going to be a cripple, but he's alive."

"Can I see him?" she asked, hurrying to him and hugging him. "Oh, I miss him so!"

"Well, I'd give him some time to gain his strength. He's gone through a terrible ordeal. But probably in a week you'll be able to drive over. It would probably boost his morale to see you."

"What good news! I can hardly wait!"

"Now run along. I want to talk to your mother. Ellie May, come into the library."

He crossed the hall and went through the door beneath the center of the swooping stair. "There's total confusion in Richmond," he said after Ellie May joined him, closing the door. "Jeff Davis is a fine man, but I fear he may not be up to the job. He's not flexible enough."

"What do you mean?"

"He's becoming convinced that time is on our side, that all we have to do is keep the Yankees out of Virginia and wait. However, he realizes we have to get recognition from England and France and, as you know, he sent Senators Mason and Slidell on a British mail steamship to England to argue for recognition."

"Has something happened to them?"

"Yes. A Federal naval commander stopped the *Trent*, the British mail ship, and removed the Slidells and the Masons, who are now in a Boston prison. Thank God, Mrs. Slidell managed to hide the documents we had sent in her crinolines, but still her husband's in jail, and Lord Lyons, the English Minister, is furious. So is Jeff Davis, and he's authorized me to go in their stead. I'm sailing from New Orleans on an English ship next Sunday. . . ."

"But the blockade! How will you get through?"

"The same way everyone else is getting through: we'll sneak through. At any rate, with my English connections—in particular, Horace Belladon—I think I can succeed, if I can get there. The English textile manufacturers desperately need our cotton, and we have reason to believe Lord Palmerston and most of the ruling class are sympathetic to our cause. So pray for me, Ellie May. I'll need your prayers."

She looked surprised. "But am I not going with you?"

"Of course not. It's too dangerous."

"Oh dear," she sighed. "And I was so looking forward to doing some shopping in London."

Her husband snorted. "Shopping? By thunder, madame, this is war! There'll be time enough for shopping after we win. And if we don't win . . ." He shook his head.

"What? What do you think, Phineas?" She looked frightened.

"Well, there's no need for alarm."

"No, I want to hear the worst."

"If we don't win, Ellie May, we may not be able to *afford* to go shopping for a long, long time."

His name was Roscoe, he was the overseer of Elvira Plantation, he was six-feet-two with the physique of a bull, and he was crazy about Dulcey. As the giant black made love to her in the cottage behind the main house that was now the Confederate Hospital, his thoughts were not on the war, nor the neglected tobacco fields he tried to cultivate with only seven males left at Elvira, nor on Dulcey's rather dubious reputation. His thoughts were on one thing alone: coming. When he did, he let out a yelp.

"Roscoe, you hush," whispered Dulcey. "You want Aunt Lide to hear? She only next door. She catch you in here, she whup us both *good.*"

"Dulcey, honey, why don't you marry me? Then we wouldn't have to sneak."

"I don't feel like marryin' nobody yet," she said, getting out of the rumpled bed to go sponge herself at the basin. It was another hot night in this interminably hot summer. "Maybe when the war's over we can talk about marryin'. Maybe when we're free."

"Huh. Free. Don't look like nobody's gonna be free 'roun' here that *I* can see. I wouldn't count on no Yankees comin' in here sayin', 'Hey, Roscoe, you free. Hey, Dulcey, you free.' "

He stretched out on the cot and looked through the window above his head at the full moon as flies buzzed his sweaty chest.

"Uh-huh. Well, I *was* free till that Senator Whitney forced me back here to work."

"Yeah, free an' expensive. I heard what you was doin' in Yorktown in Miss Rose's fancy house, an' I heard what you was chargin'."

"You hush up, Roscoe, or I'll start chargin' *you.* I'm too good to you anyway. Probably *should* charge you."

He grinned. "You love it, and you know it," he said.

"There's others just as good as you. There's Cap'n Carr, for instance."

"Him? The white boy what lost his leg?"

"Uh-huh. He didn't lose his horns, though. When I come in his room, he looks like he could pounce. And when I give him sponge baths . . ." She snickered.

"What's so funny?"

"He gets hard as a rock. And so embarrassed! He turns all red in the face an' starts gulpin' and puffin' till I think he's gonna explode. An' I tell you somethin', Roscoe: I'm gonna let him get his way real soon. An' that's gonna be my revenge."

"Revenge for what?"

"You know his daddy-in-law is one of the meanest slave owners in the South. I heard stories of him whuppin' his slaves till they almost dead, an' there was a boy named Tucker they say he put in a rain barrel with nails in it and then pushed the barrel down a hill. Well, it's time the mighty Senator Whitney get a little of his own back. It's time we colored folk start showin' some fight."

Roscoe sat up. "What you gonna do?" he asked.

"You'll find out soon enough."

Lizzie could hardly believe that the morning she lost her love could have such beautiful weather. There should have been a storm, or a drizzle at the very least. But it was a sensationally beautiful day, not a cloud in the sky, the sea shimmering in the sun, sequins on blue-green silk.

"Papa, do you *have* to go?" asked Amanda, hugging Adam.

"Yes, darling. I have to go."

"But you'll be back next month, and you'll remember to bring me another surprise."

"Yes, I'll remember."

He was standing in front of the cottage. Lizzie was in the doorway, watching him. Angus, carrying Adam's bag, was climbing into the carriage, preparing to drive him to the Ayr train station. It was all so ordinary, so everyday, so suburban, even. Yet Lizzie kept thinking: I'll never see him again. This man I adore. Never. Is it possible?

"You know what I'd *really* like?" Amanda said.

"What?"

"A pussycat. Would you bring me a pussycat, Papa? A white one, if possible. I'd really like a white pussycat."

"Then you'll get one, my darling. Now give me a kiss. Then you go in with Mrs. Parker."

Adam picked his daughter up and hugged her. She threw her arms around his neck. "Oh Papa, you're the best Papa in the whole wide world," she exclaimed. "I just wish you could be here all the time."

"Yes, I wish that too, darling."

He kissed her.

"Why are you crying?" Amanda said.

He forced a smile. "It's just something in my eye. Now you run in. I want to . . . to speak to your mother a moment."

"All right. Good-bye, Papa."

"Good-bye."

He set her back on the brick path bordered by pink and white impatiens, and she scurried back to the house, brushing by her mother before vanishing indoors. Lizzie closed the cottage door, then came down the path to Adam. He took her hands.

"How do we say good-bye?" he whispered.

"I don't know."

"You'll write?"

"Yes, of course. To Mr. Lowery, in London."

"Where are you going?"

"I'm not sure. Perhaps to see my sister, to try and make it up with her. But I can't make any decisions yet. I have to . . . well, get used to . . ."

She was trying not to cry, but she couldn't help herself. Suddenly she was in his arms.

"Oh Adam," she sobbed, "we *are* doing the right thing, aren't we?"

"You know what I think about that. You know you're sending me away from the one thing that means anything to me: you."

"That's not true. There are the children. . . ."

"Oh, I know. The children. My so-called political career. My position. The Marquess of Pontefract. All the pomp and show. But the circumstance is that I love you, and what is it all without you? What is life without love?"

"Please, darling, don't say these things. You're just making it more difficult."

"Remember Newfield Abbey? Remember two children on the moors?"

"And you said you would be my knight. You have been, my love. The truest knight that ever was."

"If you're ever in trouble . . ."

"I know."

"Now, kiss me."

She pressed her lips against his. They kissed for almost a minute.

"You are my soul," she whispered. "Now, go, my love."

He raised her hands to his mouth.

"I don't believe this is the end," he said. "If nothing else, we'll meet again in another life."

He kissed her hands, squeezed them, then turned and went to the carriage. As Angus whipped the horses, he took one last look at her out the window. Then he was gone.

She walked slowly, numbly, back to the cottage, wondering if there were any more life left for her. At the door, she put her hand on the knob.

"Oh God," she said, "what have I done?"

CHAPTER 18

Charlotte Whitney Carr was met at the door of Elvira Plantation by Charles, Lizzie's former butler who now was literally stooped by age.

"I've come to see Captain Carr," she said.

"Yes'm."

"I'm his wife."

"Yes'm, I knows. We expectin' you. You de daughter of General Whitney."

"You have an excellent memory. It's been years since I was here."

"I never forgets kinfolk of General Whitney, no ma'am. You come in. De Captain, he upstairs in Miss Lizzie's room."

Lizzie Cavanagh! How often Charlotte had heard her parents tear that woman's reputation to shreds. She remembered the notorious Mrs. Cavanagh from the Christmas ball that now seemed so long ago and far away. As she entered the beautiful house, what she didn't remember was Elvira Plantation, because it had changed so drastically. Now the front hall, the drawing room and the dining room were all filled with cots, not one empty. Dozens of soldiers were stretching, sleeping, smoking, groaning, talking. It was a hot day, and the windows were open, but even so the place stank of smoke and sweat and medicine. Charlotte wrinkled her nose as she walked through the cots to the stairs. She was attracting stares, and the noise died down as the soldiers became aware of her presence.

"You got a relative here, ma'am?" asked one soldier, half of whose face was covered with bandages.

Charlotte paused on the first stair. "Yes, my husband,

Captain Carr. He was wounded at Bull Run. This is my first opportunity to visit him."

"Your husband's a fine soldier, ma'am."

"Why, thank you. You're all fine soldiers," she added, smiling at them. "And we're all mighty proud of you."

"This war'll be over by Christmas!" yelled one teenager who had lost his right arm at Manassas.

"Christmas, hell: Halloween!" yelled another, and they all laughed.

"All our prayers are with you," said Charlotte. Then she followed Charles up the stairs. She was wearing a white dress with a matching bonnet and was carrying a white parasol as well as a leather satchel. She had wanted to look as pretty as possible, meeting Clayton, but her anxiety was high. In his letters he had seemed so despondent about his missing leg—as well he might be—and she wanted to do her best to cheer him up. But at the same time she was nervous about how she would react to seeing his wound. Rather to her embarrassment, she had found she enjoyed the physical side of marriage much more than she had expected. The thought of a stump where a leg had been made her rather squeamish, though she was determined not to show it.

"Dulcey, dis here am Cap'n Carr's wife," said Charles, halfway up the stairs. Dulcey was at the top, watching Charlotte. "You show her to his room. I's gettin' too old for stairs."

"Thank you," said Charlotte. Then she continued to the top, where Dulcey awaited her. What a beautiful girl! she thought.

"Yo' husband's at de end of de hall," Dulcey said, leading Charlotte to the left. "I'm one of his nurses. Mah name's Dulcey."

"Well, I hope you take good care of him, Dulcey."

"Oh, I take *very* good care of Cap'n Carr. Extra-special care."

Charlotte thought her tone was rather curious.

"Cap'n Carr, he got de bess room in de house," Dulcey went on. "All private by hisself. Dat 'cause yo' daddy's so important."

"Is my husband in pain?"

"Not so much anymo'. In fact, he's gettin' what you might call real frisky lately." She gave Charlotte a suggestive smile as she opened the bedroom door. "Here's yo' wife, Cap'n, come to see de great hero."

Charlotte went by her into the room. Clayton was sitting up in bed, wearing a white nightshirt, the sheet over his waist. He looked tense.

"When we heard you was comin', we got him all bathed an' shaved. Don't he look purty?" Dulcey said from the door.

Annoyed, Charlotte turned and said, "Would you leave us alone, please?"

"Oh, sure."

Smiling at Clayton, Dulcey closed the door. Charlotte hurried to her husband's bed.

"Oh, my dearest Clayton," she said, taking his hand. "How I have prayed for this moment!"

She leaned over and kissed him.

"Charlotte, I—"

There was a laugh outside the room. It was Dulcey. Charlotte, frowning, turned to the door. "That despicable girl!" she said. "Surely you have white nurses?"

"Yes, there's Miss Wilson and the Pruitt twins on this floor. But Dulcey does the cleaning and serves meals."

His wife turned back to him. "Does she really *bathe* you?"

Clayton turned red. "Uh . . . well, uh . . . yes."

"How extraordinary. I'll have to talk to the authorities about that. But let's not discuss her. Oh my dear, brave husband, I can't tell you how proud I am of you! We *all* are so proud. Oh, I almost forgot. I've brought you some presents. Let's see." She put the leather satchel on a table and reached in. "Mother sent you a jar of the quince jelly you're so fond of. And I've brought you two books . . . I know you must get a bit bored here . . ."

There was another laugh outside the door. Charlotte put the books and jelly on the table and went to the door. She opened it. Outside was Dulcey smiling impishly.

"You're eavesdropping," Charlotte exclaimed angrily.

"Oh no, miss. I'd never do *dat.*"

"Go away! That's an order!"

"Yes, miss. Sorry." She waved past Charlotte at her husband. "See you later, Clayton." Then, smiling at Charlotte, she walked down the hall.

Charlotte closed the door and turned to her husband. "These darkies are getting terribly uppity, if you ask me," she said. "I suppose they think they're going to be freed by the Yankees someday, but they'd better get that notion out of their heads."

"Dulcey already was freed, by Mrs. Cavanagh. Your father forced her to come back here to work, so she's got a legitimate gripe, I suppose."

"Perhaps. But I think you should speak to her about calling you 'Clayton.' The servants have to remember their place. Now, where was I? Oh yes, the presents." She went back to the table. "The blockade's making it difficult to find certain things, so I knitted you a scarf. Of course, you won't need it for a few months, but I wanted you to know I'm thinking of you every moment. Here, try it on."

She had pulled a red scarf from the satchel. Now she put the scarf around his neck.

"It's lovely," he said. "Thank you. It's a bit hot, though."

"Of course. Take it off."

He handed it back. She replaced it in the satchel, then looked at Clayton. There was a tense, awkward silence. Then he said quietly, "Do you want to see what's left of your husband?"

She bit her lip. It was the moment she had agonized over. "Only if you want me to see."

Clayton closed his eyes, took the sheet and slowly lifted it off. Charlotte clasped one of the bedposts as she looked down.

"Pretty, isn't it?" he said, opening his eyes to look at her.

"It's a badge of honor," she said hoarsely. "Of course I wish it hadn't happened, but . . . oh, dearest Clayton, you should be proud of it. For the rest of your life, everyone will know you gave so much for the Glorious Cause!"

"I wonder," he said, putting back the sheet, "how glorious the Cause really is."

Charlotte stiffened, remembering the letters he had written her from Princeton. "Surely you're not having doubts again," she said. "After what you've gone through, after having been so wonderfully brave, surely your faith in what we're all fighting for cannot waver!"

"I never had that much faith in the first place, and you know it."

"But Clayton, this house is filled with brave men who have given so much . . ."

"Most of them joined the war just because they were looking for a good fight and wanted to take potshots at the Yankees. Most people don't think what they're fighting for, they just fight."

"I can't believe what I'm hearing!" she gasped.

"Well, believe. Charlotte, what you and practically everybody else in the South refuse to admit is that black people are human beings just the same as you and I are, and it's damned immoral for one human being to own another. It's that simple. That's what this war's being fought about, and we're wrong. I lost my leg for a wrong, immoral reason, so don't rattle on to me about any 'Glorious Causes,' or our Southern 'way of life,' or our 'right to secede' or whatever. This war is about slavery, and we're *wrong*. Period."

Charlotte clasped her hands together and closed her eyes, turning her face toward the ceiling and moving her lips.

"What in the world are you doing?" Clayton asked.

"I'm praying to Almighty God to bring truth and reason back into your heart."

"Well, you're wasting your breath and God's time. If God's on anybody's side in this crazy war, you'd better face the fact that He's probably on the Yankees'."

Her eyes opened, and they were blazing.

"I came here to bring my love and pride for my husband whom *I* consider a hero," she said with a good deal of asperity. "Even though some mad, perverse devil has temporarily taken possession of your mind and your tongue,

I will continue to think of you and respect you for what you were, and I'll pray that you return to what you were. And I might add, Clayton, that it would not be wise for you to talk this . . . this treachery to anyone else, in particular my father."

"I gave my left leg for the Confederacy, and I can say whatever I goddamn please! Now perhaps it would be better if you leave. I don't feel up to fighting with my wife."

She put her hands to her mouth and burst into tears. "Oh, how horrible!" she cried. "My own husband, speaking like a . . . like a damned Yankee!"

Grabbing her valise, she ran to the door and hurried out of the room. Clayton sighed. Then he leaned over and pulled out a drawer in his bed table. Reaching in, he brought out a small iron flask. Opening the lid, he put it to his mouth and took a long swallow. He leaned back in his pillows, letting the whiskey penetrate his system.

Then he took another long swallow.

Dulcey slowly ran her hands over his buttocks, kneading the flesh.

"Miss Pruitt done tol' me I'm not to bathe you no mo'," she whispered as she squished her naked breasts into Clayton's back. "So I guess dat mean all we can do is make love."

It was midnight. The windows were open, but there was scant breeze. Both Dulcey and Clayton were naked and slick with sweat. He was facedown on the bed, she on top of him.

"But you lak makin' love wid Dulcey."

"Yes," he whispered. As put out as he was at Charlotte after their fight that afternoon, he still felt guilty betraying her. But Dulcey had awakened in his maimed body a sensuality Charlotte had failed to arouse when his body was whole.

"Dr. Mainwaring, he say you doin' real good wid yo' crutches," she went on. "Purdy soon you gonna be able to go back home to Miss Charlotte. You gonna miss Dulcey?"

He gulped. He felt ready to explode with desire. "Yes," he whispered.

"Miss Charlotte, she not as purdy as Dulcey, is she?"

"No."

"An' I bet she not as good in bed eeder, huh?"

"No."

" 'Course, I learnt a lotta tricks at Miss Rose's. You lak Dulcey's tricks, don't you?"

"Yes."

"Turn over, honey. I'm gonna make you happy again. You gonna forget all your troubles."

She got off him as he turned over. He was in a state of intense ruttiness. He knew her "tricks" were dirty and debased, and it embarrassed him how much he enjoyed them.

She leaned over him and ran her tongue over his stump, licking it sensuously, something he found made him feel less like a cripple, as if she accepted his amputation without distaste.

Then her mouth moved slowly to his right.

"Look at de happy family all togedder agin!" Dulcey said to Roscoe ten days later as the two stood outside Elvira Plantation, watching Zack and Dr. Mainwaring help Clayton hobble on his crutches to the open carriage. In the carriage, also watching, were Charlotte and her mother, both holding parasols against the hot sun. In another carriage sat Brandon Carr. A number of Confederate soldiers watched from the open windows of the hospital. "Look at Clayton's wife, so snooty-lookin'. Wait till she finds out de little present I done gave her husband."

"What you talkin' about, Dulcey?"

"If she ever has any chillun wid Clayton, dey may come out wif two heads."

"Two heads? Is you crazy?"

"Miss Rose done tole me all about it. De white folks, dey got a disease dey call syph wot rots de insides an' drives dem crazy an' finally kills dem. Miss Rose tole me only white folk suffer from it an' dere ain't no cure an' it git passed on by makin' love. An' she say all her gals got it, so I figure I pass it on to de great Confederate war hero, Cap'n Clayton Carr. An' *dat* is Dulcey's revenge. Look: he's lookin' at me like a lovesick puppy, an' his wife she don't like *dat* no-how."

Dulcey chuckled. The carriage had pulled away. Clayton was looking back in Dulcey's direction, but Charlotte stuck her parasol behind his head to block his view.

Roscoe grabbed Dulcey's wrist. "You mean you got de pox?" he whispered.

"Uh-huh."

"But dat means *I* got it!"

"It don't matter. It don't do nuffin' to us."

"Why, you dumb nigger . . ."

"Doan call me dat!"

"Doan you know nuffin'? Miss Rose, she tole you dat so you wouldn't get scared, but if you got it, *I* got it, Massa Clayton *he* got it, so we all *three* gonna go crazy an' have two-headed chillun!"

"Roscoe, you doan know nuffin'. We're *safe*. Now, let go my hand."

Roscoe let go her hand, then slapped her face so hard she fell back into a rosebush.

Now it was Dulcey's turn to stare.

"My dear Sybil," said Mr. Disraeli a half-world away in the ballroom of Pontefract House, "you're to be congratulated. This ball is almost as brilliant as the ones I describe in my novels. If you don't watch out, you may become London's leading hostess."

"You make it sound like a fate worse than death, Dizzy," replied Sybil, who looked refulgent in an aubergine silk gown designed by Lucien Delorme. In her chestnut hair she wore the Pontefract tiara, a sunburst of diamonds and cabochon emeralds that had belonged to Adam's grandmother, and around her long, slim throat she had clasped a magnificent new diamond-and-emerald necklace she had designed for herself at Asprey, sending the fifteen-thousand-pound bill to Adam's agent, Mr. Lowery.

"It is a cruel fate only in that you will never be able to

believe what anyone says to you again," said Dizzy, whose monocle was firmly screwed into his left eye. He stood beside Sybil, surveying the gilded ballroom filled with waltzers, one of the first great balls of the 1861–62 winter season.

"I never *do* believe what anyone says to me except you, dearest Dizzy." Sybil smiled, putting her hand on his sleeve. She had fallen under the spell of the Conservative leader. She found him fascinating, witty and magnificently clever at weaving his way through the jungle known as London society and English politics, which were so closely intertwined. Though the successful middle class was elbowing its way upward, England was still controlled politically by about fifty families who were intermarried almost to the point of incest. In those days of feeble taxes, there was little incentive to hide one's wealth, and the razzle-dazzle of balls and dinner parties during the London Season was as much a part of the game as the endless house parties at the great estates in the country during the rest of the year. Sybil had every intention of leading the pack in both categories.

Her only problem was Adam. He had gone along with her increasingly heavy social schedule, not saying a word about the expense of the balls and dinners, accompanying her to the round of parties, ever the proper husband in public. To her surprise, he had also taken to politics with gusto, listening to Dizzy's many suggestions and maneuvers, seeming to enjoy the nuances of politics. Rather mysteriously, he had started making forays on his own into various sections of London, sometimes in strange disguises. When she would ask him what he was doing, he merely said, "Politics," leaving her baffled.

The problem was, still, Lizzie. While he had been able to see her once a month, his relationship with his wife had been warm, even loving. But now that Lizzie was out of his life, his marriage had resumed its old tensions, and Sybil knew why: Adam blamed her for losing Lizzie. But Sybil was in for the long haul. She loved her husband, and she had gotten rid of Lizzie. If she endured, she told herself, ultimately she would win Adam back.

However, tonight a new and potentially troubling element had been introduced: that stunning redhead from India, Emily McNair. Sybil had not understood when Adam inserted the McNairs' names on her invitation list for the ball. He had told her they were friends he had met in Calcutta who had extended to him their hospitality.

When she saw Emily, in her white ball gown with pink bows, she understood.

"She's beautiful, this Miss McNair," drawled Dizzy. "And your husband seems quite taken by her."

"Yes, doesn't he?" said Sybil, trying to remain unruffled as she watched the attractive couple dancing. Adam and Emily were the cynosure of all eyes.

"Miss McNair's mother contracted a liver ailment in India—a fierce climate, as you're undoubtedly aware. She's being treated in a sanatorium near Brighton. The family will be in England for perhaps a year. It would be most unfortunate if Adam's pristine reputation, which we have achieved at such considerable expense, were to be, shall we say, sullied again."

"Indeed it would."

"Especially since he's progressing so well politically. By the way, you'll be interested to know that he told me this morning he wanted to make his maiden speech in the Lords against British recognition of the Confederate states. You know that General Whitney has arrived in Southampton to rally support for the Confederacy, and General—formerly Senator—Whitney brings to mind unpleasant memories, if you know what I mean."

"Oh, I certainly do." Lizzie, she thought. Again. "I hope you dissuaded my husband?"

"Yes. I told him it would harm him in the Tory party, since by and large we Conservatives favor the South. He didn't like it, but he gave in."

"I'm delighted to hear it."

"We've kept him away from Scotland, but here he is ogling the fair Miss McNair. I fear Adam has a roving eye, but perhaps not. We must wait and see how things develop. Perhaps your husband has learned his lesson and now values the joys of the family hearth. I read a recent statistic that says over eighty percent of English men are faithful to their wives. On the other hand, I have always thought there were lies, there were damned lies, and then there were statistics."

"You don't offer much encouragement to us poor English wives, Dizzy. But you're right: we'll watch and wait for developments."

Meanwhile, to be on the safe side, she began to look around the crowded ballroom for attractive young men who might divert Miss McNair's obvious interest in her husband.

"Yes, India has settled down since the Mutiny," Emily was saying to Adam five minutes later as he gave her a tour of the house. "But much as I love India, I hope to be able to live here in England."

"Why so?" said Adam.

"The Mutiny left so much ugliness between the natives and the English. Now that India is part of the Empire, one would think that ugliness would naturally diminish, since we are all subjects of the Queen. But just the opposite has happened. If your skin is white in India, you are the master. And if your skin is dark, you're treated like a dog. Of course, it was always that way to a certain extent, but it's much worse now. I've seen Englishmen kick their servants, scream at them . . ." She shook her head. "I hate it. It doesn't seem fair, and it certainly doesn't seem Christian, which is part of what the Empire is supposed to be about."

India flooded back into Adam's memory, all its gorgeousness and all its squalor. His Indian blood surged into his memory, too. It was then he decided he had been wrong to give in to Disraeli that morning. Slavery of black men was wrong. He was in a position to influence Englishmen, and he should speak out against it.

"But let's not talk about India," Emily went on, brightening into a smile. "I must confess I was delighted when Mama was told she had to come to England to be treated. I was hoping I could see you again."

They looked at each other. Adam remembered the last time he had seen her at Government House in Calcutta.

She had certainly been blunt then about her feelings toward him.

"Ah, there you are!" said Sybil, coming into the library with a young man in tow. "Dear Miss McNair, I have a young gentleman who has begged me to introduce him to you. Miss McNair, this is the Honorable Richard Faversham, Lady Chalfont's son. I am told he's the best dancer in London. You must give me a report later on. Adam," she added, turning her eyes on her husband, "you are missed in the ballroom."

Adam nodded to Emily. "You will excuse me?" he said as his wife took his arm.

Emily watched them leave the room. There's trouble between them, she told herself. And that's good news for me.

"Dizzy, I've changed my mind," Adam said twenty minutes later after he had finished a Sir Roger de Coverly, the popular dance, with Sybil. "I intend to speak in the Lords against the Confederacy."

Disraeli lowered his champagne glass. "My dear Adam, why?" he said. "I told you what harm it would do to you in the party."

"If the Conservative Party favors slavery, then the Conservative Party is wrong."

"It's not a question of favoring slavery, dear boy. It's more a question of economics, that dreary science. Our textile mills have depended on the South's cotton for years, and this blasted Federal blockade is ruining business."

"Our textile manufacturers are buying cotton from Egypt and elsewhere. The point is, Dizzy, we have to take some sort of moral stand about the Confederacy, and I've decided I'm the man to do it. I think that when the average Englishman hears how strongly I feel, he'll be in favor of letting the South hang."

Disraeli frowned. "Of course, you must follow your conscience," he said. "But as your political mentor, I can only warn you that you're making a grave error. And before you take this rash step, let me tell you in strict confidence that when I get in office, I have every intention of naming you to a Cabinet post, probably as Secretary of State for India. But of course, if you go against the party's wishes . . ." He shrugged.

Adam hesitated. Secretary of State for India: it was a dazzling prize, and it was not the first time Disraeli had brought the matter up, though previously his allusions had been hints and Adam was sophisticated enough to know that the slippery Dizzy had not exactly committed himself. But still, it was a tempting carrot. And if what Emily had just told him about racial animosity in India was true—and he had little doubt that it was—it might mean he could improve conditions for his blood brothers in the subcontinent.

He and Dizzy were standing at one side of the ballroom. Now Adam took the statesman's arm and led him through the house to the library where he closed the door, giving them privacy.

"You told my wife," Adam said, "that your country estate in Buckinghamshire has caused you a great deal of financial trouble in recent years. As I understand it, you bought Hughenden a dozen or so years ago in order to acquire a safe political base for your seat in the Commons."

"That's so."

"Your financing was provided by the Duke of Portland, who lent you twenty-five thousand pounds to buy the freehold. It was more or less understood that the loan was a gift—or something you could repay the Duke whenever you wished."

"Yes. The Duke was immensely rich and the money wasn't that important to him. Unhappily, he died five years ago, and his son, Lord Titchfield, succeeded. I need hardly tell you the Bentinck family are noted for their eccentricities, but the present Duke is exhibiting signs of being barking mad. He's built a series of tunnels beneath Welbeck Abbey where he spends most of his time like a mole, and if one of his servants dares to speak to him, he sacks the poor fellow on the spot. It's this lunatic who demanded I repay him the twenty-five thousand pounds, which has caused me severe financial embarrassment. I've had to go to the moneylenders, and the interest on the principal is, for a man of my modest financial resources, a severe burden."

"Then let me buy up your debts, Dizzy. You can owe *me* the money, and I'll charge you only two percent interest."

Dizzy's monocle dropped from his eye. "My dear Adam," he said, "are you serious?"

"Very. Let's say it's an investment in my political future, as well as the future of England. You'll make a first-rate Prime Minister, Dizzy, and I want to be a part of your team. All I ask in return is that you smooth things over for me with the party after I make my speech in the Lords against the Confederacy."

Dizzy slowly smiled. "You're a sly fox," he said. "I think you'll go far in politics."

Letter from Queen Victoria to Lord Palmerston.

Windsor Castle
1 December 1861

The Queen is so *very* distressed by the mysterious illness of her beloved husband that it is only with the *greatest* difficulty that she can attend to affairs of state. Oh, if anything should happen to her dearest . . . But the Queen must not dwell on such morbid speculations. Surely He who watches over the destinies of our beloved nation would not allow such a disaster to occur.

Ld. Palmerston is aware that the Queen was shocked and outraged when the Americans boarded the *Trent* and forcibly removed the two Southern senators, Messrs. Mason and Slidell, who were on their way to England to plead the Confederate cause. The Federals are such ruffians! To break maritime law thusly was an outrage, and the Queen will admit that for a time she was in agreement with those in the Government and the Opposition who were clamoring to declare war on the North. However, the Queen's beloved husband convinced her of the inadvisability of such a course of action and persuaded her that it is to England's advantage to remain neutral in the conflict raging in America. Thus, it came as something of a shock when the Queen learned that Ld. Pontefract is planning to speak in the Lords against the Southern cause. And yet, on reflection, she has concluded that the great moral issue of slavery cannot be ignored by our nation and that perhaps no one is better qualified to speak out against it than the man whom all true English men and women look up to, the admirable Ld. Pontefract.

Signed,
V.R. (Victoria Regina)

The snow was whirling around his carriage as Phineas Thurlow Whitney pulled up in front of the grim, fortress-like mansion set in a pine wood outside Manchester, England. The house, which Horace and Lettice Belladon had completed the year before, was built of dark stone and was dominated by a four-story clock tower. Though the local press had rhapsodized over its "Florentine-style architecture," as Phineas climbed out of the carriage, his private opinion was that the place was a horror. He went to the heavily carved front door and rang the bell. A butler admitted him and took his top hat and cloak. A fire blazed in a baronial stone hearth above which hung an enormous Landseer painting of two soulful-eyed dogs. Then the butler led Phineas across the hall to two sliding doors, which he opened.

"Senator Whitney," he announced.

Phineas went into a darkly paneled library where he was greeted by the Belladons. After pouring the American a whiskey, Horace said, "Well, Phineas? Any luck in London?"

The tall, white-haired Virginian, who was beginning to show his years, shook his head.

"No. The sympathy of the Tories for the most part is with the Confederacy, but Lord Palmerston is dead set against recognizing us, so I got nowhere. And now, to make it worse, none other than our old friend,

Lord Pontefract, is making a speech in the House of Lords condemning slavery and the South. And if he does that, my friends, I might as well leave England." He looked at Lettice. "I don't suppose, Mrs. Belladon, that there would be any way you might influence him through your sister? I'm told in London that he still has . . . How can I put it delicately?"

"Don't bother to put it delicately," said Lettice. "Everyone knows Lizzie is still his mistress. And as far as my influencing Lizzie, that would be wishful thinking. I'm sure she detests me for what I did to her, although I was only trying to have justice done. I *still* think she murdered my poor, unfortunate father."

Phineas frowned.

"If we could prevent Lord Pontefract from speaking," Horace said, "would there still be a chance of getting English recognition for the Confederacy?"

"My best hope would be from you and the other textile manufacturers," Phineas said. "If you bring enough pressure on the Government, there would be a good chance of changing the Cabinet's mind. And, as I wrote you, if you can help the South in its darkest hour, the South will be extremely grateful to Belladon Textiles after the war."

"Assuming you win."

"Exactly."

Horace raised his glass and took a sip of the strong whiskey. In his letter, Phineas had pledged the Confederacy to sell Southern cotton to Belladon Textiles at a rate ten percent cheaper than any of its competitors—that is, if the South won. It was an incredibly sweet deal for Horace. It would make him the biggest textile manufacturer in England.

"You said," Phineas prompted, " 'if' we could prevent Lord Pontefract from making his speech. Is there a way to do it?"

Horace took another sip. "My dear Senator," he said, "there's always a way to do anything. All it requires is the wit and the will. In the past, when I've had labor unrest in my mills, I've used the services of professional strikebreakers. Not to put too fine a point on it, these are people from the criminal class. With the stakes so high and time so short, I think we must consider employing their unique talents."

"Exactly what," Phineas said, eying the portly manufacturer with new interest, "do you have in mind?"

The sea crashed angrily as Lizzie walked along the sandy beach, a black cloak wrapped around her, a golden curl escaping from her hood and flapping in the stiff wind. A winter storm was blowing in, but Lizzie had come to love the sea in all of its many moods, including the infrequent storms, and she loved walking the beach while bracing against the wind. Whitecaps curled on the waves, spraying the spume into the air. An occasional sea gull swooped in the wind, cawing wildly. She had come to know the shore intimately, taking her daily walks. If anything had saved her sanity during the long months since Adam's departure, it had been walking the beach, greeting the occasional fisherman but otherwise alone with her thoughts and her memories of Adam. Sometimes she would see a man far down the beach, and for a moment her blood would surge, thinking it might be Adam defying her ban and returning to her. Then it would turn out to be a stranger and she would tell herself she was foolish to harbor such fantasies, that Adam was a beloved thing of the past—memories of his kisses notwithstanding—and life had to go on. Perhaps there would be someone else someday, but she knew in her heart no one could ever be as exciting as Adam. She was lucky to have had one such perfect love in her life, which was probably more than most women were allotted.

About ten in the morning, as the black clouds piled ominously in the western sky, she turned around and started back to the cottage. The shore was mostly empty, aside from an occasional fisherman's cottage. Flocks of sheep roamed the hills above the beach, tended by fresh-faced boys with their collies. She sometimes asked herself if she could spend the rest of her days in this lovely, peaceful place. Having experienced more turmoil in her short life than most people experienced in long lives, the prospect was not unappealing. She passed Culzean Castle, a dark, brooding pile high above the beach with its gorgeous oval staircase designed by Robert Adam and its view of the Firth of Clyde and the distant island of Arran. Yes, she thought, she could live out the rest of her days here.

She sensed something was wrong when she walked up the brick walk, because the cottage door was open, banging in the wind. Suddenly tense, she hurried into the house. She screamed. Mrs. Parker, a gag over her mouth, was tied to one of the chairs by the fire.

"Mrs. Parker!"

She hurried to her and untied the gag.

"Amanda!" cried the old woman. "They took my baby! Oh God. . . ."

"Who?"

"Two men in masks! They took my precious Amanda!"

"What do you think, Mr. Ridley? Too much eyebrow?"

The man sitting in front of the makeup mirror in the basement of Pontefract House was applying false gray eyebrows to his face, which sported a long, false gray beard. Mr. Ridley, the butler, stood next to the man, inspecting the transformation from young nobleman to old peddler. For the person in the ragged black coat at the dressing table putting on theatrical makeup was Adam.

"Perhaps a touch too much, milord," Mr. Ridley said. The butler was baffled by his employer's strange new hobby, which Adam had taken up with enthusiasm several weeks before. Behind Mr. Ridley was a steel rack which held a variety of costumes. On the dressing table in front of Adam were jars of makeup and greasepaint, with pencils for drawing in wrinkles. "Where is milord planning to go this afternoon, if I may be so bold as to inquire?"

"I thought I'd take a trip to Whitechapel."

The butler gasped. "Whitechapel, milord? I beg of you to reconsider. It's one of the most dangerous slums in London! Even the police won't go there unless there is some terrible crime. To go to Whitechapel without a personal bodyguard is madness, begging milord's pardon."

Adam looked up at him and grinned. "Do you want to come with me, Mr. Ridley?" he said.

The butler coughed.

"You see, when I was in India," Adam went on, returning to his makeup, "I was forced to disguise myself as an Indian. It was an interesting experience, Mr. Ridley, because when you put on a disguise, it's almost like becoming invisible. You can go where you wouldn't be able to go as yourself, if you see what I mean. For instance, if I go to Whitechapel dressed as Lord Pontefract, I probably wouldn't come out of the place alive. At the very least, they'd rob me blind. But if I go dressed as an old peddler, nobody will pay any attention to me. I'll be invisible."

"But why go at *all*, Sir?"

"Because I want to see it. I know you think I'm mad—"

"Oh *no*, milord."

"—but these past few weeks I've gotten to know London well. I'll wager I know it much better than most of my other noble colleagues in the House of Lords, who wouldn't set foot in Whitechapel or anywhere else except the West End. I want to see how the poor live in this country, because how can I possibly help them if I don't know anything about them? And I *want* to help them. That's why I'm in politics."

"Mr. Ridley?" It was Dorothy, one of the scullery maids, who had appeared at the top of the basement steps. "Excuse me, but this envelope was just pushed under the service door."

Mr. Ridley went to the stairs and took the envelope.

"It's addressed to you, milord," he said, returning to Adam and handing it to him.

Adam opened the envelope and pulled out a note.

"Pontefract," read the crudely scrawled note, "we have your daughter, Amanda. She won't be hurt if you don't speak out in the Lords on slavery. But if you *do* speak, Amanda dies."

The note was signed, "Friends of the Confederacy."

CHAPTER 19

An hour later, Adam, dressed as himself, pulled up in his carriage at number four Whitehall Place. He jumped out and ran to the door, barging into the reception room of Scotland Yard.

"The Marquess of Pontefract to see Inspector Quaid," he blurted out to the receptionist. The young policeman looked up, bug-eyed.

"Lord Pontefract?" he said. "The bleedin' 'ero of Cawnpore?"

"The same."

The receptionist almost jumped on top of his bench to reach down and shake Adam's hand. "This is a great moment in me life, sir! I'm 'onored to make your acquaintance. Me uncle, 'e was killed at Meerut, 'e was, by the bloody wogs."

"Yes, uh, if you don't mind, this is an emergency."

"Right you are, guvnor! Come this way. My my, Lord Pontefract! Wait till I tell me wife, she won't believe it."

He led Adam down a short corridor to a small office on the right. "Lord Pontefract to see you, Inspector."

Adam, top hat in hand, entered the office which was lined with bookcases filled with law books and tomes on criminal investigation, including two recent publications, *The Detective's Note Book* and *The Diary of an Ex-Detective*, both by a certain Charles Martel, and an article by Charles Dickens published in his periodical *Household Words* called "The Modern Science of Thief-taking," as well as several examples of that newly popular genre, the *roman policier*, or detective novel. Adam hadn't seen Inspector Quaid for over four years, since their work together on the "Moors Murder," but he looked much the same: a short, wiry man with brown hair, bright red cheeks and rather squinty eyes, although he had since grown a mustache. He came around his cluttered desk to shake Adam's hand.

"Milord, I'm delighted to see you again. I trust there's no new difficulty?"

"In fact, there is. This note was delivered to my house an hour ago."

Adam, who was wearing a heavy cloak, pulled his wallet from his jacket, removed the piece of paper and gave it to the inspector, who quickly read it. "Is Amanda your daughter by Mrs. Cavanagh?" he asked.

"Yes, though I prefer to try to keep that confidential. I've sent a telegram to Ayr to confirm whether she's been kidnapped, but I have no doubt she has. I also have no doubt the same villain is behind this that was behind those trumped-up charges against Amanda's mother."

"General Whitney? Yes, I've read he's in England. 'Friends of the Confederacy' certainly sounds like him."

"On the way to Scotland Yard, I stopped at Claridge's Hotel, where Whitney has been staying. He checked out four days ago to go to Manchester. He left a forwarding address—in care of Mrs. Cavanagh's brother-in-law, Horace Belladon."

"Of Belladon Textiles? There's a break. Excuse me, milord. If memory serves, I have a file on Mr. Belladon."

The inspector went to a wooden file cabinet. Adam waited impatiently. He knew that the Metropolitan Police, which had been founded almost thirty years before by Sir Robert Peel to curb the criminal violence in London, called its headquarters Scotland Yard because it stood on the site of a place that, during the time of the Saxon kings, was used for visits of the Kings of Scotland. He also knew that all the crimes in London were investigated by a mere eight plainclothes inspectors, each earning one hundred pounds per year, the best of whom was Inspector Quaid, who had helped Adam save Lizzie from the gallows.

"Here we are," said Quaid, bringing a folder back to his desk. "I thought so. Mr. Belladon glories in the title of Chairman of the North England Manufacturers' Association, but he's a proper villain. Two years ago, there was a general strike at two of his mills—he pays some of the lowest wages in the industry, by the way. After four days, he brought in the Rogue Boys."

"Who are they?"

"A gang of ruffians who hire out as professional strike-breakers. It's quite a common practice among industrialists. In the ensuing brawl, a total of fourteen of Belladon's workers were wounded, including a twelve-year-old boy who suffered a broken skull."

"A twelve-year-old boy?" said Adam, amazed. "But what about Lord Shaftesbury's child-labor laws?"

Quaid shot him a dry look. "Milord, if you believe those laws are strictly enforced, then I fear you are either naif or ill-informed. Unscrupulous manufacturers like Belladon do what they can get away with. If they're caught, they pay the fine and go on about their business. Besides, Belladon is a heavy contributor to the Liberal party. The M.P. for Manchester is generally considered to be in his pocket, as is the Mayor. Belladon gets away with . . . well, I won't say murder."

"Would you say kidnapping?"

"It wouldn't surprise me. My point is, he has used the Rogue Boys before, so it's not inconceivable he's using them again. And if that's the case, we may have a lead. I'll send a wire to the Chief of Police in Manchester. I may have some news for you in the morning. I'll also send a wire to the police in Ayr to find out if they've started searching for the child. But for the moment, I fear that's about all we can do. I'm assuming none of your servants saw who delivered the note to your house?"

"No, it was slipped under the service door."

"Then I'd advise you to go home and wait. In kidnapping cases like this, my experience is that the best advice is patience and a cool head."

"But dammit, man, Amanda is in these scoundrels' clutches! God knows what they may do to her!"

Quaid waited a moment till Adam cooled down.

"It is to their advantage to leave her alone. I understand

your concern, milord. But I repeat myself: go home and wait. I'll contact you when we have news."

Adam started to say something. Then he picked up his hat and left the office. He was frightened for Amanda and frustrated by Quaid's advice to do nothing, though he thought he was probably right for the moment. But Adam was a man of action: he wouldn't wait too long. And he had a new goal.

Phineas Thurlow Whitney had gone far enough trying to frame the woman he loved. But by kidnapping his daughter, Whitney had gone too far.

As he emerged from Scotland Yard, Adam vowed that someday, one way or another, he was going to ruin Horace Belladon.

The young woman with the curly brown hair unlocked the door and pushed it open. It squeaked on its hinges. Ducking into the cold attic room, she lifted her candlestick high. The room was empty except for a sagging bed and a pitcher of water on the wooden floor.

"How are you, dearie?" said the woman, who wore a filthy brown dress. There was a shawl over her shoulders.

"I'm cold," said Amanda, who was sitting on the side of the bed. Her eyes were red from crying. "And I'm hungry. Where's my mama?"

"All in good time, dearie. All in good time. And if you're cold, get under the covers."

"But I haven't any nightgown."

"Don't be such a spoiled little brat. You'll do as I say or you won't get any supper. And stop whining."

Amanda started crying. "I hate you!" she sniffed. "And I'm afraid."

"There's naught to be afraid of, dearie, as long as you're a good girl. I'll be back in an hour with supper . . . that is, if you're a good girl. Good-bye, dearie."

She left the room and relocked the door. Then she put her ear to the planks. She could hear Amanda sobbing.

"Little brat," she muttered. Then she started down the sagging stairs.

Her name was Betsy.

* * *

" 'Mrs. Cavanagh's Daughter Kidnapped!' " Sybil read the headline. " 'Police Search Border Country!' " She put down the newspaper. As much trouble as Lizzie had caused Sybil over the years, as many pangs of jealousy as Sybil had felt because of Lizzie's hold over her husband, as a mother she couldn't help but feel a surge of pity for her rival. Kidnapping! The very word was terrifying. Sybil had seen the effect of the news on Adam: he was devastated.

A towheaded boy ran into the drawing room where Sybil had been reading the paper. "Mama!" exclaimed the boy. "Arthur stole my biscuits!"

"Shh! Henry," said his mother. "Stop making so much noise. Your father's upstairs trying to get some rest. Where's Miss Partridge?"

"In the nursery with Arthur."

"Well, go back upstairs. And please keep quiet."

"Yes, Mama."

"Come here and give me a kiss before you go."

Henry ran across the room. Sybil leaned down so he could throw his arms around her. She smiled as she kissed him.

"You look like an angel, darling," she said. "And you must behave like one."

"Yes, Mama. But Arthur's no angel. I think he's a devil."

"Don't say things like that. And you two boys stop fighting."

"Oh, all right."

She released him and he ran back out of the room. Sybil stood up, a sad look replacing her momentary smile. The guilt she felt about Edgar Musgrave had been compounded by Amanda's kidnapping: neither Henry nor Arthur even knew they had a half-sister to worry about. But one day, surely, they would have to know, wouldn't they?

Mr. Ridley, the butler, came in the room.

"Pardon, milady, but Inspector Quaid has just arrived. He has some news. Should I wake His Lordship?"

"Oh yes, definitely. And send the inspector in here."

"Yes, milady."

"We've had a bit of luck," Quaid said fifteen minutes later as Adam joined him in the drawing room. "Your very celebrity in England has helped us: even the worst criminals want to help you."

"Do you know where she is?"

"We think we do. An informer told us she's being held here in London, in a house in Wapping. I sent a wire to Mrs. Cavanagh, and staked out guards to watch the place. We're organizing a raid on the house—"

"No," Adam interrupted. "Amanda might get hurt."

"I fear, milord, that a certain amount of risk is inevitable."

"Not if I can help it. I have another way, Inspector. Let me try my way first."

Quaid was about to protest, but after a moment he gave in. "Very well."

It wasn't easy to say no to the hero of Cawnpore.

The young man from New York had been sneaking looks at the beautiful woman sitting opposite him in the railway carriage. He had come aboard the London express at Manchester; finding himself alone in the compartment with this angel of beauty, he thought he must have used up all his excess luck for the next month. His mind raced to think up an opening gambit to begin a conversation. However, she looked so sad as she stared out the window at the passing countryside, he found it difficult to find an appropriate ice-breaker. But whatever Alex Sinclair's many faults, lack of nerve was not one of them. Fifteen minutes south of Manchester, he took a deep breath and leaned slightly toward her.

"Excuse me, ma'am, but being a vulgar American, I don't know the niceties of train travel in England. Is it considered rude to speak to strangers?"

Lizzie turned from the window and looked at him. What she saw did not displease her. He was well-dressed—perhaps even a trifle too well-dressed—and had slim, dark good looks that reminded her a little of Adam.

"I beg your pardon?"

"I said, is it considered rude in England to talk to

strangers on trains? It's not in America. In fact, in America you can't get people on trains to shut up."

"Yes, it is considered rude," she said. "Especially to an unaccompanied woman."

She turned back to the window. The young man cleared his throat. "Well, a lot of people have told me I'm rude. My name is Alex Sinclair, and I'm from New York. Of course, I suppose you think America is farther away than Mars."

"On the contrary, I've lived in America. My late husband was American."

"No kidding? Where was he from?"

"Virginia. He was a tobacco planter."

"Oh. Well, you're well out of *that* mess. Looks to me as if that war's going to last a lot longer than people thought. And if you ask me, Abe Lincoln is a big disappointment—and I voted for him."

Lizzie looked at him again. "Oh? How so?"

"Last July, the North was whipped at Bull Run. Then in August, Northern troops were beaten in Missouri. In October, the North was whipped at Ball's Bluff in Virginia. It just seems to me Abe can't find a decent general. All he's good for is telling jokes. It's a shame, because the war's bad for business, at least so far."

"You're a businessman, Mr. . . . ?"

"Sinclair. Alex Sinclair." He smiled, flashing straight white teeth. "Yes, I own an emporium in New York, Sinclair and Son. I'm the son. The store was founded by my father thirty years ago, but he's passed on. If you're ever in New York, drop in. I'll give you some irresistible discounts. My prices can't be beat."

She didn't know whether she disliked his brash Yankee cockiness or was intrigued by it.

"I take it you're not interested in fighting in the war, Mr. Sinclair?"

"My mother had a bad stroke—just like my dad—and I'm her only support. Are you going all the way to London?"

"Yes."

"Me too. You know, I've developed a theory about you

English. You pretend to be reserved, a bit shy, a bit snooty—"

"Do you find me snooty?"

"A little. But when you get to know you, *if* you can get to know you, which takes work, you generally turn out to be nice people. Now, you must have a theory about Americans?"

She frowned. "I have several theories about *Southern* Americans, and they're not very flattering. I hardly know any Northern Americans."

"Well, now you do, so you have several hours to come up with a theory. Let me predict: you'll say that I'm rude—which I've already admitted—much too *un*reserved, not shy enough, and, let's see: oh yes, I'm a flashy dresser. But when you get to know me, I'm really a wonderful fellow."

"Is that what you think I'll think?"

"That's what I *hope* you'll think. But you have the advantage. You know my name, but I don't know yours."

She hesitated. "Mrs. Cavanagh," she finally said.

He stared at her. "Wait a minute . . . not *the* Mrs. Cavanagh, who's in all the papers?"

"Unfortunately, yes."

"Why, you're famous. Oh . . . your daughter . . . I mean, is she . . . ?"

"There's reason to hope she'll be all right."

"Say, that's wonderful. I'll keep my fingers crossed. And I'll understand if you . . . if you'd rather I stop talking."

She smiled at him. "I'd appreciate that, Mr. Sinclair. I am rather . . . tense."

"Of course. But it's been swell meeting you, Mrs. Cavanagh. And if you're ever in New York, look me up. Sinclair and Son. Union Square. Finest emporium in New York, though we're starting to call it a department store. I'll give you a terrific discount."

Despite being preoccupied by her fears for Amanda's safety, Lizzie found that she rather liked the brash young man from New York.

* * *

The boy kneeling in the muck beside the Thames River was filthy, his curly brown hair beneath his cap so dirty that the individual hairs were in many places matted. Even though it was a cold day with swirling fog, the boy wore no coat or hat or shoes, and his only protection against the elements was a piece of a blanket he had stolen from a horse.

"What are you looking for, young man?" said the tall, bearded Indian lascar whose rags were almost as pitiful as the boy's. It was Adam's "poor Indian sailor" disguise, and he adopted the musical accent of Hindus speaking English.

The boy looked up. "It's none of your bleedin' business, you dirty wog," he said, his Cockney accent mangling his English almost to incomprehensibility.

"What a sweet little boy you are." Adam smiled, leaning down and grabbing his ear. The boy howled as Adam jerked him to his feet. "Now you will answer my questions, please, or I will shove your rotten teeth down your throat. Why are you searching through the mud?"

"I'm lookin' for coins, I am, an' you're 'urtin' me bloody ear!"

"Yes, I know. You have a very pretty older sister, I believe. I've seen her come in and out of your house. Very, very attractive she is. How much does she charge?"

The boy began pounding his fists into Adam's stomach. "She ain't no 'ore!" he yelled. "She ain't!"

Adam stuck his free hand in a pocket of his ragged trousers and pulled out a shilling, which he held in front of the boy's face. He stopped hitting Adam and stared at the coin.

"This is for you, young man, if you answer my questions."

He released the boy's ear and handed him the coin.

"She charges 'alf a quid, but she'd charge more to do it with a bloody wog."

"I see. Is it possible she's at home now?"

"I dunno. Probably. She rests durin' the daytime."

"For another shilling, would you be so kind as to lead me to your house, young man?"

The boy looked suspicious. "If you know where me 'ouse is, wot do you need me for?"

Adam smiled, pulling another shilling from his pocket. "Because I like your company, young man, and I want you to negotiate with your sister for me. She might not want to let a 'bloody wog' in the house, if you know what I mean. There's a third shilling in it for you."

The boy took the second shilling. "Well, all right. But I don't guarantee nuffing. Me sister's pretty picky. Come on."

He began squishing out of the mud up to an embankment, and Adam followed. They were near the Black Lion Wharf in Wapping, a district that stretched from the London docks to Brunel's railroad tunnel under the Thames, one of the engineering marvels of the day. Adam followed the boy along the riverside, catching glimpses of taverns and grog shops through the fog, stepping out of the way of drunken sailors. The river was a forest of masts and rigging.

In the months since his separation from Lizzie, Adam had come to know London inside out. He had also come to know the subtle—and not-so-subtle—nuances of class distinction which were so important to Londoners. The class of an Englishman was instantly recognizable to his fellow countrymen: it was not just a question of accent, though that was important, but the upper class, with their predominant Norman genes, even looked different with their high cheekbones, light coloring and sardonic blue eyes. In terms of both accent and looks, Adam realized he was different: but in terms of dress, he had become as elegant as his fellow peers, who dressed so differently from the middle and lower classes. They wore top hats indoors and out, except at home or in church. Their frock coats were exquisitely sewn by the world's best tailors; their trousers swept the ground at the heel, but rose over the instep. Since dry cleaning was unknown, garments had to be taken apart at the seams, hand-washed, then restitched together. Only expensive tailors knew how to do this properly, so only the rich could afford to look natty. The middle class, whose men wore bowlers instead of top hats, always looked slightly shopworn and wrinkled. And the poor had no choice but to wear castoffs of the superior classes, so that a costermonger might look like a tatty caricature of a banker in a ragged frock coat and battered top hat.

But when Adam began to explore the slums of London, often called the "stews," he saw firsthand the horrible world of the poor. Using his basement as a wardrobe room, he donned his various disguises and left by the service door for such grim-sounding destinations as Houndsditch, Bluegate Fields, Shoreditch and Seven Dials. Here he saw the vast underbelly of the Empire. And now, as he followed the beggar boy through the slum of Wapping, he was assaulted by the stink of the poor—the sweat, human and animal urine and general stench of a humanity that never bathed. But such varieties of stinking humanity! They passed oyster women, costermongers, lucifer-match boys, lemonade vendors, street urchins, Negro minstrels, shoeblacks, ice vendors, ginger-beer hawkers, chimney-sweeps, ratcatchers, rag dealers, dog sellers, flower girls, flypaper merchants, tinkers, ragmen, apple sellers, orange girls . . . and of course whores.

After a time, the boy turned down a narrow lane overhung with lines of washing that the coal dust of the city kept a permanent gray even when freshly laundered. Adam and the boy passed courtyards filled with offal and rubbish, through which children were poring, eating pieces of garbage. They were almost black from soot and dirt and seemed barely human in their rags. Yet they, like everyone else Adam had seen in the slums, for some peculiar reason wore some sort of hat. They passed a grimy gin shop, in front of which a woman lay passed out, an empty bottle in her hand. They passed so many drunks stumbling in and out of pubs, Adam began to wonder how the huge city functioned at all.

" 'Ere's me 'ouse," the boy said, stopping in front of a dilapidated three-story wooden house. "Wot you want me to do now?"

"Go in and see if your sister's available for me."

The boy shrugged, walked up the steps and knocked.

After a moment, the door was opened by a heavyset, bearded man.

"Is Betsy 'ome?" the boy said. "I got a customer for 'er."

The man shot Adam a suspicious look. "She's 'ome," he said. "You!" He addressed Adam. "You got any money?"

Adam pulled a small pouch from the pocket of his coat and held it up. He smiled as he said, "The very nice gentleman should know this is full of coins. The very nice gentleman should know that I just did a little job in a pub in Shoreditch."

The man frowned.

"Were you followed?" he said to the boy in a low voice.

"No."

"All right, you. Come in."

"You are very kind, sir. Very, very kind."

Adam hurried up the steps and followed the boy into the house, which smelled of stale beer and cooking onions.

"Go in the parlor," said the man, pointing to a room off the narrow stair hall. "I'll fetch Betsy. It's money in advance, you know. 'Alf for most, but for you she'll want more."

"You are very, very kind."

"I'll tell 'er to close 'er eyes and think of England."

Adam went in the parlor, which was filled with surprisingly expensive-looking furniture and a small upright piano draped with a fringed shawl.

"All right, you got me sister, but I ain't got me third shilling," said the boy behind him.

Adam handed him another coin, saying, "You are a very nice boy. Thank you very, very much. Now run along and play."

"To 'ell wif playin'. I got me three shillings. I'm goin' to buy me a pint or two."

The boy hurried out of the house, slamming the front door. Adam listened for a moment. The house was quiet. He pulled a pistol from beneath his coat and went to the hall door. The man had vanished. The informer had told them that Amanda was being kept in the attic. Moving quickly, Adam went into the hall and up the stairs to the second floor, then up another flight to the top of the house. Behind a closed door at the top of the stairs he heard a girl softly crying. He turned the key in the door and opened it. Amanda was sitting on the side of the bed.

"Don't make any noise," Adam whispered. "It's Papa. Come with me."

She ran to him, grabbing his hand. He led her down the stairs to the second floor, where they stopped to listen. Downstairs, two people were talking.

" 'E was 'ere a minute ago." Adam recognized the man's voice. "Where'd the bloody wog go?"

"Wot's a bleedin' 'Indu comin' 'ere for, anyways? It don't make no sense. They go to Lime'ouse . . ." said a woman's voice.

"God damn! The girl! Shit!"

The sound of someone running up the stairs. Adam let go Amanda's hand and ran to the head of the stairs. The man was halfway up and holding a gun. Seeing Adam, he raised it to fire. Adam fired first, point-blank at the man's chest. He didn't even grunt, although his gun went off, firing into the ceiling. He fell backward down the stairs, head over heels. The woman at the foot of the stairs screamed.

"Don't move!" Adam yelled. "Get your hands in the air or I'll fire!"

Whimpering, Betsy obeyed.

"Amanda!"

She hurried to her father's side and they both ran down the stairs, Adam jumping over the dead man's body.

"I hate you, Betsy!" Amanda cried into the woman's face as her father opened the front door. Inspector Quaid and five Bobbies poured into the house. Amanda ran to her father.

"Oh Papa, I missed you so!" she cried as he picked her up and kissed her.

"I missed you, darling. . . ."

"I was so scared!"

"Everything's going to be all right."

"Why do you look so funny?"

He laughed and kissed her again. Amanda now knew for certain she had the most wonderful father in the world.

Lord Pontefract Rescues Mrs. Cavanagh's Daughter!
Daring Police Raid in Wapping!
Gang Leader Killed!

All England thrilled at the headlines. At Windsor Castle, the Queen, desperately worried about the state of her husband's failing health, nevertheless devoured the details of the Wapping Raid, then read the accounts to Prince Albert, who was in bed in the famous Blue Room, the King's Room where both George IV and William IV had died. Albert, who for days had been drifting in and out of delirious hallucinations, mumbled, "That Pontefract . . . a most remarkable fellow. . . ."

"Oh, he is the noblest of heroes!" gushed the Queen. "Such an example to us all! If only . . ." She sighed. "But they say he has left the Cavanagh woman."

"From the pictures I've seen of her, *Liebschen,* I can understand why Pontefract deceived his wife."

"Albert!" gasped the Queen. But then she realized her husband must be hallucinating again. The doctors had diagnosed his illness as cholera, caught, it was believed, from the effluvia of the medieval drains at Windsor Castle. The Queen was praying with all her heart, but her beloved husband had only days to live.

"We knew from the informer that there were three brothers in the house guarding Amanda," Adam said to Lizzie the afternoon of the raid. Inspector Quaid had taken Amanda to her mother, who was staying at the Westminster Palace Hotel, while Adam went home to change out of his disguise. "The brothers were named Brock and the eldest, Tom, was the man I shot. When the two other brothers heard the shot, they ran out the back door where the police caught them. How's Amanda?"

"She's sleeping," said Lizzie, indicating a closed door at one side of the suite. "She's exhausted. Mrs. Parker bathed her and put her to bed. I had the hotel doctor look at her and she's all right, thank heaven."

"I think we have to face the fact this may happen again. The damnable thing about you and me, Lizzie, is that we're good copy for the press. Now that Amanda's been kidnapped once, it may give others the same idea. We have to find you a safe haven, and I want to hire bodyguards. You know that my father died?"

"No, I didn't. I'm sorry to hear it."

"It was just a matter of time. He'd drunk his liver into scar tissue. The point is, Thorne Manor is now empty. You and Amanda could live there where you're known, and we could hire locals to guard you. I understand that your younger sister is still at Wykeham Rise. Perhaps she could move in with you."

"Minna," said Lizzie. "Dear Minna. That would be nice."

Adam had kept a respectful distance from Lizzie since he came into the high-ceilinged living room of the suite with its splendid view of the Houses of Parliament. But now he crossed the room to Lizzie, who was seated on a sofa, and took her hand, raising it to his lips.

"Most important," he whispered, "we could be together again. Oh my darling, my life has been hell without you."

"Adam, don't. . . ."

"Why? To hell with being moral. You're as miserable as I am, and life's too short to be miserable! We must snatch happiness and hold on to it, and my happiness is you."

He pulled her out of the sofa into his arms and began kissing her. After a moment, she pushed him away, her taupe silk skirts rustling.

"We mustn't! I can't go through another separation, and it would come to that, Adam. You *know* it would!"

"It doesn't have to! We could make it work!"

"How? If I moved into Thorne Manor, Sybil would find out in short order, and then where would we be? The same dilemma, and Sybil is right. You have your two sons to consider, your political career—"

"Lord Palmerston has had more mistresses than the Sultan of Turkey, and he's done quite nicely with his political career."

"But don't you see?" she said angrily. "I don't *want* to be your mistress!"

Her anger surprised him.

"Don't you want to be with me?" he said softly.

"You *know* that, my darling. We are one—we always have been and always will be. But it won't work! I have to think of Amanda, if nothing else. There's only one real solution to this: I have to find her a new father. I have to remarry."

Adam thought a moment. Then he exclaimed, "Sybil's brother, Lord Ashenden. He's nice-looking, twenty-three, not a thought in his head nor a farthing in his pocket, but he's the heir and will be Earl of Nettlefield. He's looking for a wife, and with a little prodding from me . . . well, you could be the Countess of Nettlefield. Perfectly respectable, Amanda would be raised properly, and we'd be neighbors."

Lizzie laughed. "What a pretty picture that would be! And I suppose while Sybil and my husband are playing whist, you and I sneak off to have a tryst in the gazebo? Really, Adam . . ."

Again he took her in his arms. "I'm serious. It could work. Neville's a perfectly pleasant fellow, and he'd take one look at you and I guarantee he'd fall head over heels."

"But darling, it's deceitful and immoral. Probably even more immoral than our being together in Scotland. I don't want to marry a man under such grossly false pretenses."

"Lizzie, you're making this difficult . . ."

"It's not difficult: it's impossible. It's been an impossible situation from the very beginning."

She felt his hands grip her arms hard. A cold look came into his eyes.

"It's not impossible," he whispered. "There *is* a solution."

"What are you talking about?"

"Yes . . . that *has* to be the answer."

He released her and went to pick up his coat.

"Adam, what do you mean? What's the 'answer'?" she said, suddenly alarmed.

"Lizzie, I don't intend to give you up. I've done it once and I hated it. Perhaps people might call me a hopeless romantic, but I'm in love with you and always have been since I was a boy. By the way, wish me luck. I'm giving my maiden speech in the House of Lords tomorrow. Since General Whitney has left England, I believe there's no more threat to Amanda from him, at least, so I see no point in delaying the speech any longer."

He went to the door, putting on his coat.

"Adam, you haven't answered me," Lizzie persisted, hurrying to the door. "What is the 'answer'?"

He looked at her a moment, and she saw something new and terrible in his eyes.

Then he left the room, closing the door.

The following afternoon, Adam, looking striking in his impeccably tailored frock coat and trousers, walked into the House of Lords. The chamber was surprisingly small, only eighty feet long—twice the length of a large drawing room. With its extravagantly ornate decorations and deep red stained-glass windows, the place had the look of a rich private chapel. On either side of the hall were long red-leather sofas facing each other across the gangway, with dark wood choir stalls at the back. A huge red pouf with a backrest in the middle sat between the two sides. This was the Woolsack, the traditional seat of the Lord Chancellor. Facing the Woolsack were three men in wigs sitting at a large desk with inkpots. At the far end of the gallery was an immense gilded canopy, stretching halfway to the roof, with twenty-foot-high candlesticks on either side. In the middle of the canopy, on a red carpet, sat the throne from which the Monarch opened Parliament.

The House of Lords! thought Adam, trembling with nervousness, never having given a public speech before. But as he took his seat on the Conservative side of the house, something besides stage fright was bothering him. Sybil . . . the block to his happiness . . . after all, killing was so easy . . . he had killed Nana Sahib and become a hero.

What was driving Adam to the point of madness was not only seeing Lizzie again after so many months. At a political lunch given by Disraeli the previous week, Adam had been introduced to Edgar Musgrave..

Adam had seen with his own eyes that Edgar was an older version of his son, Henry.

CHAPTER 20

Sybil was awakened from a deep sleep by a noise. She sat up in her bed. The bedroom was dark, but there was enough light from the gaslights outside in Pontefract Square for her to see that a man was in her room.

"Who is it?" she whispered, trembling.

The man moved closer to her bed. Now she could see it was Adam. He wore a black robe over his naked body. There was a wild look in his eyes.

"Adam?" she whispered. "What is it?"

He was beside her bed now, staring down at her with those wide, wild eyes.

"I've met him," he whispered.

"Who?"

"Your lover. Edgar Musgrave. It's true, isn't it? He's Henry's father."

She stared at him. She was frightened. Suddenly, he lunged on top of her, grabbing her throat with his strong hands, pushing her back onto the pillows as he began choking her. "It's true, isn't it?" he said, almost sobbing. "You whore! It's true, isn't it?"

"Adam . . ." she gasped.

"Admit it! ADMIT IT!"

"Yes . . ."

She could hardly breathe. Her consciousness began swimming. He's going to murder me, she thought.

Then, suddenly, he released her. She was gasping for breath. He stood by the bed, trembling with rage.

"Henry must never know," he whispered. "Do you understand? He must *never know.*"

Then he turned and walked out of the dark bedroom.

"Madame," the bellboy said to Lizzie, "the hall porter says the Marchioness of Pontefract is in the lobby and asks if you will receive her."

Sybil! Lizzie was stunned. "Yes, of course. Please show her up."

The bellboy bowed and left. Lizzie closed the door and hurried across the living room to the second bedroom of the hotel suite. She opened the door and saw Mrs. Parker sitting inside.

"She's sleeping," whispered the nanny, coming to the door. She pointed to Amanda, asleep in the bed.

"Lady Pontefract is coming up. If Amanda wakes up, I don't want her coming in."

"She won't wake up. She's still exhausted, poor thing." Mrs. Parker closed the door. Lizzie went to a mirror and checked her reflection. For some reason, she wanted to look her best. Sybil! The longtime nemesis.

There was a knock. Lizzie went to the door and opened it. There was Sybil, looking magnificent in a sable cloak, for it was snowing in London and icy cold. For a moment the two women looked at each other in silence. Then Sybil said, "I can see why my husband is so infatuated with you. You are even more beautiful than I imagined. May I come in?"

"Please."

Sybil entered the suite, looking around as Lizzie closed the door. Then she took off her cloak and gloves. Underneath, she wore a beautiful burgundy dress. A diamond-surrounded cameo brooch was on her bosom.

"I decided it was time we met," Sybil said. "I don't intend to *faire de l'esclandre.* I don't like scenes. But we must come to some sort of understanding. You see, last night my husband almost murdered me."

Lizzie remembered what Adam had said to her just days before in the very same room.

"Why?" she said, gesturing to a chair. Sybil sat down.

"He's quite capable of it, you know. There's madness in his family. He had a great-aunt who was convinced she was a bald eagle and leapt from the roof of Thorne Manor to her death. And then look at what he did in India. Oh, the public loved the fact that he disguised himself as an Indian, but what he did no *sane* person would do. Do you realize he has a room in the basement of Pontefract House that is filled with costumes? He disguises himself as a beggar or organ grinder and goes out to roam the most wretched slums of London. I fear he's gone mad, and last night . . ."

She stopped, panic in her eyes.

"Yes, but murder!" said Lizzie, sitting next to Sybil. "Perhaps you're right and he's become mentally unstable, but surely Adam isn't capable of . . ."

"You don't think he would murder me to get you?" Sybil interrupted, turning to her. "You underestimate your power over him, my dear. His seeing you again has rekindled the old flame to a searing point. If only," she hesitated, a sad look coming over her face. "If only he loved me the way he loves you."

"You love him, don't you?"

"Very much, I've tried so hard to win him, and I was fairly successful until recently. But then . . ." Again she hesitated. "He has reason to murder me," she whispered. "I did a terrible thing to him after he left for India."

"Is it about your son?" Lizzie said.

Sybil looked startled. "You know?"

Lizzie nodded. "He told me in Scotland. He's suspected for some time that he's not the father of Henry."

"He's not," Sybil said. "Now that Henry has grown, there's no doubt about it. He's Edgar's son. Oh, it's all my fault . . . but I can't help but be afraid. I don't know what to do! I thought perhaps *you* could bring him to his senses."

Lizzie stood up. "You've done the right thing," she finally said. "We must make certain he doesn't harm you. I'm going to write Adam a note, which you must deliver for me. In it, I'll tell him there is absolutely no future for us together. I'll even lie and tell him I don't *want* a future with him. I'll make certain he'll never harm you. And then I'm taking Amanda to New York."

"New York?" Sybil said. "Why New York?"

"I'll wait out the war, at which point I should be able to get my property in Virginia back—or what's left of it." And she knew why she was choosing New York. She was thinking of the young man she had met on the train. "Perhaps you would be so kind as to wait downstairs. It's not going to be easy for me to write this letter."

Sybil stood up.

"Yes, of course." She went to get her cloak and gloves. When they were on, she turned to Lizzie, whose face looked drawn.

"For years," Sybil said, "I've been jealous of you. I fear that in moments of anger I said unpleasant things about you. I see now that I totally misjudged you. You are a fine person, Lizzie. It is mortifying for me to say this, but perhaps my husband would have been a happier man married to you."

"I think Adam married extremely well."

Sybil came to Lizzie, put her hands on her arms, and placed her cheek against hers. "Thank you," she whispered. Then she left. Lizzie closed the door. She leaned back against it, her eyes closed. Then she opened her eyes and went to a desk in front of the windows looking out over the Houses of Parliament. Sitting down, she looked at the view, thinking of Adam's political career. She hoped he would be happy. She pulled out a piece of writing paper and took a pen.

"Dear Adam," she began to write. But her tears blotted the ink. She took another piece of paper and started again.

An hour later, Sybil returned to Pontefract House. As the butler opened the front door, she asked as she came in, "Is my husband at home, Mr. Ridley?"

"Yes, milady. He is in his study."

"And my sons?"

"Lord Arthur is in the nursery with Miss Partridge, and Lord Henry is in the classroom with the French tutor."

"Thank you."

He took her hat and coat; then she went through the house to Adam's study, where she knocked.

"Come in."

She opened the door and went in. Adam was seated at his desk reading a parliamentary report on the condition of labor in the English textile mills. When he saw his wife, he stood up.

"I have been to see Mrs. Cavanagh at her hotel," Sybil said, coming to the desk. "She asked me to give you this letter." She handed the envelope to Adam, who looked amazed.

"You . . . saw Lizzie?" he said.

"Yes. It was a great revelation to me. I like and admire her."

She sat down in a wing chair as Adam resumed his seat and opened the letter. It read:

10 December 1861

My dearest Adam:

I have made up my mind to take Amanda to America. I will not lie to you by saying I don't want to be with you: you would never believe me if I did. I think that no two people have ever been closer than you and I, but we have to think beyond ourselves. As I tried to tell you in Scotland, we are both doing a terrible thing to Amanda. We *must* put the interests of our children ahead of our own interests, no matter how deeply we love each other. Perhaps we are Romeo and Juliet, star-crossed lovers. But their passion led only to the tomb, and when love becomes that destructive, then perhaps even love, the sweetest and most tender emotion, becomes something ugly. If life has any meaning, surely it is to bring children into the world and give them every opportunity to flourish. And you, of course, have your two sons to consider.

Having met Sybil, I think you must try to start anew with her. She does love you and wishes only good for you. You must never—I repeat, *never*—try to harm her. If my love means anything to you, you will lose it forever if you do anything ignoble or ugly. Remember that you are my true knight, and you must continue to act like one, even though I am going out of your life. I now realize the truth of what my poor father used to say in his sermons: that to be wicked is easy; what is truly difficult in this treacherous life is to be good. And Adam, *we must be good!*

I remember telling you that to leave you once would be hell to me, but to leave you twice would kill me. This is the second time and, yes, it is killing me to write these words. But it must be! You must not attempt to see me again. You must put me out of your life. When I am settled in America, I will make arrangements for you to see Amanda.

I will never forget you, and I will never stop loving you. You are my life. You said last summer that we would meet in another life. I think, dearest love, we shall. Perhaps a love like ours was not meant for this ugly world, but for another, more beautiful world; and there we will surely be reunited.

Until then, I love you.

Your own Lizzie

He put the letter down and rose from the desk. Sybil watched as he walked to one of the tall windows overlooking the rear mews where the carriages were kept. For a long time he said nothing, his back to her. She saw his hand go to his eyes several times. Then, finally, he turned to her.

"I apologize for last night," he said in a hoarse voice. "I don't know what got into me. . . . I wasn't thinking clearly. At any rate . . ." He came to her and took her hand, raising it to his lips. "From now on, you have nothing to fear from me." She saw his eyes were red from weeping. "Come," he said. "Let's go upstairs and see the children."

She stood up. She realized that, at long last, her husband was her own.

CHAPTER 21

Zachary Carr bolted upright in his bed on the second floor of Carr Farm. It was a hot, sticky night in June 1862, and the windows were open, which was why he had heard the hoofbeats. Jumping out of bed, he ran to one of the windows and looked out. A band of about a dozen horsemen were galloping toward the house, some of them carrying burning torches. One man fired at him.

"Yankee raiders!" he yelled, ducking. The bullet shattered one of the upper panes. He ran to pull on his pants as more shots were fired. He heard the men yelling: "Burn the Rebs! Burn 'em!"

His pants on, he pulled on his shoes without bothering to lace them and ran to the door then into the upstairs hall. There was enough moonlight for him to see that his father was already halfway down the stairs.

"Pa! Yankees!" he yelled.

"Get your gun!" Brandon yelled back as Zack started down the stairs. He knew that General McClellan's army was fighting Lee northwest of Richmond. McClellan had brought the Army of the Potomac down the Potomac by boat, then down Chesapeake Bay to Fort Monroe at the tip of the great peninsula separating the York and James Rivers. Then he had marched up the peninsula to Mechanicsville, where, two days before on the twenty-fifth of June, he had encountered Lee's forces and a great battle was raging. Zack had heard reports that Yankee raiders were taking advantage of the battle by riding into Virginia and spreading havoc.

He ran into the study to grab his rifle off the wall. Then

filling his pockets with bullets, he ran to the kitchen, beginning to smell the smoke and hear the flames. There was more gunfire outside, and he heard a scream. When he came to the kitchen, he had to back away: it was burning.

"Pa!" he yelled. "Are you all right? Pa!"

He saw through the flames that the back door was open and assumed his father had gone outside to fire at the intruders. But it was impossible to go in the kitchen now: the entire rear of the house was on fire. Zack ran to the front hall and looked through a window. Nothing. The shouts and shots had died out and now all he heard was the crackling of the spreading flames, and the snapping of old wood as the house immolated. He ran to the front door, opened it and looked out. Nothing. The moonlight reflected peacefully on the Rappahannock.

He went outside and ran around the corner of the house. In the distance he saw the raiders galloping through the fields, returning north. He ran to the back of the house, which was rapidly becoming an inferno. In the backyard he saw his father lying facedown on the ground. Some of the slaves were coming from the quarter.

"Get water!" Zack yelled at them as he ran to his father. "Water and buckets!"

He knelt by his father and gently turned him over. A bullet had gone through his forehead; another had pierced his neck.

"Pa!" he groaned. He closed his father's eyelids and stood up.

"Bastards!" he yelled, facing north. "You goddamn Yankee bastards! I'll pay you back! BASTARDS!"

The flames of Carr Farm licked the summer sky as a gibbous moon shone with indifference.

"Mr. Sinclair, there's a Mrs. Cavanagh to see you."

Alex Sinclair was squatting beside a customer sticking pins in his cuffs. He looked up.

"Who?"

"Mrs. Cavanagh," repeated the young salesman. "She's a stunner. English accent. Said she met you on a train from Scotland last year."

A smile came over his face as he stood up. "*That* Mrs. Cavanagh! Excuse me, Mr. Vanderbilt. Jerry, take care of the gentleman. . . ."

Alex hurried out of his richly appointed menswear section, where he personally tailored such New York notables as William Henry Vanderbilt, the son of the "Commodore," August Belmont and assorted Astors, van Renssalears and other swells. Though Alex was, with his mother, the store's owner, he was such a whirlwind of energy that there was no detail, no matter how small, that he didn't attend to, including Mr. Vanderbilt's cuffs. But such had been the impact of Lizzie's beauty on the young retailer that he even risked offending the son of the richest man in America to see her.

And he wasn't disappointed. Lizzie was looking at some earrings in a display case in the front of the store when Alex came up to her.

"Mrs. Cavanagh!"

She turned and smiled at him. He was dazzled.

"You remember me?" she said.

"Of course. The London express. Your daughter had been kidnapped, but I read that it all turned out fine. Welcome to New York. Welcome to Sinclair and Son."

"Thank you. It's such a lovely store, and you have such beautiful things. I love these gold earrings, but the price seems a trifle high for me." Her eyes twinkled mischievously. "I remember you said you'd give me a discount, and here I am, claiming it."

He laughed. "I have a big mouth," he said. "But you're right. I promised and I don't go back on my word. In fact, I'll give you an irresistible discount. Bob." He turned to the well-dressed young salesman behind the display case. "Gift-wrap these earrings for Mrs. Cavanagh. There'll be no charge."

Lizzie looked startled. "Mr. Sinclair, I couldn't accept *that!* I was just looking for a bargain."

"There's no better bargain than a gift. And you can wear them tonight when you have dinner with me."

She laughed. "I remember you said you were too unreserved. I can see you were right. But Mr. Sinclair—"

"Alex."

"Alex, I know nothing about you. Is there a Mrs. Sinclair?"

"Yes. My mother. Unfortunately she was paralyzed by a stroke several years ago and can barely talk, but she'll serve as chaperone. And I have one of the best cooks in New York. Where are you staying?"

"At the Fifth Avenue Hotel."

"The fanciest hotel in town! I admire women who do things first-class. I'll call for you at seven. Now I really have to get back to Mr. Vanderbilt."

He started toward the menswear department.

"Alex."

He turned. "What?"

"I didn't say yes."

A worried look came over his face for a moment. Then he flashed that cocky grin. "You couldn't possibly say no."

And he hurried off again.

"So: what do you think of New York?" he asked that evening as he sat opposite Lizzie in the dining room of his mother's brownstone on East Fourteenth Street, not far from the store on Union Square.

"It's dirty," Lizzie said as she picked at a dainty quail.

"Dirty? It's filthy. I have to hire private contractors to cart away the store's refuse."

"I'm told Madison Square is the center of town, but this morning I saw a pig eating cabbage on the street in front of my hotel."

"There are wild pigs in the slums. Sometimes they wander into the better sections of town."

"And the traffic! It's as bad as London."

"Someone counted fifteen thousand vehicles passing one corner downtown in a single day. But Lizzie, isn't it an *exciting* city, smells and all?"

His enthusiasm was infectious.

"Yes, it *is* exciting," she admitted.

"Are you staying long? What are your plans?"

Her plans? They were simple: to find a husband so that Adam would finally give up hope of ever having her and abandon his insane threat against Sybil. Lizzie wondered if this intense, exciting young man opposite her might be that husband. But there was a bizarre element in that dark-paneled room: the old woman in black, sitting silently in the wheelchair at the end of the table, a black veil over her gray hair, her brilliant dark eyes fixed on Lizzie. Naomi Sinclair, Alex's mother, looked much older than her chronological age of fifty-two. Alex had explained that the stroke had aged her. But it was unnerving having this wreck of a woman, who once must have been beautiful, sitting—or, more accurately, slumping—in her chair, her mouth pulled down at one side, her hands gnarled and lifeless, but her eyes riveted on Lizzie. Though Naomi couldn't speak, her hostility toward the guest was palpable. Lizzie felt sorry for the woman, but she wished to God she'd stop staring at her.

"My plans are to try to get my property in Virginia back if this war ever ends," she said, sipping the excellent Chablis the butler had poured. The Sinclair brownstone was not especially opulent: most of the houses in New York were very much alike and none of them was anywhere near as grand as Pontefract House, for example. But Lizzie had noticed that everything—silverware, china, furniture—was of the highest quality. Someone in the family bought only the best, and she suspected it was Alex. One look around his store had told her here was a man with a discerning eye as well as a flair for salesmanship.

"Ah, the war. I'll have to admit I've changed my mind about its being bad for business," Alex was saying. "It's turned out to be fabulous for business—the store has never been so profitable. You see, with the Union blockade of the South, we've been unable to get cotton for clothes. That's why I was in Manchester last year, buying dry goods, shirts and dresses for the store because I couldn't get them here in the States."

"Did you meet my brother-in-law, Horace Belladon?" she interrupted.

"Yes, in fact, I did. I had no idea you were related."

"He married my elder sister, Lettice—or rather, I

should say Lettice married him. I'm convinced he was involved with the kidnapping of my daughter."

"That I could believe. Horace struck me as a man not overly burdened with scruples. I remember it said in the newspapers that the kidnapping had something to do with England's recognizing the Confederacy. Well, from what I hear in Washington, that's no longer in the cards, which is good news for the North."

"Do you go to Washington often?"

"More and more. You see, this is turning out to be a different kind of war. Wars are no longer professional armies fighting battles on a field somewhere while the rest of the nation goes on about its business. This war is involving everyone, and the businessman is turning out to be almost as important as the soldier. The Government in Washington is terribly confused—half the Congressmen are running around like chickens with their heads off, and old Abe is a farce. They can't handle this war because it's turned out bigger than anyone dreamed. They need blankets, uniforms, tents—all the things my store sells. So I've rented rooms at Willard's Hotel in Washington and I'm finding these things for the government. For instance, last May the Union forces took Memphis in Tennessee. Now, I happen to know a cotton dealer in Memphis, so I went out there and got him to sneak through the lines with me. The Southern planters are being starved out by the war, so we found plenty of planters who had literally tons of cotton in storage and were itching to sell. I got a line of credit and bought over two million dollars' worth of the finest cotton in the South. We sneaked it into Memphis, I shipped it to the factories in New England, they manufactured what the government needs and I sold the dry goods to Washington for a million dollars' profit."

"A *million*?" she exclaimed. "That's a huge profit."

He shrugged. "It was a fifty-percent markup. My markup in the store is a hundred percent. I took the risk, why shouldn't I be paid? If I'd been caught going through the lines, Johnny Reb might well have shot me. I'm not ashamed of anything I've done. In fact, I'm proud of it. Ah, and here's dessert. I hope you like loaf pudding?"

"I've never heard of it."

"You're in for a rare experience."

The butler brought in a steaming pudding in a silver dish. As he served, Lizzie realized this intense young man sitting opposite her was not only a war profiteer but also a bit of a pirate. And yet what he had told her had intrigued her.

"Time for bed, Mrs. Sinclair," said a nurse, who had come into the dining room with the butler. Alex stood up and went to kiss his mother.

"Good night, Mama," he said.

"Good night, Mrs. Sinclair," said Lizzie.

Naomi's hate-filled eyes burned into her soul.

"Why does your mother dislike me?" Lizzie asked an hour later as Alex drove her to Madison Square in his luxurious carriage.

"Why do you think that?"

"She never took her eyes off me through the entire dinner, and her looks were anything but loving."

Alex, who was sitting beside her, sighed. "Mother never has been very subtle about her likes or dislikes. I suppose it's because you have an English accent. My father was a Scot who lived in Belfast, but Mother is Irish through and through and she hates the English. Father had a store in Belfast, but after the potato famine pretty well ruined his business, he brought us all over here and started over again in New York. He died seven years ago, and I've run the place since."

"You don't have an Irish accent. To me, you sound pure American."

He grinned. "Ah well, I put on a wee bit o' the brogue for St. Paddy's Day, but the rest of the year I make sure to forget it. The Irish are looked down on in New York as trash, and we want the carriage trade."

"I hope *you* don't dislike me because I'm English?"

"Now, what do you think the answer to *that* is? And here's your hotel."

"It was so charming of you to invite me to dinner. And I love the earrings."

He got out of the carriage and helped her down as the Negro doorman held the door. Her hat flapped against the stiff breeze as she smiled at him.

"Good night, Alex," she said, extending her hand.

"May I buy you a cognac?" he asked, raising her glove to his mouth.

"I think not."

"May I show you the city tomorrow?"

"But you're so busy . . ."

"I'll pick you up at ten. Bring your daughter, and I'll give you both a royal tour. Then we'll have lunch at Delmonico's."

"That's very kind of you, but—"

"You couldn't possibly say no." Again the cocky grin.

She laughed. "You're incorrigible, but you're right. I couldn't. I'll see you at ten."

She walked into the hotel, wondering whether she was trying to hook him or not. Whichever, it was becoming increasingly obvious he was hooked.

After Adam's rescue of his kidnapped daughter, Phineas Thurlow Whitney decided it would be wise to absent himself from England, where he had correctly concluded that any hope for recognition of the Confederacy was doomed. He crossed the Channel to Calais then on to Paris where he had hopes of a more friendly reception from the government of Emperor Napoleon III.

It took Phineas two frustrating months to get an interview with the Emperor, which in itself demonstrated Louis Napoleon's slipperiness: the French government was involved with the Mexican adventure of the Archduke Maximilian, whom Louis Napoleon was backing, but the French Emperor was extremely reluctant to commit himself to either side of the Civil War.

"But Sire, Lincoln's hands are tied as long as he's fighting the Confederacy," Phineas insisted as he sat next to the Emperor's desk in the Tuileries Palace. "Therefore, it's to France's advantage to recognize and—if I may be so bold as to suggest—*help* us with arms and money. France seeks to establish an empire in Mexico. If you recognize the Confederacy, you will have a friend and ally on Mexico's northern border. The Empire of Mexico and the Confederate States of America are natural friends and trading partners."

"True," mused the Emperor, sitting at his desk in the center of the austere study smoking a cigar. A monumental map of Paris hung over an enormous filing cabinet. Opposite was a marble bust of the Emperor's mother, Queen Hortense. "On the other hand, Monsieur Whitney, what if the tide turns for Lincoln?"

"It hasn't and it won't. His generals are incompetent."

"Ah, but he might be lucky and find a competent general. Wars have curious ways of surprising people. If Lincoln won, then Mexico would have an enemy at her northern border. Then, too, there is England. If England were to recognize the Confederacy, then I would not hesitate. But England hasn't, and my ambassador tells me it won't. So . . ." He shrugged as he exhaled cigar smoke toward the distant ceiling.

When he left the Tuileries, Phineas knew he had failed. The European powers were going to remain neutral, despite everything he had done—despite, even, kidnapping Amanda, the failure of which had infuriated him. He was almost wild with despair, because beneath his cool and unruffled facade was a heart full of hate. He hated the damned Abolitionists, he hated the North, he hated Lincoln, and he hated what he saw as the future of the South after a Federal victory: a South where freed slaves might someday challenge the white man's supremacy.

But for the moment he had no choice but to go home and do everything in his power to support the Southern cause, even though he now perceived that hopes for a Southern victory were dwindling, despite its military victories.

Phineas Thurlow Whitney had to go home for the simple reason that he had run out of money. Both the North and the South were printing paperbacks and bonds as fast as they could to finance the war, but Europe was on the gold standard and Europe was expensive. When Phineas ran out of gold in Paris, no banker would honor a letter of credit or check drawn on a Southern bank. The harsh fact was that just as Phineas was running out of cash, so was the South.

Pawning most of his clothes, his gold watch and diamond cufflinks to finance his passage home, he took a leaky boat from Cherbourg to Bermuda, the base for most of the British blockaders slipping through the Union Navy. Then he boarded one of the blockade runners, landing at Mobile in the middle of the night. Rather, he thought grimly, like a fugitive criminal—and he a former United States senator, a former ambassador! It was galling. He sent a wire to Fairview Plantation, then took a train to Richmond, where he was met by Elton, his aged driver.

"We was expectin' you yestidday, Genral," said Elton, taking his master's one bag. "We didn't know de train was gonna be a whole day late. Looks to me lak de train drivers, dey doan know what dey's doin' no mo'."

"The engine broke down and they had no spare parts," Phineas said irritably. "And I don't want you saying things are bad, Elton."

"Yessuh, Gen'ral. I guess tings is goin' fine."

They arrived at Fairview in the middle of the night—again like a criminal, thought Phineas—and a cold, snowy night at that. It was November 7, 1862, the same day Lincoln gave command of the Union forces to General Burnside.

"Guess dey all went to bed, Gen'ral," said Elton, climbing down from the driver's seat. "We got a houseful, what wid Massa Clayton and Miss Charlotte livin' here."

"What do you mean?" Phineas was looking at the dark plantation house as he climbed down. A misty moon hovered above the chimneys of the house he had been born in, the house he had loved for sixty years.

"Well, Miss Ellie May, she tole me to keep mah mouf shut, 'cause she wanted to tell you de bad news herself. But while you was away in Eur'p, de Yankee raiders dey come an' burn down Carr Farm. Massa Brandon, he was done shot daid. Massa Zack, he done gone off to join de army, an' Massa Clayton an' Miss Charlotte, dey had to move in here wif Miss Ellie May. An' it sorta hard, what wif Miss Charlotte bein' in de fambly way an' Massa Clayton he ain't good fo' much wid only one leg, an' he drunk half de time."

"Clayton? Drunk? I never saw him even tipsy in my life."

"Well, he sure do lak it now, Gen'ral. Yessah. Dat boy sure grown mighty fond of de bottle."

"Here: give me my bag. You put the horses away and go to bed."

"Yessah, Gen'ral. An' welcome home."

Home? Phineas thought as he started up the path to the house. Home? He was losing his home, his way of life, his wealth, his neighbors, his world . . . it was all going up in smoke because of the damned Abolitionists . . . that damned Lincoln. . . . The President's homely face flashed in his mind. He envisioned putting a pistol to that hated head and pulling the trigger. . . . Phineas might not have been much of a humanitarian, but he was a first-class hater.

A cold wind was moaning as he walked across the verandah and let himself in. The house was silent. He set his bag on the floor of the entrance hall and fumbled for an oil lamp on one of the tables. He lit it with a lucifer match. Its flickering light illuminated the portraits of his ancestors.

"Goddammit!" he yelled at the top of his lungs. "I'm home! Why isn't there a goddamn welcoming committee? I'm home! General Phineas Thurlow Whitney is home from France and England and the bastards aren't going to support us! I'm home! 'Oh, I wish I was in the Land of Cotton . . .' " Maniacally he kept singing "Dixie." " 'Look away, look away, look away, Dixie Land!' "

"Phineas!" Ellie May was looking over the railing of the second floor. "My darling, you're home!"

" 'I wish I was in Dixie, Hooray, Hooray! In Dixie Land I'll take my stand to live and die for Dixie . . .' "

"Phineas, why are you singing? What is this? Charlotte . . . Clayton. . . . He's gone mad!"

Ellie May, who had a white nightcap on her head and had flung a flannel robe over her nightgown, started running down the stairs.

" 'A way down south in Dixie. . . .' "

"Phineas, my dearest—"

She ran across the hall to him. He was sobbing as she ran into his arms.

"We're going to lose, Ellie May," he said softly, choking on his words. "We're going to lose. I did everything I could to convince them in Europe, but they don't care. . . . We're going to lose."

She stared at her sobbing husband. The once-elegant Senator now looked a bit seedy, a bit frayed around the edges.

He also, suddenly, looked old.

Phineas may have had a momentary breakdown of despair—he was, after all, only human—but by the next day, after recharging his batteries with ten hours' much-needed sleep, his normal iron will reasserted itself. As he bathed and shaved, he told himself there was still hope, no matter how dim. And, as a reader of Schopenhauer, he believed that if nothing else, he could *will* a victory. He cursed himself for his emotional display the night before. And, after finishing dressing, he went back to his bedroom where Ellie May was still in bed, reading.

"Ellie May, I want to apologize for last night," he said, coming over to the four-poster and sitting beside her. "I was tired and upset and . . . well, I made an ass of myself."

"Is it so bad?" she asked, putting down the out-of-date novel she was rereading for the third time. New books had become unheard-of because of the blockade.

"Between you and me, it looks bad, and my failure in Europe is a blow. By the way, I'll have to go to Richmond today or tomorrow to make a report to Jeff Davis. But meanwhile, it's important we keep our spirits up, and my breaking down last night was inexcusable. Now, Elton tells me that Carr Farm was burned and Brandon was shot."

"Yes, it's true. I wanted to tell you myself, but I should have known that old darkie couldn't keep a secret. It happened last summer, while the Yankees were in Virginia before *dear* General Lee drove them back out. They were sending out raiding parties to do as much damage as they could—those filthy pigs! And they attacked Carr Farm in the middle of the night. When Brandon came out his back door with his rifle, they shot and killed him, then set the house on fire. By some miracle, dearest Charlotte was here for the night with Clayton, else they would have been killed too. And then, of course, they had nowhere to go so they stayed here. Oh, it's been too horrible! And food's getting so hard to come by . . ."

"Elton said Charlotte is in the family way?"

"She's due any day, poor child. What a terrible world to be born into!"

"And Clayton's drinking?"

Ellie May sighed. "Well, I suppose I can't blame him. For such an active young man, losing a leg has been a terrible blow. And his father dead, his home burned, Zack off to the war now, and we may lose him . . . Oh Phineas, what dark times these are! When I think how lovely our lives once were, I . . ."

She held a lace hankie to her eyes. Her husband put his arms around her and gave her a comforting hug.

"There, there," he said. "Yes, times are bad, but we'll pull through somehow. I can't chide you for despairing since I did it myself last night. But we must be like iron, Ellie May. Like iron. And we mustn't let the servants see that we have any lack of confidence or resolve."

"Servants?" she sniffed. "What servants? They're all gone except for Elton and Cordelia and a few others."

"Gone?" Phineas released her and stood up. "What do you mean?"

"Dear Phineas, you've been away for over a year, you have no idea of the unbelievable things that have happened. That awful man Abraham Lincoln freed the slaves in September."

"Yes, I heard. But surely that has no force *here*?"

"Who's to control things? We've gone through three overseers, and the last one went to the army a month ago. No able-bodied white men is left to hire. The darkies think they're free, so they run off, just like that"—she snapped her fingers—"with no sense of loyalty or devotion after *all* we've done for them. And the few that didn't run off have been conscripted to do work for the army. The fields are in ruin, and of course we had to close the tobacco factory for lack of labor. Oh, everything . . ." she shrugged helplessly, then started crying again. "Oh, everything's a *mess*!"

"I see," said Phineas. "Things are more grim than I supposed. I trust I can get some breakfast?"

She nodded, blowing her nose. "There's still some bacon left, and Elton's got laying hens, so there's eggs. But the coffee—oh, the coffee! It's like drinking mud. I don't know what they make it out of!" She wiped her eyes again, then looked up at her husband. "I don't want to sound frivolous, but did you manage to buy me anything in London or Paris? It would be such a help if you brought any clothes. My wardrobe is getting so shabby, I'm ashamed to be seen in polite company."

"Ellie May, I hate to tell you this, but the only thing I bought in Paris was my passage home. I ran out of money."

"What?" she cried. "Oh, it doesn't seem possible all this is happening. It's like some horrible nightmare. You, Phineas Thurlow Whitney, penniless? It doesn't seem possible!"

She gave way to hysterical sobs. Her husband, a grim look on his patrician face, turned and left the room. Closing the door softly, he walked around the upstairs balcony to the stair, which he started down.

A door to another bedroom opened slightly, and a dark face appeared. It was Sarah, the laundress, who now, with Cordelia, the cook, was the only domestic female help left at Fairview Plantation. Sarah had been changing the sheets of Charlotte's bed. She looked at Phineas walking down the stairs and remembered the mangled corpse of her son, Tucker, that she had watched Mr. McNally, the overseer pull out of the rain barrel. The nails on the inside of the barrel had pierced Tucker's body in a hundred places, including his eyes.

Now, Sarah watched her former master, and there was murder in her eyes.

In a way, Phineas reflected as he walked down the curving staircase, he was perversely lucky. Carr Farm was only a quarter-mile down the road. The Yankee raiders could have as easily burned Fairview Plantation, but from what he had seen so far, the house, while perhaps not as pristine as before the war—he ran his fingers over the wooden banister and checked the dust—was unharmed. It still was a glorious symbol of the aristocratic way of life he had such a passion for. If a Yankee ever comes through the door, he thought, I personally will—

"I heard you last night."

The voice startled Phineas out of his murderous reverie. He had just reached the bottom step when he saw Clayton hobble out of the dining room on his crutches. Except this was not the dashing young officer he remembered from Bull Run. This looked more like a derelict. His hand-knit sweater was spotted, his trousers, with one leg pinned up, were filthy, and he hadn't shaved for days. His eyes were suspiciously bloodshot.

"What do you mean?" said his father-in-law.

"I heard you when you came in the house. I heard you singing 'Dixie.' Were you drunk?"

"I resent that, sir. And I suspect *you* are the one who's been drinking."

"All day, all night." He grinned. "When the Yankees come, I'll blast them away with my breath. It's all over, isn't it? We're losing the war."

"It's too early to call. And you might welcome me home."

Clayton snickered. "Oh yes, I forgot. Welcome home, sir. Welcome to beautiful Fairview Plantation. Did you hear about my pa?"

"Yes. I'm sorry, Clayton."

"Oh, we're all sorry. I expect Jeff Davis is sorry, and General Lee. Did they tell you I got the medal? Yep, a bright, shiny medal. 'For valor and bravery at the Battle of Bull Run,' the letter said. The letter was signed by Jeff Davis himself—isn't that impressive? You know what I did with the medal? No, you couldn't know, of course. You were in Europe. I threw the medal into the privy. And you know what I did with Jeff Davis' letter? I wiped my ass with it."

Phineas stiffened.

"My ASS!" Clayton shouted. "I shat on Jeff Davis' letter! I'd love to shit on the whole goddamn Confederacy—do you hear me, *SIR*? Do you hear me, *General*? Shit! The Confederacy is SHIT!"

"If you don't retract these disgusting words," Phineas said, "by God, I'll throw you out of this house."

"I don't retract one goddamn syllable. I lost my leg—what for? So you could go on whipping and killing darkies? Is *that* what I lost my leg for? Is that what my pa lost his life for? Is that what my brother's fighting for? I say Zack's a fool to fight. I say fuck the Confederacy! Fuck the Glorious Cause! Fuck *everything*!"

He was sobbing. Phineas walked across the hall to him and slapped his face so hard, Clayton lost his balance and fell on the floor, his crutches scattering.

"By God, sir, you'll leave this house! *Now!*"

Clayton was laughing and sobbing at the same time. "Fuck the Confederacy! Fuck it!"

His father-in-law kicked him viciously in his stomach. As Clayton howled with pain, Phineas stepped over him and walked into the dining room.

Watching from upstairs, Sarah smiled.

" 'Oh, I wish I was in the land of cotton,' " Clayton started singing as he crawled across the floor to retrieve his crutches. " 'Old times there are not forgotten . . .' "

He clutched one crutch.

"Well, well," he said to himself, "old One-Leg has got to find himself a new home. Wonder where I should go?"

As he grasped his second crutch, a memory of fleshly pleasure assaulted him and suddenly he knew where he would go.

CHAPTER 22

The twelve-year-old boy's fingers moved with amazing speed over the keyboard as he raced with thrilling accuracy through Chopin's "Revolutionary" Etude. Lizzie, sitting in the austere drawing room of the Gloucester Academy, could hardly believe what she was hearing. Gabriel Cavanagh (Lizzie had given him Jack's name since she had no idea of Moses' surname: in the slave ledger at Elvira Plantation, he had been listed merely as "Moses, male") was a handsome boy with skin even lighter than his father's. But what stunned Lizzie, who had taken the train to Boston, then hired a carriage to drive north to the fishing village of Gloucester, was his musical talent. Mrs. Ogilvie, the matron of the Academy, had mentioned in her annual reports that she was encouraging the boy to take piano lessons. But this! Above the tempestuous storm of passages for the left hand, the melody rose aloft, passionate and proudly majestic. Then the bravura descending whirlwind of notes and the final stirring clouds, evoking images of Zeus hurling thunderbolts at the world. Then silence.

The boy looked at Lizzie as he rose from the piano bench. He was burning with curiosity about this beautiful woman he had met for the first time a half-hour before.

"Gabriel, I don't know what to say," she remarked, standing up. "I had no idea you were so wonderfully gifted. Your playing is brilliant."

"His teacher is a Polish gentleman who lives in Marblehead," said Mrs. Ogilvie, a gray-haired lady. "Mr. Karasowski says Gabriel has one of the greatest talents of any boy he's ever taught. And he has an incredible memory.

He can sight-read anything and never have to look at the score again."

"I can improvise, too," the boy said proudly. "Listen."

He sat back down at the piano and began the "Revolutionary" Etude again, except this time the melody in the right hand came out as "Yankee Doodle."

Lizzie laughed and applauded. "He's marvelous!" she exclaimed.

"He's a sweet boy," Mrs. Ogilvie said, "but a bit of a show-off. He's one of our brightest students, except for history. He doesn't much like history."

"I want to take him to dinner at my hotel," Lizzie said.

Mrs. Ogilvie lowered her voice. "You'll have to take him to your room," she said. "They won't let him in the dining room."

Lizzie frowned.

"Why do you pay my tuition?" Gabriel asked an hour later. He was sitting opposite Lizzie at a small round table that had been brought to her second-floor room by two waiters, both of whom had looked suspiciously at the neatly dressed black boy.

"I promised your father I'd take care of you," she said.

Gabriel was devouring a lobster.

"How did you know my father?"

"He . . . worked at my plantation in Virginia."

"You mean, he was a slave?"

"Well, yes."

"What was he like?"

"You don't remember him?"

"Not much. I was four when my mother and I were sold."

"Well, your father was very strong and very proud. He was a good man. And I know he loved you very deeply. When he ran away, he told me he was going to try to find you and take you North to freedom. And then . . ."

"Mrs. Ogilvie told me he was killed."

"Yes, unfortunately."

"How did it happen?"

"Well, my husband struck me. And your father . . . shot

my husband. And then the overseer shot your father."

Gabriel put down his fork and stared at her. "Why did my father shoot your husband?"

Lizzie toyed with her fork a moment. "That's rather complicated," she finally said. "I think . . . well, your father liked me a lot."

"Did he *love* you?"

Another pause. "Perhaps. I'm not sure."

"Do you think a black man can love a white woman?"

Yet another pause. "I suppose. Yes, why not? Othello loved Desdemona."

"But that was in Venice. It couldn't happen in America."

He returned to his lobster.

"I owe you a lot, Mrs. Cavanagh," he continued. "You've given me an education. I wonder what I can do with it in this country."

"Things are changing, Gabriel. Mr. Lincoln has freed the slaves, and—"

"Excuse me, ma'am. Did you see the way the waiters looked at me tonight? Until I can eat in the dining room downstairs, I'm not really going to be free. I don't fool myself. But Mrs. Ogilvie and the other Quakers have taught me not to be bitter about that. It's just that I have to be realistic, and realistically I'm always going to be a black man in a white country. But I've been terrifically lucky." He expertly cracked a lobster claw. "I've had you and I have my music. This lobster's wonderful. Don't you like lobster?"

"Oh yes."

"You're not eating yours."

"I'm more interested in you. Have you considered making a career of the piano?"

"Yes, ma'am. That's my dream. My piano teacher, Mr. Karasowski, knows Franz Liszt and he said he'd write him a letter if I ever went to Europe. Franz Liszt is the greatest pianist in the world, Mr. Karasowski says, and if he backs you, you can make a wonderful career. Even if you're black. In *Europe*."

He was watching her with his intelligent eyes. Lizzie smiled.

"I'm getting the idea you'd like to go to Europe," she said.

He looked sheepish. "I guess I wasn't very subtle," he said. "But oh, Mrs. Cavanagh, if I could get there and study with Maestro Liszt, I could make you so proud of me!"

"I already *am* proud of you," Lizzie said. "Now tell me something about Mr. Karasowski. How old is he?"

"He just had his thirty-fourth birthday. He was sort of a child prodigy and studied with Chopin in Paris. But about fourteen years ago, he came to America because of some revolutions in Europe. He's very nice."

"Where does he live?"

"In a cottage in Marblehead. It's on the ocean, with a beautiful view. And Anna's a wonderful cook."

"Who's Anna?"

"His wife. She's French. They're always babbling at each other in French."

"I see. Well, I think in the morning I'll pay a call on Mr. Karasowski."

The next morning, Lizzie emerged from a carriage in Marblehead. A nor'easter was blowing, and her cloak whipped around her as she started up the walk to the cheerful, small cottage which, as well as the crashing of the sea, reminded her of Ayr and, inevitably, her happy years with Adam. But that was all gone now. She knocked at the door. After a moment it was opened by a nice-looking young woman in an apron.

"Yes?"

"My name is Mrs. Cavanagh. I'd like to speak to Mr. Karasowski about Gabriel."

The woman's face lit up. "Oh, yes . . . come in, please," she said in a French accent. "Tadeuz—zat eez my hoosband—'e eez geeving a lesson, but 'e weel be right out." She lowered her voice as she closed the door. "Zeez eez one of 'ez worst pupils. 'E weel be glad to 'ave an excuse to leave."

In fact, Lizzie could hear someone butchering a Mozart sonata in the next room. Anna led her into a low-ceilinged parlor, then went to fetch her husband. When he emerged from behind a closed door, Lizzie saw that he was tall, slightly stoop-shouldered, but nice looking with curly brown hair and myopic eyes behind gold-framed spectacles. His clothes were a bit tired-looking, and his coat was worn at the elbows. He came into the parlor and kissed Lizzie's hand.

"You are the famous and rather mysterious Mrs. Cavanagh," he said in a heavy accent as he indicated a chair for Lizzie. "Mrs. Ogilvie told me you were coming to see my star pupil. I am eager to hear what you think of him."

"I think he's amazing," said Lizzie, sitting down, "but I know little about music. More important, what do *you* think of him?"

Tadeuz didn't hesitate. "I tell you frankly my opinion. I have studied with Chopin. I have heard him play—he played divinely. I have heard Liszt play. I have heard Mendelssohn play. Gabriel is not as polished as these giants, naturally, nor does he yet have the emotional maturity, the depth of expression. But I would swear, madame, that Gabriel's natural talent is as great as theirs. I have heard Gabriel turn 'Chopsticks' into a whirlwind of beauty."

" 'Chopsticks'?" smiled Lizzie, amused by the mention of the old Russian nursery tune that, in later years, would inspire variations by Rimsky-Korsakov and César Cui.

" 'Chopsticks.' The boy is a genius. But of course . . ." He shrugged. "What to do with him? There's nothing more I can teach him. His talent is much greater than mine. And where does a black child go?"

"Perhaps to Europe to play for Maestro Liszt?"

"Ah yes, that would be wonderful. But Europe takes money."

"Mr. Karasowski, I am not a spendthrift, and I don't like to throw my money out the window. But I have already invested a good deal of money in Gabriel. Do you think it would be a prudent investment if I sent Gabriel to Europe to play for Liszt?"

"Of course, these things can never be guaranteed. But I swear to you, madame, it would be worth the gamble."

"Still, there are other problems. Gabriel has never traveled, he doesn't speak foreign languages . . . Mr. Karasowski, if I paid you and your wife's expenses and compensated you for your time, would you consider taking Gabriel to meet Liszt?"

The tall Polish Jew looked surprised. "I would be delighted, of course. My wife and I haven't been to Europe for years. But may I ask why, aside from the money you have already spent on Gabriel, you are doing this?"

Lizzie stood up. "There are many reasons, not the least of which is a promise I made to his father. But also, I'm frankly curious to see how far Gabriel can go with the proper backing. And it might be a useful thing, in the middle of this horrid war over slavery, if a black child managed to stupefy the world."

There was excitement in Tadeuz's eyes as he took Lizzie's hand. " '*Stupor mundi*'!" he said thoughtfully. "Yes, that's what Gabriel might be: '*Stupor mundi*'!"

It was a Currier-and-Ives scene. Amanda, looking adorable in a fox-trimmed coat with a fox-fur hat tied under her chin, was skating on a pond with Alex Sinclair. Snowflakes drifted down, bending the boughs of the pines and spruce trees that dotted the beautiful Harlem Valley. Lizzie watched her daughter and Alex from a sleigh at the side of the pond, a fur throw pulled up to her waist. Alex had invited them for a weekend excursion to an inn a hundred miles north of the city and had rented a private railroad car for the trip, a lavish gesture Lizzie had learned was typical of him. The young retailing "genius," as she had seen him described in an article in *Harper's Weekly*, had fallen unabashedly in love with Amanda, and his love was wholeheartedly reciprocated. Which fact delighted Lizzie, because she knew her daughter missed Adam fiercely. Lizzie, who had told Amanda "Papa" was staying in England for political reasons, had also told her not to mention "Papa" to Alex, a deception Lizzie didn't like but one she thought necessary if she wanted a chance to catch Alex. Lizzie missed Adam too, but Alex was beginning to fill the void in her life and although she wasn't in love with him, she liked him a lot. So far, Alex had behaved like a perfect gentleman. But Lizzie sensed that this weekend in the rural reaches of Dutchess County, in an inn that was mysteriously empty except for the three of them and Mrs. Parker, had been well-planned. Alex's familiarity with the innkeeper and the staff led her to suspect this wasn't the first time he had come north for a weekend and she thought he hadn't come north alone. From offhand remarks he had let drop, Lizzie inferred he was no stranger to the pleasures of the female sex.

"Alex!" squealed Amanda as her skating partner flew into the air and landed on the ice. As he sat up, a sour look on his face, Amanda began laughing.

"You're supposed to be the expert," she said. "Mommie, doesn't Alex look funny?" At which point, Amanda fell on her bottom and they both were laughing.

He'd be a good father for her, Lizzie was thinking, and she's never had a full-time father.

Mr. Carpenter, the jolly, adipose innkeeper, served the four of them a turkey dinner with all the trimmings. After dessert, Mrs. Parker got up to take Amanda upstairs to bed.

"Good night, Alex," Amanda said, hugging him and giving him a kiss. Then she came to Lizzie and kissed her. "Good night, Mama. You know something? Alex is almost as nice as Papa."

Lizzie smiled wanly as the nanny took Amanda upstairs, leaving her alone with Alex. They took their coffee to the big stone hearth while Mr. Carpenter cleared the table. Outside, it was still snowing, but in the snug, low-ceilinged living room of the eighteenth-century inn, it was warm.

"Happy?" Alex asked. He was standing in front of the fire; Lizzie was seated on a cushioned Colonial settle.

"Very happy." She smiled. "This was a wonderful idea, Alex. And I appreciate how kind you are to Amanda. I fear she's totally captivated by you."

"Well, she's captivated me. She's an enchanting girl."

He hesitated, waiting for Mr. Carpenter to leave the room. When they were alone, he looked at Lizzie. "You told me Jack Cavanagh was murdered five years ago. Yet Amanda's only five and a half. How can she remember 'Papa'?"

In for a penny, she thought. "Jack was not Amanda's father," she said.

"Then who was?"

She smiled slightly. "I suddenly feel rather naked. But you might as well know all my lurid past. Amanda's father is Adam Thorne, the Marquess of Pontefract."

Alex let out a whistle. "So *that's* why he was so anxious to save her from the kidnappers."

"That's right. Of course, we've tried to keep it confidential."

He was looking at her rather strangely. Well, *that* did it, she thought. She stood up and put her hand on his sleeve.

"Dear Alex," she said, "I know what you're thinking. It's been so wonderful being with you these past few weeks, but we can go back to the city tomorrow and go our separate ways. There'll be no hard feelings on my part." A clock on the mantel began striking. "It's late. I think I'll go up to my room. Good night."

She turned to go, but he took her hand and pulled her to him. Hugging her, he kissed her mouth with a passion that surprised her.

"Lizzie, Lizzie," he whispered, "I'm crazy about you. I don't care. . . ." He kissed her again, her chin, her nose, her cheeks, her eyes. "I don't give a damn who Amanda's father is. I want *you*. . . ." He kissed her mouth again. She felt his hands hungrily squeezing her back.

Gently she pushed him away. "Now it's time *you* told me a few facts," she said. "Why do I have this odd feeling you've been in this inn before?"

He smoothed his hair. "I have been. I don't deny it."

"And I have an odd feeling you didn't come alone."

"I don't deny that, either. I hope you're not going to give me a sermon?"

"I'm in no position to sermonize, God knows. But I want to make one thing clear: I'm far from being the Holy

Virgin, but if you think I'm going upstairs with you—"

"Lizzie, those girls were different. They were cheap actresses, tarts. . . . I want to *marry* you. I want you to be my wife!"

Silence.

"And your mother?"

For a moment he looked troubled. "This sounds cruel, but I don't care about Mother. She's had her life, I have mine. Say yes, Lizzie. Or do you want me to get down on my knees and do a proper proposal?"

She was staring at him, her mind confused.

"All right, by God, I *will* get down on my knees!" He knelt on one knee and put his hands over his heart. "Fair Lizzie, you have driven me wild with passion and desire. Since I cannot live without you and since neither of us is a paragon of virtue . . . What's wrong?"

She had turned away, putting her hand to her face.

"Lizzie, you're crying! Why?"

He stood up and came to her, putting his hands on her arms.

"Oh Alex, you're so good and kind and wonderful. . . . I like you so *very* much. But I have to be honest with you. I don't love you. If you believe in curses, the curse of my life is that I've always loved one man and I fear I always will."

"Adam Thorne?" he said softly.

She nodded as she wiped her tears. "Damn," she exclaimed. "Why am I so bloody honest? You'd be the perfect husband for me and the perfect father for Amanda. Why can't I just say yes and shut up? But Alex—dear Alex—I can't lie to you. You're too good for me. You deserve a woman who can love you with all her heart. And always, in a corner of my heart, will be a man I'll probably never see again. A man I've tried my best to forget but can't. A man who . . . well, I suppose you could say we're soul-mates, though that doesn't begin to describe it. So there you have all the truth about the notorious Mrs. Cavanagh. I'm deeply flattered you want me to be your wife, but go find someone better than me."

He took her hands. "I don't want anyone better than

you," he said. "And I still want you to be my wife. Someday, by God, I'll make you forget Adam Thorne."

Again he kissed her, again with such passion she wondered if he just might not be able to do it.

"Say 'yes,' Lizzie. Say 'yes.' "

The strength of his body began to excite her.

"Even knowing—?"

"Even knowing everything. I don't give a damn. Say yes or by God I'll hold you here all night!"

She closed her eyes. Adam . . . the moors . . . her true knight. . . . But her true knight was married to Sybil, who, perversely enough, she had to protect. . . . She needed a husband. . . . Adam, my love . . . she opened her eyes.

"Yes!"

He blinked with surprise. "My God, it worked!"

CHAPTER 23

"Miss Charlotte, she done gave birf to a baby boy who's daid!" Elton said, coming into the kitchen of Fairview Plantation.

"Good," said Sarah, the housemaid.

"What does you mean, 'good'?" exclaimed the old slave whose wife, Cordelia, had helped deliver the stillborn baby upstairs minutes before. "How can you say dat 'bout Miss Charlotte?"

"I wants nuffin' but evil fo' dis house," Sarah said. "Nuffin' but evil. Massa, he kilt mah boy, Tucker. As far as I care, he can spend de rest of his life payin'."

"Dass no Christian attitude," Elton admonished her. "Revenge is de Lord's bizness, dass what it say in de Good Book."

"I don't care what it say. I wants nuffin' but evil fo' dis house."

Upstairs, Charlotte was crying hysterically. "Clayton? Where's Clayton? I want my Clayton! Please, Mama, tell me where he went!"

Ellie May was standing by her daughter's bed, holding her hand, a strained look on her face. Now she glanced at Phineas, who was standing at the foot of the four-poster. A fire burned in the hearth and oil lamps illuminated the high-ceilinged room. Charlotte had gone into labor as the sun was setting on a cold November day, and Dr. Cooper had arrived just in time to deliver the dead child. Charlotte had been hysterical ever since.

"Papa, what *is* it?" she cried. "Why did Clayton leave? Where *is* he? Oh, I want him so, especially now, with my baby dead . . ."

She started sobbing again. Phineas shifted uncomfortably. Ellie May let go Charlotte's hand and came around the bed. "Come outside," she whispered to her husband. "Cordelia, stay with Miss Charlotte."

"Yes'm." The fat cook curtsied as Phineas and Ellie May passed her out of the room.

"You must get Clayton," Ellie May whispered after closing the bedroom door.

"I won't have that traitor in this house," said Phineas. "You don't know what he said to me the other day. He spoke obscenities about the Confederacy—"

"I don't *care* what he said! Charlotte needs him! Her heart's breaking in there!"

"But you know where Clayton went. I told you."

"It doesn't matter where he went. Bring him back for our daughter's sake. And you have to have a *little* sympathy for Clayton. No matter what he says now, he gave his leg for the Glorious Cause."

"Damn!" muttered Phineas. "All right, I'll leave first thing in the morning."

He walked down the upstairs hall toward the stairs, his daughter's sobs still ringing in his ears.

"Dulcey," Clayton muttered as he lay beside the beautiful slave. "Oh Dulcey, you make me so goddamn happy."

"Uh-huh. Well, jes 'cause I been good to you the lass few days, doan get no fancy notions 'bout movin' in here permanent. Dat is, unless you come up wid some money."

"Who's got money? I haven't, you haven't, nobody has." He smiled as he rubbed his hand over her bare breasts. "Besides, you like me. I can tell."

"You all right fo' a white boy. But whass gonna happen when you run out of de likker you done stole from de gen'ral? I knows how you drunks go crazy."

"I'm no drunk."

"Huh. Sure puttin' on a good imitation of one."

"Oh Dulcey, let's not quarrel. Let's just make love."

She smiled as he maneuvered himself on top of her. They were both naked, under a horsehair blanket on her sagging bed in the cold cottage at Elvira Plantation.

"All I can say is, honey, you sure got one big itch in dat ting o' yours."

The door opened, and Phineas filled the frame. Dulcey gasped and pushed Clayton off.

"Clayton," Phineas said, "get dressed. Charlotte's baby was stillborn. My daughter needs you."

"Stillborn?" Clayton exclaimed.

"Yes. It was a boy, if you're interested. Get dressed, man! And get out of that filthy nigger bed. I'm taking you home."

Clayton's temper flared. "Why? So you can throw me out again? No thanks. I'd rather stay here. And if Dulcey throws me out, I'll live in the fields."

"Have you no concern for your wife, sir? Charlotte's hysterical! And if that doesn't influence you, perhaps this will: there's a major battle shaping up at Fredericksburg, and we'll need every man we can find to help protect Fairview. You may hate the Confederacy, but Fairview will be yours one day, Clayton: yours and Charlotte's. So if you can tear yourself away from this slut, I suggest your better interests lie at Fairview. I'll wait outside while you get decent—if the word is applicable."

Shooting Dulcey a savage look, he backed out of the cabin and shut the door.

Clayton hesitated, then got out of bed. "He's right," he said. "I have to go. Thanks for everything you've done, Dulcey. When things calm down . . ."

"You'll what? Come back to Dulcey? Forget it, white boy. I doan want you. I felt sorry for you when you come in here lak a sick dog de udder day, but I doan want nuffin' to do wif dat man de gen'ral. No, sir."

Clayton was pulling on his trousers. "I can understand why you feel that way," he said. "The general's been bad to his slaves—I know that. But, well, we'll see. And I'll send you some money if I ever get some."

"Too bad 'bout yo' baby," she said, watching him. "Wonder what went wrong? Two fine, healthy parents lak you an' Miss Charlotte. It doan seem right yo' baby ain't healthy, too."

"Yes, it *is* odd. We'll just have to try again."

Dulcey smiled. She had a good idea why Clayton's baby had been born dead.

His awareness of the horrible conditions in the London slums had convinced Adam that making speeches in the House of Lords was not enough to change anything. A far more practical approach to the problems of the poor was to buy up a section of Wapping, raze the rat-infested buildings and put up new, low-cost housing that would incorporate the new technology of plumbing and heating which had so revolutionized the lives of the better-off classes. Adam set about to do just that, and he hired the eminent architect Sir Joseph Paxton to draw up the plans. Sir Joseph, who had designed the world-famous Crystal Palace that had been the star of the Great Exhibition of 1851, was excited by the challenge. Adam and he liked each other immediately, and the two were going over some preliminary drawings in Adam's office at Pontefract House when Mr. Ridley knocked on the door.

"Excuse me, milord, but this note was just sent round by messenger." The butler offered an envelope on a silver tray.

Adam opened it. Inside, a note read: "Sir: I have something I believe will be of interest to you. If you are curious, please present yourself at Suite 2-A, Claridge's Hotel, tomorrow at one P.M."

The note was unsigned.

Claridge's had begun its long career at the beginning of the century as a town house where the Prince Regent kept his various paramours. In time it developed into a hotel, retaining some of its risqué flavor, but gaining respectability as that most respectable of centuries, the nineteenth, progressed. Eighteen-year-old Sean Griswold, who had worked at the hotel as a porter for two years, knew that the management prided itself on its respectability. Nevertheless, Sean was aware that certain noblemen, if they had sufficient cash and social clout, were allowed to use the hotel for a trysting place. Therefore, when he saw Lord Pontefract come into the hotel lobby the next day shortly before one, he wondered what the great Hero of Cawnpore was up to. He recognized Adam not only because he had seen pictures of him, but because he had seen him in person many times since his aunt was the housekeeper at Pontefract House. When Adam asked at the desk to be taken to Suite 2-A on the second floor, Sean grinned. He knew who was in Suite 2-A.

Adam followed the bellboy up the stairs to the second floor, then down a hallway to the suite. He was burning with curiosity as to the authorship of the note. Knocking on the door, he waited for it to be opened, not having any idea who would do so. His surprise was genuine when it was opened by Emily McNair.

"Emily!" he exclaimed. "What in the world are you doing here?"

Emily was wearing a beautiful ivory silk dress with much bosom exposed, a dress that anyone, including Adam, knew was proper for dinner but outrageous for lunch. She smiled.

"I'm taking you to lunch," she said. "Since you've never asked me, I decided to ask you. Come in."

Adam glanced nervously at the bellboy, who was staring at the ceiling, trying not to snicker. Adam gave him a half-crown tip, then went into the drawing room of the suite. He looked around as Emily closed the door. A small circular table had been put up in the middle of the room. Lunch for two had been laid, and a waiter was standing beside it, holding a bottle of champagne which he now, on cue, uncorked with a loud pop.

"Do you like Veuve Clicquot?" Emily said. "If you prefer some other brand, we can change it. As for me, I've acquired quite a taste for the Widow."

Adam was a bit dazed. "Uh, no, that's fine."

Emily signaled the waiter to pour.

"Do you smoke, milord?" she asked. "I bought some of the finest Havana cigars—"

"I'm allergic to cigar smoke."

"Of course, I forgot. I should have remembered that from India. That first glorious night we met on my father's terrace in Calcutta, you had gone out to escape the cigar smoke. Would you like some caviar with your champagne?"

"Emily, what *is* this?"

"It must be obvious: it's luncheon. *Do* you want some caviar? It's the finest Persian beluga."

"Do your parents know you're doing this?"

She laughed. "What in the world difference does it make whether they do or don't? Really, milord, you're not being a very good guest. I keep offering you things, and you keep asking me questions as if I were some naughty child. Where are your manners?"

"I'm not used to receiving anonymous invitations. And what is it you think will interest me?"

She smiled coquettishly. "Would I be wildly conceited if I hoped it were me?"

Adam frowned. He turned to the waiter, who was passing a bowl of iced caviar. "Leave us."

"Milord?"

"I said, leave us. Put the caviar on the table and go."

The waiter, unnerved by Adam's sharp tone, nodded and quickly obeyed.

When they were alone, Adam turned to Emily. "I can't believe you'd be this foolish," he said.

"Foolish? I think you're horrid! I've gone to a great deal of trouble and expense to entertain you, and you're behaving like a boor."

"Whatever made you think I'd want to be entertained *this* way?"

"Well, all the heroes in the novels I read from Mr. Mudie's want to be entertained this way."

"Mr. Mudie's? You mean, the lending library?"

"Of course. I'm one of his biggest customers. Papa is furious at me because he says my overdue fines are sinful."

Adam stared at her a moment, then started to laugh. Emily, whose red hair hung in glorious curls, stiffened.

"I'd like to know what's so funny?" she said.

"I hate to tell you this, Emily, but *you* are. I can't believe you'd go to these lengths to imitate the trashy novels you read—"

"They're not trashy! They're romantic! And *I* can't believe you'd behave this way! Aren't I beautiful? This dress cost Papa a fortune. Why aren't you besotted by me? Why aren't you sweeping me off my feet and covering me with hot kisses? Do you know what this lunch is *costing* me? I pawned my pearl necklace to pay for this."

Adam groaned. "Good God . . . *un*pawn it. I'll give you the money—"

"I don't care about my pearl necklace! I want *you!* Can't you understand? From the first moment I saw you, I was madly in love with you. You know I'm not demure—God knows, it's no secret. But I don't care. Adam, you're my every thought, my every dream. All I want out of life is to be held in your strong, virile arms. All I want is your love!"

For a moment he was tempted. As silly as she was, she was radiantly beautiful. Then he turned and looked at the love seat by the door. Her ivory cloak and bonnet were on it. He went over, picked them up, and brought them to her.

"Put these on. I'm sending you home."

"No!"

"Emily, you're playing with fire! Don't you realize you're compromising yourself *and* me?"

"I don't care! Nothing is more important than love!"

"You're wrong," he said quietly. "There are many things more important than love."

"Name one."

"I'll name several: Honor. Dignity. Self-respect."

She laughed. "Really, Adam, with *your* reputation you have the nerve to say that to me? I never thought you were a hypocrite."

"Yes, I suppose I am a hypocrite, and if I hadn't learned anything in my life, I'd probably do what you want. But I like to think I've learned something."

"What have you learned?" she said scornfully.

"Well, for one thing: if I seduced you, I'd hate myself for the rest of my life because I would have ruined you, and you're too sweet a girl to ruin."

"I don't care. I want to be ruined."

"No you don't. And I'd never be able to look at your

parents again, who were, after all, kind to me in India. But even more important, frankly, I'd ruin *me.*"

"What do you mean? How can a man be ruined?"

"Easily. The Queen told me this. My Aunt Sidonia told me, my wife told me. Listen: love is wonderful. Passion is wonderful. But I've been passionately in love with a woman since I was ten, and it's done nothing but cause both of us trouble. You ask what's more important than love, and I'll tell you: my two sons, whom I adore. My wife—God knows we've had our fights, but she has earned my respect and love, despite the fact that I don't love her the way I love Lizzie. And if you think I'm going to betray her by seducing you, you couldn't be more wrong. And there's something else: I'm trying to help the poor. Oh yes, you can call me holier-than-thou and a hypocrite because I live in beautiful mansions, but I'm *trying* to do something for the ghastly poverty in this country. And if it got out that Lord Pontefract was bouncing in and out of bed with a beautiful young girl at Claridge's, it would compromise what I'm trying to do in, of all places, Wapping. So here: put on your cloak and bonnet. I'm sending you home to Berkeley Square, and I'm going home to my family."

He put the cloak around her shoulders as she burst into tears.

"This is the most horrible day of my life!" she cried.

"No, it isn't. Someday you'll look back and thank me for being intelligent."

She wiped her eyes on a napkin, then looked at him with angry eyes.

"And someday when we're both old and gray, perhaps you'll look back and realize what a fool you were to be so damned intelligent!"

Now it was his turn to stare. She walked to the door and slammed out of the room.

"Oh, Dizzy," Sybil said sadly the next afternoon as she and Mr. Disraeli took tea in the music room of Pontefract House, "I have reason to believe Adam is deceiving me again."

"What do you mean?"

"Mrs. Griswold, my housekeeper, has a nephew who works at Claridge's. He told her that yesterday Adam entertained Miss McNair at lunch in a private suite. It hardly takes a genius to figure out what that means."

Dizzy sighed. "It's a pity that Adam's moral views seem so Chaucerian. But since he has become my political protégé, I can see that I will have to take matters into my own hands—for the good of the party, of course. Perhaps, Sybil, you should give a ball and let me furnish the guest list. I think it's time we found a suitor for Miss McNair. I have one attractive and thoroughly unscrupulous young man in mind."

"Who is that?"

"Edgar Musgrave." He and Sybil exchanged meaningful looks. "It would perhaps put to rest some—shall we say?—unfortunate gossip."

"Am I ever going to see Papa again?" Amanda asked Lizzie, who was sitting at her vanity preparing for dinner. "I mean, my real papa, not Alex."

"Yes, darling. Someday." Lizzie tiptoed carefully around this subject. "But you like your new papa?"

"Oh, Alex is wonderful. And so kind. I just love all the presents he gives me. Is he *awfully* rich?"

"Yes, I think he is." Lizzie had not *quite* squared her conscience about Alex's war profiteering. After the wedding, they had honeymooned for a week in upstate New York, then Alex had taken off for Washington where, he told her after his return, he had made almost a half-million dollars brokering a deal selling the Union Army one hundred thousand uniforms. But then, American businessmen seemed to have a rather casual attitude toward the war.

His surprise wedding gift to her was a new house. He had bought two of what he called "boring" brownstones on Fifth Avenue, ten blocks south of the huge stone reservoir, shaped like a truncated pyramid, that squatted uptown at Forty-second Street. The houses were being torn down so that he could build his beautiful new English bride a "palace you'll be proud of," as he told her. When he showed her the architectural plans, they had dumbfounded her. The house was a five-story stone mansion in the Gothic style that looked more like a miniature cathedral than a home. When she protested that it looked rather big, he told her they had to put on a show to teach New Yorkers how best to spend all their war-boom millions, particularly at Sinclair and Son. It was all heady and giddy and probably, she reflected, gaudy and vulgar as well. But Alex's energy dazzled her, as well as wearing her out. She thought that in the back of his mind was a desire to create a life as grand as Adam's in England: for he had developed an intense jealousy of Lizzie's former lover.

Alex's paralyzed mother had died of a heart attack. Alex sold her house and rented a brownstone on Fifth Avenue one block south of the construction site of the Gothic mansion. Now he came into the bedroom, saying, "How's my sweet Amanda?"

"Alex!" squealed Amanda, running to him. He picked her up, kissed her, swung her around twice, then put her down. "Now, run to the kitchen. Mrs. Parker has supper for you. And Lila baked you some chocolate cookies."

"I *love* chocolate!"

She literally zoomed out of the room. Alex came up behind Lizzie, put his hands on her bare shoulders and leaned down to kiss her neck. "And how's the most beautiful woman in New York?" he said.

Lizzie watched his reflection in her mirror. He was, as always, beautifully dressed, and she was not immune to his dark good looks.

"Frankly, I'm a little tired. I think I'm catching a cold. At any rate, I'm glad no one's coming tonight. It will be a relief to have dinner alone."

"Didn't you get my message?"

"What message?"

He straightened. "I sent a message boy from the store this afternoon. I had lunch today with a swell fellow, a real corker of a man whom I've had some dealings with in Washington. I asked him to dinner tonight."

"Oh Alex, *really*. The messenger never came! How can

I feed a total stranger? Lila just has a chicken for us . . ."

He looked worried. "Damn!" He stuck his hands in the pockets of his slim trousers. "Those message boys are so damned unreliable. I'd better send Lila out for another chicken, maybe two . . . Jim's fat as a pig and eats like a trencherman. But you'll like him, Lizzie. He's a lot of fun and bright as a penny. I may be doing some business with him—he's got a lot of ideas. I'd better run downstairs and tell Lila."

He hurried out of the bedroom. Lizzie sighed. Since their return from their honeymoon a month before, their social schedule had been unrelenting, almost every night either out or entertaining at home. Alex said good social contacts made for good business; besides, he obviously took great pride in showing her off. But the pace was wearing her down, and she often thought back wistfully on her peaceful days in Ayr, on her walks along the beach, on, inevitably, Adam. How different the two men were. How different the peaceful coast of Scotland from money-mad New York. Putting on the diamond earrings Alex had bought her, she wondered who in God's name Jim was.

"Why Alex, my boy, I'd eat bone-marrow soup till Judgment Day if I done ever seen me a prettier gal than your wife," exclaimed Jim Fisk, Jr., an hour later as Alex led the rotund, flashily dressed former circus carny into the drawing room. "My God, she's a queen! A veritable queen! Mrs. Sinclair, ma'am, even though I was born on April Fool's Day, I never tell a lie. And believe me, ma'am, when I assure you that one look at your beauteous visage and I hear the heavenly choir singin' 'Hosannah! Hosannah!' and I see cherubim playin' on golden harps! This day will live in my memory forever because I done met me Venus herself!"

Lizzie could barely refrain from laughing in his face at this bombast, delivered in a nasal Vermont twang. Jim Fisk was twenty-seven, with bulging blue eyes and a walrus-size mustache. He had three gold-and-diamond rings on his pudgy fingers, a diamond stickpin in his gray silk tie and a gold watch chain swooped across his immense belly.

"Why, thank you, Mr. Fisk," she managed to get out without guffawing.

"Alex, I thought you was braggin' up a storm at lunch, but now it turns out you was tellin' the truth: you married the prettiest gal in New York. Say, and I like your house, too," he added, looking around the overly fussy drawing room which Alex had rented furnished. "Mighty fancy place, in the best taste, and on Fifth Avenue. I hear Fifth Avenue's the place to be, and prices are goin' sky-high."

"Yes, it's a bull market for real estate," Alex agreed.

"Mr. Fisk, would you like a sherry before dinner?" Lizzie asked as she sat on a settee.

"A sherry?" he snorted. "Tarnation, ma'am, that's no drink fit for a man. I say give me whiskey or give me water. You got any rum, Alex? I got me a hankerin' for some good old rum."

"I have no rum, but I have some prewar bourbon."

"Bourbon'll do fine. Well, now, ma'am"—he settled his bulk into a fragile-looking armchair—"you bein' a furriner, what do you think of this here crazy war we got on our hands? Huh? And I say 'crazy' because ain't it crazy for brothers to be shootin' at each other? I think of Johnny Reb as my brother even though he'd like to blow my head off. But say, looks like we got us a real fight shapin' up down at Fredericksburg, don't it? I wonder if Burnside might win us one, for once. Nah. Come to think of it, the North don't win battles. What do you think, Alex? Want to make a bet? I'll give you three to one that Burnside gets his tail whupped by the Rebs."

"One hundred dollars?"

"You got a bet."

Lizzie thought it was somewhat cynical for two men of fighting age to be betting on the outcome of a battle that promised to be bloody, but she held her tongue.

"So what do you think of the great Jim Fisk?" Alex asked that night as he undressed for bed.

"He's a buffoon," Lizzie said. She was already in bed.

"And not to sound like a snob, but he really is the *most* vulgar man."

"Oh, he's vulgar, all right. Just a farmboy from Vermont who's got the instincts of a Bengal tiger."

"Did you see his table manners? He held his fork as if it were a dagger, and I'll have to have the tablecloth washed twice, he slopped so much chicken on it. And the belches!"

Alex laughed as he put on his red flannel nightshirt. "He used to work in a circus, so he's not exactly the refined type. But he's making millions down in Washington working for the Jordan, Marsh store in Boston."

"Is that where you met him?"

"Yes."

"Is he profiteering, like you?"

"That's right." He climbed in the big bed next to her. "I know he's crude, but they're all crude down on Wall Street, and from what he was saying at dinner, it sounds as if he's headed that way. It makes you sort of dizzy to think of the fortunes being made down there."

"It makes me dizzy thinking of the fortune *you're* making down in Washington. Oh Alex, couldn't you stop what you're doing with the Government? Don't we have enough money?"

"How much money is enough?" he said, looking at her coolly.

"You told me you've made over two million dollars this year. That strikes me as enough."

"They say Commodore Vanderbilt's worth *fifty* million or more, but that doesn't stop him from trying to make more. You can never have enough money. That's what this country's all about: making money. And the more money you make, the better man you are."

"That's the most absurd statement I've ever heard. You mean you think Commodore Vanderbilt is a better man than you?"

"Yes. He's a better businessman, at least. But he's old, and I'm young. I'll be in his league one day, and maybe Wall Street's the quickest way to get there."

She stared at him. "I'm beginning to see you—*really* see you—for the first time. Money is your god, isn't it?"

"You got a better one?"

She turned down the bed lamp and pulled the duvet over her shoulder, her back to her husband. "Good night, Alex."

"Wait a minute! You're making me look like some sort of greedy monster just because I like money! Don't *you* like money?"

"I don't wish to discuss it further."

"Well, *I* wish to! I repeat: don't *you* like money?"

She sat up and turned the lamp back up. "Yes, of course I like money," she said, "but I'm not obsessed by it. Do you realize we've been married six weeks and *all* you ever talk about is money? There's nothing else in your life: no art, no books, no music, no love . . ."

"I love you! And I love Amanda!"

"Only a monster couldn't love Amanda, and you love me only because you like to show me off, as if I were a new-model dress available at your store."

"That's a damnable thing to say!"

"But it's true, Alex. You have many wonderful qualities, I won't deny that. But what you know about love could be written on one of your Sinclair and Son price tags."

"Oh? And I suppose Adam Thorne knows all about love?" His tone became soft and vicious.

"Adam Thorne *is* love."

"Is that why you're so unenthusiastic about *my* love-making?" he whispered. "Because you're still in love with that damned limey?"

"I'm unenthusiastic about your lovemaking because you do it so fast it's like a white sale at Sinclair and Son. Adam made love like a symphony. You make love like the Minute Waltz."

His pale face went even paler.

"Damn you!" he whispered. "*Damn* you!"

He threw off the duvet and got out of bed.

"I'm sorry, Alex . . . that was a cruel thing to say."

"The 'Minute' Waltz!" he snorted. Grabbing a coverlet from a chaise longue, he went to the door.

"I'll sleep downstairs," he said. "The 'Minute' Waltz my foot!"

He slammed out of the room. Lizzie sighed and turned down the lamp again. Twenty minutes later, just as she was dozing off, she heard the door open. She sat up. The gaslight from Fifth Avenue spilled through the windows, faintly illuminating the room. She saw Alex, still in his nightshirt, come across the room. He knelt beside the bed, took her hand and brought it to his lips. "I'm sorry," he whispered, kissing her hand. "I'm so in love with you, Lizzie, that when I think of Adam Thorne, it just *kills* me. Teach me to make love like Adam. I want so much for you to love me."

She put her free hand on his hair, which was thick and black like Adam's. "Well," she said, "my first suggestion would be not to make it seem like a relay race."

"Am I *that* bad?"

She nodded. After a moment he snickered. Then she snickered.

"All right, I'll slow down."

He climbed in bed. This time, she thought a while later, there was a definite improvement.

CHAPTER 24

Phineas's black carriage drove up to the entrance of Elvira Plantation. It was a cold, snowy day, the onset of December, and the windows of the Confederate hospital rapidly filled with faces as the men, bored to distraction, looked out to see who was coming. Old Elton got down from the driver's seat and opened the door to hold Clayton's crutches and help him out. Once on the ground, Clayton took his crutches and hobbled up the walk to what had once been one of the most beautiful plantations in Virginia but was now showing the effects of the war. Clayton's breath fogged in the cold air as he rang the bell. The door was opened by Miss Pruitt, one of his former nurses.

"Captain Carr!" She smiled. "It's so nice to see you. I do declare, you're looking quite strong again. I'm so glad."

"Thank you, Miss Pruitt. I wanted to see Dr. Mainwaring. Is he in?"

"Yes, he's just finished his morning rounds and has gone to his office."

The nurse led Clayton through the packed cots to the back of the house where, in Jack Cavanagh's former office, the hospital's director now reigned. After knocking, Clayton went in. Dr. Mainwaring, a short man with gold-rimmed spectacles, stood up and shook his hand.

"It's good to see you, Clayton. How is everything?"

"Well, not too good. We're sitting uncomfortably close to the battlefield at Fairview, and we're all a little nervous. General Whitney is with General Lee at Fredericksburg, and we're mighty shorthanded at the plantation, so he sent me to get Dulcey."

The mild-mannered doctor looked startled. "Dulcey? But we need her here. We're shorthanded too!"

"It's my wife, Doctor. She had a stillborn baby three days ago and she's just not mending well. General Whitney is very nervous about her. He got you Elvira Plantation and most of your staff, so he's calling in a favor."

"In that case, there's not much I can say. I think Dulcey's in the kitchen with Aunt Lide."

"Thanks."

Clayton hobbled out of the office and went to the kitchen, where Dulcey was wiping dishes with her grandmother.

"How are you, Aunt Lide?" he asked, coming in the room.

"Captain Carr," exclaimed the old woman, giving him a suspicious look. Aunt Lide knew about Clayton and her granddaughter. "I's pleased to see you's mendin', but I hope you's not plannin' to move back in wid Dulcey. It's bad enuf dat Elvira Plantation's become a hospital, but I sho' don't like de idea of it turnin' into no sportin' club. You unnerstan' what I mean?"

"Yes, I understand. And no, I'm not moving in with Dulcey again. Dulcey, may I speak with you a few minutes in private?"

Dulcey put down the dish towel and followed Clayton into the adjacent butler's pantry. Clayton pulled a wad of Confederate bills from the pocket of his ragged coat and put it in her hand.

"Here's fifty dollars," he whispered.

Dulcey stared at the money. "Where'd you get dis?" she asked.

"My father-in-law. He's got a lot of cash locked up in Fairview Plantation—I don't know where it's coming from, but I found the key and took this for you."

"Why?"

"I owe you for putting me up."

"Warn't worth no fifty dollah."

"Well, I thought maybe you could buy something pretty for yourself. Anyway, it's for you. Now, go pack your things. I'm taking you to Fairview Plantation."

"Maybe I doan wanna go."

Clayton took her hand and raised it to his lips. "Dulcey, please," he whispered. "I miss you. My father-in-law's gone now, so he can't hurt you. Please come."

Her eyes narrowed. "You a strange man, Clayton. But yo' wife not gonna be very happy seein' *me* around."

"My wife's sick. She's recovering very badly. . . . Dr. Cooper's not sure what's wrong with her. Please come, Dulcey. There'll be more money for you."

"I ain't a whore no mo'."

"I didn't mean that—"

"Get down on yo' knee—I said knee—and beg me."

He winced. "You'll have to help me."

She smiled. "You don't have to do it. I jes' wanted to see if you *would*."

"I'd do anything for you, Dulcey."

"Clayton, have you done gone an' fallen in love wid me?"

"What if I have?"

"You askin' fo' a lot of trouble."

"I don't care. My life's hell without you, and with you it's . . ." He bit his lip. ". . . heaven."

"Huh. Dass sweet. You're not only cute, Clayton. You're a poet. You go wait in the carriage. I'll pack my tings."

Giving him her sultriest smile, she went into the kitchen.

They returned to Fairview Plantation just before sunset.

"So dis is where you live," said Dulcey, looking around as she got out of the carriage.

"Yes," said Clayton, who was being helped out by Elton. "Do you like it?"

"It's all right. But it's not as purdy as Elvira Plantation."

"Sorry to disappoint you. Elton, take Dulcey to the kitchen. Tell Sarah she's going to stay in the room next to Miss Charlotte, so she can be on hand."

"Yessah, Massa Clayton." The old man started toward the rear of the house.

"On hand fo' Miss Charlotte?" whispered Dulcey with a mischievous grin. "Or fo' *you*?"

She laughed as she hurried after Elton.

"Zack!" Clayton exclaimed. His younger brother had just come out of the house onto the verandah. He was wearing a rather dirty gray private's uniform. "When did you get here?"

"This morning. I got three days' leave." He came down the steps as Clayton hobbled toward him.

"You're looking wonderful, Zack!" he exclaimed, squeezing his hand.

"Well, I'm dog tired, that's for sure. We've been doing nothing but digging ditches for the past week. The Yankees have taken Fredericksburg, but they haven't done a damned thing except sit and stare up at us. We think Burnside's either chickenhearted or dumb, we're not sure which." He looked back at the house, then lowered his voice. "Clayton, did your father-in-law send a trunk here last week?"

"Yes. We put it in the basement. It's filled with cash—must be thousands of dollars in it. Where'd he get it?"

"General Whitney's in charge of issuing the licenses to the sutlers for the entire army. They're making money by the ton selling everything to us from bacon to stationery, and they charge wild prices. The rumor in the camp is that your father-in-law is taking kickbacks from the sutlers."

"Doesn't surprise me. Phineas is a sly old bastard. Well, so much for the Glorious Cause. What a waste this whole stupid war is. Come on in, Zack. It's time for lunch, and I'm starving."

Leaning on his crutches, he started toward the house. Zack put his hand on his arm to stop him.

"Clayton," he said "you don't *mean* that?"

"Mean what?"

"What you said about the war being a waste."

"You're damned right I mean it."

"But we're fighting for our homeland!"

"Maybe our homeland isn't worth fighting for. Come on, I'm hungry."

He hobbled up onto the verandah, but Zack didn't follow him. He just stared at his older brother as if he couldn't believe what he had heard.

CHAPTER 25

Sybil was in bed reading a novel when there was a knock at her door.

"Yes?" She and Adam and the two boys had come north to Pontefract Hall in Yorkshire for the Christmas holidays. Now the door opened, and a dirty-looking stranger came in. Sybil tensed.

"Who are you? Get out immediately!" Greatly alarmed, she started to reach for the bellcord to ring for her maid when a familiar voice said: "Don't you recognize your own husband?"

She hesitated. "Adam?"

He took off his workman's cap and came to the bed, a smile on his face. "I'm sorry if I frightened you," he said, "but I wanted to try out my new disguise. Do you like it?"

She stared at him. He was dressed like a beggar in a long black coat that was filthy and worn.

"Like it?" she said. "Am I supposed to?"

"Well, perhaps not. What I meant was, what do I look like?"

She gave a confused shrug. "A beggar?" she said. "Or a workman?"

"Bravo. What I hope to look like is an out-of-work laborer." She wrinkled her nose slightly, and he laughed. "Ah yes, I smell a bit, don't I? It's these clothes. I bought them at a flea market in York the other day. They don't have fleas—at least, I think they don't—but I daresay whoever wore them didn't bathe too frequently. Don't you see? It gives the disguise a certain authenticity."

"But why in the world are you disguising yourself as an out-of-work laborer?"

"An excellent question. And if you'll wait till I change, I'll come back and tell you all about it."

He left her bedroom. Fifteen minutes later, he returned, wearing a bathrobe. "I took a quick shower," he said, coming to the bed. "I expect I smell a bit better." He sat on the bed next to her. "Things are changing in England," he said. "The working class is beginning to feel its muscle. It wants the vote, and Dizzy wants to give it the vote—or at least extend the franchise by as much as is politically feasible. But the average Englishman has no idea of what the working class is like . . . what it's like to work in a cotton mill, for instance. Most of the press lords are on the side of the millowners and don't print the truth, and nobody reads the radical press except the radicals. But I intend to change all this."

"How?"

"By going to Manchester disguised as an out-of-work man named Adam Fielding. I'll try to get a job at Belladon Textiles. If I can, I'll work there for several weeks to see what it's *really* like. Then I'm going to London and tell my experiences to the House of Lords. If my hunch is correct, life in the Belladon mills is sufficiently colorful so that I ought to be able to wake the noble lords out of their slumber and maybe stir the Commons enough to get them to pass some social legislation with teeth. Dizzy thinks it's a capital idea, and if it works, it may help us win the next election."

Sybil looked at him with undisguised admiration. "Adam, it's brilliant," she said. "But mightn't it be dangerous? I've heard that those millowners have spies on the work force. What if you were discovered?"

Adam shrugged. "It couldn't be more dangerous than India."

"Yes, I suppose." Sybil paused. "Why do I think it's no coincidence you've chosen Horace Belladon's mills to attack?"

"Of course it's no coincidence. I know Belladon hired the Brocks to kidnap Amanda. They never said his name, but I know it in my bones. It's time I squared accounts with him."

Sybil shook her head. "What a bizarre husband I have," she said. "To smear dirt on your face, put on clothes that stink to high heaven, and go to find work in a horrible cotton mill. But I admire what you're doing. Have you told the boys?"

"No. They probably think I'm dotty enough without seeing me in my beggar's rags. I'll tell them when I get back."

"When are you leaving?"

"In the morning. I have to go to London first, for some business. But the next morning I go to Manchester."

"Then this is our last evening together?"

"Yes." He hesitated. "I thought perhaps you'd like me to spend the night . . . here."

Her face lit up. "Oh yes," she whispered, putting her book on the bed table. He took her in his arms and kissed her. After a moment, she pushed him away. "No," she said, frowning. "You'd better go back to your room."

"What's wrong?"

"I know about Emily McNair," she said. "I'm not going to make a scene about it, but as long as you're involved with her, you're not going to be involved with me."

"What are you talking about?"

"Oh Adam, don't play innocent. I know all about your little escapade at Claridge's. You seem to forget that the housekeeper's nephew is a porter there. You should have used a bit more discretion in choosing your trysting place."

"Sybil, I swear I am not 'involved' with Emily McNair. Yes, I did see her there, but it was anything but a scandalous affair. She sent round an anonymous note last week, saying if I came to Claridge's the next day I'd find something that might interest me. I went, and of course it was Emily—I say 'of course,' though at the time I had no idea. To put it bluntly, she asked me to seduce her. The whole thing was almost laughable. I got rather angry with her and told her to go home, which she finally did. But I swear to you: nothing happened. I like Emily, but I'm not about to make her my mistress—or anyone else, for that matter. I happen to love my wife."

She looked at him, tears in her eyes. "If I could only

believe that . . ." she whispered. "I'd be the happiest woman in England."

"It's the truth."

"Oh, my darling . . ." She moved over in the bed and threw back the coverlet. "Climb in," she ordered. "And I'm not letting you out—ever!"

"Cet enfant noir est un prodige de la nature," said the most famous pianist in the world.

Gabriel Cavanagh had just finished a bravura performance of Franz Liszt's "Dante" Sonata, playing on an Erard piano in the Salon des Muses in the Hôtel Lambert in Paris. Liszt was sitting near the piano with his long-time mistress, the Polish-born Princess Carolyne Sayn-Wittgenstein, a heavy-set woman in voluminous skirts with a shawl around her shoulders, who was smoking a large cigar. Liszt was fifty-one and rapidly losing his romantic good looks that, along with his thunderous piano technique, had, a quarter century earlier, made him the toast of Europe as he concertized across the continent, creating a sensation.

"The Maestro says you are a wonder of nature," Tadeuz Karasowski translated for Gabriel. When they had arrived in Paris, Tadeuz had used his Polish connections to make contact with Princess Carolyne who had arranged the recital in the spectacular Hôtel Lambert on the Ile de la Cité in the middle of the Seine. The house had been built by Jean-Baptiste Lambert, secretary to Louis XIII, and had in the eighteenth century been temporary home to Voltaire; but now it belonged to Princess Czartoryska, the wife of the immensely rich Polish Prince Adam Czartoryski who had taken refuge in Paris after the Polish insurgency against Russia in 1831. The Hôtel Lambert was now the capital of the Polish circle in Paris and had been a natural choice of Princess Carolyne. But the grandiose setting of the house, as well as Liszt's celebrity, had put Gabriel into a near tongue-tied state of awe. Although he had nerves of steel and was extremely unusual in that stage fright was unknown to him, being in the presence of the great Maestro who had been lionized by society, fought over by women, and decorated by kings and governments like a military hero was almost too much for Gabriel. He stared at the Hungarian-born genius (who, since moving to Paris at age ten, had forgotten how to speak Hungarian) and thought: That's what I want out of life—fame and glory.

Liszt got out of his chair and came to Gabriel, taking the boy's hands and examining them.

"Les mains sont extraordinaires," he mumbled to himself. Then he released them and looked at the boy's face.

"When I was younger even than you," he said in his tortured English, "I played for the sublime Beethoven. He kissed me for good luck. I now kiss you for good luck." He leaned forward and kissed the boy's forehead. "God has given you a great talent," he went on. "You are a *wunderkind*, as I was, and Mozart. No one knows why these things happen, they just do. But there is nothing in life more important than art. You must serve music like a priest in a temple. There is nothing I can teach you, but I can help you to start a career. I will write a note to my friend, Monsieur Pleyel. He will arrange for you a concert in his hall. Conquer Paris and you will conquer the world." He patted Gabriel's lamblike black hair and smiled. "And remember: the worst audiences are the Italians. They talk while one plays."

"Maestro," Gabriel said, gulping with nervousness, "will you play for me?"

"Ah, no," Liszt said. "I have no desire to come off second-best to a child." Then he turned to Tadeuz. *"Je prévois une carrière époustouflante, en dépit de sa couleur. Ou peut-être à cause de sa couleur."*

"What did the Maestro say?" Gabriel asked as they walked out of the Hôtel Lambert onto the rue Saint-Louis.

"He says he predicts an amazing career for you," replied Tadeuz.

"But he said something about my color?"

"He said, 'despite your color. Or perhaps because of it.' "

"In other words, I may be a freak?"

"I don't think the Maestro meant that, exactly."

"I don't care if they *do* think I'm a freak. I'm still going to be famous."

As Tadeuz hailed a cab, a pretty girl passed by on the sidewalk. She gave Gabriel an interested look. He watched her as she continued down the sidewalk.

Gabriel didn't care if she had looked at him because he was black. The point was, she had looked.

"A letter arrived from your brother," Ellie May said, holding the envelope out to Clayton. "Zack's such a fine young man," she went on, giving Clayton a sour look. "So brave and loyal to the Cause." She emphasized the last words. Clayton, no fool, got the dig, but he refused to rise to the bait and snap back at her. The cold winter, the lack of food, and Charlotte's mysterious illness had made everyone at Fairview Plantation tense and snappish. As Ellie May went out of the room, Clayton hobbled over to the fireplace to keep warm while he read:

Dec. 12, 1862
Marye Heights, Fredericksburg, Va.

Dear Clayton:

Stationery is getting so expensive that it is costing me dearly to write to you (the sutler charged me $1 a sheet), but as you are all the family I have left, I expect it's worth the money. The sutlers rule the roost here. You can buy just about anything from these rascals, but they charge what the traffic will bear and must be all becoming millionaires. You recall, I trust, what I told you the rumors are about Gen. Whitney. But life goes on here as we await what we all assume will be the great battle. The Yanks have been trying to build pontoon bridges across the Rappahannock, but our sharpshooters, many stationed in basements of houses destroyed by the bombardment of Fredericksburg, had been giving the Yankee engineers merry hell. Finally, yesterday morning, General Burnside, the Yankee commander, must have got tired waiting for the bridges because he sent over a wave of infantry in boats. Our commander, General Longstreet, withdrew our men from the town up here to the safety of the heights, and thus Fredericksburg—or what's left of it—is now in Federal hands. The Yankee guns have reduced most of that lovely old town to rubble. Today, we hear that they have ransacked the town, pulling furniture out of the houses, looting, and getting drunk. They turned pianos into watering troughs for their horses, and many of the drunken oafs danced around the streets in dresses and bonnets they stole. What a sorry spectacle that must have been! But it proves that these northern invaders of our beloved homeland are nothing more than vandals, as vile and beast-like as those who invaded the Roman Empire.

It has been so damned cold, but happily we finished our little house last week. There are six of us in "Buzzards' Nest"—that's the name we've given it—and while it's not exactly a palace, we're surprisingly warm, all things considered. Our house is about twelve feet square and made of sticks and pickets chinked and daubed with mud. The roof is a tent flap, and we have the best fireplace in the company, the bottom made of brick and the rest mud and sticks. Everyone is building houses like ours to live in, but we are conceited enough to think ours the best. Our utensils consist of one skillet, a stew pot, bread pan, frying pan, and kettle. We take turns cooking, but Tom Moore from Georgia is generally conceded to be our best chef. We try to keep ourselves as clean as possible, but I suppose we must all stink to heaven, as soap is expensive.

I am sad to report that the state of morals here has sunk to an ugly low. *Nymphs du monde* have swarmed up from Richmond's bawdy houses to ply their lewd trade, and they have no reason to complain about bad business: they have customers galore, though I am proud to tell you, dear brother, that I have not succumbed to temptation. This is not due to virtue on my part as much as plain common sense: the bawds are badly infected, and the worst-kept secret in the camp is the horrifying number of men with gonorrhea and syphilis. Smoking, chewing, and drinking are also common, and when you think of how we Southerners have all been given the benefits of Christian training and Bible reading, it makes you wonder how easily all that good work can come to naught. The Devil is king here, and in his train are his handmaidens, the Pox and Clap.

I have not been so virtuous about the whiskey. The names we give it can give you an idea of its taste and potency: "burst-head," "pop-skull," "old red-eye," and "rifle knock-knee" are examples. I'd give a lot for a glass of fine old bourbon like Pa used to drink. There are many ways of fighting boredom here aside from boozing and whoring, snowball fights being the most innocent. Gary Laidlaw is another of the boys in Buzzards' Nest, and he plays a mean banjo. We spend many a whiskey-fueled evening singing "Annie Laurie," "The Girl I Left Behind Me," "All Quiet Along the Potomac Tonight," "The Bonnie Blue Flag," "My Maryland," and of course endless choruses of "Dixie."

But I suppose the most prevalent vice here is gambling, and you can't imagine how much of it goes on! There's a real gambling den near here called the Devil's Half-Acre, where half the pay of the Confederate Army changes hands. Poker, twenty-one, euchre, keno, chuck-a-luck, raffles, shooting crap—you name it and it's going on. As a man who is proud of what he's fighting for, it brings tears to my eyes to see the finest flower of our Southern youth give way to so much dissipation and wickedness.

Which brings me to a painful moment. I can't tell you how distressed I was when I was on furlough at Fairview Plantation to hear you express loss of faith in our great cause and that you think slavery is not worth fighting for. Oh, Clayton, if you are right, then this terrible conflict is a horrible mistake, and the oceans of blood that have already been spilled on both sides are nothing but tragic waste! But I cannot believe you are right. I would be the first to say that the institution of slavery on these shores was a mistake, and that the Africans were brought here cruelly and against their will. But justly or unjustly, slavery is the foundation of our Southern way of life, and what can possibly be the alternative to it except ruin and chaos? It is for this reason I am risking my life to fight for it. It has given me great sadness that you, my dear brother, have espoused the enemy's view. I can only pray that this letter may perhaps bring you back to your senses.

Yr. devoted brother, Zack.

After finishing the letter Clayton shook his head sadly. Then he wadded it into a ball and threw it in the flames.

"Charlotte has developed a pelvic inflammatory disease," said the white-bearded Dr. Hilton Cooper that night as he closed the door to her bedroom and came into the upstairs hall at Fairview Plantation.

"Is that serious?" Clayton asked.

"If it's what I think it is, it's very serious." The old doctor took Clayton's elbow and guided him a few feet away from the door to Charlotte's bedroom. "May I be blunt, Clayton?"

"Yes, of course."

"Have you been unfaithful to your wife?"

Clayton's face turned red. "Yes," he finally whispered.

"Who was the woman?" Clayton gulped as he stared at the doctor who had brought him and Zack into the world. "Come come, man, this is no time for gallantry! This is important to Charlotte's health! Who was the woman?"

"The nurse."

Dr. Cooper's eyes widened. "The darkie in there? What's her name—Dulcey?"

"Yes, Dulcey."

"Think back, Clayton. Have you had any sores on your private parts?"

"Well . . . yes, come to think of it. There was an odd sore on my pecker. It went away after a few weeks."

"When was that?"

"About ten months ago."

"Come here, Clayton. Over by this lamp. Show me your wrists."

Clayton hobbled to a half-moon table on which stood an oil lamp. Dr. Cooper took his hands, turned them palm-up and rolled back his sleeves.

"When did you get this rash?" he asked, pointing to the red marks on Clayton's wrists.

Clayton stared at them. "I don't know . . . I hadn't even noticed it till now. What is it, Doc?"

The old man sighed. "I don't like to tell you this, Clayton. You've had enough misery out of this war, losing your leg. But you have syphilis, and it's rather advanced. The rash indicates it's already in the second stage. The sore on your penis was the first stage."

"Syphilis?" Clayton repeated the word disbelievingly.

"Yes, and I fear you've passed it on to Charlotte. That's what's causing the inflammation in her uterus. That's also probably why her baby was stillborn. You'll have to be strong about this, son, but there's a definite possibility Charlotte will not be able to bear children again. The good Lord displays His infinite wisdom in strange ways. Syphilis kills the reproductive system's functions, and it's just as well because the child could be infected."

"But . . . is there a cure?"

The doctor sadly shook his head. "None that I know of," he said. "Though being cut off from Europe by the blockade, there may be developments I'm not aware of."

"What . . . will happen?"

The doctor patted his arm reassuringly. "We can talk about that some other day," he said. "No need to burden you now."

"No. I want the truth. Tell me: what will happen?"

Dr. Cooper looked at him with sad, blue eyes. "Nothing for a while. Perhaps nothing for years. But the spirochete is in your blood and it's vicious. Someday it will go to your brain."

"My brain?"

"Yes."

"You mean I'll go mad?"

"Yes, and then . . ." He shrugged.

"Oh my God . . ."

He started whimpering. Even though it was chilly in the drafty hallway, beads of sweat appeared on his brow. He wiped his mouth with his sleeve.

Down the hall, the door to Charlotte's bedroom opened and Dulcey stepped out. Clayton looked at her, then at the doctor.

"Do you think I got it from her?" he whispered. "She worked for a madam in a Yorktown bawdy house."

"In that case, it's highly likely. The disease is spread sexually."

The doctor pulled out his gold watch and checked the time. "I have to be going now, Clayton. Mrs. Thornton's expecting. And I'm sorry, son. Deeply sorry."

"Yes . . . thank you. Good night, Doc."

Clayton's attention was riveted on the beautiful slave he had fallen in love with. Dr. Cooper picked up his black bag and headed for the stairs as Dulcey came to her one-legged lover.

"Go to your room," he whispered.

Dulcey obeyed, opening the door beside the half-moon table and entering the bedroom next to Charlotte's. Clayton waited until Dr. Cooper was downstairs. Then he hobbled into Dulcey's room and closed the door with one of his crutches.

"What's wrong?" Dulcey asked.

"Everything," he whispered. "Did you ever hear of a disease called syphilis?"

"Oh, sure. You mean de pox."

"I've got it. And Dulcey, I don't want to frighten you, but I think I got it from you."

Dulcey frowned. Then she went to one of the bedroom windows and looked out. It was another cold, snowy night. Below, she saw Dr. Cooper climbing in his buggy.

"Well?" Clayton said. "Don't you have anything to say? Do you know what it does? I'm going to go crazy and die!

And Doc thinks I gave this to my wife, so she'll die too! And we never can have children . . ." He started sobbing. He hobbled over to Dulcey's four-poster bed and sank down on it, burying his face in his hands as his crutches clattered to the floor.

Dulcey looked at him for a moment with compassion. Then she came to the bed and sat next to him, taking him in her arms.

"Oh Clayton, I done a terrible ting," she whispered, tears forming in her eyes. "A terrible ting. Oh God, you gotta try an' forgive Dulcey."

"What are you talking about?" he sniffed, looking at her.

"You see, I used to hate you," she went on. "I hated you 'cause you was white an' you was kin to Gen'ral Whitney, wot tuck away mah freedom an' sent me back to Elvira Plantation to nurse. But lately, since you fell in love wid me . . . I mean, you bein' so sweet an' kind an' gentle to Dulcey . . . well, I tink mebbe I done fell in love wid *you.*"

He stared at her with red, runny eyes. "You did?" he whispered. "You sure picked a helluva time to tell me."

"I know. An' I wouldn't tell you, sept . . . Oh, God . . ."

"What? What *is* it?"

She bit her lip, terror in her eyes. "Oh Clayton, I done giv' you de pox on purpose! I was so dumb, I didn't tink de pox hurt colored folk, jes white folk, an' I was hopin' you'd get it so you'd give it to yo' wife. An' oh, Jesus, de worst ting happen: what I was hopin' done come true."

"You bitch," he whispered. "You black bitch."

He grabbed her throat with both hands and pushed her down on the bed.

"Clayton!" she gasped. "You stranglin' me . . ."

"Bitch!" he roared, rolling on top of her. "You damned BITCH!"

"Clayton!"

It was Charlotte, standing in the doorway that connected the two bedrooms.

Clayton looked at her and released Dulcey, who was

moaning. Panting, he leaned down for his crutches, then got up.

"Do you know what this bitch did?" he shouted. "Do you *know*? She gave me the pox on purpose! That's why our baby was stillborn, because this black BITCH gave me the pox and I gave it to you!"

"An' who done give it to ME?" screamed Dulcey, getting off the bed. "You keep callin' me names, callin' me a black bitch, who done gave the pox to Dulcey? Huh? It warn't no black man, I can tell you dat, 'cause no black man ever had enough money to go to Miss Rose's an' she wouldn'ta let 'em in if dey did! Mah customers was all white, Clayton! WHITE! De white man done give me de pox an' so it only fair dat I done give it back to you! We're all in dis togedder, Clayton, white an' black! We all in dis togedder!"

Bursting into tears, she ran to the door and out into the hall. Charlotte, who was leaning against the door frame, looking pale in her ivory nightgown, stared at her husband.

"You disgust me," she said, softly.

CHAPTER

26

Many places might have been said to be the heart of the vast, cocksure British Empire, but as good a claim as any might have been made by the London clubs. Here, in magnificent houses, the rulers of the Empire could get away from it all in a tawny setting of leather armchairs, fine crystal and mellow whiskey. It was an all-male world where the problems of wives, mistresses and children could be forgotten over an excellent game pie, a backgammon match or a snooze in the Silence Room. A few of the clubs were essentially political. The Carlton Club in Pall Mall was the home of the Conservatives, and when Adam was proposed for membership by Disraeli he had been easily elected. It was in the dining room of the Carlton that Adam entertained his old friend from the glory days in India, Bentley Brent.

"So you're retired?" Adam asked, cutting into his *pâté maison.*

"Yes. Twenty years in India and it seems like a wink." Bentley, who had been retired a colonel with several medals besides his V.C., had put on twenty pounds since Adam had seen him last and his black beard was now streaked with gray.

"What are you going to do now?"

"Ah, Adam, I haven't given it much thought. I suppose I'll go find me a cottage somewhere and grow roses, though it certainly sounds boring after Cawnpore and Nana Sahib."

"Would you be interested in working for me on a part-time basis? It would involve going to America twice a year."

"America?" Bentley wrinkled his nose.

"I'll grant you it's not as exotic as Cawnpore, but I'm told the climate's better. You see, I have a daughter there, in New York City actually. She's my . . . natural daughter, if you see what I mean."

"Ahem. Yes, I see."

"We, uh, try not to advertise that, naturally. Her mother is very dear to me, as is Amanda. I'd pay you to go to New York twice a year and make sure all is well with them. The mother has remarried a man who owns a department store and apparently they're happy. But I'd like to keep an eye on them. I thought perhaps you could be my eyes."

"It would be a pleasure, Adam."

"Excellent. My London agent has retired and I've placed my money with Coutts and Company."

"The bank of the royal family?"

"Yes, I figured they'd be reliable. When I get back from Manchester, I'll arrange the financial details with them."

"You're going to Manchester?"

"In the morning. I wanted to talk to you about that, too."

The Victoria and Albert pub on the outskirts of Manchester was as working-class as its neighborhood. It was a cold, blustery day when Adam walked in the grimy pub where a few men were drinking ale at wooden tables. Adam, who was unshaven and filthy, went to the bar and ordered some ale.

"You're new here," said the burly barman as he filled a glass from the tap.

"That's right. I'm looking for work at the mills."

"Well, good luck to you, lad. From what I hear, they're not hiring. Leastways here. Someone said there was a sweeper's job at Mandeville, but they wouldn't want you."

"What's wrong with me?"

"You're too old." Adam, who was twenty-four, looked surprised. "Besides, only a fool would work there."

"Why?"

"It's got a bad reputation, that place. Old man Belladon

puts on a good show here, but he sweats his labor at the other mills, and Mandeville's the worst of the lot, they say. That'll be sixpence."

Adam took some change from his pocket and carefully counted out the pennies. The barman watched as he put the coins out one by one.

"Mighty careful with your money, ain't you?"

"I haven't got much to be careful with."

"You sound like a Yorkshireman."

"That's right. Tell me more about Mr. Belladon. You say he puts on a good show here. What do you mean by that?"

"Look: Horace Belladon is chairman of this organization of manufacturers, right? So when some high muckymuck comes up here from London to take a look around, Belladon takes him to this mill where everything's clean and the weavers all have rosy cheeks and the pay is decent. And the muckymuck goes back to London and says that Horace Belladon is a bloody saint! Because the poor chap's been hoodwinked, you see? You can lay a safe bet they never get a peep at the other mills. Especially the one at Mandeville."

"You make Mandeville sound like something satanic." Adam purposely used the adjective "satanic," which he had read in the William Blake poem. He correctly assumed the barman wouldn't know the reference.

"Aye, it tis, lad. That's the very word for it." He leaned forward and lowered his voice, his ruddy face assuming a sinister expression. "The place is *evil.*"

"What's evil about it?"

A bearded man came in the pub. The barman straightened and began wiping glasses. "I wouldn't know, lad," he said. "And if I knew, I'd be a fool to tell you."

The bearded man was coming to the bar.

"Good day, Mr. Creevy," the barman said, smiling unctuously. "The same?"

The man took a place at the bar next to Adam, giving him a curious once-over. "The same."

The man was well over six feet tall and looked as if he could wrestle an ox and win. He had dark brown eyes, one of which had a cast in it, so it was difficult to tell which way he was looking.

"This lad wants work," said the barman. "Mr. Creevy works for Mr. Belladon. He can tell you more."

"Do you have any experience?" said Mr. Creevy.

"No sir."

"I told him there's a sweeper's job at Mandeville," the barman said.

Mr. Creevy shot him a look, then returned his wayward eyes to Adam. "You want a job as a sweeper?" he asked.

"I can't be choosy, sir. I'll take what I can get."

Mr. Creevy studied his face a moment, as if, Adam thought, he were looking for something. Then he said: "You look strong, lad. Ask for Mr. Hawkswood at the mill. Tell him Mr. Creevy sent you. He'll take care of you."

"That's very kind, sir. I appreciate it. Thank you."

Adam finished his ale and wiped his mouth on his sleeve.

"There's a coach that leaves by St. Bartholomew at three," Mr. Creevy said, still looking at Adam.

"Can't afford a coach, sir."

"Then how will you get there?"

"I expect I'll have to walk."

As he left the pub, Mr. Creevy kept his good eye on him. When he was outside the door, he said, more to himself than to the barman, "I swear I've seen that man before."

Alex Sinclair handed the black velvet box marked "Tiffany & Co." to his wife. "Happy anniversary, darling," he said, kissing Lizzie.

"Anniversary? What anniversary?"

"We were married four months ago today. How can you forget?"

"Alex, you're mad," she laughed, but when she opened the box, her laugh was replaced by a gasp. Inside was a magnificent diamond-and-emerald necklace. "Alex!" she exclaimed. "For me?"

"No, it's for the cook. Of course, I realize you're not interested in money, but sometimes it has its advantages."

He lifted it out of the box and put it around her neck. She was sitting at her dressing table in the main bedroom of the Fifth Avenue house. She had just taken a bath and was wearing a bathrobe when her husband had come home to surprise her with the gift. The jewels felt cold on her bare flesh.

"God," he whispered, leaning over her. "Those jewels on your breasts really *could* drive me mad. Take off your robe. I want to make love to you with nothing on but your necklace."

"No more 'Minute' Waltz, remember? And we don't have much time. We have to be at dinner in an hour, and you have to change."

"To hell with dinner." He put his hands inside her robe and squeezed her breasts. "You know how much that necklace cost me? I deserve a little enjoyment out of it—"

She pushed him away and stood up. "You have a wonderful knack for saying the wrong thing," she said, angrily unclasping the necklace. "You *can't* buy me, Alex. I'm not for sale."

She threw the necklace on the bed, then started for the bathroom. He ran to her and grabbed her wrist.

"You still love him, don't you?" he said. "You still love Adam?"

She sighed. "Oh, what does it *matter*?"

"I want you to love *me*, dammit!"

"I'm going to give you a child. Isn't that love?"

He looked startled. "A child? You are?"

"Dr. Logan came this afternoon. I'm with child."

His face lit up. "Why didn't you tell me?"

"I didn't have a chance, with you pawing me."

"Oh Lizzie, Lizzie . . . I'm going to be a father! Damn!" He hugged her. "I'm sorry I said that about the necklace. . . . I just wanted to make you happy, and now you've made me happy. . . . Oh, Lizzie, I adore you! Say you love me!"

Again she sighed. "All right, I love you. Now, get dressed. You've been dying to meet the Astors socially, and now that they've finally invited us, we mustn't be late."

"Yes, you're right. Um . . . Lizzie, *will* you wear the necklace?"

She gave him a dry look. "Yes," she said. Then she went into her dressing room and closed the door. She knew Alex had bought the expensive jewelry as much to show off his wealth as to please his wife.

Fifteen minutes later, when she was dressed, she came back into the bedroom, went to the bed and put on the necklace.

"Alex?" she called. "Are you ready?"

Silence. She turned to look at the door to his bathroom. It was slightly ajar. She went to the door and pushed it open.

"Alex!"

Her husband, wet and naked, was lying facedown on the tile floor. She hurried to his side, knelt and felt his wrist. Then she heard him moan. Gently she turned him over. "Alex, what happened?"

His eyes were fluttering open. "Lizzie . . . I don't know . . . I got out of the tub and felt dizzy . . ."

She was drying his face with a towel. "I'll send for Dr. Logan."

"No, no, I'll be all right . . . we have to get to the Astors'."

He was sitting up.

"Alex, you have to see a doctor! This might be serious!"

"Lizzie, I'm thirty-one years old and haven't had a sick day in my life. It must have been the excitement about the baby. I guess I fainted. Anyway, I'm fine now."

They both stood up.

"Will you promise to see the doctor in the morning?"

"All right. Now, don't worry. I'll get dressed, and we're off."

She left the bathroom. But she was worried.

"To the best of my ability to judge these things, Alex had a minor stroke last night," said Dr. Logan, removing his pince-nez. He had just come out of the bedroom where he had examined Alex. "Of course, it might be something else. But because of his mother, I think we have to consider the possibility of a stroke."

"His mother?" Lizzie recalled the wreck of a woman sitting in her wheelchair staring at her.

"There is a school that says a tendency to have strokes is inherited. His father died of a stroke at a young age, so there's a double reason for concern."

Lizzie turned away, clasping her hands nervously. "He's so young, so vital," she said. "I've chided him for being too energetic, too fast. To think that he might—"

"We don't know for certain, Mrs. Sinclair. But I think Alex must make some changes in his life, to be on the safe side. He should slow down, take better care of himself. I've told him to spend several days in bed, and—"

The bedroom door opened and Alex came out. He was dressed in his business clothes.

"I'm off to the store." He smiled and came over to give Lizzie a kiss.

"Alex, Dr. Logan told you to stay in bed."

"Nonsense. I've never felt better in my life. Thank you, Doc. I appreciate your advice, but I'm a little too young to bury yet. Remember, darling, we have that dinner at Delmonico's tonight. See you this evening."

He started down the stairs.

"Alex!" Lizzie cried. "You have to listen to the doctor! You have to slow down!"

"Slow down? Hell, in this town if you slow down, you're dead."

And he was out of the house.

Lizzie turned to the doctor. "What can I do?" she sighed.

"Perhaps there's nothing you can do. Except pray."

The mill at Mandeville was a long, ugly brick building with tall chimneys. A large sign read: "Belladon Textiles, Ltd. Mill No. 3." Adam, cap in hand, entered a door marked "Employment" and walked down a narrow hall to a grilled window. An enormously fat man who was completely bald was sitting behind the grille eating a chicken leg.

"Excuse me, sir," said Adam. "I'm looking for Mr. Hawkswood."

"You're looking at him."

"I understand you have a job as a sweeper. Mr. Creevy sent me."

Mr. Hawkswood put down his chicken leg. "Creevy, you say? Well, that makes a difference. Being sweeper's a hard job, but if you're diligent you could work your way up to overseer one day, and I imagine that's what Mr. Creevy has in mind for you. But as sweeper, you'll be at the bottom of the heap, just below the scavengers. And the hours are long: five-thirty in the morning till seven-thirty at night." My God, thought Adam, fourteen hours a day! "We have two ways of paying," Mr. Hawkswood went on. "One shilling a week with free room and board at the bothy—"

"The what?"

"The bothy. That's where most of the work force sleep. It's behind the mill, next to the victualing shack, where you eat. Or we pay two shillings, sixpence a week and you fend for yourself."

"Excuse me, sir," Adam said, "but that's not much choice. How can a man live on two shillings, sixpence a week?"

"That's why a smart man chooses the former. We pay the piecers two and six a week and let them stay at the bothy, but the sweeper gets less."

Adam was appalled. Nothing he had read in any of the Parliamentary reports had suggested wages as low as this. And because of the Ten Hours Bill, working men fourteen hours a day was illegal. "I guess I'd better be smart, then," he said.

"What's your name?"

"Fielding. Adam Fielding."

"Can you read?"

"Yes sir."

"Read this and if you agree to it, sign it."

He pushed a piece of paper under the grille. Adam took it and read:

ARTICLES OF EMPLOYMENT

The undersigned agrees that while he is employed at Belladon Textiles, Ltd., he will not seek to join any organization the purpose of which is to syndicate the working force of the company.

Agreed ______

"Well? Do you sign?" Mr. Hawkswood asked. "If you don't, don't bother to come round in the morning. Mr. Belladon wants no truck with latter-day Chartists and radical union organizers."

"That's fairly obvious," Adam said, thinking: It's slavery! It's bloody slavery!

"Give me a pen."

"Give me a pen, *sir.*"

"Give me a pen, sir."

Mr. Hawkswood dipped a quill in an inkwell and handed it through the grille to Adam. As he signed his pseudonym, Adam calculated that at the rate of one shilling a week, to earn his actual income of one hundred thousand pounds would take a little over 228 years.

"Might I take a look around the mill, Mr. Hawkswood?" Adam asked after he had signed the articles and pushed them back under the grille.

"No reason why not, now that you're one of us," the fat man said, taking the articles and putting them in a drawer. He heaved his massive bulk off the stool. "Come around to Gate One and I'll let you in for a look."

Adam went back to the door and let himself outside. Bending into the wind, he walked down the building to a large wooden double gate marked "Gate 1." He could hear the roar of machinery through the closed windows. After a moment Mr. Hawkswood opened a door in the gate.

"Come in, Fielding," he said. Adam stepped inside. "Lovely, ain't it?"

His first impression was heat, noise and stench. The mill, its machinery run by steam, must have been eighty-five degrees, and the noise of the machines, the ceaseless whirring of a million hissing wheels was a hellish din. But what shocked Adam—although he had suspected it from the references to his age—was that no one in the room, aside from himself, Mr. Hawkswood and two rough-looking men holding leather straps, was over the age of fifteen! Boys and girls, filthy and in rags, some as young as seven or eight, were the entire work force of the mill.

"Yonder is Cliff Burton, our chief overseer," yelled Mr. Hawkswood over the din. "The lads and lasses respect him, I can tell you that. If they doze off, or make a mistake that causes a flying, which makes bad yarn, Burton takes the taw to them or the billy-roller."

"What's that?" Adam yelled.

"The taw is those leather straps they're holding. And the billy-roller is one of those heavy iron rods on top of the cording, like that yonder." He pointed at a murderous-looking nine-foot pole. "That keeps the little bastards on their toes. And most of them *are* bastards. We go up to London two or three times a year and recruit them from the slums. They come from such dirt, they think the bothy is bloody paradise."

Adam was staring at the children, most of whom had sunken cheeks and sallow complexions, many of whom had deformities like bowed legs, hideously swollen ankles or missing fingers.

"Do they all sleep in the bothy?" Adam yelled.

Mr. Hawkswood gave him a lecherous wink. "Aye, lad."

"Boys and girls together? Without chaperones?"

"Chaperones?" Mr. Hawkswood guffawed. "Not bloody likely. Some of the girls ain't bad-looking, though we send the best-looking elsewhere. A lad like you should have some fun, if you're so inclined."

The suggestion was so lewd, Adam had to restrain himself from punching Mr. Hawkswood's fat face. But he kept his temper. He was, after all, receiving an education from the man. He had learned that Horace Belladon was disobeying the Ten Hours Bill by working the children fourteen hours a day. Belladon was disobeying sanitary regulations in this unventilated steambath, and he was ignoring the bill, passed in 1844, requiring dangerous machinery to be fenced in.

But Adam was soon to learn more.

"Burnside's attacking at Fredericksburg!" exclaimed Alex Sinclair. He threw down the morning paper and jumped up from his breakfast table in his Fifth Avenue brownstone.

"Alex, where are you going?" said Lizzie from the other end of the table.

"I've got to get down to Wall Street," Alex said as he hurried to the door. "Jim Fisk told me every time there's a battle, the Market goes crazy! I'm going down to his office and catch the action. See you tonight, darling."

Blowing her a kiss, he ran out of the room into the central hall. Moments later, she heard the front door slam.

"Where's that man off to now?" said Lila, the fat black cook who came in from the kitchen holding a silver tray. "Miss Lizzie, you done married yourself a jackrabbit, not a man."

"I expect you're right, Lila," she sighed.

"I hear you tellin' Mr. Alex to slow down, slow down, an' all he do is run faster. Huh. What am I gonna do with his breakfast? Ain't no use keepin' it, 'cause eggs ain't no good leftovers. You want his sausages?"

"I'd better not. I'm getting fat as a pig."

"Miss Lizzie, you carryin' a baby. You suppose to get fat. Now you eat another sausage."

Lizzie smiled at her. "No, really, I've had enough. But I will have some more coffee."

"Well, all right. But you lookin' a little peaky, if you ask me."

Lila set the tray on the sideboard and brought the coffee pot to refill Lizzie's cup.

"Mr. Alex, he told me this morning he done rented a cottage by the sea for next summer, and that's mighty good news, 'cause New York ain't no place to be in the summer, no, ma'am. It get so hot here in July, even the cockroaches faint."

"Lila, please."

"Oh-oh, I done forgot you don't like bugs. Anyways, you an' me an' Miss Amanda, that little angel, we all can go sit on the shore an' enjoy the ocean breezes while Mr. Alex, he run around makin' money. Don't that man ever get tired of makin' money? Makin' money, makin' money—that's all he ever think about!"

Lizzie laughed. "I think he's beyond reforming."

"Huh. Anyways, we'll all be cool down by the Jersey shore."

Amanda came into the room. "Good morning, Mama. Good morning, Lila."

"Good morning, darling."

"Now I got you some nice scrambled eggs an' sausage, honey," Lila said as Amanda kissed her mother's cheek then took a seat at her left. "You been eatin' like a bird lately, so I want to see you clean your plate. You want some toast?"

"Oh yes, Lila. And some of your strawberry preserves. They're *so* good."

"Huh. They oughta be. Made 'em myself. Now, who's that ringin' the front bell?"

She waddled into the central hall as Amanda pulled off her napkin ring.

"What are you going to do today?" her mother asked.

"Jimmie Brady's coming over and we're going to play in the garden."

"Well, it's a lovely day to play outdoors. You like Jimmie, don't you?"

"Oh, he's all right, I suppose. But he's always ragging me about my accent. He says I sound 'funny' and that I'm a foreigner. He makes me so mad."

"Tell him *he* sounds funny to you."

"I did already. He sulked for ten minutes."

"Excuse me, Miss Lizzie." It was Lila at the door. "There's a police gentleman out here wantin' to see you."

"A policeman?"

"Yes ma'am."

Lizzie stood up and left the dining room. In the front

hall, a tall, bearded policeman was standing, his bobbylike helmet under his arm.

"Good morning, officer," Lizzie said, coming up to him. "I'm Mrs. Sinclair. You wanted to see me?"

"Yes, ma'am. It's about your husband."

"Is something the matter?"

"I'm afraid there is. Mr. Sinclair was getting in his carriage a few minutes ago when he collapsed."

"Alex!"

"Your coachman is taking him to Dr. Logan's office. We thought it was best, under the circumstances."

She tried to keep calm. "I'm sure you did the right thing. Lila, get me a hat . . . the gray bonnet."

"Yes'm. I sure hopes Mr. Alex is all right."

She hurried to the coat closet while Lizzie turned back to the policeman.

"Thank you so very much," she said. "Could you possibly get me a cab?"

"I'd be glad to, ma'am."

Dr. Logan lived five blocks down Fifth Avenue in a brownstone similar to the Sinclairs'. Ten minutes later, Lizzie climbed out of a cab and hurried up the steps to ring the bell. After a moment a nurse opened the door.

"I'm Mrs. Sinclair."

"Come in, please."

"Is my husband . . . ?"

The nurse closed the door. "He's with the doctor. Take a seat in the parlor, please. Dr. Logan will be right with you."

"But my husband . . . is he all right?"

"Doctor will explain."

Lizzie went into the parlor. She remembered Alex's collapse in the bathroom. She remembered Dr. Logan's warning, but as Lila had said, the more she tried to slow Alex down, the more he seemed to speed up. When Jim Fisk opened a brokerage firm on Wall Street, Alex began playing the Market, which only accelerated his already frenetic pace. And now this. Oh, that maddening nurse! she thought. Why wouldn't she *say* something?

"Mrs. Sinclair."

She turned from the tall window overlooking Fifth Avenue and saw Dr. Logan coming into the room, wiping his gold pince-nez on a handkerchief.

"How is he, Doctor?" she said anxiously.

"Please sit down."

"Please, someone *tell* me!" she exclaimed with exasperation. "Is he all right?"

"No. I'm afraid your husband has suffered a serious stroke—perhaps a massive one. It's too early to tell for certain, but for the moment, at least, he is paralyzed."

"Dear God, Alex . . . paralyzed!"

"We knew this was a possibility. God sent him a warning."

"I know, but he wouldn't listen to us. . . . May I see him?"

"Yes, of course. But I must warn you: he can barely speak. And he's frightened, which is only to be expected. We must do nothing to upset him. No tears. No scenes."

"I understand."

"Come this way."

He led her out of the parlor, down the hall to his office. Alex, his tie off and his collar open, was lying on his back on a leather sofa. The nurse was removing his expensive shoes.

Lizzie came over to him. Alex looked up at her, terror in his eyes.

"Darling . . ." She smiled, trying not to show her fears, which had doubled since she saw him. She took his hand and squeezed it gently. "Everything's going to be all right." Oh God, is that a terrible lie? He was trying to say something, moving his lips. "Don't exert yourself."

"I . . ."

She knelt beside the sofa and put her cheek against his.

". . . love . . ."

"Ssh, darling. Please. You *must* rest."

". . . you."

She had to turn away to hide her tears.

CHAPTER 27

Zack Carr thought he must be as close to Hell as he could be. It was just past midnight, December 14, 1862, it was bitterly cold, and the sky was aflame with the most extraordinary display of the Northern Lights he had ever seen, certainly a rarity in Virginia. He was crouched behind the stone wall that had saved his life that day, staring at piles of naked corpses sprawled on the slope in front of him. The battle that day had been his baptism of fire, and what a baptism! Rumors flying around the Confederate troops estimated the Yankee dead as high as fifteen thousand in that one horrible day, and Zack could believe it. All day the Yankees had come up the hill from Fredericksburg, wave after wave of them assaulting the Confederate forces dug in on the hill known as Marye's Heights overlooking the town and the Rappahannock River. Zack and the other Rebs had mowed them down with almost nonstop fire from behind the stone wall. General Burnside, the Union commander, was throwing everything he had at the Rebels, and the Yankees never stopped coming and they never stopped dying. And now he could hear the groans of the wounded. He could see the scavengers from his own side who had gone across the stone wall to steal clothes, shoes, guns and ammunition from the dead. It was so bitterly cold that the corpses were freezing solid, adding to the grotesqueness of the night.

But horrible as it all was, Zack was jubilant. There could be no doubt that that day had been a great victory for the South. Abe Lincoln was increasingly unpopular in the

North, and this defeat might just be enough for him to call it quits.

That bitterly cold December night might just be the end of the war.

"Charlotte told me what happened last night," Ellie May Whitney said to her son-in-law. Clayton was sprawled on a sofa in the drawing room of Fairview Plantation drinking a bottle of Chambertin he had taken from the basement. "I just can't believe it, Clayton. I can't!"

"Well, you'd better start believing it. It's true."

"You . . . making love to that darkie . . ."

"If you think that's never happened before, you don't know what's been going on down here for the past two hundred years."

"But you've given my daughter that horrible disease! You're vile, Clayton. Vile! You've betrayed everything we're fighting for, all the goodness and nobility of the South—"

"Oh to hell with Southern nobility and goodness!" he yelled, emptying the bottle and sitting up.

"When Phineas hears about this, he'll horsewhip you!"

"Like he whips his slaves? It might not be as much fun whipping a white man, but I expect he'd enjoy himself anyway." He was getting off the sofa onto his crutches. "Let me tell you something, Mother dear: you know where that trunk full of cash in the basement comes from? It comes from kickbacks your husband, the great General Whitney, takes from the sutlers! Southern boys are getting killed and maimed—like me—while your husband lines his pockets with gold! That's blood money down there, Ellie May. So don't say one more goddamned word about nobility. The South is rotten to the core, and the rot comes from slavery, the most disgusting institution that ever befouled the face of this earth."

He was hobbling across the room toward the door. Ellie May was staring at him.

"I don't believe you!" she whispered.

"Ask my brother. He says everybody in the army knows about it. Now if you'll excuse me, ma'am, I'm going to get me another bottle of wine. The only way to blot out the stench of corruption around here is to get stumble-down drunk."

He opened the door and hobbled out. Alone, Ellie May put her hand to her mouth, nervously biting her index finger. "I don't believe it," she whispered to herself. "I *don't* believe it."

That night, it rained at Fairview Plantation. It rained hard. As Ellie May lay in her bed, staring at the dark ceiling, she listened to the pelt of the rain on the roof and wondered what future there was for her family. What Clayton had done was so unspeakable, she didn't know how to cope with it.

It was then she heard him singing "Dixie."

"Oh, I wish I was in the land of cotton, old times there are not forgotten, look away, look away, look away, Dixie Land!"

It was Clayton, coming up the stairs to bed, drunk as usual. The jaunty tune, written shortly before the war for the famous Bryant's Minstral Show in, of all places, New York City, sounded slightly off-key, certainly anything but jaunty. Ellie May ascribed it to his drunkenness. She had been bred a lady, but her mountain of woes had brought her to the breaking point. She started to get out of bed to yell at him, when the singing abruptly stopped. She remembered the night when Phineas had returned from Europe, singing "Dixie" as he told her the heartbreaking news that the war was lost. But surely, the great victory at Fredericksburg meant the war was won? Oh God, she didn't know, but she wished Phineas were home. He would know how to handle Clayton. And she didn't for a moment believe that horrible lie about her beloved husband taking kickbacks.

A shot echoed through the house. She froze for a moment, then hurriedly lit a lamp. There was a scream from Charlotte's bedroom next door, then another shot.

"Oh my God!"

Ellie May got out of bed, grabbed the lamp, and hurried toward the door to the upstairs hall.

There was a third shot, then the sound of something heavy hitting the floor.

Ellie May ran into the hall and tried the door to Charlotte's bedroom. It was locked—she remembered that her daughter had locked the door to keep her husband out. She saw that the door to Dulcey's room down the hall was open. She ran to it and went in. She looked at the bed and screamed. Half of Dulcey's face had been blown away by a shotgun blast.

Screaming again, she ran to the door that connected to Charlotte's room. It was open and a light was burning inside. She went in.

Clayton was lying on the floor, Phineas' hunting gun beside him along with his sprawled crutches. He had shot himself in the mouth.

"Charlotte!" she screamed.

Her daughter was in her bed. Like Dulcey's, half her face had been blown away.

"Elton, you was right," Sarah said fifteen minutes later as she brought the old slave a cup of coffee in the kitchen. Upstairs, the hysterical cries of Ellie May rang through the house, competing with the rain. "Revenge should be left to de Lord. De Lord done 'venged dis family better dan I ever could."

The old man shook his head sadly. "De Lord knows bess," he said. "But I sho' feel sorry for Miss Charlotte. An' poor Miss Ellie May, I tink she 'bout to go crazy."

All Sarah could remember was the mangled body of her son, Tucker, that had fallen out of that rain barrel of death.

Review printed in *La Presse*, Paris' leading newspaper, written by the music critic, the pseudonymous Salieri, dated January 3, 1863:

> Last night, a most extraordinary event occurred at the Salle Pleyel. A piano recital was given by a young American named Gabriel Cavanagh, and it was extraordinary on several levels. First, M. Cavanagh is only twelve years old: although the music

world is becoming used to prodigiously talented *wunderkinder*, it is still somewhat awe-inspiring to hear a boy thunder his way through the "Hammerklavier" Sonata without missing a note. Second is the fact that M. Cavanagh is an American, the first virtuoso from that distant shore to be heard in Paris since the dazzling Louis Moreau Gottschalk. Perhaps it is time that we in the "old world" begin to reexamine the cultural level of the new: it is possible there is more to be found in America than Indians, tomahawks and slavery.

Which brings me to the third, and perhaps most amazing aspect of last night's concert. The boy—that is, M. Cavanagh—is a Negro, the son of a slave. This had created a great deal of speculation in Paris, which fact, along with the sponsorship of Franz Liszt, caused the recital hall to be packed. Before M. Cavanagh appeared onstage, one heard the expected number of vulgar jokes: Would he have a bone in his nose? Would he do a cakewalk? Would he eat a banana? But when the young man walked onstage, the jokesters were silenced. Far from looking like a Ubangi, M. Cavanagh was strikingly handsome and carried himself with dignity. He seated himself at the Pleyel and, without further ado, launched into the most electrifying rendition of the first Chopin Scherzo in B minor this critic has ever had the pleasure of hearing. From the first thrilling chords to the tumultuous opening theme—so frequently muddled by less-skillful artists—the boy exhibited a mastery of the keyboard that astounded all. But what was most surprising was the subtlety of his art: in the *agitato* section, instead of the furioso banging one is accustomed to hearing, the playing, though marvelously swift, was a silkily elegant whisper, M. Cavanagh bringing out themes in the music that I had never before encountered. The luscious B major *molto più lento* section was heavenly, a musical chocolate mousse. Then the return to the main theme, the barbaric cross-country gallop of the coda, with its shrill dissonances assaulting the eardrums, and the final charge up the keyboard of the chromatic scale, played in the Liszt-Taussig manner of interlocked octaves. The final chords brought the audience to its feet. Cheers filled the room, as if the people present sensed a legend was a-borning.

But this was the *hors d'oeuvre* of a musical feast. M. Cavanagh resumed his bench to play the enchanting Liszt transcription of themes from Gounod's *Faust*, and his almost casual handling of the monumental technical difficulties of this bravura piece dispelled whatever wispy doubts were left as to his mastery of the keyboard. Then, after a brief intermission, he returned onstage to tackle Beethoven's "Hammerklavier" Sonata; and if here he showed the limitation of his youth—for I found his interpretation somewhat callow—still one can only respect his audacity for taking on such a thorny masterpiece.

At the conclusion, one is reduced to clichés to describe what happened: the audience went wild. And what is embarrassing to report is that many of the women in the hall comported themselves like frenzied *bacchantes*, screaming and even swooning into the arms of their escorts. That aging society pianist-cum-*salonière*, the Princess Belgiojoso who, a number of years back, rounded up the six greatest European pianists for one of her *soirées*, ran up on the stage and shamelessly threw herself at M. Cavanagh's feet, crying: "Sublime! Sublime! Thou art a divinity!" This prompted others of her sex to follow her example and soon the stage was thronged with females, tearing at the boy's clothes and person until the astounded M. Cavanagh had to run into the wings for safety, his tailcoat in tatters and his shirt half off his back. Thus, celebrity-mad Paris has created a new idol. Surely the fact that he is of African descent is part of the boy's glamour: France is intrigued by its new empire in the dark continent. The fact that he has striking good looks is also part of the reason for his galvanic effect on the women last night.

> But it would be sad if all this eclipsed what was most remarkable: a truly major musical talent. If his skin were green, it would still be a pleasure for this critic to say, mimicking Herr Schumann's reception of Chopin's debut many years ago: "Hats off, gentlemen: a genius!"
>
> —Salieri

The young Confederate soldier stood in the rain and urinated on his brother's grave.

"Zack!" yelled Phineas Whitney, hurrying out the back door of Fairview Plantation, umbrella in hand. "What the hell are you doing?"

"What does it look like I'm doing, General? I'm pissing on Clayton's grave. I'm pissing on the grave of a murderer and a traitor, and I don't care who knows it."

Zack buttoned the fly of his gray trousers. He had no umbrella, and the rain running down his face almost concealed his tears.

Phineas, also in uniform, put his hand on the boy's shoulder. "I know how you feel, Zack," he said, glancing at the grave of his daughter nearby. Clayton and Charlotte had been interred in the family burial plot; Dulcey's body had been sent back to Elvira Plantation for burial in the slave cemetery, for even in death the two races were kept apart.

"I loved him, General," Zack said, his eyes red. "He was the best brother anyone could ever have. And then when he turned . . ." He put his hands to his eyes. "God *damn*, the Yankees are bad enough, but when your own brother . . ." He took his hands away and looked at Phineas. "It was the Yankees who sowed the seeds of doubt in his mind, when he was up at Princeton. Those goddamned Abolitionists!"

"We have to carry on the fight, Zack. We have to carry on, no matter what happens."

"Believe me, sir, you don't have to worry about me. I'll hate those nigger-loving Yankees till the day I die."

"That's the spirit, son. As long as we have men like you, the Glorious Cause will never die. *Never*."

CHAPTER 28

After only one day on the job at the Belladon Textile Mill in Mandeville, Adam was marveling at the durability of the children working the cotton spindles. Fourteen hours work had exhausted him, and he was in the prime of his manhood. How children seven years old could stand fourteen hours, with only a half-hour break for a lunch of gruel and a hunk of coarse bread, without collapsing seemed incredible. In fact, he found out that the many grotesquely swollen ankles were caused by the long hours of standing, and all this for the miserable wage of two shillings, sixpence a week.

The mill was run by terror, and the overseers, like their counterparts on the plantations in the American South, ruled by brute force. On his first day, Adam saw Tim, a frail boy just turned eleven, savagely beaten by Cliff Burton for dozing on the job. Adam watched with horror as the overseer slammed the leather taw on the boy's back and shoulders, and then, as further punishment, hung a twenty-pound weight around the boy's neck to wear for the rest of the day. It was galling to Adam that he couldn't stop the overseer, but he knew it would only result in his being fired, and he wanted to see more. Soon enough, he would be helping not only this child but many others as well.

Girls called scavengers were continually scrambling to pick the fluff off the machinery and floor, for the weaving machines were constantly throwing off clouds of flying pieces of cotton. The girls often had to crawl under the swiftly moving drivebelts to collect the fluff, and Adam thought it miraculous they didn't get their hair caught in the machinery. The scavengers would bring their fluff to one end of the room where Adam's job was to sweep it into great white mountains and carry it outside in heavy metal bins. He could see why they had to hire an adult for the job: even the strongest child couldn't carry the iron bins. The work, in the steamy millroom with the continual deafening roar of the machinery and with no drinking water available to replace the quarts he sweated out, was physically exhausting and deadening to the mind. Adam realized that these wretched children-slaves were not only losing their childhood and ruining their health, they were receiving no education at all except the horrendous school of hard knocks. And this was the future of England!

But as bad as conditions in the mill were, the bothy was in ways worse. The grim brick house behind the mill housed over fifty children of both sexes with no bathing facilities except a pump outside the building and no toilets except two filthy privies. Inside, the house was simply one large open space filled with primitive cots—a dirty, smelly, dreary dormitory.

"There's bedbugs galore," one boy named Larry told Adam. "And we makes pets out of the rats."

Adam was no prude, but as the only adult present he was shocked at the way these children exhibited no modesty at all either to him or each other. But then, they were so exhausted that most of them fell asleep immediately to be awakened by the mill's steam whistle at five the next morning, when the night shift came to sleep through the day in the same filthy beds.

Larry, the redhead whose cot was next to Adam's, seemed a bright boy and the second night Adam struck up a whispered conversation with him.

"Why do you work in this awful place?" Adam asked.

"It ain't so bad," the boy said. "It was worse where I come from."

"Where's that?"

"Whitechapel in London. Rats as big as bloody elephants."

"Who are your parents?"

"I dunno. Never had none. Leastways here I makes

some money, and I ain't on the street. And if I do me work right, Mrs. Abernathy won't come for me."

"Who's Mrs. Abernathy?"

"She's the lady wot takes the bad boys and girls."

"Where does she take them?"

"I dunno. No one ever sees them again. She come here last month, it was, and took Jennie and Nellie and three other girls. The pretty ones. And sometimes she takes boys, too."

"Shut up," muttered the boy next to Larry. "I needs me sleep."

"Sorry."

Larry turned on his side. Adam tried to sleep, but as exhausted as he was, this new information was pounding his brain. After a few minutes, he got off his cot and went to the door to go outside, get some fresh air and think. The implications of the mysterious Mrs. Abernathy taking the "pretty" children away were appalling. Were these children being taken to become prostitutes? He remembered Mr. Hawkswood saying that they sent the best-looking children "elsewhere." Were the mill owners selling children to organized vice rings?

He filled his lungs with the cold night air, then went back into the stinking bothy to try to get some sleep.

It was ten thirty the next morning when the accident occurred. Adam was sweeping the cotton fluff at one end of the shed, which held twenty huge Jacquard power looms, when he heard Cliff Burton, the chief overseer, begin yelling. He turned to see Burton beating little Larry, the orphan from Whitechapel, with the leather taw. The boy was screaming. Throwing aside his broom, Adam ran down the stone alley between the huge looms with their flying shuttles. Most of the children had stopped work to watch the beating in terrified silence. Adam ran up to Burton and grabbed the taw.

"Beat someone your own size!" he yelled, tearing the taw from his hands and slaming Burton over the head with it. The children began yelling, excited to see someone turn the tables on the hated overseer. Burton was a big, bearded man. Though he was not entirely sober, he was a good fighter. He jumped Adam, grabbed him around the waist and threw him on his back on the stone floor. As the children cheered, Adam and Burton rolled over and over, exchanging punches. Burton plowed his hammy fist into Adam's nose, causing blood to spurt out, but Adam hit the overseer in the stomach so hard the man howled with pain, releasing Adam who scrambled to his feet, wiping the blood from his face with his sleeve.

Burton got to his feet, and the two men slowly circled each other as the power looms continued to roar and spin, the shuttles flying back and forth across the warps. Suddenly Burton lunged at Adam, almost literally throwing himself at him. Adam jumped to one side, and Burton fell into one of the looms instead, his left arm catching in one of the thick vertical belts. Burton was jerked upward toward the iron ceiling. The overseer, screaming in horror, frantically tried to free himself from the belt, which ran over a large iron flywheel at the ceiling. The flywheel was rotated 120 times a minute by a long steel rod that ran the length of the shed, propelling via the flywheels all twenty looms. Now Burton was thrown violently against the ceiling. He fell down into the maze of shuttles, tappets, wheels and gears of the power loom and was mangled to death.

The children, cheering, surrounded Adam, hugging him and pounding him affectionately with their fists.

Adam had once again become a hero, this time to a most unlikely audience.

"In view of your many charitable donations in the past," said Lady Gwendolyn Despard, who was taking tea with Horace and Lettice Belladon in the paneled library of Belladon Manor, "we hope to persuade you to make a generous donation to the Manchester Society for the Preservation and Notation of Birdsong."

Horace, who was adding an inch to his waist each year, looked puzzled. "Pardon me, Lady Gwendolyn, but I don't quite understand. How does one preserve and notate birdsong?"

"A most enterprising young man, a Mr. Whipple, has

devised a method to write on paper the songs of various birds. We hope, with the proper funding, to be able to distribute pamphlets to schools throughout England. Whereas only a few generations ago the average English child spent his formative years in the fields, today he is much more likely to live in a city and thus is deprived of intimacy with our wildlife. Our Society hopes to rectify this by bringing birdsong, as it were, into the schoolroom."

Mr. Clyde, the Belladons' butler, entered the room and came to Horace's chair. "Excuse me, sir," he whispered. "Mr. Creevy is here and wishes to see you. He says it's urgent."

Horace frowned. "Excuse me, Lady Gwendolyn," he said, getting up. "I'll be back in a moment."

He left the library and went into the entrance hall with its huge Landseer painting of sad-eyed dogs. Mr. Creevy, hat in hand, was standing by the front door. There was fear in his good eye.

"What is it, Creevy?" Horace grumbled as he came up.

"Sir, there's been an accident at Mandeville. Burton, the chief overseer, fell into one of the looms and was mangled to death."

"Damn. Burton was a good man. Well, hire a replacement."

"Excuse me, sir, there's something else. Apparently, Burton had had a fight with the new sweeper down there, Fielding. And I just realized who Fielding is."

"Do you realize you're taking me away from tea with Lady Gwendolyn Despard?" Horace fumed. "She may be from some damn-fool charity, but she's the wife of the Lord Mayor!"

"Excuse me, sir, I wouldn't interrupt you if it wasn't important. A few days ago there was a young chap at the Victoria and Albert asking about a job at the mills. I thought he might be overseer material, so I sent him down to Mandeville for that sweeper job. I thought at the time I'd seen this man somewhere, but then I dismissed the idea until today. My son's greatest hero is Lord Pontefract, and he has a picture of him in his room. The boy has measles, and I was in his room a few hours and I noticed the picture.

I'd swear the man I sent to Mandeville is Lord Pontefract!"

"Are you mad! What would a rich nobleman . . ." Horace stopped, his face turning red. "Disguises," he whispered. "He likes disguises . . ." A look of horror came over his face. "And you sent him to *Mandeville*?"

"Sir, if I'd had any idea—"

"You fool! You thickheaded fool!" He raised both fists, almost striking Creevy but deciding against it.

"Get down there," he whispered. "Get rid of him!"

"You mean—?"

"I mean, get *rid* of him! If he tells what he's seen, I'm ruined—ruined!"

"But how far dare I go? The man's a hero—"

"*Kill* him!"

Horace turned his back and stamped his way across the hall to return to the library, where Lady Gwendolyn was still holding forth on birdsong. But at the door, he changed his mind and came back to Creevy. "Take him to the old watermill first. I want to ask him some questions."

"Right, Mr. Belladon."

"He might have somebody else involved."

That night, around midnight, Adam stepped out of the bothy to get some fresh air. It was a cold, moonlit night. He saw Creevy and two other men standing near the door.

Then something slammed down on the back of his head, and his world went black.

CHAPTER 29

Every time I look at Alex, it just about kills me," Lizzie said as she dined with Jim Fisk in her brownstone on Fifth Avenue. The fat Fisk was devouring a canvasback duck. "Alex, who was so vital and active—far too active, of course—now like a child upstairs, barely able to talk. It breaks my heart."

"Does Doc Logan think he'll ever improve?" Fisk asked, shoving the duck into his mouth.

"Oh, he doesn't know. He's supposed to be the best doctor in New York, but what do doctors know? Yes, he says there may be some improvement, and there's a Swedish masseur who comes every day to work on Alex and that seems to be doing a little good. But there's no medicine . . . It's the worst thing that could have happened to him. The worst! And he's so young, not thirty-two."

"What are you gonna do with the store? I know Alex ran that thing single-handed, everything from countin' the cash to sweepin' the floor, practically. Who's gonna run it now?"

"I don't know. That's why I wanted to talk to you. Dear Mr. Fisk, you know about business, which totally baffles me. Might I ask for your advice?"

"Well sure, Mrs. Sinclair. Alex is a pal of mine, as well as a client of my brokerage house, so I'll be glad to give you all the advice I can. 'Course, I can't guarantee nothin', but I'll be glad to help. But I'll tell you one thing: a store's a tricky thing to run. It's a day-by-day operation, and you gotta be right *there*, watchin' everything, or you're gonna lose your shirt. You can hire yourself a manager, but *he'll* steal you blind if you don't watch him like a hawk. Now, Alex'd kill me if he knew I said this to you, but I think you gotta consider sellin' Sinclair and Son, unless you're willin' to go in there and run it yourself."

"I can't! It's not only that I don't know anything about business, I'm in the family way, I have Amanda to raise, and I have to take care of my husband. I'm in no position to run a business."

"Then I think you have to consider sellin'. And listen: I just might have a buyer for you. I used to work for Jordan, Marsh up in Boston, and I happen to know they're itchin' to get into the New York market. I'll bet I could get you a real good price out of them for Sinclair and Son. Yessir, *real* good. And because of my friendship with Alex, I'd set the deal up and not even charge a commission, except expenses, of course."

"Mr. Fisk, you're a true friend. To be honest, I've already come to the same conclusion. I have to sell. I simply have no choice. How much do you think you could get?"

"Well, I'll have to check the books, of course. But offhand I'd say, maybe, three million. May I make a suggestion?"

"Please do."

"If we're gonna do this, maybe you shouldn't tell Alex, what with his delicate condition. Just get him all riled up, which is the last thing he needs."

"I'm sure you're right." She hesitated. To sell the store. She knew it had been Alex's pride and joy. She knew it would hurt him, perhaps even turn him against her, which was the last thing she wanted. But he was helpless, barely able to move, taken care of by round-the-clock nurses who had to feed him, bathe him, take care of his natural functions. She really had no alternative.

"Then let's do it," she said.

"You got yourself a deal. Say, this duck's so tasty, I don't suppose I could have just a tiny bit more?"

"Of course." She rang for Lila. "Oh Mr. Fisk, you are turning out to be the greatest treasure of all: a friend in need."

"Please, ma'am: my friends call me Jimmie."

And he smiled at her.

After Jim Fisk had left the house, Lizzie passed the entrance to the dining room where Lila was blowing out the candles. "That was such a good dinner, Lila," she said, coming into the room. "Mr. Fisk raved about your duck."

"Uh-huh. If I'd had any sense, I'd have stuck some rat poison in it."

"Why in the world would you say that?"

Lila turned to her. "Miss Lizzie, you a fine woman, a nice woman. You treat your colored help like we was human beings, not just niggers. An' I heard what you done down in Virginnie, freein' your slaves before the war even broke out, an' how you's payin' for that boy, Gabriel, so he can get to Europe an' have a chance to make something of hisself. I respects you an' I likes you. Now, you can tell me this is none of my business an' I don't know nuffin' 'bout business, but I wouldn't trust that Jim Fisk further than I could spit. There, I said it an' I'm glad."

"Lila, Mr. Fisk is a friend!"

"Huh."

"He *is*! Tonight he made the most generous offer to help me—"

"Oh, I heard when I was feedin' him his third helpin' of duck—that man eats like a warthog. If you ask me, he's nuffin' but Wall Street trash who'd sell his grandmother *cheap*. An' you can fire me if you like, but all I can say is, if you give one penny of your money to that man, you're gonna live to regret it. Now, I's goin' off to bed. Good night, Miss Lizzie."

She went into the butler's pantry, leaving Lizzie alone. After a moment, she shook her head, turned down the gas sconce, went into the hallway and started up the stairs. She had become fond of Lila, who lived on the top floor. Lila had a heart of gold, and Lizzie had always thought she was shrewd. Had she seen something about Jim Fisk that she hadn't? Yes, the man was crude, but that was no crime, and his offer that night had been, in her opinion, extremely kind. And he wasn't even asking for a commission.

When she reached the second floor, she told herself Lila had just taken an irrational dislike to him. She walked down the hall toward her bedroom, pausing by Alex's bedroom door.

"How is he?" she whispered to the white male night nurse, Joe, who came to the door.

"He's having a bad night. He can't sleep."

Lizzie went in. Alex was on his bed. She leaned down to kiss his forehead.

"Lizzie," he whispered with difficulty. His speech had improved slightly, but she knew it was still an agony for him.

"Jim Fisk was here for dinner," she said. "I've come to like him after all."

"How's . . . the mar . . . ket?"

"It went up eight points today, and don't worry about the stock market."

"How's . . . the store?"

"Business is fine, darling. Just fine. Now you go to sleep."

She kissed him again, then left the room. In a way she felt as helpless as Alex. She didn't know what to do about the house they were building farther up Fifth Avenue. She had seen the bills, which were staggering, but the place was so far along now she wasn't sure she could stop it, and selling a half-completed Gothic mansion might not be easy. On the other hand, mightn't it be ruinous to continue with it? The place had been designed to flaunt Alex's success in the face of the world. Now, in his state of paralysis, it might seem more like a mausoleum.

There were so many decisions she had to make, which was why she was glad to have Jim Fisk. She went in her room and closed the door. She suddenly felt exhausted. She lay on her bed and closed her eyes for a few moments before undressing.

It shamed her to admit it, but her heart ached for Adam. Adam, her true knight, would know what she should do. But Adam was half a world away.

"I'll have to do it myself," she said. "There's nobody else but me."

When Adam came to, he found that his hands were tied behind him so tightly it was impeding his circulation. His head ached from the savage blow. He was seated on a wooden chair, his ankles tied to the legs, in the middle of an empty room that once had been a mill but was obviously abandoned. A small fire had been lit in an ancient brick chimney, and by its feeble light he saw rusty remnants of machinery scattered about the floor. Most of the windowpanes were broken out and above him, part of the roof had rotted away so that he could see the night sky, clouds racing across a pale moon.

"He's awake," said one of the four men who had attacked Adam outside the bothy. One, John Creevy, held a gun. "Go tell Mr. Belladon," he said. One of the men went through the door as the others came over to Adam's chair.

"Cawnpore," said Creevy. "What was it like killing Nana Sahib?"

"What are you talking about?"

"The game's up, milord," Creevy said. "We know who you are. Did Nana Sahib and them other wogs really rape Englishwomen during the Mutiny?"

Before Adam could answer, he saw Horace Belladon come through the door with the first man. Horace was wearing a silk hat and a fur-collared black overcoat, looking every inch the rich industrialist that he was. He came to Adam. A smile crept across his face, his muttonchop whiskers silvery-gray in the moonlight.

"What an interesting situation," he said. "I don't believe we've ever formally met, milord, but I've heard so much about you from my wife who, as you know, is the sister of Mrs. Cavanagh. In case you aren't aware, I am Horace Belladon, your—shall we say?—employer."

"Oh, I'm aware," Adam said. "And you're a pretty rotten employer to work for. Don't try to pretend you don't know what goes on in your filthy mills." He looked at Creevy and the others. "You, Creevy: do you know Belladon sells children into prostitution?"

"*I'll* ask the questions!" Horace shouted. "Who else is in this with you?"

"That's my business."

Horace turned to one of his goons and pointed to the fire in the chimney. "Bring me one of those sticks," he ordered. "One that's burning." The man obeyed as Horace turned back to Adam. "You've cost me a considerable amount of business over the years," he said. "The deal I could have worked out with General Whitney and the Confederate Government would have made me millions, but you ruined that with your fuzzy-headed speech in the House of Lords. I was extremely displeased by that. Extremely."

"Did you and Whitney hire the kidnappers of my daughter?"

"As I said, *I'll* ask the questions. Open his shirt."

The first man brought Horace a piece of wood from the fire, its end burning, the flames fluttering in the night wind. Horace took the stick as one of the men leaned over and ripped Adam's shirt open.

"Now," Horace said, "I repeat: who else is in this? I want names."

"Well, Queen Victoria got a job as a scavenger, and the Prince of Wales is working as a piecer."

"Quite a sense of humor he has, eh boys? Now then, milord, make a joke out of this."

He stepped forward and rammed the burning end of the stick into Adam's stomach. Adam writhed and howled with pain as the smell of burnt flesh stank the room. When Horace pulled the stick away, there was a smoking scar on Adam's skin three inches wide.

"Wasn't that fun?" he said. "The old Grand Inquisitors may have been a bit humorless, but they had a point about physical pain: it can break a man's spirit. Shall we do it again, milord? Or will you answer my question?"

"I'm alone, you bastard," Adam gasped. The pain was excruciating. "Do you think anyone else would be crazy enough to do what I've done?"

"You have a point there. And what was your plan? To expose me in Parliament?"

"You're damned right, and it would be a pleasure to do it! You're scum, Belladon. No, you're worse than scum. To turn children into prostitutes is about as low as it comes! How much does Mrs. Abernathy pay you for the girls and boys?"

"Kill him," Horace snapped. "You, Creevy: blow his brains out, put a weight on his leg, and toss him in the river. The rest of you come with me."

He turned and walked toward the door.

"Mrs. Abernathy?" whispered one of the goons to Adam. "You mean, the Manchester Madam?"

"You're damned right!" Adam yelled, bluffing. He had never heard of the Manchester Madam, but obviously she was a local celebrity. "The man you work for sells children to her! Square that with your conscience!"

"Blimey," whispered the man, looking at the others. "Did you know that?"

"Of course," said Creevy. "They're just scum from the London slums. Get the hell out of here so I can finish this."

The other men hurried out of the mill. Creevy turned to Adam. Holding the gun with both hands, he raised it slowly and pointed it between Adam's eyes. Adam stared at the barrel, less than six inches away. Death. The ultimate adventure. He wondered if it would hurt.

The shots from outside the mill jolted Cheevy. "What the hell . . . ?"

He turned to the door. Bentley Brent and three other men ran in. Bentley raised his pistol and fired. Creevy was hit in the chest. He twirled and fell forward on his face, dead.

"Jesus," said Adam, "I was wondering where you were!"

Bentley hurried over. "Sorry, old man," he said. "Got a bit delayed outside. Wouldn't have let you be shot for the world."

Adam, who had hired Bentley to cover him during his

dangerous Mandeville adventure, said, "I'm glad to hear . . . Oh God, my stomach . . ."

Despite the cold night air, Adam was covered with sweat. As Bentley cut his ankle ropes, Adam slumped forward off the chair and fell to the floor, unconscious. Bentley looked at the scar on his stomach, which was still smoking.

"Let's get him to a doctor."

Letter from Queen Victoria to Lord Palmerston:

Windsor Castle
23 January 1863

The Queen has read with shock and outrage the newspaper reports of Ld. Pontefract's revelations of conditions in the Belladon mills. Once again, this noble man has done a great service to England. I am told Ld. Pontefract is out of physical danger and has been released from the hospital, but that he will carry the scar on his stomach for the rest of his life. To think that an English businessman could resort to physical torture, like some Bulgarian or Turk! It is too infamous! This time, happily, no domestic moral issue, such as Ld. Pontefract's romance with Mrs. Cavanagh, can prevent the Queen from rewarding him with the Garter, which she fully intends to do.

But as Ld. Pontefract is to be rewarded, this vile monster, Mr. Belladon, must be punished; and the Queen will lend her heartfelt support to Ld. Pontefract's call on the English nation to refuse to buy any of the goods manufactured by Belladon Textiles. Bringing this ignominious man to his knees financially will be his just desert, though I have instructed the Home Secretary to investigate the possibility of bringing criminal charges against Belladon, not only for his violations of the Ten Hours Bill and the Law of 1844 requiring the fencing of dangerous machinery, but also for his loathsome traffic with the woman, Abernathy. However, the Queen has been advised that dragging this odious man through the law courts might have a negative side effect by exposing to the public the lurid details of his crimes, for we must always bear in mind our duty to protect the purity of the English household.

Signed,
V.R. (Victoria Regina)

Seven-year-old Lord Henry, the first Earl of Castleford and future Marquess of Pontefract, sat on his father's lap and stuck his finger through Adam's shirt.

"Is that where the bad man burned you, Papa?" he asked.

"Yes," said Adam. The burn was healing, but it still hurt.

"That was a terrible thing to do. He must be very, very wicked."

"Yes, he is."

Henry threw his arms around Adam's neck and hugged him. "Oh, Papa, it makes me so proud to have a father who is a hero!" he exclaimed.

"What's a hero?" asked four-year-old Arthur, who was sitting at his father's feet in the nursery of Pontefract House playing with lead soldiers. Arthur had dark hair, like his father. Both children were stunningly beautiful.

"Well, that's a good question," Adam said, wondering about the ball he and Sybil were giving that night. Sybil had told him Disraeli had invited Edgar Musgrave to the ball, with the hope of fostering a romance between him and Emily McNair. Adam had no idea whether this would work, but he had great respect for Dizzy's flair for conniving. And he had to admit that if Edgar and Emily became involved with each other, it would be a double relief. Sybil had told him of Edgar's second blackmailing attempt, and he had agreed, however reluctantly, to the annual payment of ten thousand pounds to shut him up. Now, as he looked at the two sons he adored, he inwardly groaned at the cloud that hovered over both their heads. The heir that actually wasn't the heir, the younger son who actually *was* the heir. For all his honors—and Adam was proud that the Queen was presenting him with the Garter—the future of his children was still gravely in doubt.

"I'm no hero, Arthur," he said. "I only do what I think is right."

"*I* think you're a hero," said Lord Henry. "All the newspapers say you are, and the Queen is giving you the Garter, so if you're not a hero, who is?"

"Maybe Larry is a true hero," his father said.

"Who's Larry?"

"An orphan I met at Mandeville who had none of the wonderful advantages you and Arthur have. A little boy to whom life has been nothing but ugly. Maybe Larry's a *real* hero."

"I don't know anything about Larry," said his son, "but he doesn't sound like a hero to *me*. You're my hero, Papa."

"And mine," echoed Arthur from the floor.

"Dizzy tells me the Liberals in Parliament are furious at you for what you did to Mr. Belladon," Sybil said that night as she and Adam walked from their bedroom to the top of the grand staircase. Sybil looked spectacular in a lemon-colored silk dress with rubies and diamonds draped around her neck, dangling from her ears and blazing from her tiara.

"That's because Belladon contributes so much money to their party," Adam replied. He looked equally superb in his tailcoat, his blue Garter ribbon slashing across his starched white shirtfront, his diamond Garter star attached to the left side of his coat. The twenty-two-year-old Prince of Wales was coming to the ball, and the word "Decorations" had been engraved on the invitations, as was *de rigueur* when any member of the Royal Family was to be present. The Prince, who had recently announced his engagement to the beautiful Danish Princess Alexandra, was carrying out all the social functions of the Royal Family since his mother, Queen Victoria, had retired into virtual isolation in mourning for her beloved husband, Prince Albert. "Belladon ought to be glad I don't prosecute him for attempted murder, but I think ruining his company is enough. And I didn't want to subject you and the boys to another courtroom drama."

"That was thoughtful of you, darling, and I appreciate it. The boys are so very proud of you, as am I. And you look very handsome in your Garter regalia."

"Thank you." They started down the stairs. "But I have to tell you, I'm very nervous about Edgar Musgrave coming tonight. I know that Dizzy is scheming to pair him off with Emily, but Edgar is a loose cannon, in my opinion. This whole scheme could go miserably wrong."

"I know. I'm nervous too. But Dizzy seems sure of what he's doing, and I think in this instance we have to leave things in his hands. He tells me he has high hopes for your political future. He even thinks you might be a possible future Viceroy of India."

"Dizzy can be extremely glib."

"I know, but oh Adam, wouldn't that be a dazzling prospect? Viceroy!"

"I'll have to admit it *sounds* nice. But we'll see. Ah, I think our first guests have arrived."

They stationed themselves on the landing to receive their guests.

Emily McNair had never seen such a glittering scene. Dizzy's guest list included the power brokers of London and the rulers of approximately one-fourth of the planet Earth were jammed into Pontefract House. Emily was with her parents inching up the stair with the other guests waiting to be greeted by Sybil and Adam on the landing. Suddenly the chatter of the crowd was hushed. Emily looked down to the entrance hall, where the Prince of Wales and his gorgeous fiancée had just arrived. Quickly the people on the stairs made a passage for the royal couple, bowing and bobbing as they climbed the steps. Emily curtsied, at the same time noticing a strikingly handsome man with blond hair who was behind her on the stairs.

Emily told herself she was still in love with Adam. But as she resumed the slow climb toward the landing, she found herself looking back down over the heads of the crowd at the intriguing stranger.

"I have a young lady I want you to meet," Dizzy said fifteen minutes later as he came up to Edgar Musgrave. "Her name is Emily McNair. Her father is Sir Carlton McNair from Calcutta, possibly the richest tea planter in India. I think it will be to your advantage to meet Miss McNair. She's quite charming."

Edgar was hardly lacking in nerve, but he was more than a little awed by Disraeli. That such a powerful politician would even remember his name, much less go out of his way to be nice to him, struck him as amazing.

"You're very kind, Mr. Disraeli," he said, following him across the ballroom which was filling up as the guests passed through the receiving line.

"I am a matchmaker at heart." Dizzy smiled. "People think of me as an old cynic, but the truth is, I'm an incurable romantic. Poor Miss McNair knows few people in London, and I thought you might show her some of the sights." He lowered his voice. "I happen to know that Sir Carlton is a millionaire many times over and Emily is the only child. One can only speculate what the dowry for such an heiress might be, eh?" He raised his voice again. "There she is: the redhead in the white dress with the pink bows. Isn't she a stunner?"

"Yes, she is," Edgar said truthfully.

"There are so many unscrupulous men in London who will soon be after her dowry like bloodhounds. Alas, the House of Commons is filled with such unscrupulous—if attractive—young men. But I know Emily will be safe with you, Edgar. I am told you are a man of lofty principle and character."

"Who told you that?"

"Lady Pontefract." Dizzy smiled. Edgar had the grace to turn slightly red.

"Sir Carlton!" Dizzy exclaimed, coming up to the fat planter. "And Lady McNair. Might I present Mr. Edgar Musgrave? And this charming creature is Emily."

Emily turned to see the good-looking man with the blond hair she had admired on the stairs.

"Miss McNair," Edgar purred as he raised her gloved hand to his lips, "might I have the honor of the next waltz?"

Emily looked as pleased as her parents.

"Where is Lord Henry's bedroom?" Edgar asked one of the forty white-wigged, liveried footmen who were serving the party. It was twenty minutes later. Edgar had danced two waltzes with Emily and felt certain he had made a favorable impression on the girl.

"One floor up, sir, at the rear of the house. It's the left-hand door, next to the nursery."

Edgar looked back. The orchestra was playing a snappy galop, and the dancers were thumping around the ballroom, shaking the house enough to jiggle the crystal chandeliers. Edgar, who was holding a glass of champagne, climbed to the third floor. He wondered why Disraeli was maneuvering him. Like everyone else in London, he knew that Dizzy was close to Sybil. Was it possible the two of them—and even Adam perhaps—were dangling Emily as a bait to get him out of their hair? That didn't seem unlikely. As he walked down the third-floor hall, he thought it was time to make the move he had been contemplating for a number of years. Henry, his son—not Adam's—was a powerful weapon.

Reaching the end of the hall, he knocked on the door.

"Who is it?"

Edgar opened the door and looked in. Lord Henry, in his nightshirt, was reading in bed. The fair-haired boy looked at the fair-haired man in the doorway.

"May I come in?" Edgar said, not waiting for Henry to say yes. He closed the door and came to the bed.

"Who are you?" asked Henry.

"My name is Edgar Musgrave. I'm a friend of your mother's. I've heard so much about you, I wanted to meet you. What are you reading?"

"My French grammar."

"French grammar is hideously boring, isn't it? Do you mind?"

He pulled a stool over and sat down next to the bed. Henry was studying him curiously.

"Do you know my father?" he asked.

"Oh yes."

"My father's a hero, isn't he?"

"Yes. He's also very rich. You're going to be rich one day, aren't you?"

The boy looked confused. "I suppose."

"Do I look at all . . . familiar to you?"

Henry frowned. "Yes, a little," he finally said.

Edgar finished his champagne, stood up and went to a bureau where he picked up a hand mirror. He went back to the bed and held the mirror in front of Henry's face. The boy looked at his reflection. Then he looked at Edgar, who was watching him intently.

"Are we . . . related?" Henry asked.

"Yes, we are."

"How? I never heard your name mentioned before."

"It's a long story, Henry," Edgar said, taking the mirror back to the bureau. "One day I'll tell it to you. In the meantime, I wanted to meet you. We have so many things in common." He went to the door. "Good night, Henry."

"Good night, Mr. Musgrave."

Edgar let himself out and softly closed the door. Alone, Henry left his bed and ran across the room to the bureau. Picking up the mirror, he looked at his reflection again.

Then he looked at the door, puzzlement on his face.

Five minutes later, Edgar came up to Adam, who was standing at one side of the ballroom watching the dancers. "A lovely evening, milord," Edgar said with a smile. "And I congratulate you on your bubbly. I've just helped myself to a fresh glass. It's first-rate. But then, everything you have is first-rate."

Adam looked at him coolly. "Musgrave," he said in a soft voice, "it's bad enough that you blackmail my wife. But by God, I don't have to pretend to like you, or even be civil, for that matter. I'll thank you to drink *my* champagne with somebody else."

"Really, old boy, that seems rather unfriendly. Yes, decidedly unfriendly. And we have so much to be friendly about. I was just upstairs having a chat with Lord Henry. Delightful boy."

Adam's eyes widened. "Stay away from him, Musgrave," he whispered, "or by God I'll . . ."

"You'll what?" Edgar smiled. "He is, after all, my son, not yours. I see no reason why I shouldn't be able to see him whenever I choose. I suspect a court of law might see it my way, for that matter."

Fear came into Adam's eyes. "Did you tell him?"

"No, but I might." Edgar sipped the champagne, enjoying watching the mighty Lord Pontefract squirm like a worm on a fishhook. "A moment ago, you used the word 'blackmail,' " he went on. "A word I don't like much. Such an unattractive word. But I suppose a rose by any other name, et cetera. However, it's occurred to me that perhaps I've been blackmailing the wrong person all these years. I should have been blackmailing *you*." He took another sip of champagne. "And perhaps I shall, old boy."

He walked away.

"We're in a fine mess now," Adam said at four that morning. The last guests had just left with the Prince of Wales, and the host and hostess were climbing the stairs as the servants cleaned up. "Edgar went to Henry's room and introduced himself."

"What?" Sybil looked shocked.

"I told you he's a loose cannon. And now he's hinting broadly that he may start blackmailing me rather than you. He threatened to tell Henry who his real father is."

"But that's not fair. After all the money we've paid him . . . thousands of pounds . . ."

"Edgar's not much interested in fairness. The damned man's a bloodsucking leech! I don't know *what* to do. It's such a hellish dilemma. Either way, one of the boys is getting terribly hurt."

"Kill him!" Sybil whispered, putting her hand on his

arm. "You know how to kill—it's the only way to silence him. Oh Adam, I know it's my fault. Edgar was my childhood passion . . ."

"As Lizzie was mine."

"Yes, exactly. But you were lucky with Lizzie, and I've had nothing but rotten luck with Edgar. But we must protect Henry. It would be so cruel to that adorable child to lose his inheritance—"

"Just as it's unfair and cruel to Arthur to lose the inheritance that *really* is his. But there are other ways to deal with Edgar than slitting his throat, as enjoyable as that might be. I'll talk to Dizzy tomorrow. He's better at this sort of thing than I am. Meanwhile, I think perhaps I've made a mistake not telling Henry myself."

"Adam, you mustn't!"

"I thought that at first too. But I went through childhood not knowing who I really was, and I don't want to wish that on my own son—pardon me, Edgar's son. No, Henry must know the truth. It's the only fair thing to do. And we'll let Dizzy handle Edgar."

They had reached their bedroom.

"Do you love Henry as if he were your own son?"

"Yes."

"Thank God for that." She paused. "But Adam, what if he hates us for it? What if they both hate us?"

"Don't think I'm not terrified of that. But if it happens, it happens."

"This is all my fault. Can you ever forgive me?"

He took her in his arms. "I forgave you a long time ago," he whispered. "After all, I deceived you for years with Lizzie. I'm no one to moralize. But pray for us, Sybil. I think this is going to be the most difficult thing I've ever done in my life."

"Perhaps we should do it together?"

He thought a moment. "Yes, perhaps we should. We'll both talk to him in the morning."

"You're . . . *not* my father?" Henry's eyes were wide with shock.

"No."

Adam was sitting on the side of his son's bed. Sybil stood beside him, watching nervously.

"Then that man last night . . . Mr. Musgrave . . . ?"

"He's your father," Sybil said softly.

Henry looked at his mother, then back to Adam. Tears began running down his cheeks. "You were my hero," he whispered. "What are you now?"

"I hope you'll let me continue to be your father," Adam said. "To me, you're still my son, and always will be."

"Is Arthur your son?" Henry asked.

"Yes."

"Then he should be the heir, not I."

Adam and Sybil exchanged looks.

"We want you to continue to be the heir," Sybil said. "Otherwise . . . well, there might be a scandal."

The boy sitting in the bed looked numb. He didn't say anything for a long while. Then he said, "I'll have to take good care of Arthur, won't I? I'll have to be especially fair with him because I'm cheating him out of so very much. I don't like cheating my own brother." He looked at his parents again. "Oh Mama and Papa, how *could* you have?"

Adam leaned forward and hugged him.

"Can you forgive us?" he whispered.

After a long moment Henry said, "May I be alone now?"

Adam released him and stood up. Sybil leaned forward and kissed her son. Then they left the room, closing the door quietly.

They waited silently in the hall. After a moment they heard Henry begin sobbing.

They walked down the hall together, avoiding each other's eyes. Then Adam took her hand.

"He had to be told," he whispered.

"I know. But I feel so . . . dirty."

"Edgar's asked me to be his wife!" Emily McNair exclaimed the next week in the drawing room of Pontefract House. She was looking unusually pretty in a dark blue silk dress.

"Congratulations," Adam said. "It's been a whirlwind courtship."

"Hasn't it? But oh, Adam, I'm so much in love. And Mr. Disraeli is arranging a knighthood for Edgar, so I'll be Lady Musgrave. Isn't that thrilling?"

"Yes, Dizzy told me Edgar's to be the new English Consul in Florence."

"Edgar's mad for Italy, and he tells me I'll love it too. Hasn't everything turned out splendidly?" She turned to Sybil, who was sitting on a sofa. "You know, Lady Pontefract, I have a confession to make. There was a time when I was in love with your husband. I threw myself at him quite shamelessly. It makes me blush to admit it, but I even hired a room at Claridge's and invited Adam to lunch. My intentions"—she turned her eyes rather defiantly on Adam—"were dishonorable, I fear. But your husband was the perfect gentleman. I think it was then I fell out of love with him." She laughed. "Isn't life bizarre?"

"But you *are* in love with Edgar?" Sybil asked.

"Oh yes! He's the most wonderful man. Of course, I'm not blind to his faults. He's a bit of a rogue, I think. But roguishness makes men so attractive." Again she looked at Adam. "Your husband was a bit of a rogue . . . *once.*" This, rather dryly. "By the way, Adam, Edgar asked me to give you this note. I have no idea what it's about."

She pulled an envelope from her purse and handed it to Adam, who opened it. It read: "Pontefract: I have accepted Mr. Disraeli's deal. I get the title and the Consulate in Florence. You get my son. Tell Sybil she need send me no more money, since Emily's dowry has made me a rich man. Neither of you has to worry: I'll keep my mouth shut and play the game. After all, we mustn't let the Empire down, must we? Signed, Sir Edgar Musgrave."

It was so beautifully cynical, Adam couldn't help but smile. He remembered what Disraeli had once told him: "What are empires for if not to buy off your poor relatives and enemies with jobs and titles?"

CHAPTER 30

There's action in Gettysburg!" Captain Zack Whitney yelled to his men. "Some of our boys went into town this morning looking for shoes, and they ran into Yankee cavalry. General Lee has ordered all companies to head for the town. Forward *march*!"

It was the blistering hot morning of July 1, 1863. As Zack's company moved forward, the faint sound of artillery booming could be heard in the distance. Phineas Whitney had arranged a commission for Zack the previous winter after the Battle of Fredericksburg. And, in light of the deaths of Charlotte and Clayton, Phineas and Ellie May had adopted Zack, making him their heir—if there was anything left to inherit.

Both sides felt that the long and bloody war was nearing some sort of climax. Lee's string of victories had left Virginia decimated, and the Southern commander had decided he must take the action into the enemy territory. Thus the rebels had moved into Pennsylvania through the Shenandoah Valley, and the past few weeks had been something of a lark. Pennsylvania was as rich as Virginia had been before, and most of the farmers had been willing, albeit somewhat nervously, to sell food to the Southern soldiers in return for Confederate currency. The rebels went on a vast shopping spree, shoes and boots being the hottest items since leather had become so scarce in the South. Phineas had sent his newly adopted son five thousand dollars in Confederate money, part of his kickback cash in the trunk in the basement of Fairview Plantation, and Zack had bought himself a beautiful new pair of boots, some much-needed underwear, a dozen bars of soap and a steak dinner with some of his fellow officers at a tavern in Chambersburg in the Cumberland Valley southwest of Harrisburg. That these purchases used up most of his five thousand dollars indicated the value of Confederate currency outside the South, but his belly was full, he felt clean, well-shod, and he was ready for a little glory.

The next morning, when news of the encounter at Gettysburg came, he thought perhaps it might be his chance to get that glory. But as he marched down the Chambersburg Pike at the head of his company, he was also feeling apprehensive about what lay in store for him. He remembered the ghastly corpses piled up in the freezing night the previous December at Fredericksburg. He knew that in a matter of hours, or even less, he might be a corpse himself, and while he didn't dwell on the morbid thought, it was a bit unnerving. The sweat rolled down his face in the blistering heat as he neared Gettysburg. Zack was a brave man who was scared.

About eleven o'clock in the morning, Zack began to make out a wide ridge to the east where fighting was going on. This was called McPherson's Ridge, though Zack didn't know it. The ridge was about forty feet high, and at one point Zack saw that a deep cut had been dug through the hill for the railroad. As Zack's men marched past yet another hill called Herr Ridge, they could see the butternut uniforms of the rebel army running down the ridge toward McPherson's Ridge, just past a meandering creek called Willoughby Run.

"This is it, men!" he yelled back to his hot, dusty company. "The enemy's on that ridge! Let's join the others on the double!"

Letting out the fabled rebel yell, the company broke ranks and began running with the others, bayonets fixed, their guns loaded and ready to fire.

As at Fredericksburg, once Zack was in combat his nervousness and fear were replaced by a searing excitement. The yells, the screams of the wounded, the noise of the guns and the fierce July heat created a "high" in all the men. The Union forces on McPherson's Ridge were under the command of Major General John F. Reynolds, who had good reason for wanting to hold the ridge. As long as the Rebels came from the west, McPherson's Ridge covered the approaches to the town of Gettysburg. The stand of timber in approximately the center of the ridge afforded protection for the Yankees because they could send an enfilading fire on enemy columns moving along either the Chambersburg Pike or, to the south, the Fairfield road—or both at once. The greatest defect of Reynolds' position was the exposure of his right flank to artillery fire from Oak Hill to the north and attacks from infantry which could use nearby fields of tall wheat as a cover. This was where Zack led his men. Running through the wheat, bullets hissing over his ducked head, sweat soaking his uniform, he thought it was a grand moment to be alive—if it lasted.

By the time Zack was out of the wheatfield, he could see the whole panorama of the battle. Butternut rebels were swarming up McPherson's Ridge, and the fighting was intense. "Up the hill!" he yelled to his men. "The enemy's on top! Up the hill!" They ran until they were within range of enemy fire. Then they began to fire back, pausing to reload their Enfields as Zack had trained them, getting off an average of three shots a minute. It was all confusing, but Zack had the sense that his casualties were, at least so far, not great. But he couldn't look back. He was leader going up the hill, and he was so fast that within minutes he found that he had lost his men—or, more accurately, all the Rebels were jumbled together in one great mass of firing, shouting soldiery.

Zack paused behind a tree to catch his breath and reload his rifle. Then he peeked out around the tree. He saw a Union officer mounted on a horse about one hundred feet away, surrounded by a few other officers. Zack didn't know who the man was, but he looked important. Zack took aim and fired. The officer's horse reared backward, and the officer fell forward onto the ground. The other men with him quickly dismounted and ran toward the fallen figure. Zack grinned. "I think I got him," he mumbled.

He had. The man was dead. What Captain Zachary Whitney didn't know was that he had just killed Major

General John F. Reynolds, the Union commander of the forces on McPherson's Ridge. By dumb, blind luck—always a major factor in warfare—Zack gave the Confederate forces their first big break in the first encounter on the first day of the three-day Battle of Gettysburg. By early afternoon, the Union forces were in retreat, regrouping on the next ridge to the east, Seminary Ridge. By dusk, the Union forces, primarily the crack Iron Brigade, were making a last stand on Seminary Ridge. For seven or eight minutes there ensued probably the most desperate fight ever waged between artillery and infantry at close range without a particle of cover on either side. Bullets hummed and whistled everywhere; cannon roared. It was all crash on crash, peal on peal, smoke, dust, splinters, blood, wreckage and carnage. The Iron Brigade was decimated. The Twenty-fourth Michigan lost eighty percent of its men. By evening Seminary Ridge was in Confederate hands and the Yankees had retreated into Gettysburg, attempting to take up a new position on Cemetery Hill, near the looming gate to the Evergreen Cemetery south of town.

As an exhausted but exhilarated Zack tried to get some sleep, he thought that the battle was over—perhaps even the war—and that his Beloved Cause had triumphed.

Zack was wrong.

"It seems there's been a Union victory at that little town in Pennsylvania," Lizzie read to Alex three mornings later. They were sitting on the porch of the house on the Jersey Shore she had rented for the summer.

"Gutenburg?" Alex said. He was in his wheelchair, a shawl wrapped around his shoulders to protect him from the sea breeze.

"No, darling, Gettysburg. General Lee's army is running back to Virginia—'stumbling' might be the better word. It looks like it's a rout, though the casualties on both sides are appalling."

"About . . . time the North had . . . a victory," Alex said. Though still partially paralyzed, his recovery from the stroke had been encouraging, and his speech was much improved. He even had some color in his cheeks. "This will be good for business," he went on. "What's the . . . Market doing?"

"It went up a few points yesterday, but today, with the news of the victory, I imagine it should soar. We stand to make a great deal of money."

He was watching some children on the beach playing ball. It was a beautiful morning. The Atlantic shimmered in the sun.

"What . . . stocks have you . . . bought?" he asked.

"Alex, you know I'm wretched about business. I leave it all to Jim Fisk. The last time I talked to him, he said he was buying heavily into some railroad or other. The Erie, I think."

"Don't . . . trust Jimmie . . . too much. He's a sly fox."

"*You* trusted him!"

"Yes, but . . . I kept an eye on him."

"Darling, he's making *so* much money for us! Why, last month alone he sent me over twenty thousand dollars."

Alex looked at her with surprise. "How . . . much money have you . . . invested with him?"

Lizzie put down the New York *Times*, mentally kicking herself. Alex still didn't know she had sold the store.

"Miss Lizzie," Lila said, waddling out of the white house onto the porch, "that baby of yours done wet himself again. I swear that boy's worse'n the Hudson River."

"Did you change him?" Lizzie asked, thankful for the interruption. She had been delivered of a fine baby boy six weeks earlier whom she had named Somerset.

"Yes'm. Does you want another cup of coffee?"

"No thanks."

"How 'bout you, Mr. Alex? More coffee?"

Alex shook his head.

"Miss Lizzie, you gonna feed Somerset at the reg'lar time?"

"Yes."

"Then I go up an' make the beds now. Gotta wake up that sleepyhead, Amanda. That girl's gettin' lazy as a mule."

Lila went back into the house. Alex was still looking at his wife. "How much . . . money?" he repeated.

Lizzie stood up, going to the porch rail. The breeze blew her golden hair.

"Oh, several thousand dollars," she lied.

"You don't make . . . twenty thousand dollars in one month on . . . several thousand dollars."

She turned to him. "Alex, I've told you over and over not to worry about business. The doctor's so pleased with your improvement, but you can't think about business."

"The store," he said. "Did you borrow . . . money on the store?"

"No. The store's doing well. You know that."

He looked at her with suspicion. "I want to . . . go back to the city."

"We can't. It's hot and they're having riots. It's in the paper . . . something about the new draft law." She came to him, leaned down and kissed him. "Now, please: relax. You're getting stronger every day. The doctor says by Christmas . . . well, we don't want to get our hopes up too high, but—"

"Lizzie, you . . . didn't sell the store, did you?"

She straightened. "Why ever would you think that?" she said. "Of course not."

"I miss my store," he said wistfully. Lizzie knew that someday he would have to know. But not yet, she thought. She knew how much Sinclair and Son meant to him, but she had had no choice. Jim Fisk had come to her with an offer of two and a half million dollars from Jordan, Marsh, and she simply could not turn it down. Now she had a new worry, though. She had let Fisk invest almost all the money in the market, and whereas she had great confidence in his business ability, the market was going up and down so wildly that at times she had severe attacks of "what if?" What if Jim Fisk turned out to be wrong? What if he turned out to be more a crook than a business genius? What if Lila had been right in her assessment of his character?

Then she told herself she *had* to trust him, for who else was there to trust?

* * *

"Happy birthday, Alex!" exclaimed Lizzie three days later as Lila carried the big white cake into the dining room of the summer cottage.

"Happy birthday, Papa!" chorused Amanda.

Alex, slumped in his wheelchair, tried to smile. Lizzie and the male nurse had dressed him in a loose-fitting white suit for the occasion, but Alex had shown little enthusiasm.

Lila put the cake in front of Alex. "Make a wish, darling." Lizzie smiled.

Alex looked at her with dull, resentful eyes. "I wish," he said, "I was . . . back in my store."

Then he leaned forward and blew. Only seven of the thirty-two candles went out.

"Mrs. Sinclair?"

There was a knock on her bedroom door. Lizzie sat up, yawning, and looked at her bed clock. It was almost four in the morning, a week after the birthday party.

"Yes?"

"It's Joe. I'm afraid something's happened."

She was suddenly wide-awake. "Oh God . . . I'm coming . . ."

Turning up the bedlamp, she got out of bed, threw on her slippers and a robe and hurried to the door. She opened it. Joe, the nurse was outside. "What's wrong?"

"I think he had a heart attack."

"Is he . . . ?"

Joe nodded yes.

Dead of a heart attack, just like his mother. She closed her eyes a moment, leaning on the door frame.

"He was such a good man," she said. "How very unfair."

PART IV

PEACE

CHAPTER 31

On a foggy November night in 1868, a carriage pulled up in front of the Carlton Club in Carlton House Terrace, London, and Bentley Brent stepped out. The big, bearded man entered the club. After checking his top hat and black opera cape, he said to the porter, "Lord Pontefract is expecting me." The porter led him to the library, where Adam rose from a leather armchair to shake hands with his old companion. After ordering whiskeys, the two men took seats next to each other.

"So," Adam began, "how was America?"

"Booming. At least, the North is. Now that they've gotten slavery out of their system, the country seems to be in a sort of economic explosion."

"And how is my Lizzie?"

"Ah well, old boy, I wish I could say the same for her. What's happened is shocking."

"What *has* happened?"

"When I got to New York, I went to her house on Fifth Avenue. Big, bloody thing it is, looks like Salisbury Cathedral. One can't imagine what notions of taste these Americans have! Bloody barbarians!"

"Yes, yes—but what happened?"

"Doing my best to tell the story, Adam. Well, I rang the bell and a butler answered. I saw right off he was different, because I'd been there only six months before. I asked for Mrs. Sinclair, as I always do. And the chap said, 'She doesn't live here anymore. She sold this house two months ago to Mr. . . . ' Well, I forget his name. So I asked the butler where Mrs. Sinclair was living now, and he told me she and her children had moved to a certain Hotel Davenport."

"Where's that?"

"On lower Broadway, and it's not a very good hotel, I'm sad to report. I mean, it's respectable enough—but it's slightly down at the heels, if you know what I mean. Lizzie and her children are living in two rooms on the second floor."

"Two rooms?" exclaimed Adam. "But she was worth millions! What happened to her money?"

"Jim Fisk. She told me she'd given that Falstaffian character all of her money to invest, and it all got swept away in the Erie Railroad War. Surely you read about that?"

"I read something . . . didn't pay much attention . . ."

"The biggest swindle in Wall Street's history. She admits she was a fool, and she feels horribly guilty about having lost the money. But there it is: gone. She had to sell her Fifth Avenue mansion to pay her debts."

"What about her plantation in Virginia?"

"Gone. Burned by the Yankees in the last year of the war. She sold the land to a Carpetbagger for three dollars the acre. The South is devastated. The price of losing the war is that they're all poor as church mice. It's rather sad, actually."

"You're telling me she was wiped out?"

"Yes. You know she has no head for business. She's just a woman, after all. Still a damned pretty one, but can a woman deal with money? Preposterous idea."

"And Amanda? She's all right?"

"Well, yes. She's eleven now and pretty as a picture, but she's been spoiled, Adam. And I can tell you she's not very happy about being poor. Then there's Somerset, the son by Alex Sinclair. He's five and a handsome lad, but she has two children to take care of in a two-room flat. It's not easy, as you can imagine. Fortunately, she has the colored maid, Lila, who's remained loyal."

"Then what are they living on?"

"Now, this is the interesting thing: she could be quite well-off despite having lost her money. You remember the son of the slave that she educated?"

"Of course. Gabriel Cavanagh, the pianist."

"She told me he was in New York last spring trying to arrange for a concert—it didn't work out, no one would rent him a hall—and he came to her and offered her any amount of money she needed. A bit of an irony there, wouldn't you say? Tables turned, and all that? But she refused him. Nicely, but she won't take charity, she said. Actually, *I* offered her money, because I was sure you'd want me to, and she turned me down too. She has a lot of pride, that Lizzie."

"Pride's very nice, but it doesn't pay the rent. Again, what is she living on?"

"She's become an actress."

Adam looked shocked. "An *actress*?"

"Well, she is a stunner, you know."

"But actresses are—"

"I hope you're not going to say 'indecent,' old boy?"

Adam had the grace to look embarrassed.

"Is she any good?" he finally asked.

Bentley chuckled. "She's *ghastly*," he said. "She gave me a ticket to a show she's in, *Virtue Regained*, I think it was. I went to see it, and she's like a stick onstage, could barely get out her lines. To be fair, she told me it's only her second role, but still I don't think she's ever going to be a Sarah Siddons. But the amusing thing is, the audience loved her because she's so deuced pretty."

"You don't have to tell *me* that. So Lizzie's an actress? A bit of a come-down from Fifth Avenue."

"Oh yes, but she has a good deal of notoriety. Everyone knows who she is. She sells tickets."

"Perhaps, but I don't like the idea of her and Amanda living in a hotel. I don't like that at all."

Bentley ordered another whiskey, then leaned closer.

"Now look here, Adam. Dizzy's Prime Minister now, and you're in line for a large political plum. Don't start hatching any schemes."

Adam gave him a cool look. "I don't consider trying to help dear friends as 'hatching schemes.' "

"No offense intended. Just looking after your better interests."

"Bentley, all my life I've been trying to figure out what exactly *are* my better interests, and I still don't know."

"I'd say being Viceroy of India is a 'better interest.' "

"Yes, I suppose you're right. But Dizzy keeps promising and so far, at least, he hasn't delivered."

"Isn't that the definition of a politician?"

Adam laughed. But he wasn't laughing about the sudden reversal of fortunes for Lizzie and Amanda, and he knew what he had to do about that. No matter how happy he was with Sybil, he was still Lizzie's true knight.

The young man with the narrow face and wide black mustache in the fourth row of the Broadway Theatre was watching the play onstage with rapt attention. The play, *Don't Fool with Love*, was a translation of de Musset's *On ne Badine pas avec l'Amour* and was, by New York standards, risqué. The star of the show was a slightly over-the-hill French actress named Edwige Mercier, but the young man's eyes were glued to the maid, being played by Lizzie. The nineteen-year-old Yale student, home in New York for the Christmas holidays, had never seen anyone so radiantly beautiful. For the first time in his life, he had fallen wildly, passionately in love.

When the curtain fell on the final act, the audience applauded politely when the stars took their curtain calls. But when Lizzie came out to curtsy, looking very sexy in a black maid's costume that had been designed to show a considerable amount of her legs, the audience, almost totally male with a heavy sprinkling of college students, exploded. Lizzie might not have learned to become a very accomplished actress, but she had learned how to take curtain calls. She smiled seductively, blew kisses, then stepped back behind the curtain where Mlle. Mercier, the star, was ready to strangle her.

"Beech!" she hissed at Lizzie. "You upstage me once more in the last act and I weel bite you!" And she flounced off to her dressing room.

Out front, the crowd was drifting up the aisles. The young man, Jeffrey Schoenberg by name, made his way to the cloakroom to get his hat and coat, then struggled through the crowd to emerge into the icy December night. He was nervous, but determined that tonight he would meet this woman of his dreams who was listed in the playbill as "Elizabeth Sinclair." Darting into an alley, he went to the stage door, tipped the aged attendant five dollars, then went backstage to the dressing rooms. Even if he hadn't been told, the six college men his age waiting in front of one of the doors would have indicated Lizzie's whereabouts. The blond English beauty was taking New York by storm.

"Oh I say, what have we here?" said one of the college boys as he spotted Jeffrey. "Jeffrey Schoenberg thinks *he* has a chance with the divine Mrs. Sinclair? Oh I say, that's good for a few chuckles, eh, lads?" The speaker, a senior from Harvard, affected the most languid of pseudo-English accents. The others laughed as Jeffrey burned.

"And what's wrong with *me*?" he said.

"Oh I say, *must* we tell him?"

"Go to hell, van Brunt."

Theodore van Brunt raised a pince-nez to his face and inspected Jeffrey down his long, patrician nose.

"Should we Harvard Christians teach this Yale Jewboy to show a little respect?" van Brunt said, stepping up to Jeffrey and giving him a shove in the chest. Jeffrey shoved back. Van Brunt tried to punch him in the face, but Jeffrey, who boxed in college, took a defensive stance, shot out his right fist and pummeled van Brunt's patrician nose, sending his glasses shattering to the floor. The others jumped Jeffrey, and a *melée* began. Some stagehands were running over to try and pull the collegians apart when the dressing-room door opened and Lizzie appeared, wearing a yellow Japanese wrap. Seeing her, the brawling boys stopped, almost as if the teacher had walked into the classroom.

"What *is* this?" she said with annoyance.

"Merely some of your devoted admirers trying to protect you from garbage," van Brunt said, brushing off his sleeves as he sneered at Jeffrey. "We are a contingent from Harvard who have come to pay our respects and beg the privilege of escorting the divine Mrs. Sinclair to Delmonico's for a champagne supper—"

"You're bleeding!" exclaimed Lizzie, pointing to Jeffrey's nose which had blood streaming from the left nostril. "Really, you college boys are like babies! Come in, young man. I'll get a wet towel."

Jeffrey, hardly believing his luck, pushed through the collegians, giving van Brunt a slyly superior smile.

"Sit down," said Lizzie, closing the door and indicating a chair in front of her makeup table. He obeyed as she soaked a towel in the basin, then brought it to him, taking his silk hat from his head. "Lean your head back." He did as he was told and she put the towel to his nose. "Now, what was that all about? And who is that ridiculous Harvard fop?"

"Ted van Brunt," Jeffrey muttered through the towel. "His father owns a shipping company. Ted spent a month in London and came back sounding like Disraeli."

Lizzie laughed. "He's hardly the first American to do that, nor the last. I take it you're not at Harvard?"

"Yale."

"And why did you come backstage?"

"To tell you that . . . that I'm in love with you."

Lizzie removed the bloodstained towel and stepped back, putting her hands on her hips. "The bleeding's stopped. You can go now. And *stop* falling in love with actresses. You'll end up in trouble and your father will spank you."

Jeffrey got up from the chair. "That's not fair, Mrs. Sinclair. I'm nineteen and know what I'm doing. Please let me take you to dinner. Once you get to know me, you'll see that my affection for you is not just the passing fancy of a callow youth, but a deep and sincere emotion."

"Yes, I'm sure. What's your name?"

"Jeffrey Schoenberg."

"That name sounds familiar."

"My father is Otto Schoenberg, president of the Schoenberg Bank and Trust."

Lizzie's face turned to ice. "Wall Street," she said, practically spitting the words. "Thank you, my friend, but I've had enough to do with Wall Street to last a lifetime. Now run on home and ask your father if he knows how to get my money back from that overweight scoundrel, Jim Fisk. Here's your hat."

She practically shoved it into his hand, then went to the dressing table to finish removing her greasepaint.

"I take it you lost some money with Fisk?"

"*Some* money? He robbed me blind! Why do you think I'm on the stage? I should have listened to Lila."

Jeffrey looked confused. "Who's Lila?"

"My maid. She told me Jim Fisk was trash and she was a lot more perceptive than I."

"Well, Jim Fisk *is* trash! I agree with that. But my father's very honest."

"I'm sure. Now, I'm extremely tired, so if you don't mind . . . ?"

She looked at him in her mirror.

"Mrs. Sinclair, I don't suppose you'd be free for supper tomorrow night?"

She sighed. "Jeffrey, I'm ten years older than you and I have two children. So let's not indulge in any puerile fantasies. Really, you're wasting your time and mine."

He frowned. "Most women find me very attractive," he said. "Even older women."

"That's wonderful. Good night."

"I'm *very* persistent, you know." Then he left the dressing room. Lizzie shook her head, then went back to removing her makeup.

"Miss Lizzie, there's a package for you," Lila said the next morning as she came into Lizzie's bedroom in the Hotel Davenport. With Lizzie's growing drawing power at the theatre, she had been able to negotiate a raise from the management and move her family from the cramped two rooms they had been squeezed into up to the top floor to an "apartment," which had a commodious living room overlooking Broadway, a tiny kitchen that was nevertheless workable, two bedrooms and a private bath. While the entire apartment could have fitted comfortably into a corner of the Fifth Avenue mansion, it still was vastly better than what they'd had before. Lizzie, sitting in bed, took an envelope from Lila.

"What's in the package?"

"I don't know, but it sure am big."

Lizzie opened the envelope. Inside was a thick card with "Jeffrey Lyman Schoenberg" engraved on it. A handwritten note over the engraving read: "I love you. I am persistent. I will be at Delmonico's today at one P.M. If you do not show up for lunch with me, I cannot be held responsible for my actions. Affectionately, Jeffrey. P.S.: My nose is better today. Thank you for stopping the bleeding."

Lizzie frowned. "Listen to this." She read the note.

"Who's Jeffrey?" Lila asked. Lizzie told her about the previous evening. "Huh. He sound like a crazy man to me. What's he mean, he won't be responsible fo' his actions if you don't show up? He gonna shoot somebody or somethin'?"

"Of course not. It's just teenage bravado." She hesitated. "I think. Let's open the package."

"I'll do it. Miss Lizzie, I tol' you when you started bein' an actress you was lettin' yourself in fo' a lotta trouble. This New York City's full of crazy people."

She left the room. Lizzie re-read the note. She remembered the intensity of his dark eyes. At the time, she thought it was merely the look of a young man infatuated with an older woman. But might it be something else? She remembered her terror in Ayr when she returned to her cottage and found Amanda gone. New York was a city filled with violent crime, as the many newspapers never let their readers forget for a moment. What if . . . ?

She told herself that was ridiculous. Jeffrey Schoenberg was just a young man too much in love with love.

"Oh Mama, look what was in the box!"

Lizzie turned to see Amanda holding up a chinchilla coat that was so big it almost made her disappear behind it. Lila was next to her.

"This Jeffrey may be crazy," Lila said, "but he sure must be rich. Look what he done sent you!"

Amanda ran to her mother's bed and threw the chinchilla over her, then climbed on top of the fur.

"It's so beautiful," she cried. "And so soft. May I have it, Mama?"

"Of course not. Nor may I. Lila, I don't understand Americans. They're always trying to *buy* me."

"I knows what you mean, Miss Lizzie. I 'spect it's in their blood. They been buyin' and sellin' slaves for so long, they jes' got in the habit. What you gonna do with this Jeffrey?"

Lizzie shooed Amanda off the bed.

"I suppose I haven't much choice, have I? I'm going to lunch at Delmonico's. And believe me, I'm going to order the most expensive thing on the menu."

Lila chuckled as Lizzie got out of bed. She held up the chinchilla, then put it over her shoulders a moment and modeled it around the room for Amanda and Lila.

"That sure am pretty, Miss Lizzie."

"Wouldn't he be surprised if I kept it?" Lizzie said with a suggestive smile. "I'll bet anything he charged it to his father. Where'd it come from?"

"Where else? Sinclair and Son."

"Mr. Schoenberg—" Lizzie said three hours later.

"Jeffrey. Please."

"All right, Jeffrey. I'm very annoyed with you. I don't like to be threatened and I don't like to be bribed, and you've done both to me this morning."

Lizzie was sitting opposite Jeffrey at the best table at Delmonico's, the best restaurant in New York just north of Madison Square near the Fifth Avenue Hotel and the marble-fronted Hoffman House.

"If you think the chinchilla was a bribe," Jeffrey said, "you couldn't be more in error. I bought it for you as a visible expression of my devotion to you. May I hold your hand?"

"No, you may not."

"More champagne?"

"Please."

Jeffrey signaled the waiter, who refilled their glasses with Veuve Clicquot.

"I'm mad for you, Mrs. Sinclair. May I call you Lizzie?"

"No. Now, what did you mean when you said you wouldn't be responsible for your actions if I didn't come to lunch? And don't try to tell me that wasn't a threat."

"I'd commit suicide."

She looked at him. Then she laughed.

"I would!" he insisted. "You don't seem to understand that I have determined to win you at any cost. And any cost includes my life."

Her laugh faded. "Let me tell you something, Jeffrey. Life is nothing to throw away so lightly, even if only in jest. You remind me of my late husband. He was intense, like you. He was in a rush, like you, and he died at the age of thirty-two. If I thought for a moment you were remotely serious about committing suicide over a lunch, I'd despise you as a fool. As it is, I will thank you never, under any circumstances, to entertain such a ridiculous notion. Now, I'm hungry. Let's order."

He looked at her worshipfully. "I adore you," he whispered.

Lizzie rolled her eyes. She knew what had to be done next.

The Italianate mansion on Fifth Avenue filled an entire block and looked like a Medici palace in Florence, which had been the intent of the architect. The Civil War had created a bull market on Wall Street the likes of which was not to be seen for another sixty years; and while many were left ruined in its wake, like Lizzie, the fortunes made by others were creating a class of multimillionaires America had never encountered in its brief history. The most visible manifestation of this huge new wealth was the building of great mansions that made the respectable brownstones of the past look like privies in comparison. Alex had been in the vanguard of this expensive movement with his Gothic pile he never lived to see completed. But Otto Schoenberg had been swift to follow, and by Lee's surrender in 1865, the Medici Palace, as it had been quickly nicknamed, was already rising on Fifth Avenue, its grim stone walls looking as much like a fortress-prison as a palace.

Fifty-year-old Otto Schoenberg was one of New York's most successful bankers, American correspondent for some of the great European banks that were pouring capital into the booming American economy. Otto not only wanted a New York palace, he wanted to fill it with the treasures of the past: like most newly rich men, he wished to buttress his social position with the religion of the powerful, art. Thus, great, gloomy Italian paintings in heavy baroque frames were hung on the limestone walls of the soaring salons and drawing rooms. Tapestries were bought from impecunious European noblemen, as well as furniture fit for a palace. When all was in place, Otto moved in. This tycoon of finance, born the son of a Munich tailor, was now content.

Until that Sunday afternoon in December.

When Jeffrey came home from his lunch at Delmonico's, he went up to his bedroom to sleep off the effects of the considerable amount of wine he had drunk with Lizzie. At about five, he was awakened by a knock on the door.

"Yes?" he said sleepily.

"Master Jeffrey." It was one of the footmen. "Your father wishes to see you in the game room."

"Bother," muttered Jeffrey. "All right, I'll be down in a minute."

After washing his face and gargling with cologne, he left his room and went down the huge stone stair to the two-story great hall with its priceless Titian. He crossed the marble floor, his footsteps echoing in the gloomy recesses of the second-floor loggia that surrounded the hall. He entered a long, carpeted hall lined with yet more paintings, consoles and eighteenth-century bombé chests strewn with statues, bibelots and jeweled snuffboxes collected by his father to attempt to appease his insatiable appetite for the exquisite, the rare and the beautiful. Finally, he stopped before a walnut door and knocked.

"Come in."

It was his father's familiar, deep voice, made to sound

even deeper by the German accent. Jeffrey opened the door and went in. Even though the mammoth house was heated by huge coal furnaces in the basement, the latest technology, and even though a fire blazed in an eight-foot-high marble hearth in the game room, Jeffrey felt a definite chill as he confronted his father. But then, he felt the same chill when he confronted him in July. Otto Schoenberg was a formidable parent.

"You wanted to see me, Father?" Jeffrey said, standing in front of the ormolu French desk on which the great banker was playing a game of solitaire. Otto Schoenberg was a handsome man, tall, stiff and lean. He wore a bulging Bismarckian gray mustache, but the top of his head was totally bald, a pate so smooth it reflected the light of the gilt gas chandelier above him. To anyone with a sense of humor, the game room was hilariously named: the dark paneled walls, the heavy billiard table with its fat round legs, the backgammon tables were all about as "fun" as a museum. But Otto liked it.

Now he looked up at his only son. His dark blue eyes seemed to bore through Jeffrey's skull.

"A while ago, I received a note from the Sinclair woman," he said. "The actress, the widow of Alex Sinclair. She claims you have been harassing her. Is this possibly true?"

Jeffrey shifted uneasily. " 'Harassing' is not the word *I* would use, sir."

"Then it is true you know this woman?"

"Uh . . . yes, sir. As a matter of fact, I took her to lunch today at Delmonico's."

His father stared at him. "You . . . were seen in public with this woman? Are you out of your mind? Don't you know who she is? Don't you know *what* she is?"

"I know she's the most beautiful woman in the world!" Jeffrey burst out. "And if I can get her to marry me someday, I swear I will!"

"*Marry?* This is more serious than I imagined. You will be brought to your senses, sir, or I'll know the reason why! She tells me she is returning the fur coat you bought her. Might I ask *how* you paid for it?"

"I charged it to your account at Sinclair and Son."

"Damnation, sir! Dam-*NA*-tion! This will cease immediately! Buying fur coats for an actress, for a woman of her reputation!"

"Father, you keep attacking her—why? What has she done?"

Otto simmered down.

"Perhaps I'm being unfair to you," he said. "Perhaps you don't know about her. Let me tell you a few of the facts about Mrs. Sinclair, facts I've learned from my London friends. Did you know that she is notorious in England for having been the mistress of the Marquess of Pontefract?"

"Oh yes," Jeffrey said offhandedly. "Fascinating, isn't it? I really admire that man."

Again Otto stared. "You have a curiously adaptable sense of morality, sir," he said. "Perhaps the expensive education I have bought for you at Yale is somewhat lacking in the fundamental truths of decency and honor. You are aware that it is rumored that her elder child, Amanda, is the natural daughter of a certain nobleman?"

"I've heard that, yes."

"You know she stood trial for the murder of her father in London?"

"Yes, and she was pardoned. The whole thing was set up by slave owners in Virginia. Father, what you're saying doesn't alter the fact that she's an absolute angel, and that I adore her."

"I am only thankful your dear mother is not alive to hear you speak these vile words." Otto stood up, straightening his frock coat, then went to stand before the fire, his hands clasped behind his back. After a moment he turned and looked at his son.

"I forbid you to see this woman again," he said firmly.

"You can't stop me."

"By God, sir, I *can* stop you!" Otto roared. "I can throw you into the street!"

"You can, but you won't," Jeffrey said, amazed at his own gall. "The last thing you want is a scandal in the family. Father, if you'd just accept the natural flow of things, everyone would be happy. I know that, given enough time, I can win Lizzie over, and that's all I want. I'll be the happiest man in the world."

"Man? You're not a man, you're a child with a child's obsession. The only reason she'd possibly marry you is for my money, and I've worked too hard in my life to let my money end up in the greedy hands of some . . . some money-hungry trollop!"

Jeffrey laughed. "Father, you're so wrong, it's funny. The one thing you can't do with Lizzie is buy her. Why do you think she's sending back the chinchilla? It really was the most stupid thing I could have done. I don't mean to offend you, sir, but when it comes to Lizzie, you don't know what you're talking about. And . . ." He leaned forward, his knuckles on the desk. "I intend to have her. By the way, the red six goes on the black seven."

Pointing to the solitaire game, he walked to the door and left the room. Alone, Otto pulled a handkerchief from his pocket and mopped his brow.

"Damn! I must stop this," he muttered. "But how?"

He walked over to the desk and put the red six on the black seven.

"You are a *beech*!" yelled Edwige Mercier as she stood in the door of Lizzie's dressing room at the Broadway Theatre. "I tell you one thousand times to stop upstaging me, yet you continue to do eet. You step on my best lines, and you make leetle *moues* at the audience—I *keel* you!"

Lizzie was putting on her maid's costume. "Edwige, that's a lie and you know it. I don't make faces at the audience, and if I step on your lines, it's certainly not intentional."

"Hah! So say *you*! I complain to Monsieur Montgomery again and he weel fire you!"

"Perhaps. But since I'm getting all the applause, maybe he'll give me your part instead."

"Oh! You *beech*!" Edwige ran into the room and began pulling Lizzie's hair. The two women were in a real cat fight when a man in a sable-collared coat appeared in the door. What Otto Schoenberg saw made him gasp. Lizzie, her costume torn at the bodice, pushed Edwige away.

"Who the hell are *you*?" she blurted out.

"My name is Otto Schoenberg."

"Half an hour!" a stagehand yelled in past Otto. "Curtain going up in thirty minutes!"

He vanished.

"I pay you back for zeez!" Edwige snapped at Lizzie. Then she pushed past Otto and left. Lizzie went to her dressing table and began briskly brushing her hair.

"I apologize for the street brawl," she said. "Edwige plays a *comtesse* in the play, but she was raised on a pig farm outside Toulouse. Did you get the chinchilla coat?"

"Yes, and I appreciate your sending it back. Jeffrey was entirely out of line. He charged it to my account without telling me."

"At least he has good taste. The coat was beautiful, but then, all the furs at Sinclair and Son are gorgeous. The store used to belong to me, you know, until one of your colleagues on Wall Street stole all my money."

"Yes, I understand you were one of the wounded in the Erie War."

"One of the wounded? I was one of the dead. I hope you convinced Jeffrey to stop bothering me. I'm sure he's a sweet boy, but I have enough teenage Romeos pestering me."

Otto watched as she pinned the costume where Edwige had torn the bodice. Then she powdered her bosom with a big white puff. She turned to look at him.

"Was there anything else, Mr. Schoenberg?"

He cleared his throat. "Jeffrey has been out to Long Island to see his grandmother for several days. I wondered if I could take you to dinner after the play to discuss the boy?"

Lizzie hesitated. "Yes, why not?" she said.

"Perhaps we could dine at my home. It's only three blocks away from your former house."

"I didn't realize we had been neighbors. Yes, that would be nice. Wall Street made me leave Fifth Avenue, it at least owes me a dinner. Would you like to see the play? I can get you one of the house seats."

"Thank you, I bought a ticket. Actually"—he looked a little embarrassed—"I've already seen it. Twice."

Like son, she mused, like father.

CHAPTER 32

"*Der junge schwarze Mann ist ein wunder,*" exclaimed the Prince of Prussia to his wife, the Princess Frederick. They were seated on gold chairs in the music room of the New Palace in Potsdam, with half the German court behind them. All were applauding enthusiastically. Eighteen-year-old Gabriel Cavanagh, handsome in his white tie and tails, was standing by the Bechstein bowing to the distinguished audience. He had just played the solo part of the "Emperor" Concerto with Franz Liszt playing the orchestra part on a second piano.

"I must tell Mama to ask him to play at Windsor," said the Princess Frederick to her husband. She was the eldest child of Queen Victoria and the mother of the future Kaiser Bill.

"Encore!" cried a voice from the audience. "Encore!"

The noise quieted as Gabriel reseated himself at the piano and, in deference to the Maestro, began playing Liszt's "Mephisto Waltz."

"How many kings have you played for?" asked Ilsa, Gabriel's Berlin-born mistress three hours later. She was sitting, naked, on the bed in Gabriel's suite at the Hotel Adlon at Number One Unter den Linden, Berlin's most luxurious hotel and one of the premier hotels of Europe. The Adlon was infinitely more lavishly furnished than the rather dowdy royal palace, which had no bathrooms. When the King of Prussia wanted to take a bath, six footmen had to go to the nearby Hotel de Rome and carry a tub back to the imperial quarters.

"He wasn't the king," said Gabriel, who was lying beside

her, filing his fingernails. He also was naked. "He was the Crown Prince."

"Sorry. I forgot you've become an expert on royalty."

"Why not? I've played before three kings, one dowager queen, two grand dukes, three archdukes and the Pope. Besides, I'm the king of pianists."

"Modest, too."

"Well, I am."

"I suppose you are." She yawned and stretched, displaying her superb breasts. Ilsa was a sensational blond. She also was beginning to wonder if she was pregnant, which prompted her next question. "Tell me, Gabriel, where did you get your talent?"

He didn't answer. She looked at him. "Why don't you answer?"

"Because I don't know!" he snapped.

"There's no need to get angry. I was just curious."

He threw the nail file across the room, got off the bed and walked to the window to look out over the Unter den Linden.

"The fact is . . ." He stopped.

"What?"

He sank into a chair and buried his face in his hands. "The fact is, I don't know anything about my past—except that my father and mother were slaves." He looked up. Ilsa was surprised to see he was crying. "Mrs. Sinclair doesn't know much more than I, except that I have white blood in me. The whole thing's so damned confusing. It's like coming out of nowhere! I'd give anything to know more."

"Then why don't you go find out?"

"Where?"

"Back to your father's plantation."

"It was burned in the war."

"But some of the slaves must still be there. They would know something, wouldn't they?"

Gabriel wiped his nose. "I hate America. They won't even let me rent a recital hall."

"Because you're black?"

"Because I'm a nigger. There's a difference."

"What is it?"

"A black man has a future. A nigger just has a past."

"And you don't even have *that.* I think you should go back to Virginia and find out what you really want to know."

Gabriel didn't say anything.

Two mornings later, as they walked through the beautiful, snow-covered Tiergarten, Gabriel stopped and said, "You're right. I'm going back to Virginia. I'm going to find out who I am."

Lizzie hardly recognized Gabriel when he came into her living room at the Hotel Davenport.

"You're so tall! she exclaimed, taking his hands. "And so very distinguished! Now I understand those reports of women tearing at your clothes."

"They've stopped doing that." He smiled. "There's a twelve-year-old Bulgarian violinist they're after now. One woman in Rome stole his underdrawers. But I understand you're becoming quite a star yourself. I saw your posters all over town. You're playing Kate Hardcastle in a new production of *She Stoops to Conquer*?"

"Yes, I'm very excited about it. And also scared out of my wits. Here: sit down. May I get you anything?"

"I'd love a cup of coffee. That's all we do in Germany: drink coffee." He thought of Ilsa. "Well, we do a few other things, too."

He sat on a sofa as Lizzie turned toward the kitchen door, where Lila was standing.

"Lila, this is Gabriel, whom I told you about."

"Uh-*huh*. That is one good-lookin' man!" Lila said. "Mr. Gabriel, you gonna play somethin' fo' me befo' you leave?"

"I'd be delighted if I can find a piano."

"That singin' teacher downstairs, he got one an' Lordie! do he play it bad, all night long! I'll get some coffee."

Lila went into the kitchen as Lizzie sat in a chair.

"I'm so eager for you to meet my children," she said. "They've heard so much about you. They should be back from school soon. How's Tadeuz?"

"Oh, he and Anna are fine. They've bought a house in Fontainebleau, where they stay when we're not touring."

"And you? Do you have a house?"

"Not yet. I live in hotels. But I guess I'll buy one soon."

"Do you have a girlfriend?"

He smiled. "Yes. A German girl."

"So you're happy?"

The smile vanished. "Yes . . . and no. I mean, of course I'm happy about my career, which I owe to you."

"All I did was give you the opportunity to develop. You had the wonderful talent."

"But where did *that* come from? Was it my white blood or my black blood?"

"Does it matter?"

"It does to me. You see, I don't know who I am. I'm an American who lives in Europe. I'm a black man, but I live and talk like a white man. I'm a black pianist who plays white men's music for white audiences. Maestro Liszt once said I might be a success as a freak, and I sometimes wonder if that's not true. That's why I'm going back to Virginia: to see where I came from, to find out my past."

Lila came in from the kitchen with a cup and saucer. "Mr. Gabriel, does I hear you correct?" she said. "You say you goin' back to Virginia?"

"Yes."

"Excuse me, but you gotta be crazy."

Gabriel frowned. "Why?"

"They got the Klan down there."

"She's right," Lizzie said. "You'd better be careful."

"Why would the Klan be interested in me?"

" 'Cause you beat the system," Lila said, putting the cup on a table. "You made somethin' outta yourself. They don't like that down there. They don't like it up *here*, as far as that goes. But down there they can do somethin' about it. The last thing they wants to see is some colored man like you what dresses well and is worl'-famous an' got a lotta money. Talk about 'uppity.' Huh. You'll drive them crazy!"

Gabriel smiled as he sipped his coffee. "I'll be careful, but I still have to go." He turned to Lizzie. "I seem to remember an Aunt Lide when I was a boy. Is she still alive?"

"Oh yes. She's still at Elvira Plantation, living in her cabin behind the main house which was burned in the war. She'd be the one who could tell you your past. She knows all the slave histories."

"Huh," Lila mumbled, returning to the kitchen. "Only a crazy man'd go to Virginia."

"The rich nigger is in Richmond," said Zack Whitney after he galloped up to Fairview Plantation and dismounted. Phineas had come out on the verandah. It was the middle of February.

"Which rich nigger?" Phineas said as his adopted son climbed the steps to the verandah. "There's so goddamn many of them now." The once-wealthy tobacco planter was now wearing a suit that was nine years old and looked it. Phineas was seventy years old and looked it. Fairview Plantation hadn't been painted since before the war. Most of the furnishings of the great house had been sold off to pay debts and raise much-needed cash. The war had wiped Phineas out financially. All that was left was hate.

"This is a special rich nigger," Zack said. "This is the one from Elvira Plantation. The one that nigger-lover Mrs. Cavanagh sent to Europe. The one who became a pianist."

"Ah yes, him." Phineas' eyes lighted with interest. "I read that he's been quite successful in Europe. It's hard to imagine why anyone would want to listen to a nigger play Mozart. For that matter, it's hard to imagine that any nigger *could* play Mozart. Come in, Zack."

He put his arm around Zack's waist and they went inside. Ellie May was sitting by the fire in the nearly empty drawing room, knitting. When her son came in, she looked up and smiled. Never a beauty, Ellie May was now a wrinkled hag. Lack of dental care had caused her to lose her buck teeth, and Phineas couldn't afford to buy her false teeth, so her mouth was caved in onto her rotting gums.

"Dearest Zack, welcome back," she said. "How was Richmond?"

"How do you expect?" Zack said, kissing her forehead.

"Things are still dead, and I still can't get a paying job."

She patted his hand. "Never mind, Zack. We'll get by. We've gotten by since the war, and we'll continue to."

"Zack has interesting news," Phineas said, warming his hands at the fire. "Mrs. Cavanagh's fancy nigger is in Richmond. What's he after, Zack?"

"They say at the hotel—"

"They let a *nigger* in the hotel?" Ellie May gasped.

"Oh yes. If you have money, you can do anything you want in Richmond. Anyway, they say he was asking how to get to Elvira Plantation."

"Whatever for?" Ellie May said.

"Perhaps he wants to visit his father's grave," Phineas said. "Whatever the reason is, I'm beginning to think this gives us an excellent opportunity to settle old scores with that nigger-loving Mrs. Cavanagh."

"Terrible woman," Ellie May said. "Jack Cavanagh made the worst mistake of his life when he married her."

"What are you thinking of, Father?" Zack asked.

"Oh, that maybe we should give the fancy nigger a real welcome home. One he'll never forget—or anyone else, for that matter."

Ellie May looked up from her knitting at her husband and her son. A smile slowly crossed her toothless mouth.

CHAPTER 33

It was snowing as Gabriel climbed out of the rented carriage and looked at the ruins of Elvira Plantation. He had dim memories of how it had looked before the war. It had been a beautiful house, he supposed, but he had always thought of it as ugly. Now only the walls remained, and the bricks were burned black from the flames. The roof was gone, the windows empty, the yews uncut. It was a tomb of a way of life.

He noticed a young black boy staring at him from behind a tree.

"You!" he called. "Can you help me?"

The boy came around the tree and walked toward him warily.

"What's your name?" Gabriel asked.

"Buford."

"Do you live here, Buford?"

The boy pointed past the house in the direction Gabriel remembered the slave quarters had been. He remembered peeing in a communal bucket. He remembered the stench of urine.

"What does your father do?" Gabriel asked.

"He a sharecropper fo' Mr. Boone."

"Who's Mr. Boone?"

"He own Elvira Plantation."

"I see. How many sharecroppers are there here?"

" 'Bout twenty. Is you a politician?"

"Why do you ask that?"

" 'Cause you dressed so fancy."

Gabriel laughed. "I hate to disappoint you, but I'm just a pianist. Can you take me to Aunt Lide? Here." He pulled a five-dollar gold piece from his pocket and tossed it to Buford. The boy looked amazed as he stared at the coin.

"Thank you!" he said. Then he beckoned. "Come on. Aunt Lide back here in her cabin."

"Is Charles still alive?"

"Oh no. He died two year back."

They walked through the snow around to the other side of the ruined house. Gabriel recognized the small brick buildings where the senior house servants had lived. He pointed to the second to the left.

"That's where I grew up," he said.

"You was *here*? At Elvira Plantation?"

"That's right. My father was the coachman."

They came to the first cabin. Buford knocked on the door, then pushed it open. "Aunt Lide," he called in. "Dey's a man here to see you. He say his daddy was de coachman here."

Gabriel went inside after Buford, who closed the door. An extremely old woman with a shawl around her gingham dress was sitting before the fire. She looked at him with curiosity. Gabriel realized, with a sense of awe, that he was looking at his family history.

"My name is Gabriel Cavanagh," he said. "My father was Moses, the coachman who was murdered. Do you remember Moses?"

"Oh yes," said Aunt Lide. "You must be de boy Miss Lizzie done bought and sent to school up No'th."

"That's right."

"I hear tell you done right good fo' youself playin' music in foreign lands."

Gabriel smiled. "I've played for kings," he said. "I even played for the Pope."

"My my. Do tell. Well, dass mighty fine, boy. Mighty fine. Guess you seen tings most colored folk never will. Whaffo' you come back to Elvira Plantation?"

Gabriel pulled up a stool and sat next to her as Buford watched from the door. "Miss Lizzie told me I have white blood in me," he said. "Who would that have been?"

"De Cap'n," said Aunt Lide unhesitatingly. "De Cap'n

was Moses' father. He was always playin' roun' in de slave quarter."

"Who was the Captain?"

"Cap'n Cavanagh, Massa Jack's father. Dass why Massa Jack hated Moses so much: he was his brother, jes lak Dulcey was his sister. Poor Dulcey, she daid now. Dey's all daid. Guess dey's all pretty much equal now."

"Master Jack?" whispered Gabriel, dimly remembering the man he had hated and feared as a child. "Then I'm related to Mrs. Cavanagh?"

"Looks lak. You her in-law."

"I'll be damned. Then at least my last name, Cavanagh, is real. Tell me, Aunt Lide, was the Captain musical?"

"Naw. Couldn't carry a tune."

"Then . . . where would I have gotten my talent?"

"Your granny Ida. Moses' slave mother. She had the sweetest voice. She used to sing in church and everyone would cry their eyes out when she quit. I can hear that sweet voice now, singin' spirituals. Dass where you got yo' talent. An' you got yo' looks from yo' daddy. Han'somest black man I ever lay eyes on."

"Ida," Gabriel repeated. "Thank you, Ida, wherever you are."

"She in de slave graveyard wif everyone else. Spect I'll be dere soon enough myself."

"Where's that?"

"Next to our church. If you wants, I can take you dere. An' maybe, since you played fo' kings an' de Pope, maybe you could play somethin' fo' us. Dey's a nice piano in de church. We all paid fo' it ourselves."

"I'd be proud to."

"Buford!"

"Yes, Aunt Lide?"

"You run an' tell everyone to come to de church in an hour. Tell dem dat Mr. Gabriel Cavanagh, who has played fo' kings an' de Pope, has come home to play fo' us. Get Reverend Peale, tell him to light de candles. Now run along, boy."

"Yes, Aunt Lide." He opened the door and hurried out into the snow.

"Help me up, Gabriel."

Gabriel got to his feet and helped the old woman out of her chair.

"I can't thank you enough for telling me about Ida," he said. "I'm glad I got my talent from . . . from my people."

She patted his arm. "We're all proud of you, Gabriel," she said. "Very proud. Now, you play real good fo' us colored folk. You play jes' as good as you played fo' de Pope."

"I'll do my best."

He led her outside, around to his carriage.

It was growing dark by the time they arrived at the little church in the woods. Gabriel helped Aunt Lide out of the carriage, and they walked to the graveyard beside the church.

"Dere's my Charles," said Aunt Lide, pointing to a simple stone that was heaped on top with a half-inch of snow. "Hello, Charles. An' over here is poor Dulcey. Hello, Dulcey. Den here is yo' daddy, Moses. Hello, Moses."

Gabriel paused by the grave. Though he found it strange that the old woman talked to the dead, he couldn't help saying, "Hello, Father."

"An' over here is Ida."

He came to another stone. "Hello, Ida," he said. "And thank you."

He found himself crying.

By six o'clock, the small church with its wooden pews had filled with former slaves and their wives and children. Reverend Peale, the church's minister, a big man with gray hair, was standing in his pulpit, watching his congregation. The church was lighted with candles.

"We have a treat tonight." The reverend smiled. "One of our own people has become famous all over the world, and he has come home."

Home, Gabriel thought. This isn't my home. Or is it? He was sitting on the front pew with Aunt Lide.

"Gabriel Cavanagh's father was coachman here before

the war. You all know the story, how he was murdered and how Miss Lizzie, may the Lord bless her name, raised his son up on high, amen!"

"Amen!" chorused the congregation.

"Now, Brother Gabriel is going to play for us on our own fine piano. Brother Gabriel, I just wish we'd had time to have it tuned."

Gabriel stood up and climbed on the platform. The piano, a battered upright, had been wheeled to the center of the stage. He went to it, then turned to look at the faces of his people. Strangely, for the first time in his life he felt stage fright.

"I will play . . ." He hesitated. ". . . the eighth Prelude in F sharp minor by Frédéric Chopin."

He sat down on the creaky stool. The church was cold. He blew on his fingers, checking the piano's manufacture. It had been built by an obscure company in Philadelphia. Gabriel, used to playing the finest instruments in Europe, decided he was going to make this piano sing like it had never sung before.

He attacked the prelude. The gorgeous music, a whirlwind of notes, filled the tiny church. Gabriel played it at dizzying speed. He played it flawlessly, magnificently. He made the tiny upright sound like a Steinway.

When he finished, silence. Confused, he looked at his audience. Then Reverend Peale began to applaud, and the former slaves, taking his cue, applauded also. Gabriel stood up and bowed, but he knew that he hadn't pleased them. When the applause died down, Reverend Peale smiled at him. "Thank you, Brother Gabriel," he said. "That was beautiful. But perhaps now you could play us some of our own music?"

Then he understood. Chopin meant nothing to them. Chopin was white music.

"Uh, like what?" he said, feeling awkward.

"Perhaps you could play us a spiritual, Brother Gabriel?"

"I . . . I don't know any."

There was a murmur from the congregation, as if they

were shocked that a black man would not know any spirituals.

"You don't know any spirituals?" said Reverend Peale. "Oh, Brother Gabriel, what a treat we have in store for you. Why, spirituals are the sweetest music this side of heaven—amen!"

"Amen!" chorused the congregation.

"We'll teach you a spiritual. Then you can play it for us. How's that?"

Gabriel smiled. "I think that's lovely," he said.

Reverend Peale turned in his pulpit to his congregation. "Let's sing him 'O Canaan, Sweet Canaan,' " he said, raising his hands. The congregation rose. Then he began beating time, and they all sang: " 'O Canaan, sweet Canaan, I am bound for the Land of Canaan. . . .' "

The doors burst open. Eight men in white robes and hoods came into the church. They held rifles. The congregation stopped singing and started screaming. Reverend Peale waved his arms for silence.

"This is the House of God," he cried. "How dare you come in here?"

"Shut up, nigger!" yelled one of them. It was Zack. "No one will be hurt," he went on, running down the aisle with the two others. "All we want is the fancy nigger."

Gabriel realized they meant him.

"This is blasphemy," cried the reverend. "Blasphemy! This is the House of God!"

Zack ran up to him and jammed the butt of his rifle into his face, knocking the elderly man backward. He stumbled out of the pulpit and fell over a choir bench.

"I told you to shut up," Zack yelled.

Two other Klansmen had grabbed Gabriel and were pulling him up the aisle to the rear doors.

"Help!" he screamed. "Somebody help me! Sweet Jesus, help me!"

One former slave, enraged to see Reverend Peale struck, now started out of his pew to help Gabriel. It was Broward, who, as a teenager, had taken Moses' job as coachman for Jack Cavanagh. He was now a sharecropper, father of two, a strapping black man. Now he ran up behind a tall Klansman and pulled off his hood. Everyone in the church froze when they saw who it was.

"General Whitney!" exclaimed the Reverend Peale as he pulled himself back onto his pulpit, blood running down his forehead. "I can't believe you would do this. You, a former Senator, a former Ambassador—you would put on a white hood and desecrate the House of God? For shame, sir! When you meet your Maker, sir, what will you say to Him when He asks you of this vile crime?"

Phineas looked at the preacher coolly. "I'll tell Him," he said in ringing tones, "that I am proud of what I did."

Slowly he put his hood back on. The two Klansmen had Gabriel at the church doors. Broward started toward them, but Zack aimed his rifle at him and fired over his head. The congregation screamed as the Klansmen hurried out of the church, slamming the doors behind them.

"The shame is on us," cried Reverend Peale from the pulpit. "We let them do it. The shame is on us!"

"He's right!" Broward cried out. "If we don't fight back, we gonna be slaves forever. De Guvmint, it say we be freemen, but I say we ain't nevah gonna be free as long as de Klan can come in our homes and churches an' drag us off to be killed. Dey's gonna kill Gabriel Cavanagh, an' we gotta stop 'em. Dat man, he what we might be able to be someday in dis country if we fight. We can't let the Klan kill Gabriel Cavanagh!"

Wild cheers broke out.

"Brothers!" cried Reverend Peale, waving his hands for silence. "We can't resort to violence. We must stop them, but we must do it with prayer."

"Reverend," Broward shouted, "we can pray till we's outta breath, but dat ain't gonna stop dem from killin' Gabriel Cavanagh! I say, if dey use violence, *we* use violence! Come on, men! An' bring yo' guns! It's time to *fight*!"

Gabriel was lying on his back on the floor of a covered wagon. His hands were tied behind him, and a gag had been put around his mouth. The wagon was bumping through the cold night. Eight hooded Klansmen were sitting on benches on either side of Gabriel, looking down at him. It was terrifying. Now, two of the Klansmen pulled off their hoods.

Zack and Phineas were smiling.

"We hear you played for the Pope," Phineas said. "That's lucky for you, because you're going to need his prayers."

The Klansmen began laughing.

"Look, he's shivering," said Zack. "Do you think he's frightened? Nah, he's just cold. You're cold, aren't you, nigger? But that's all right, because you're going to be real warm very soon."

More howls of laughter from the Klansmen. Zack pulled a knife from under his robe, got off the bench and knelt on top of Gabriel, his knee in his chest. He stuck the point of the knife to Gabriel's throat.

"We fought a war for you, nigger," he said. "You know what I lost in that war? I lost my father, my home and my brother. You know how many relatives of the men in this wagon were lost in the war? It's something like forty-five. Forty-five dead men, nigger, that are in heaven right now because they fought for you niggers. We used to be rich, but now we're poor. And you fancy niggers have the nerve to strut your money in front of us, throw it in our faces, force yourselves into political office . . . You played for the Pope? Well, Pope this!"

He turned and raised the knife over Gabriel's genitals. Gabriel, gagging with horror, tried to roll to one side. Phineas leaned forward and put a restraining hand on Zack's shoulder.

"Don't," he said. "We have something better."

Reluctantly, Zack got off Gabriel and sat back down. Gabriel was whimpering with fear.

The wagon rolled through the snowy night toward its ghoulish destination. Twenty minutes later, it stopped. The Klansmen began climbing down. Zack, his hood still off, grabbed one of Gabriel's arms as another hooded Klansman grabbed the other. They jerked him to his feet and pulled him to the rear of the wagon. Four Klansmen were standing in the snow, their rifles pointed. Zack pushed Gabriel from behind, and he jumped to the ground.

They were in a clearing in a pine forest, and the snow weighing down the soft branches of the trees gave the place a look of eerie beauty. Then he saw what they had built in the center of the clearing, and his skin crawled.

They had built a large, wooden barbecue over a pile of logs almost six feet high. A dozen flaming wooden crosses had been set in the ground around the bonfire, illuminating the scene.

"Guess what's going to be dinner tonight?" Zack said with a smile as he poked his finger into Gabriel's chest. "*You,*" he said. "We're going to have barbecued nigger."

The Klansmen laughed. Gabriel started to run, but Zack stuck out his foot and tripped him. Gabriel fell face-forward into the snow.

"All right, who's our chef?" Zack called.

"As a former Ambassador," said Phineas, coming up beside his adopted son, "and a man not unacquainted with the finer restaurants of Europe and Washington, I suggest my claim is not unworthy."

"Hear, hear!" cried the Klansmen.

"Then, sir chef, please prepare the main course."

"With pleasure, son," Phineas said. "I need some help."

The two men knelt beside Gabriel and started to take off his boots. Gabriel kicked wildly.

"Hold his knees," Zack said. One of the Klansmen knelt on Gabriel's knees. Phineas and Zack pulled off the boots, then Gabriel's socks.

"All right; his pants," Zack ordered. The third Klansmen got off Gabriel's knees. He began kicking again, thrashing on the ground like a terrified animal. With some difficulty, Zack and Phineas pulled off his trousers. Then they jerked him to his feet. Using a knife, Zack ripped the back of his coat in two, then his shirt. He pulled the rags off, leaving Gabriel shivering in his underdrawers.

"Bring the spit," Zack said.

Two Klansmen lifted the wooden log off the two Y-shaped wooden crutches it had rested on and brought it over.

"Pull off his drawers, then lash him to the spit," Phineas

said in a cool, almost clinical tone. Zack and another Klansmen pulled down Gabriel's drawers and ripped them off his bare feet. He was naked now, shivering from cold, sweating from terror.

The spit was laid in the snow. Zack grabbed Gabriel from behind as another Klansmen took his ankles. They lifted him up.

"Stick the spit under his wrists, then tie his ankles."

This was done.

"All right, let's put this nigger on the barbecue."

Both ends of the spit were picked up. Gabriel's weight caused him to slip around so that he hung facedown from the pole. The macabre procession carried him to the pile of logs, and the spit was replaced in the Y-shaped crutches.

Phineas and Zack climbed up on the pile of logs till they were standing next to Gabriel's head.

"We may have lost the War," Phineas proclaimed to the Klansmen. Then he turned to Gabriel, loathing and hate in his patrician features. "But we will win the battle because when all is said and done, the white Northerner hates you niggers as much as we do. You hear me, nigger? You put on your fancy clothes and you went around Europe, but you're home now. Home in America. And where are your fancy clothes now? Nowhere. What good do they do you now? No good. Because you're with us: your masters. And you're too afraid to fight—"

A shot rang out from the woods. Phineas Thurlow Whitney, a look of amazement on his face, clasped his hands to his chest, then fell forward, rolling down the pile of logs to the snowy ground. More shots fired. The Klansmen were yelling, running for their rifles in panic. Zack scrambled down the logs, grabbed a torch from the ground and stuck it into one of the burning crosses. Its oil-soaked rag flared into flame. Holding it, he ran back to the log pile and started to stick it in to light the bonfire when another volley of shots fired. Zack was hit in the back. He cried as he pitched forward, falling on the very torch he was about to roast Gabriel alive with, lying dead next to his father, Phineas. Zack's sheet-robe caught fire, and he became a pillar of fire. Phineas, lying next to him, also caught fire.

Gabriel, still tied to the spit atop the huge pile of logs, watched in horror as the flames of his two would-be executioners began to lick at the base of the bonfire.

Five of the other Klansmen were dead, lying in the snow. Now the remaining Klansmen, yelling in terror, climbed back in their wagon and galloped off into the night.

Now all was silence as the great bonfire began to kindle.

Broward and twelve men from the church ran out of the woods into the clearing.

"Put out de fire," he yelled, throwing down his shotgun as he ran to the flaming corpses. He began throwing snow on them.

"Help me," he yelled. "An' get Gabriel down!"

Within minutes the fire was out, leaving the corpses of the former Senator and his Confederate-hero adopted son smoldering. Gabriel had been untied and a blanket had been thrown around his nakedness.

"Thank you," he mumbled in a state of shock. "Thank all of you."

"We scared de shit out of dose Klansmen," chortled Broward.

"Yeah, but dey's gonna be back," said another. "We'd all better lay low fo' a while. Dey's gonna be a lotta trouble from dis."

"Dass all right," Broward said. "We know how to fight now. What about you, Brother Gabriel? You bess go back to New Yawk quick."

"Yes, I'll go back," Gabriel said, tears in his eyes. "But I finally found my past. And you know something? For all its ugliness, it has a certain beauty. Because it takes *guts* to go through what we've gone through in America."

"Amen to that," said the others.

"I can't believe it," Lizzie said two nights later to Otto Schoenberg. She was taking off her makeup in the dressing room of the Empire Theatre where she was rehearsing *She Stoops to Conquer*. "Yes, I *can* believe it, actually," she went on. "Phineas Whitney was a madman! To try and burn Gabriel alive—it's monstrous! Thank God Whitney is dead. If ever a man deserved to die, it was he."

"And Gabriel is in New York?" said the banker.

"Yes. He had lunch with me at my apartment. He was almost in tears when he told me about it. Even so, he's glad he went back to Virginia. At least now he knows who he is."

"And what will he do now?"

"He says he's going back to Europe, because he can't perform here except in minstrel shows. Oh Otto, isn't it a crime that someone as talented as Gabriel can't even rent a beer hall to play in just because he's black! You'd think that after so much suffering in the war, things would start to change a little. But Lila tells me there's as much prejudice in New York as there is in the South."

Otto thought a moment, his eyes never leaving Lizzie. Then he stood up.

"The Academy of Music has been asking me to make a donation to improve their recital hall. And, as you know, I already am a benefactor of the New York Philharmonic. Perhaps I can arrange for Gabriel to make his New York debut."

Lizzie put down her tissues and turned to him, her face radiant. "Otto!" she exclaimed. "If you could do that, it would make me the happiest woman in the world. You know Gabriel's almost like a son to me: if he could play in New York . . . !" She jumped up, ran to him, threw her arms around him and kissed him. "Oh, you darling man! Will you do it?"

Otto turned slightly red. "You got greasepaint on me."

"I'll wipe it off." She ran back to her dressing table. "How much will it cost?"

"They're thinking in terms of six figures."

"It would be worth it—every cent. Please say you'll do it."

She hurried back to wipe the greasepaint off his cheek. The banker, who was not known to smile often, grinned.

"I'll talk to the committee in the morning," he said.

Lizzie kissed him again, smearing more greasepaint on his face.

* * *

One week later, a crowd gathered in front of the Academy of Music on Fourteenth Street. The people, all white, carried signs bearing such crudely lettered messages as "No Niggers Allowed!" "Theatres for Whites Only!" "Minstrels, YES! Pianists, NO!" They chanted as they milled around in an oval in front of the gaslit recital hall where large posters announced:

The Great American Virtuoso
GABRIEL CAVANAGH
To Appear March 3, 1868
8:30 P.M.
With the New York Philharmonic
Guest Conductor: Hans von Bulow
The Program:
Concerto No. 1 in E flat . . . Liszt
Concerto No. 5 in E flat . . . Beethoven
Tickets: $2

As Lizzie and Otto pulled up in his carriage, she groaned when she saw the crowd. "It's worse than we feared," she said.

"We were warned."

When Lizzie climbed out, the crowd started booing. She and Otto hurried into the recital hall, where an usher led them down the aisle to their seats. The hall was far from sold out, but by the time the houselights dimmed she was relieved to see that over a hundred seats had been filled, and she spotted music critics from three of the major newspapers.

The members of the orchestra filed onstage to take their seats behind the big black Steinway as the concertmaster played A.

In the wings, Gabriel stood, wiping his face with a handkerchief. The guest conductor, Hans von Bulow, Liszt's son-in-law who had been cuckolded by Wagner and was trying to forget it all with an American tour, patted him on the shoulder.

"Relax," said the German maestro. "Tonight you will make history."

"Maybe," mumbled Gabriel.

Von Bulow walked onstage and bowed to the politely applauding audience. Then he stepped on the podium.

Gabriel took a deep breath and walked onstage. Total silence as he went to the piano and bowed. Then he sat down, flipping his coattails behind him. He looked at von Bulow and nodded. The Maestro raised his baton. The dramatic opening bars of the concerto filled the hall.

Gabriel stared at the keyboard, thinking of his murdered father, of the generations of slaves who had preceded him, dim figures in an anguished history whose names he would never know. He thought of Phineas Thurlow Whitney and Zack. He thought of the Klan. Suddenly he burned with anger.

The four bars of the orchestra introduction concluded. Gabriel struck the great opening chord of the piano solo, then began the electrifying passage of climbing octaves.

Lizzie, in the third row, squeezed Otto's hand.

When the concerto came to its thrilling conclusion, again there was silence. Gabriel, soaking with sweat, stood up. He knew he had played brilliantly. He looked at the audience.

Lizzie stood up. "Bravo!" she cried, beginning to applaud. She was joined by Otto.

Suddenly the audience was clapping. There were a few "Boos!" but they were drowned out by other "Bravos!" Rather uncertainly, Gabriel bowed. But he shouldn't have been uncertain. It was a triumph.

That night, Gabriel Cavanagh had made history.

CHAPTER 34

Theatre review in the New York *Herald,* March 5, 1868:

> Last night at the Empire Theatre, Mrs. Sinclair, the noted English beauty, opened in a revival of Oliver Goldsmith's *She Stoops to Conquer*. It is my sad duty to report that Mrs. Sinclair stooped, but she failed to conquer this critic. Mrs. Sinclair is extraordinary to look at, but her acting was wooden and her timing was bad. However—such are the vagaries of the theatre—she was given an ovation by the audience, which she obviously conquered despite her acting. It would seem that there is a new star tonight in the Broadway firmament. Rumor on the Rialto has it that this star was hung by an angel from Wall Street.

On a brilliant but blustery Sunday afternoon in March, Amanda was reading a book in the living room of the Hotel Davenport apartment when the bell rang. "I'll get it," she called to Lila, who was in the kitchen. Amanda got up. She was wearing a white dress with a white bow in her blond hair and was looking, as usual, extremely pretty. She went to the door and opened it.

"Papa!" she cried. "Papa!"

Adam was standing in the door, his arms open. Amanda ran into them, hugging and kissing him.

"I can't believe how tall you are," Adam exclaimed. "And how beautiful. Oh, Amanda, you're going to be a heartbreaker. And look what I have for you."

It was then she saw the spaniel puppy, who was on a leash and threatening to pee in the hallway.

"For *me*?" Amanda said. "He's so cute! What's his name?"

"That's for you to decide."

"Oh, he's so beautiful!"

She scooped up the puppy, who started licking her face.

"Thank you, thank you! Come in! How long are you going to stay? And why haven't you come before? I've missed you!"

"And I've missed you, darling."

He took off his hat and coat, looking around the room, which was comfortably, if a bit drably, furnished.

"Lila, come here and meet my father. Somerset, you, too."

Lila came out of the kitchen.

"Papa, this is Lila, the sweetest woman in the world. Lila, this is Lord Pontefract."

"How do you do, Lila?"

Lila, looking rather nervous, curtsied. "How do you do . . ." She turned to Amanda and whispered, "What do I call him? 'Your worship'?"

"Call me Mr. Thorne." Adam smiled. "I checked my title at the boat landing. And who's this handsome young man?"

Somerset had come out of his bedroom. He was six years old, tall, with dark hair.

"This is Somerset, my naughty brother," Amanda said.

"I'm not naughty: you're the brat," Somerset said. Then he turned to Adam and gravely shook his hand. "How do you do, sir? I'm pleased to meet you."

"I'm pleased to meet you, Somerset. And where's your mother?"

"She's spending the day with Mr. Schoenberg."

Adam looked puzzled. "Who's Mr. Schoenberg?"

Lila cleared her throat. "That's Miss Lizzie's, uh, friend," she said, glancing nervously at the children.

The Marquess of Pontefract blinked with surprise.

* * *

"I'm making money off you," said Otto Schoenberg, "which is a pleasant surprise. Mr. Gray tells me he's selling out every night."

Lizzie cut into her Dover sole. "It certainly *is* a surprise, after those terrible notices," she said.

"What do critics know? If they could write a good play, they'd do it and get rich. I received a letter from Jeffrey yesterday."

"Oh dear. Is he still upset about us?"

"No, he seems to have accepted the fact that his father is the better man."

"Darling, don't be conceited."

"Besides, he's met a new girl, a Miss Lowell. He seems quite taken by her."

"Good. The sooner he forgets about me, the better."

A footman appeared in the dining room to refill their wineglasses. Then he retired.

"You've made me very happy, Lizzie," Otto said. "My only problem is that I hate sharing you with your audiences."

"Just be thankful I have an audience."

"Would you ever consider giving up the theatre?"

Lizzie laughed. "According to the critics, the theatre would gladly consider giving me up."

"I'm serious."

"Of course. I don't particularly like acting. I only did it to make some money."

The butler came in from the entrance hall. "Pardon me, sir. There is a Mr. Adam Thorne asking to see Mrs. Sinclair."

Lizzie stiffened. "Adam . . ." she whispered.

"Who is he?" Otto asked.

"Lord Pontefract."

She was standing up, her face pale.

"Where is he?" she asked the butler.

"In the drawing room."

Otto, frowning, watched Lizzie as she ran out.

Adam was examining a Rembrandt in the drawing room when Lizzie appeared in the doorway. She was wearing a beige silk dress, the skirt of which was pulled back into a bustle, the newest fashion craze.

"Adam!"

She closed the sliding wooden doors behind her. He turned to give her a cool look.

"I came from England to help you because Bentley told me you had lost all your money," he said. "I see you managed to find some."

"Otto financed my play—"

"What else has he financed?"

She frowned. "Adam, you sound so cold."

"Do I? Remember when you wrote to me, 'Adam, you must be good.' You know, I took that advice to heart. I *have* been good. I've remained faithful to Sybil and our marriage is a success. And now I find that the mother of my daughter has *not* been very good. Has become, in fact, a high-priced tart—"

She came up to him and slapped him, hard. "Don't you *dare* speak to me that way!"

"Isn't it true? My Lizzie, the woman I've loved all my life, has become the mistress of some nouveau-riche Wall Street banker."

"All right: I'll admit I'm his mistress. But he's not nouveau-riche!"

"A minor detail."

"All right, he *is* nouveau-riche, but he's an extremely cultivated man whom I'm very fond of!"

"Lizzie, you're dancing around the point! The point is, what kind of influence do you think you're having on Amanda? 'Where's Mommie! Mommie's spending the day with her friend, Mr. Millionaire.' Amanda's innocent, but she won't be for long when she finds out what Mommie's doing."

Lizzie turned away, tears in her eyes. "You have to give me time," she whispered. "I think Otto wants to marry me, but he hasn't said anything yet. You have to give me *time*. And don't be so smug. Don't be so cruel to someone who holds you so dearly."

He relented. "I'm sorry. I *have* been cruel. It's just that I was so surprised . . ."

"This is a tough country, Adam, and a tough city. It's all very fine to talk about morality, but when it comes to paying the rent, well, you have to scramble. I learned a lot from that thief, Jim Fisk. I was a pigeon waiting to be plucked, and he plucked me. But that's not going to happen again. Perhaps I sound hard, but one has to be hard to survive."

"All right, take more time. But let me take Amanda to England for a while, until you and Mr. Schoenberg can come to some sort of resolution. I want to be with her, and she wants to be with me."

Lizzie considered this a moment. "I think that's probably a good idea," she finally said. "Yes, take Amanda to England."

"Lizzie . . ."

"Yes?"

"Do you know why I came to New York? It was partially to see Amanda, but . . . it was mostly to see you again. I've missed you like the very devil."

"But you're happy with Sybil?"

"Yes, but it's . . . it's not the same. Oh God, Lizzie, I still love you! Damn!"

He took her in his arms and hungrily kissed her. Without much prompting, she responded.

The doors slid open and Otto appeared.

"My dear," he said acidly, "perhaps you would introduce me to Lord Pontefract, who seems to have made himself quite at home."

Adam released her. "I'm sorry, Mr. . . ."

"Schoenberg. Otto Schoenberg. Lizzie, the theatre critics were wrong. You're quite good at French farce."

"This is all my fault," Adam said.

"I understand, milord. Lizzie is a witch. She has obviously bewitched you as she has bewitched me. And how many others have you bewitched, my dear?"

Lizzie turned icy. "I don't have to take this from either of you," she said, heading for the door.

"Where are you going?"

"Home."

"But you haven't finished dinner."

"To hell with dinner! To hell with you! To hell with both of you!" She had reached the door. Now she turned, her eyes blazing. "To hell with *men*!"

She went into the hall. Otto started after her, but Adam restrained him.

"Let her go," he said. "I attacked her about you, which was probably a mistake. Let her cool down."

Otto turned on him. "This is my house, sir. How dare you tell me what to do? And how dare you kiss Lizzie—?"

"Mr. Schoenberg, you're becoming a bore."

The banker's face turned red. He started to explode. Then he fizzled down.

"Now," said Adam, "let's discuss this like two civilized gentlemen. Since Lizzie has no father, I suppose I'll have to act *in loco parentis*. What, sir, are your intentions toward her?"

Otto scowled, started to say something, then changed his mind.

"Do you love her?" Adam asked.

Otto sagged. "I never knew a passion could be so overwhelming. Yes, I love her."

"I understand how you feel. Do you intend to marry her?"

"I'm afraid she'll say no. After all, I'm so much older than she—"

"*Ask*," Adam prompted. "Meanwhile, I'm going to take Amanda to England. That will clear the field, so to speak, until you and Lizzie can work things out. We must always think of the children first. After all, they're the future."

Otto looked at him with admiration. "Milord," he said, "have you had dinner?"

"No."

"Why don't you join me? I think we should get to know each other."

"I'd be delighted."

They started toward the hall.

"Who is your London banker?" Otto asked.

"Coutts."

"An extraordinary coincidence. I'm their New York correspondent. Well, well, this evening, like a fine wine, is beginning to improve with time. By the way, I'm serving a Château Margaux with the beef. Do you like Château Margaux?"

CHAPTER 35

On a warm summer day in 1874, Adam and Sybil were escorted into one of Queen Victoria's cluttered sitting rooms at Windsor Castle. The Queen, a fat, dumpy, little lady in black with a white lace cap on her head, was sitting in an armchair. Adam bowed, and Sybil curtsied.

"I am delighted to see you both," said the Queen. "Of course, your exploits over the years have thrilled me, Lord Pontefract. As your sovereign, I have tried to reward you for your many services to England and the Empire. Tonight, I have yet another honor to offer you. Yet, alas, I cannot pretend that the position is entirely untinged by danger. You have, of course, heard the news about Lord Mayo? Our Viceroy was making a tour of the prison in the Andaman Islands when he was attacked by a crazed convict and most foully murdered."

"I have, in fact, heard the news, ma'am," Adam said.

"Over the years, Mr. Disraeli has spoken to me frequently of your suitability for the position of Viceroy, if the opportunity arose. Heretofore, we have thought you were perhaps a bit young for such a glittering prize. But now that you are riper, I can think of no one more qualified. Will you be our Viceroy, Milord?"

"Adam!" Sybil whispered, pride in her eyes.

"Before I answer, ma'am," Adam said, "I feel I must apprise you of a fact about myself that only my wife and a few others have known. It may cause you to change your mind about me."

"What is this fact, pray?"

Adam took a deep breath. "I am not a pure-blooded

Englishman, ma'am. My great-grandmother was an Indian woman from Calcutta."

"Indeed?" said the Queen. "My dear Lord Pontefract, I see no reason why that would disqualify you for the position of Viceroy. In fact, it makes your appointment even more suitable, if not ideal. We are not unaware of conditions in India, and we are most acutely disturbed by reports of racial animosity there. I am the Queen of all the subjects in the Empire, no matter what their color. I think it would thrill the Indian population of the subcontinent if I appointed a Viceroy who shared their blood. In fact, it is a most splendid choice."

Adam thought of the years of fear and guilt about his mixed blood. Suddenly, magically, the fear and guilt vanished. What, in fact, did it really matter after all?

"Then, ma'am, it gives me the greatest pleasure and honor to accept your offer."

"Excellent. You will both honor the office. And I must say"—she lowered her voice and, to their astonishment, winked—"few of my viceroys and vicereines have been as good-looking as you two!" She rang a bell. "Shall we go in to supper?"

"Oh, Adam," Sybil said that night as they made love in Windsor Castle. "I'm the happiest, proudest woman alive. Viceroy of India! What a supreme honor."

"I think you'll love India, Sybil."

"I love *you,* dearest Adam. I would be happy wherever I was as long as my dearest husband was with me."

After they made love, Adam said, "Speaking of romance, Henry keeps talking about Amanda. Do you think he's in love with her?"

"Of course he is," Sybil said. "It's painfully obvious. Every time she pays us a visit, he becomes tongue-tied and awkward. And she is the sweetest child." She paused. "Wouldn't it be wonderful?"

"What?"

"Don't you see that if Henry married Amanda, it would be the ideal solution. Because it would return Amanda's de Vere blood—yours—to the title and make their heir, who will be the third marquess, totally legitimate."

"Yes," mused Adam, "that had occurred to me. When Amanda comes over next week, we'll have to do some matchmaking."

Yes, that would be nice, he thought. Now that Lizzie was happily married to Otto Schoenberg, it would be sweet indeed to have Amanda, the fruit of their great love, his daughter-in-law.

"I have an idea," Sybil said, "there won't be much matchmaking for us to do."

"Amanda seventeen," mused Lizzie as she sat at the long dining table in Otto's Medici palace on Fifth Avenue. "And now on her way to England again. She told me she has the most tender feelings for Lord Henry. Wouldn't it be wonderful if they . . . ?"

She didn't finish the sentence. Her husband looked up from his dinner.

"But my dear," he said in rather shocked tones, "she's Lord Henry's half-sister."

"Not exactly," said Lizzie with a sphingine smile.

"What do you mean?"

"Adam isn't Lord Henry's father. It's all been kept very quiet, of course. But there's really no reason Amanda couldn't be the future Marchioness of Pontefract. And wouldn't that be lovely?"

It wasn't meant for me to have Adam, she thought. But my daughter being his daughter-in-law would be just as nice.

Well, almost.

The two seventeen-year-olds galloped across the moors until they came to the ancient ruined abbey. Wildflowers grew where once, centuries before, monks had chanted to their unseen god. Lord Henry dismounted, then came over to Amanda to help her off her horse.

"My father used to bring your mother here when they were children," he said, leading her through the empty door.

"It's beautiful," Amanda said. "What's it called?"

"Newfield Abbey. My father told me he pledged his love to your mother here and told her he would always be her true knight."

"Oh, I like that! It's so romantic."

Lord Henry got down on one knee and took her right hand. The June sun shone in his golden hair.

"Fair Amanda, I pledge to thee that I will always be thy true knight, and whenever thou art in trouble, wherever it may be, I shall come to thy assistance."

Amanda giggled. "Henry, you're being silly."

"Silly? I thought it was jolly beautiful. Amanda, I'm telling you I love you."

"I know, and I love you too."

"No, I don't mean *that* way. I mean . . . well . . . *that* way."

"Whatever are you talking about?"

"I mean, I don't love you like a half-brother. I love you like . . . well, as a knight loves his lady."

"But you can't, Henry. We both have the same father."

The handsome young heir to the Marquess of Pontefract turned slightly red. "Actually," he said, "we, uh, don't."

Amanda stared at him. "You mean, we're not related?"

"No. Not by blood."

"Then who was your father?"

"Someone else. Actually. It's a bit of a secret, you know. One wouldn't like to trumpet it about."

"Henry," she said softly, "I believe you really *are* going to be my true knight."

He got to his feet and put his arms around her. "Fairest Amanda," he whispered.

"Sweetest Henry."

They kissed for an unreasonably long time.

ABOUT THE AUTHOR

FRED MUSTARD STEWART is one of America's bestselling novelists. He is author of eleven previous novels, among them *Century*, *Ellis Island*, and most recently, *The Glitter and the Gold*. He lives with his wife in northwest Connecticut.